CLAIM THE LIGHT

SUPERNATURAL LEGACY 4

EVERLY FROST

Copyright © 2023 by Everly Frost
All rights reserved.

No part of this book may be reproduced or used in any manner whatsoever without the express written permission of the author, except for the use of brief quotations in a book review.

This book is a work of fiction. Names, characters, places, and incidents either are the product of the author's imagination or are used fictitiously. Any resemblance to actual persons, living or dead, is purely coincidental.

Frost, Everly
Claim the Light

Cover design by Claire Holt with Luminescence Covers
www.luminescencecovers.com

For information on reproducing sections of this book or sales of this book,
go to
www.everlyfrost.com
everlyfrost@gmail.com

Be the moonlight in the dark. The sunlight in the shadows. The quiet between bursts of thunder.

Accept your strength and claim your light.

CHAPTER ONE

*P*eace.

It's mine if I have the courage to claim it.

I hover in the shadow of the door leading out onto the moonlit rooftop of my clan leader's home, daring myself to step into the light.

I'm not supposed to be up here.

Today, we fought a battle against angels and the danger isn't over—not until word comes that the Sentinels who hunted us are finally imprisoned.

But while my clan sleeps, my fears have kept me awake.

I need to know if my dragon shadow is gone—that the danger is truly over. The only way I can be sure of that is to step into the moonlight and dare my shadow to reappear. Then, and only then, can I push away this heavy dread building in my stomach.

My hand shakes as I raise my arm, forefinger extended, but I freeze before I can go farther.

I faced warrior angels today. Fought beside dragons who had once been my enemies. I've faced fire and dared death to come for me, and yet...

Why can't I do this simple thing? Why can't I accept that I'm worthy of this peace?

"Your life is yours now," says a quiet voice from the stairwell behind me.

I spin to find Micah Grudge standing two steps down. The shadows within the stairwell only serve to accentuate his height and muscular build, casting darkness over his light-brown hair, tanned skin, and cedar-brown eyes. My heartbeat quickens at the remembered strength in his arms and the heat in his eyes.

He isn't beautiful like some dragon shifters. Not smooth or polished. He's rugged and unkempt and, as I've come to learn, he speaks from his heart.

He was once an enemy of my clan, the Dread. There was a time when I was afraid of him. Well, for all of two seconds before he put his foot in his mouth and insulted me, after which I raged at him with all my false bravado.

I sensed his true nature even then. An alluring, wild nature. I'd pulled his scent into my chest and felt like I'd been transported to another place. A place where I didn't have to hide.

"Micah." I can't stop my smile. Or the heat growing within my body. "You're back."

If he were still my enemy, I might be unsettled by his ability to creep up on me, but it's a strength I now appreciate. His father was a dragon shifter, and his mother was a wolf shifter, and Micah inherited many of her wolfish traits.

My impulse now is to propel myself down the steps into his arms, but I make myself stop, feeling suddenly vulnerable. He's held me before but always to scoop me out of danger.

This feels different.

Another fear I'm determined to face.

"We're safe now," he says, leaning back against the wall with a tired exhalation. The shadows may conceal his coloring, but not his fatigue, nor the scuffs on his brown pants and the rips in his gray T-shirt.

"The last of the Sentinels are imprisoned in the veil," he continues. "Lana and Callan will stay there tonight to make sure there isn't any trouble. They'll return tomorrow. Zahra's keeping the dragon's light safe." He takes a breath. "But you knew some of that already."

I give a quick nod.

After the fight today, Lana asked for Micah's help transporting the Sentinels into the prison within the veil.

Lana is an Avenging Angel—the first to be born in a very long time—but she's also half dragon. Her father was the dragon shifter known as the Grudge King. He was also Micah's grandfather. Which technically means that Lana is Micah's aunt. It's a little mind-bending since Lana's only a few years older than Micah.

I don't ask Micah where the veil is located. It's a secret known only to a few, and I'm happy not to be one of them. That sort of knowledge is dangerous.

As for the gold-encased diamond that we call 'the dragon's light,' Lana threw herself into raging fire to recover it from a secret place within the veil.

The stone can never again be taken behind the veil, so Lana entrusted it into the care of Callan's sister, Zahra, who's my alpha and the leader of the Dread.

"How did you know where to find me?" I ask Micah.

"Zahra told me you were out here," he says, his voice quiet.

I draw a sharp breath, guilt pricking my conscience. I'd pretended to go to bed. I thought I'd crept out without Zahra noticing.

I grimace. "I was supposed to stay indoors until you returned and gave us the all-clear. She must be going ballistic."

Micah gives a gentle shake of his head. "She's fine. The weight has lifted from her shoulders."

"Oh." The weight of responsibility. A heavy burden carried by a leader desperately trying to keep her people alive. I always understood her anger, even when it was aimed at me.

"Sophia," Micah says, taking a careful step up toward me. "Will you tell me what's weighing on *your* shoulders?"

When Lana brought the dragon's light out from behind the veil, it restored our dragon hearts and our power, allowing us to shift at will. I don't need the moonlight to shift, but I also couldn't bring myself to do it before now.

"It's the moonlight," I say without hesitation. "I don't have the courage to step into it." My shoulders hunch a little as soon as I speak my thoughts, but dammit, I want to believe that I'm safe telling him anything.

He nods slowly as he finally moves up to my side, towering over me now, so close I'm tempted to reach out and close the gap between us. "I haven't gone into the moonlight, either."

I'm surprised. "But you went to the veil."

"We reached the veil before the sun set. On the way back here, all of my old habits set in." The corners of his eyes crinkle as he casts a smile at me that nearly stops my heart.

Damn. The way his smile brightens his eyes and lifts the fatigue from his expression makes my heart beat so much faster.

I understand why his old habits would have kicked in. The Grudge, more than any other clan, became experts at hiding in the shadows and covering their tracks.

"You talk of courage," Micah continues, "but I'd rather face Sentinels than the unknown of this moonlight."

"It's the final test," I say, casting a glance across the empty, flat rooftop. "If my dragon shadow is gone, then I'm really free."

"Mine is gone," he says with certainty. "I can no longer sense or hear him."

Unlike other clans, the Grudge learned how to conceal their shadows—*and* how to communicate with them. But they were no more able to withstand the long-term destructive effects of their shadows than the Dread or the Scorn.

He reaches his hand out to me, palm up, and waits for me to take it. "As for what kind of dragons we are now, we can find out together."

I hesitate, but not because I don't want to take his hand.

It's because I'm not sure I'll be able to let him go again.

My dragon shadow was a water dragon named Bella Vorago, whose scales were glimmering, cerulean blue. When she first met Micah, she nudged her face to his in the way that dragons once bonded. Even though her form was insubstantial, I felt the connection she formed with him. But she's gone now, and I'm left to discover if her instincts were also mine.

"Hope is hard," I say.

One corner of Micah's lips twitches up. "Then let me make it easier."

Still holding his hand out to me, he steps onto the rooftop and into the light.

I gasp when the moonbeams burn across his frame, lighting up his hair and eyes, falling across his broad shoulders and glinting around his forearms where his shirt doesn't cover his skin.

His pupils slowly shift, becoming silvery and reptilian. A beast's eyes. At the same time, dark-gray scales shimmer across his visible skin, smooth and tough like the hardest stone.

I didn't see Micah's dragon shadow to know what kind of dragon it was. But in my mind, I'm suddenly whisked away to the top of a craggy mountaintop covered in ancient stones, the kind that have withstood any storm. A wolf prowls across that mountain, slipping between the jagged outcrops.

The wolf I see within my mind isn't hunting its prey.

It's searching for its pack.

Micah is both the mountain and the wolf. Steadfast and true, strong and reliable, with a heart that has space for me in it.

His eyes slowly close and his head lowers, but his hand remains outstretched toward me.

"Come with me, Sophia," he says. "Come into the light."

Every inch of my skin is tingling and my heart is pounding. Simply standing near him is shaking me to my core.

When I hesitate another heartbeat, he opens his eyes and

lifts his other hand, turning it palm up. At the same time, a shiver passes through his scales and I sense the nearness of his wings, the burst of energy that he's constraining.

"These hands will never harm you, Sophia," he says, his focus steady and calm. "No part of me will ever hurt you. Not by words or actions. I will be the solid ground beneath your feet. I'll lift you up when you need me." He pauses. "I don't have much to offer you except my heart and my home. But they're yours if you want them."

It's enough for me. It's everything.

I don't hesitate another second.

I step from the shadows into the moonlight and into the circle of his arms.

The breath catches in my chest as the moonlight falls across me, a waterfall of magic immersing me in its rays.

Cerulean-blue scales ripple across my forearms and the backs of my hands where I press them against Micah's chest. I sense the scales forming around my torso beneath my loose shirt, across my shoulders where my light-brown hair rests, up my neck, and over my cheeks. They shiver down my legs beneath my jeans and all the way to my toes.

At the same time, I'm aware of every droplet of moisture in the air. The slight sheen of sweat on his brow. And the need to explore his lips.

I exhale softly. I can't help my smile. "I'm still a water dragon."

He lifts his left hand to cup my cheek, but only lightly, the barest contact of skin on skin.

I choose to breach the gap, leaning in to his hand, sensing the roughness of the scales across his callouses and the smoothness across the center of his palm.

I lift myself up on tiptoes, slipping away from his hand and leaning into him, aware of the way his breathing hitches, the stilling of his chest where I press my palms.

The bond I want to give him carries more power even than a kiss, and I hesitate. "May I?"

"If you'll have me," he replies.

I bite my lip. Here I am asking if I can bond with him when he already asked me if I would. But in the past, I didn't have a choice about where I placed my love. Asking for his permission gives me the reassurance I need to be sure his bond is willingly given. That I will never take by force the same things that were once taken from me.

My nose touches his before I slip my face to the side and press my cheek to his.

His arms slide around my waist, supporting my back as I remain there, my eyes closed.

His breathing deepens.

So does mine.

I never thought I could feel peace like this.

It makes my eyes burn with hot tears but I don't feel vulnerable letting them fall. Rather, my dragon nature seems to welcome the tears.

Micah tugs me gently downward, our cheeks still pressed to each other's as we settle, kneeling side by side on the rooftop.

There's a soft *thump* and a rush of air as his wings finally release and then I'm enveloped in a silver-gray cocoon that folds around my back, open at the top to allow the light to radiate around us.

I haven't released my wings, and I don't feel the need to. Not yet.

Very slowly, I withdraw my cheek just a little, my lips brushing his jaw as I move and then stop. So close to his mouth that the corners of our lips touch.

This time, he whispers against my lips. "May I?"

After a lifetime of not controlling when I was kissed, his question is more valuable to me than dragon's gold could ever be.

"Yes."

He turns and his lips touch mine and that's when I know I was wrong before, because brushing my cheek to his is not more powerful than this.

As his mouth moves over mine, striking awake sensations that ripple through my entire body, the air we breathe becomes *ours*. The light pouring around us becomes ours. Every wound and every hurt from my past disappears, wiped clean, and for a small moment, I know true bliss.

Fire in the hands he presses to my back.

Need in the quickening of my breath and the heat growing in my center.

Want in the groan that sounds in the back of his throat as I press closer to him.

I slide my hands to his stomach, needing to draw up his shirt and press against his naked skin, needing to get closer to him, but before I succeed—

A shadow drops over us.

It's sudden and cold and brings so much darkness to my heart that I gasp against Micah's lips.

Our kiss breaks and it feels like glass cracking, leaving only shards that pierce my chest.

I can't breathe. My entire body is being compressed by an external force and my fingers and toes are suddenly freezing.

My heart squeezes and pounds, and my ears fill with buzzing, a low drone that sounds like a moan of wind through a dank cavern.

Every shred of hope and love drains from me as my peace shatters.

CHAPTER TWO

My gaze shoots upward.

Above us, far too close, a dark cloud has gathered.

It has no distinct shape but spills across the air above the rooftop like a mass of soot, swilling and glistening as if it were made of ground onyx.

What the fuck is that?

Micah's arms and wings tighten around me, but even the pressure of his body can't stop the shudder wracking me.

He wrenches me to my feet while I struggle to drag in enough breath to force sound past my lips.

I gasp. "We need to move!"

I don't know what this shadow is, but I know we need to escape it.

Micah's wings spread wide as he releases me from his hold. I extend my own wings, unable to take any joy from the moment they *thump* into the air. They're strong and bright even in the darkness, a reminder that I'm not as vulnerable as I once was.

Even so, I've only begun learning how to defend myself. I haven't trained for years like Lana, Callan, and Micah have. I haven't spent my life honing my body or learning how to handle a knife or a gun. I don't have any dragon's gold to use as a weapon and even if I did, my ability to control dragon's gold is modest and new.

I'm sensible enough to know that running is still my best option. *If only I could make myself fucking move!*

The very tip of my left wing nudges into the moonlight beyond the dark shadow and that small touch of light clears my head. Not by much. Just enough for me to break through my frozen thoughts and launch myself into action driven by instinct.

We have to get to safety.

I can't let this hellish shadow take hold of us.

I won't lose Micah.

Grabbing his arm, I prepare to launch myself to the side of the rooftop so we can fly out from under the dark cloud, enter the moonlight, shake off this awful dread, and fight back against whatever this new threat is.

I've barely managed to take a step before the cloud descends on us.

Before my eyes, the glistening mist draws together into the shape of clawed hands and scaled legs and wings that extend so far on either side that I can't follow them in the seconds I have left to act.

In that moment of hesitation, Micah deftly slips free from my hold to step between me and the oncoming form before I can stop him.

His wide eyes, silvery in the dark, dominate my vision as he drags air into his chest, the wheezing sound he makes telling me he's fighting as hard as I am to breathe. "Run, Sophia!"

Then he's turning away from me—whirling to face the oncoming danger, his wings held at his sides as he makes a shield of himself, just as he's done so many times for me before.

My heart wrenches as I face the choice between doing what he wants, what I know will keep me alive—running—and standing my ground because I will never break the bond I've just formed with him.

You stand beside those you love. You don't leave them to fight battles on their own. Not even when they tell you to save yourself.

I plant my feet as the cloud finishes drawing together, and finally, its form is visible.

A dragon shifter rages toward us. The black scales covering his entire body glisten in the moonlight while wisps of black mist swirl around his torso and wings. His eyes are pure black and his hair is as dark as coal. If he's wearing pants, they meld seamlessly into his form.

His low growl, the sound of a mindless predator, fills my ears and freezes me to the spot.

Even though the cloud has drawn together into the shape of the dragon, a layer of shadow remains blanketing the moon, keeping its healing rays from me, keeping me within the shadow of dread.

"Time to die, Grudge," the dragon snarls as his fist flies out, his black claws ready to slash at Micah's throat.

Pure fucking fear fills my mind and my heart.

But a heartbeat later, terror turns to rage.

This creature has stolen a moment from me that I will never get back. I don't know who this beast is, why he's here, or what he wants, but I will die before I let anyone hurt Micah and take my future away from me.

Beating my wings and rising into the air, higher than Micah's head, I dart forward at the same moment that Micah's fist flies out. My intention is to fly down on our attacker from above and my trajectory is perfect, but fear rushes through me when Micah's hand connects with the dragon's body.

Micah punches right through the dragon's scales without harming him. The dragon's body turns to mist around Micah's fist and arm, as if the beast really were made of nothing more than shadows and dust.

The momentum takes Micah forward into the path of the dragon's claw, but he manages to twist at the last moment, dropping so that the dragon's hand flies over his head instead.

Micah's arm tears all the way through the black dragon's body and exits through its side.

The beast doesn't appear remotely harmed. He's already lifting his fists, both together, preparing to drive them down onto the back of Micah's exposed head and split his skull.

My thoughts are whirling as fast as the air rushing past me as I adjust my aim mid-flight.

This creature may have the ability to disintegrate to take a blow, but if it intends to hurt Micah, its fists will have to remain solid.

I fly at the black dragon's upraised arm, grab hold of his clenched right fist, and wrench upward. His scales are icy cold within my hand, drawing a scream of pain to my lips, but I won't let go.

His head snaps back, his eyes narrowing, as if incredulous that I dared to fight back. He abandons his attack as he's forced to pivot to rebalance himself while his fist remains solid.

Within seconds, his hand opens and his palm closes over my wrist so that we're both suddenly gripping each other.

His hold is stronger than I could have imagined.

Damn!

My upward momentum and new strength lift him off his feet and he uses his hold on me to his advantage, beating his wings and attempting to fly toward me—no doubt to knock me across the air. At the same time, his other hand reaches for the lower edge of my wing as if he would pull it right off when he hurls me backward.

Micah hasn't remained still, and it seems he's learning fast.

Before the beast can leave the ground more than a foot, Micah punches through the dragon's nearest wing. His blows are rapid, his fists smashing the beast's scales into plumes of dust as he extends and retracts his arms at full speed.

It doesn't hurt the beast, but it stops him from gaining air because of the rapidly forming holes in his wing—unlike his other wing, which catches air and throws him off-balance.

The black dragon lets go of my arm and drops to the rooftop.

I tumble backward, free of his hold.

Micah's defense of me only seems to have made the dragon angrier.

With a roar, he swings back to Micah, standing taller even than Micah's towering build.

Micah's teeth are gritted, his feet planted, and in his eyes, I see even more of the wolf that lives in his soul.

"Who the fuck are you?" Micah demands to know, squaring his shoulders, watching the beast approach once more.

"I'm your death," the beast replies.

Once again, the dragon swings his claws toward Micah's throat, but Micah aims for the beast's wrist, blocking the blow and punching at the dragon's face. It's a quick jab that smacks into the beast's jaw, a solid hit before dust flies around his face, seeming to cushion the blow.

Even though the dragon is only knocked back a single step, it gives me hope that he isn't as fully in control of his power as he wants to be. If he's a dragon shifter with new powers that only emerged today, then his control will be as new to him as mine is to me.

If his face remained solid for a beat too long, then maybe other parts of him will too.

The beast shakes his head, recovering before Micah can land another blow.

He dives back at Micah.

The two men exchange hits, but nearly every time, it doesn't seem to matter how fast or skillfully Micah moves—his fists merely churn through the dragon's shadowy form. It's also clear that Micah can't put the full force of his strength into each blow since he has to be able to retract his arm quickly so he doesn't lose his balance.

What's more, his ragged inhalations tell me he's struggling to draw a proper breath, just as I am. He won't be able to keep this up.

Knowing I can't recklessly throw myself into the fight—to do so could make things worse for Micah if I get in his way—I take a moment to study the way the beast moves, watching the shadows and mist that cling to his form and then casting my gaze up to the thin, dark cloud that continues to cover the moon above us.

How can I fight a shadow?

I focus on his back and the way he keeps his wings ready, using them to gain height to give more strength to each blow. The best I can do is to impede his ability to use his wings and I need to do so fast.

Darting toward the dragon's back as he moves to once again lift off the rooftop and gain height, I aim for the spot between his wings and grab hold of his wing bones where they meet his shoulders. My hands pull right through his bones, and I tumble back through the air, but I achieved my intention.

I upset the dragon's balance.

Even so, it came at a cost. The dragon may be like a cloud of ash, but the icy feeling that flows through my palms is too real and so is the fine dust that remains on my skin. Flecks of it suddenly fill my heart with ice when they don't rub off. They're tiny, but I sense them draining my strength as sure as a blow to my heart would.

How many flecks now rest on Micah's skin?

His labored breathing tells me too many.

With a cry of fear, I throw myself back at the dragon, abandoning caution. Wrenching at his left wing with one hand, I punch through his back with the other, driving my arm right through his torso.

It's like pushing through gritty ashes. Every particle bites my skin, scratching and grinding and cutting through my scales, and when I retract my arm with a hoarse scream, my limb comes away covered in cuts and blood.

My fear for Micah grows even worse. He's punched his arms through the dragon's body over and over again and it must only be the toughness of his scales that's prevented his arms from being ripped up.

Unless I simply can't see the blood through the layer of dust that's now clinging to him.

The dragon gives a frustrated roar and spins to me, his fist flying wildly at my face.

I'm already darting backward. I narrowly evade the blow but manage to rasp a taunt. "Come for *me*, you fucking coward."

The dragon's growl is low and cold as he plows after me, his footfalls soundless. "Silly Sophia. You never learned respect."

My eyes widen at how familiarly he speaks to me. *Silly Sophia.* It's the dismissal my mother would give whenever I tried to ask for her help.

Silly Sophia, it's all in your head.

Silly Sophia, you have it far better than I ever did.

Silly Sophia, be grateful Tyler doesn't throw you out.

Silly Sophia, if you were a better wife, he would be nicer to you—

My mother called me "silly" so many times that my ex-husband took to using it, too.

A maelstrom of emotions springs to life within me, but I feel like a butterfly beating at my old cage.

If I could draw a full breath, I would let my rage loose in a scream.

All I can manage is a whisper. "Tyler."

CHAPTER THREE

My ex-husband pulls to a stop, raising himself fully upright, his shadow engulfing me in icy darkness.

"I warned you that you wouldn't survive without me." The corners of Tyler's lips rise and his eyes gleam at me, as if he's mocking me for taking so long to recognize him, but how could I have?

The Tyler I knew had blond hair, fair skin, and gray-blue eyes. He only picked fights against opponents he thought he could beat. He never would have taken on a Grudge dragon in the past, let alone their leader. *Never.*

But now…

He clearly has strength and power he never had before.

His entire form has changed, even more than mine has.

The dragon's light was created to give dragons the power to evolve. It was intended to allow each new generation to be born with traits that ensured our survival through the ages and kept us in balance with an inevitably changing environment. The ability to take human form is one of those traits. The absence of an aura is another since it helps us evade detection from other supernaturals.

By bringing the dragon's light back into the world, Lana restored our ability to have our own souls and our ability to find our hearts. No more will we struggle to shift or to have children or to blend into human society.

But the changes in Tyler are beyond anything I imagined possible.

Was his heart truly this dark that this is what he's become?

Micah's voice cuts through the frozen silence that was squeezing my insides, his command aimed at Tyler. "Step away from Sophia."

It's not the first time Micah has placed himself between me and my ex. He first did it within the Scorn's territory—the clan with which Tyler has aligned himself. I didn't need Micah's help then, but I'm not too proud to admit that I need it now.

Micah and I *both* need help. We can't fight Tyler alone. Not in his new form.

For a second, my gaze flashes to the door leading back into the building. Zahra is one of the strongest dragons alive, but to run to her would take the threat to her daughter, too. The other two dragons I consider family—the Lamonte cousins, Beatrix and Felix—are too far away. They left earlier to take the rightful leader of the Scorn, the teenager Gisela, to safety. They wouldn't have hesitated to fight, but they aren't here.

The corners of Tyler's eyes crinkle as he tips his chin at me, his posture deceptively relaxed. "You don't give me orders, Grudge."

I know that look on Tyler's face. It's the disarming smile he wears to hide the fact that he's about to lash out.

My gasped cry of warning barely breaks the air when Tyler swings toward Micah, throwing a low punch.

Tyler's black claws extend just before his fist smacks into Micah's ribs and the *crack* shatters my hope.

"No! Micah!"

The force of the punch propels Micah across the rooftop. He lands heavily on his side, his upper wing partially covering his torso and lower face. His eyes are closed and his breathing is shallow. I can't see the extent of the wound Tyler's claws will have made, but the crack signaled at least one broken rib.

I fully retract my wings, knowing they're a liability if Tyler grabs them, and dart to the side, attempting to reach Micah.

Tyler's reflexes are far quicker than they were before. He catches me before I can make it past him, pulling me back against his hard frame—my back to his chest—even as I struggle to free myself.

His arms bite painfully into my diaphragm and crush my breasts while his voice sounds in my ear.

"Where are your guard dogs, Sophia?"

Guard dogs?

His voice becomes harsher, more demanding. "Where are Callan Steele and Asper Ashen-Varr? You will tell me or I will crush the Grudge dragon's skull beneath my feet."

Tyler uses Lana's official name—her angel name. I know that she and Callan are in the veil, but I'm even more grateful now that I don't know where that is.

If I did…

My focus flickers to Micah. Overwhelming dread rises with me as he continues to lie still. But no, even if I knew where the entrance to the veil was located, I wouldn't tell Tyler.

"You're lucky they aren't here," I say.

His lips press to my ear and a shiver of revulsion wracks me.

"Oh, but I want them here," he whispers. "I want them to know that I can end them."

My brow furrows. Callan and Lana are fire dragons. The most powerful of our kind. On top of that, Lana is an Avenging Angel, the strongest angel born in centuries. She fought and defeated both the angels' leader—the Celestial Ascendant—and Dominus Audax, who was one of the most ferocious fire dragons ever born.

Now that her own dragon heart has been restored, she's powerful beyond measure.

But… Tyler sounds very certain and again my dread grows.

I tell myself: *No*. Even with all the power Tyler has demonstrated tonight, he could never survive Callan's fire or Lana's strength, especially not if they fight him together.

"What happened to you, Tyler?" I ask, hatred and a strange sort of deep pity coating my tongue.

He was never kind to me, but there was a time when he didn't scheme like he does now.

"What do you mean, Sophia?" He gives a soft laugh. "I'm more myself than I've ever been."

"You betrayed everyone who ever cared about you."

He stiffens, his arms clamping so tightly around me that my head swims as I struggle to draw breath. The press of his chest against my back amplifies the helplessness I feel. It's the same draining of hope I felt the moment he appeared in the sky.

"You talk to me of betrayal," he snaps, "but I always knew Callan would kill me eventually. I knew it the moment he ended Byron."

Byron was a Dread dragon. He'd murdered a human woman —the sister of one of Callan's human bodyguards. The punishment was death, which Callan meted out with brutal efficiency.

Tyler slides his arm away from my chest and grabs the side of my head, his big fingers wrapping around my cheekbone and forehead. In the moment that he moves, I struggle again, but my new strength is nothing compared to his.

"Now, tell me where they are," he orders me.

"I don't know. They've gone into the veil." I speak with honesty, since there's nothing I can tell him that would jeopardize my friends' safety. He knows about the existence of the veil. Most supernaturals do. It's the location of its entrance that is guarded so heavily.

But my voice lowers. "There's a prison in the veil, Tyler. An awful, dark prison. Lana will judge you and put you there."

"Bars can't hold dust," he whispers into my ear and then he pauses before he continues. "But I believe you when you say you don't know where the veil is. After all, why would your leaders share something so important with *you*?"

I squeeze my eyes shut. His words are intended to cut me and make me feel like I don't matter.

But my experiences over the last few weeks have helped me to trust in myself. To believe that I matter.

So strange that it was Lana, the angel who had hunted me, who first encouraged me to believe that there were members of my clan who truly cared for me: Callan in particular, but also Beatrix and Felix, the cruel cousins who'd scared the shit out of me for years.

They have my back now.

"You can't hurt me," I say to Tyler, feeling the truth of it to my core.

Well, physically he can, but not emotionally.

I have shields of warmth and kindness around my heart now that I never had before.

"I can," he responds. "And I will."

He spins me around so that I'm facing him, his palms as rough as the ash I drove my fist through.

I plant my hands against his chest, finding his torso solid, but I'm not fooled. The moment I try to fight back, he'll turn to smoke again.

Still, I prepare to shove him away from me, hoping to break through his steel-like grip and dislodge the arms that bite into my back.

"Come back to me, Sophia," he says, his dark eyes gleaming down at me. "Or I will end everyone you love, one by one. Starting with this Grudge dragon."

I shake my head, my response quiet but sure. "No."

His eyes widen a little, a hint of the surprise he must feel that I continue to defy him, before they narrow to dark slits.

"I don't think you understand," he says. "I will take everyone away from you until you finally realize I'm the only one who really loves you."

I sigh softly. "You never loved me, Tyler. You controlled me and acted as if you owned me. Love doesn't include either of those things."

His lips twist and his hands tighten on my arms, his claws extending and pricking my skin as he leans in. "Soon, *my* love will be the only love you'll have left."

And still, he insists that the way he treats me is love.

I will never make him see that our relationship was toxic.

But his assertions tell me one thing: He isn't here to kill me. He wants to keep me alive. After all, he can't make me suffer if I'm dead.

While that realization eases my immediate panic, my fear remains for Micah, who continues to lie still behind me.

If I don't get him out of here, Tyler will kill him.

I push against Tyler's hands and arms, struggling to free myself. There's nothing I can say that won't inflame him.

I could threaten him, cajole him, beg him, appease him, and he will respond only with violence, so once again, I speak the truth. "You have a chance for peace, Tyler. Don't throw it away."

"I don't want peace!" Tyler shoves me away from himself, a downward push. I imagine he wanted me to land on my knees at his feet. To crumple under the force of his physical strength and beg him for mercy.

Instead, I plant my right hand on the rooftop, maintaining my balance, and use the angle of his shove against him. My right leg sweeps out, my foot cutting through his calves.

The sharp ash that makes up his body swills at my attack.

I can't topple him, but I'm hoping to distract him for long enough that I can launch myself away from him and reach Micah.

My only plan now is to use every heartbeat to scoop Micah into my arms, spread my wings, and fly him to safety. I have to believe that I'm strong enough to carry his weight. At least down to the street below us, where cars and trucks continue to pass by as humans go about their nights in Philadelphia.

Tyler would never dare expose his dragon form to them.

Even if I can only force him to shift back into his human form, at least then I'll be able to fight him.

But he's faster than I am. As I fling myself backward, he grabs my descending foot, wrenches it upward, and flips me onto my back. The rush of scales across my skin protects me from the worst of the fall, but the wind is knocked out of me.

His face blurs above me as I try to clear my head.

He wears a cruel smile as he reaches down for me. "Now you're on your back where you belong."

I try to stop the sob of panic filling my throat. Fear won't help me. I have to trust that I can get myself out of this. I've seen Lana fight using her wings to balance herself, even propel herself away from a surface. I'm still getting used to having wings, but I tell myself I can do what she does.

I'm about to release my wings and push myself up and through Tyler's entire fucking body if I have to when a shout echoes across the rooftop.

"Sophia, stay down!"

The voice is familiar. It's young, female.

It sounds like Gisela Scorn, who fought beside me today, but I can't see her to be sure of her identity.

I have no reason to distrust her.

I fight the intense urge to run and plaster myself to the ground instead.

At her shout, Tyler's head snapped up and now he casts around wildly for her location, but he can't seem to see her, either.

If it is Gisela, then she's skilled at concealing herself.

I shouldn't be surprised. After all, her mother was one of the most cunning assassins.

A second later, multiple soft *pops* sound close by, coming from the direction of the shadowed rooftop next door—the one at Tyler's back.

He twists toward the sounds and then chaos breaks loose.

CHAPTER FOUR

The air explodes with golden bullets.

They're as quiet as whispers as they shoot across the space above me, nearly too fast to follow, and cut through the front of Tyler's chest in a stream of glinting gold.

His eyes fly wide. He inhales a loud breath. For a second, the confident mask on his face remains, but then his back arches.

A second stream of bullets rips through his chest from behind, tearing up his form.

Every golden projectile punches holes in his torso, arms, wings, and upper legs, sending smoke and ash swirling and causing his silhouette to bleed into the air around him.

The shooting isn't only back and forth. Each bullet carves an impossible curve through the air, circling back at full speed and cutting through him again.

And again and again.

The tornado of bullets circles and whips through his body, each one traveling in a tight arc. So fast that they're mere golden streaks within the churning ash of Tyler's form.

He tucks his wings to his sides, attempting to make himself a smaller target, but it doesn't seem to help.

A maelstrom of ash and soot swirls around his body while the onslaught of bullets drives him to his knees.

The breath has caught in my throat, but within my mind, I'm screaming at myself to get away from him while I can.

If only my arms and legs were functioning. Everywhere that Tyler's ash remains on my body, my limbs are slowly becoming numb.

Managing to turn onto my stomach, I drag myself across the rooftop and away from Tyler while keeping myself low in case of stray bullets. I can't move fast enough, progressing inch by painful inch.

The dust on my legs where I kicked Tyler is like a weight I can't dislodge while the film on my hands and arms is making it difficult to pull myself along.

I convince myself I can make it back to Micah, clawing my fingers and dragging them against the rooftop when my legs refuse to obey me.

I'm grateful that the bullets are giving me a reprieve from Tyler's attention.

Nobody but Sienna Scorn had ever had this much skill with golden bullets. She'd been the leader of the Scorn dragons, the clan of thieves and murderers who had assimilated into the supernatural underground. That is, until Lana ended her.

This new storm can only be the work of her daughter, Gisela, which confirms for me that it was her who shouted for me to stay down.

I've nearly reached Micah when Gisela finally appears and alights on the rooftop beside me, tucking her wings into her sides.

She's young, only fourteen, with blue-black hair, pale skin, and high cheekbones. Dressed in black from her boots up to her chin. Her arms are outstretched, a golden pistol bearing a silencer held in each hand. Her face is a picture of concentration as she continues to fire each weapon.

My eyes widen at the number of apparently fully-loaded

spare magazines that rest within a strap across her chest, and the speed with which she reloads the moment her guns are empty. All without missing a beat as she storms toward Tyler.

Behind him, I finally spy a second dragon shifter—the source of the bullets that shot through his back.

I recognize Dane, the fifteen-year-old Scorn dragon sworn to protect Gisela. He also holds two weapons with silencers and wears a belt with spare magazines in it.

As he alights on the rooftop, he retracts his dark green wings. Despite his younger age, he's already broad-shouldered. He has a strong jawline and muted, green eyes that appear shadowy in the dark.

"You think you can steal my clan, Tyler Dalton?!" Gisela shouts. "The Scorn are my people, and I will fight to the death for them."

Because she's Sienna's daughter, Gisela is the rightful leader of the Scorn. When I first met her, she didn't have a dragon and, as a consequence, she was despised by her mother. It was why Tyler was able to take control of the Scorn after Sienna's death.

But Gisela's powers have clearly changed and the position of alpha can be won by a fight to the death, the same way that Callan won the Dread. He later willingly handed over the role of alpha to his sister, but a peaceful changing of hands is a rare occurrence among dragon shifter clans, even when it's from parent to child.

"I'm challenging you, Tyler," Gisela calls. She lowers her guns, no longer firing new bullets while the storm of gold continues to churn through Tyler's body. "A fight between you and me to determine who leads the Scorn."

She glances back at me and then to Micah, who has remained unconscious and is still several paces away from me. "Without collateral damage."

"If death is what you want, then you'll have it," Tyler snarls, the contours of his face barely visible within the storm of dust. I'm surprised when he continues. "But not today."

Gisela gives a hiss. "You would run from this fight?"

Tyler's laugh makes my blood run cold. "I'm not running. I will simply wait for fear and darkness to spread. Then you'll realize how truly weak you are."

He pushes forward through the continuing barrage of bullets, his form seeming to waft across the ground, a mass of smoke and ash.

The sense of dread burrows more deeply into my heart.

Gisela now stands between him and me and, despite the bullets that are clearly hampering his movement, he is a tower of might filling the air in front of her.

She holds herself tall despite her young age, her hair shining brightly and her hands hovering once more over the guns at her waist.

Even within the simmering cloud of wrath that Tyler forms, I sense his focus is not on her anymore.

Gisela twitches when his next words are clearly directed at me.

"I will come for you, Sophia," he says in a low whisper that sounds once again like a moan of wind through a dank cavern. "These bullets can't kill me. Nothing can. Fear is eternal and so am I."

His lips curve into a cruel smile. "I only choose to leave now because you will tell others what you've seen here. Your terror will fester, and each night when you fall asleep, you will ask yourself if this is the night I will come for you.

"You can't hide from me. I own the darkness. Nobody can protect you. Not even your precious Avenging Angel."

There's a rush of air at my back and I'm startled when two new figures alight onto the rooftop beside me. I should have been able to hear the beat of their wings before now, but my ears are still buzzing and my heart feels like it's working overtime to keep beating.

Beatrix Lamonte lands on my left and holds her blood-red wings aloft to form a shield around me while her cousin, Felix, tucks his wings and crouches on my right, positioned close to Micah.

The cousins are both tall and lean with the same high cheekbones that belong to many Scorn dragons. They have straight, black hair; dark eyes; and pale skin. Beatrix's hair is cut at an angle along her jaw, while Felix wears his longer hair in a bun. They were born into the Scorn clan but are now Dread dragons loyal to Callan and Zahra.

"Like fuck she can't," Beatrix replies to Tyler's assertion that Lana can't protect me. "Asper Ashen-Varr will tear you to shreds, Tyler." Beatrix's sneer turns into a sweet smile. "Assuming there's anything left of you once Gisela is done with you."

At the appearance of the cousins, Tyler steps backward. No matter his confident threats, he's well and truly outnumbered now. "Don't forget what I said, Sophia."

A moment later, he bursts into a cloud of soot and ash that seems to swarm like insects before it forms a tornado and rushes upward.

Finally, he disappears into the sky and takes the darkness with him.

The haze across the moon clears. Light strikes down around us, although it's muted now that natural clouds have gathered.

The moment Tyler rises from the rooftop, the golden bullets zip in two directions: half to Gisela where she stands near me, and the remaining bullets to Dane where he crouches on the other side of the rooftop. The bullets deposit themselves neatly into the magazines resting against their chests.

I slump to the ground as Gisela and Dane rush toward me.

Beatrix bends to me first. "Sophia! Are you okay?"

I can't answer her. The worst of the pressure around my chest has lifted and my fingers and toes are flooding with feeling, no longer freezing, but my dread is quickly becoming panic.

The fine sheen of dust that gathered on my hands and arms

when I punched Tyler is still there even now that he's gone. So is the grit on my legs.

So is all of the ash covering Micah's body. A blanket of it rests across his dragon scales, layered over his entire form.

He still hasn't moved.

I can't stop my cry. "Micah!"

I claw at the ground, trying to make myself move. The weight on my legs and arms remains, and the small gap between me and Micah feels like a mile.

My focus rises to Beatrix. "You have to help him! Please!"

She's already moving, but Felix gets to Micah first, bending to the Grudge dragon and carefully peering at him without touching him.

Micah's eyes remain closed and his scales are a dull gray.

Far too dull.

"Is he breathing?" My question is panicked. The stillness of Micah's chest is scaring the fuck out of me.

Felix lifts a calming hand in my direction. "He's breathing. It's shallow but steady."

I slump with a soft cry, fighting back my tears of relief. If Micah is breathing, it not only means he's alive, but that his cracked ribs didn't pierce his lungs. It's a small mercy.

"I've never seen anything like this." Felix casts an alarmed glance at Beatrix, who has remained beside me. "What is this substance coating Micah's skin?" Felix gives me a quick onceover. "And yours, too, Sophia?"

"It was Tyler." I struggle to find the words to describe the grit that remains on Micah and me.

Is it shadow? Mist?

Fear in a tangible form?

Ash seems like the best description since it's rough and gray and leaves me feeling as if I've been burned to cinders.

"Every time Micah came into contact with Tyler, more of this ash covered his body. Just like it did with me." My arm shakes as I hold up my hand to indicate where the ash has turned my own skin a pallid gray.

Beatrix reaches down to help me up. She and I were never friends. In fact, there were times when we fucking hated each other, but now she holds her hands out for me despite Felix's quick, quiet warning.

"Beatrix, be careful," he says. "We don't know what this ash is or what it can do to us."

Beatrix's arms close around me without pause. "I'm not letting Sophia cut her elbows and knees to shreds dragging herself to Micah. She needs to be near him."

Tears burn behind my eyes as Beatrix's arms tighten around me.

She helps me upward and supports me for the four steps it takes to reach Micah's side. Then she helps me lower myself down next to him where I can kneel beside him.

Now leaning against his chest, I reach for his cold face.

Tears slide down my cheeks. "Micah was trying to protect me. He kept punching through Tyler's body and each time he made contact, more of this ash covered his body."

Beatrix kneels beside me, but I sense her sudden tension.

She checks her hands and arms where she touched me, revealing that some of the dust has rubbed off on her. She brushes at it, an increasingly panicked movement when the dust sticks to her skin. "Fuck! It won't come off."

"Oh no," I whisper.

It's spreading. Transferring from one of us to the other through touch and then sticking to us.

Beatrix shivers so violently that her scales recede. She stares at her dusty palms before she wraps her arms around herself. "It's plucking at my soul."

"Taking away your happiness," I whisper.

"Yes." Beatrix gives a low moan. "Like falling into a dark pit with no way out."

Just as Tyler threatened, fear is spreading.

CHAPTER FIVE

I can only stare in horror at the dust coating Beatrix's skin.

Dust that I transferred to her.

At that moment, Gisela and Dane approach us quickly across the rooftop, and it's clear they've been listening to our conversation when they keep their distance.

They settle into a crouch on my left.

Dane cranes his neck to study Micah's face without touching him. "It must be some kind of toxin."

He glances up at Gisela, who nods.

She explains to me, "Every Scorn dragon is taught about poisons. My mother had many different toxins in her vault, some very rare. But I've never seen anything like this. It seems to be keeping him unconscious."

"Or slowly killing him," I whisper, unable to conceal my fears.

"I agree it's some kind of toxin," Felix says, rising to his feet on my right. "It must be a new power belonging to Tyler's dragon. Just as Callan and Lana can breathe fire. Tyler can do this. Whatever *this* is."

"Like water is part of me." I swipe at my tears before I hunch over Micah, pressing my forehead to his. I'm certain I already have ash on my face—the buzzing in my head indicates it—so this contact with his skin shouldn't worsen my condition.

I let my tears fall. "How do we help him?"

Beatrix's hand lands softly on my shoulder, but her whisper is urgent. "Sophia, look."

She gestures to Micah's face where my thumb brushes slowly back and forth across his cheek, smearing my tears over his skin.

Where the liquid has fallen, his scales are glistening again. Bright and living. His eyelids flicker and, even though he doesn't open his eyes, I sense his breathing deepening a little.

"Water." I gasp, looking to Beatrix and the others for confirmation. "I can't seem to rub the ash off my palms but could it be as simple as washing it off in water?"

Of course, I'm ignoring the possibility that there could be some aspect of my tears that's helping him, but even if I wept my heart out, I couldn't create enough to bathe Micah.

"Can you summon the rain?" Beatrix asks with hope in her eyes.

I shake my head, my despair returning. "I've only ever manipulated raindrops once they were falling. I've never created them. We need a water source large enough to fully immerse ourselves, and we need it soon. Before this ash does any further damage."

Damn, my mind is foggy now. The longer I stay like this, imprisoned in a sheen of dust, the worse I feel.

"A large water source?" Felix points west. "You have it."

He's pointing in the direction of the Schuylkill River. It's only five blocks away, its swilling water a constant sound beneath the hum of vehicles and nightlife on the streets below.

"I'll help you carry him," Felix says.

"No." My response is immediate. "You'll only endanger yourself. We have no guarantees that river water will work. Beatrix and I are already affected. We'll have to manage by ourselves."

Beatrix nods to me. "We can do this." She quickly turns to Felix. "You need to warn Zahra. Tell her about this new threat so she can decide if this building is still the safest place for her and Emika to stay. She may even need to seek help from Micah's clan. They hid for decades without being found."

Beatrix then turns her attention to Gisela and Dane, giving them an apologetic grimace. "I'm sorry, but Zahra's trust is hard to win. Even though you fought by our sides today, you're Scorn dragons. You can't go with Felix into Zahra's home unless she invites you."

Don't I know it. When I brought Lana back to this building with Micah and the angel Isaac, Zahra had come out on the offense, attacking us without hesitation. It was only because of Lana's control of dragon's gold that nobody was hurt.

Gisela gives a nod. "We understand. We can fly with you to the river to make sure you reach it safely."

But Beatrix shakes her head. "I won't be able to camouflage all of us. It's better if Sophia and I go alone so I can focus on shielding her and Micah."

Gisela's brow creases with apparent worry, and Felix looks like he's going to object, but I get in first.

"Camouflage?" I ask.

Beatrix's eyes light up. "Felix and I have a new power that will help us fly without being spotted by humans."

As she speaks, muted wine-red scales form over her entire body. They don't shimmer like my scales do and at first I think she's trying to show me that she won't stand out as much, but then she plants her hand on the rooftop and its motley color floods across her hand and up her arm.

My eyes widen when her scales morph across her upper body, mimicking the color of the building and the sky in the distance behind her.

Within seconds, I can't distinguish her from her surroundings.

Her visually disembodied voice says, "As long as I'm

touching you, I can camouflage you too. In this case, I'm hoping that my power will flow through Micah so that by holding him, you'll vanish from sight at well."

"So that's how you all crept up on Tyler," I whisper.

Beatrix's scales ripple and her form returns to view. "We're still learning how to control it. I can't maintain it for longer than ten minutes, although I'll try. We'll need to move fast."

The light fades from her eyes as she rubs her palms against her black jeans, as if the darkness is pushing at her mind again.

"For more reasons than one," I say.

Beatrix turns a rueful smile up at Gisela. "You and Dane should get to safety."

Gisela pauses, as if she's about to argue, before she nods. She says to Felix, "You know how to contact us. As soon as Zahra makes a decision, let us know how we can help." Gisela draws herself upright. "I won't let Tyler win."

At Felix's firm nod, Gisela and Dane step back into the rooftop's shadows and within moments, they're gone.

Beatrix reaches for me again. "Sophia? Are you ready?"

I grit my teeth. "I'll take Micah's head. You take his legs."

I'm lucky Tyler's body didn't come into contact with my wings or they'd be no use to me. Thankfully, I'd already retracted them before he grabbed me.

It's my arms I'm most worried about. I can only pray they won't give out on me in the air. Particularly as some of the dust on Micah's body could rub off onto us and make things worse.

Beatrix seems to be thinking the same thing. Her lips press together in a worried line as she casts a glance at her arms, but without further hesitation, she scoops Micah's upper wing over his body.

Together, we turn him onto his side so we can pull his lower wing around him, wrapping him up and cocooning him.

Felix keeps watch as we work. He's always been the quieter of the two cousins, but I've come to know him as a dragon of action. The way his hands twitch and he steps toward us several times tells me he doesn't like that he can't help us.

Once Micah is safely wrapped in his wings and his head is supported within the cocoon we've created, Beatrix and I continue to coordinate our movements, crouching, sliding our arms under his body, and lifting.

"Damn," I whisper when my legs buckle before I can spread my wings.

Felix darts forward and nearly touches me, but I ward him off with a fierce glare. "I can do this."

Concentrating as hard as I can, I extend my wings, controlling the movement so I don't bump anyone. Then I force myself fully upright again, grinding my teeth with effort.

Beatrix follows my lead, lifting Micah at the same time I do. We're incredibly lucky that our wings curve enough at the sides that they don't collide as we rise into the air, but our mistimed wing beats buffet the wind around us, making us tip to one side.

"We need to be in sync," Beatrix cries. "Up, down... Up, down."

I follow Beatrix's lead, beating my wings in time with her voice as we wobble into the air.

Damn, we're like acrobats clinging to nothing but hope right now.

I don't dare look back in case I upset our precarious balance, but I sense Felix's burning gaze.

I'm not sure how I'll know when Beatrix uses her power to camouflage us, but in the next second, my body tingles, as if a low-level vibration were passing through it.

When I dare to glance back at Beatrix, her forehead is creased in concentration.

She gives me a brief smile. Even though nothing looks different to me, I hope her power is working.

It worries me a little, now that we're in the air, that she will have to use her power while fighting off the effects of the ash on her skin. I may have more of the dust on me, but her energy could drain faster than mine.

Thankfully, we can take a straight line to the river since we don't need to keep to the shadows.

I fly as fast as possible, my concentration intense as I focus on keeping my wing beats in time with Beatrix's, but I'm frighteningly aware that my arms won't hold out much longer.

I try to lace my fingers behind Micah's torso, only to find that my hands are completely numb.

Up ahead, the river is like a black snake meandering between the riverbanks. There's a bridge a little farther to the north and I'd prefer to dive into the river beneath the bridge's shadow, but I'm afraid we won't make it that far.

Groaning with effort, I push on until we pass the riverbank.

The water sparkles beneath us and the moment I see it, my muscles give way.

My arms and legs cramp up, my wings shudder, Micah's weight is suddenly unbearable, and then I'm falling.

I cry a warning to Beatrix, only to find that she's already plummeting toward the water behind me. Her wings are fully retracted, and my brief glimpse of her face tells me her eyes are closed.

Fear shoots through me. Not only for Micah, but for Beatrix if she's also unconscious. The water is meant to help us—not drown us!

I barely have time to take another breath before I hit the surface. It cracks across me before I plunge into the cold wash.

Desperately, I thrash within it, praying that the water will rinse away the ash so I can help my friends. Also desperately trying to keep their sinking bodies in my sights within the murky deluge.

But the moment the cold liquid fully engulfs me, a new fear fills my heart, icy cold and as sharp as barbs.

There's darkness in this water. A darkness that squeezes my heart harder than the ash did.

Out of nowhere, tendrils like ropes wrap around my legs and drag me down into the deep.

CHAPTER SIX

I fight the scream building in my throat, knowing that I need to hold on to my oxygen for as long as I can.

As the invisible ropes tighten around my legs, the ash on my body also seems to cling more tightly, compressing all of my limbs, as if it has formed a tether to the dark water I'm plummeting into.

I try to turn, fighting to move my arms so I can twist, seeking to find Micah and Beatrix in the wash.

All I see is churning water.

It rakes over me like daggers as I plunge farther down.

Falling... falling...

I'm forced to close my eyes while I try not to open my mouth and exhale the cry that's pushing at my throat.

Then, just as abruptly, I come to a stop.

Silence falls around me.

My eyes flash open.

Only to discover I'm now floating in a vast, dark space.

It isn't filled with water, but there doesn't seem to be any air, either. Despite that, I'm somehow breathing. At least, I *think* I'm breathing. All I know for certain is that I'm not gasping for air or choking.

I can't see the edges of this place, can't sense its boundaries. There is no bottom or top or anything to stand on. I'm suspended in *nothing* and the sheer impossibility of the area around me is tearing at my mind.

With relief, I locate Micah, who floats nearby. His eyes are still closed, but his wings unfurl, spreading out in the dark like sheets of stone that have been hammered flat and now ripple in the darkness.

A short distance from him, Beatrix is also suspended in the air, her short hair floating around her face, her lithe body like a reed swaying in the darkness.

Neither of them gives any sign of being conscious.

The ash on their bodies sparkles like deadly diamonds, glowing more brightly with every passing second, providing the only light around me.

Beatrix said the ash made her feel like she was falling into a dark pit with no way out.

Well, here we are. Apparently dragged into oblivion by this hateful substance.

My goal was to get rid of that dust, but now, my primary concern is escape.

Desperately, I reach out to Micah, trying to swim toward him, only to find that the air around me is as slippery as ice and as thick as oil.

I can't seem to move an inch.

As I struggle to swim, light refracts around me, the ash on my own body somehow reacting to my surroundings by flickering and shining right up into my eyes. The blinding flashes force me to stop.

I fight my panic as the heavy silence pushes down on me.

Fuck! If I can't move, how can I escape?

The emptiness around me is slowly shredding my sense of self. As if the pieces of my heart and soul are being dissected within my body and soon, I won't be able to hold myself together.

I inhale a deep breath—if, indeed, it's a breath I'm taking—and scream into the darkness. *"Where am I?"*

My voice echoes back at me, and that's when I sense a new presence.

As if born from the sound of my cry, a shape materializes within the darkness only a few paces away, standing terrifyingly close to me.

It's a male form, taller even than Callan and as slender as a wraith. He's dressed in black from his neck to his feet and wearing an inky cloak that sways around his figure.

I try to see his features, but a black crown, which appears to be made from some kind of dense metal, sits around his eyes. Its dark spokes rise up around his forehead, leaving only the lower half of his face visible. His skin is pale, a washed-out gray hue.

His lips twist in a cruel line as he speaks, low and soft. "That magic belongs to me."

I don't know what he's talking about until I follow his pointed finger. He seems to be gesturing to the dust coating my arm.

The ash belongs to him?

"Who are you?" I demand to know.

"I am the keeper of dark magic," he says, his cloak swishing around him as he takes a step toward me. The material makes a hissing sound that breaks the oppressive silence. "It is my burden to ensure that dark magic is claimed when creatures of dark magic die."

My eyes widen. "I'm not a creature of dark magic."

Dragon shifters, like angels, are born of light magic. When the dragon's light was taken from us, we suffered, but not anymore.

My voice hardens as I quickly continue. "And I'm not dead."

Not fucking yet.

His snarl is instant. "Yet you are here because you carry magic that does not belong to you. The moment you touched the water, it called to me. Now, you must give it to me."

A chill passes through me as his upraised hand closes into a fist, as if his fingers were gripping my heart.

Icy tendrils like the invisible ones that dragged me down into this oblivion curl around my chest, squeezing so tightly that it feels like I'm being crushed.

I'm frozen with shock, but my hesitation only seems to enrage him.

"Dark magic cannot remain untethered!" he roars, his fist squeezing more tightly in the air, causing the pressure on my heart to increase.

His eyes may be hidden, but the slight turn of his head indicates that his focus now switches to Micah and Beatrix.

"This dark magic you carry seeks only destruction," he says. "It is my burden to tether it."

He steps forward, a dark, raging form. "Give it to me, dragon, or I will have no choice but to tear out your heart and take the ash from your dead body."

I stare up at him with wide eyes, struggling to respond, struggling to unclench the muscles of my throat to allow speech through.

With an enormous effort, I whisper back at him. "Then take it! I don't want it. *We* don't want it."

The keeper leans backward, his head tilted as if I've surprised him. "You would give up this power without a fight?"

Did he expect me to fight him?

"I'm not *giving up* anything," I rasp. "This ash is killing us."

He pauses, his head still tilted. "If that is what you believe." He sounds skeptical, as if he doesn't believe me.

His response only confuses me. We're dying because of this ash. As far as I'm concerned, there's no doubt about it.

He continues before I can voice my confusion. "But as long as you're alive, you must give this power to me."

"I already told you I don't want it!" For fuck's sake, we fell into this water for the very purpose of getting rid of this dust.

"Then give it to me!" he commands me. "I cannot *take* it unless you're dead."

A scream of frustration leaves my lips. We're going round in circles. He's telling me to give it to him, but I don't know how to do that. I literally can't take it off my body and hand it over to him. If I could have willed the ash the fuck off me, or scraped it off myself, I would have done it already.

My frustration gives way to despair but I push hard against that emotion because it can only defeat me.

As the keeper continues to tighten his fist and the pressure of my own heartbeat drums in my ears, I force myself to turn my thoughts inward. To pretend that the ash doesn't scare the fuck out of me and to consider its nature in the same way I'd consider the sun. Or a tree. Or a ball. Or some other everyday thing.

The weight of the ash is like a hammer beating against me, but beneath that weight, there's also…

Power.

A glittering, seductive power.

It rests on the surface of my skin like a shield and, while it's sucking the happiness and warmth out of me, it's also making me feel untouchable. Unfeeling. Unable to be hurt.

If I let it stay… If I let it become a second skin…

No. I shake myself.

That kind of power would turn my heart to shadows and vengeance.

It would crush my soul, and I won't let it do that.

And I sure as fuck am not about to let this keeper kill me to get at it.

I tried scraping the dust off myself before and so did Beatrix, but we're in a different place now. An abyss filled with the kind of darkness with which the dust belongs. This wraith seems insistent that I can hand the ash over to him.

So I try again.

With a snarl, I claw at my arms where the ash clings to me, using my fingernails to scrub at my skin.

I don't expect it to work. Not even for a moment.

My eyes widen with surprise when the crystals lift off me, floating upward into the gloom.

The keeper's lips rise into a smile. His fist snaps open, releasing my heart, and I gasp with relief. But I don't stop, not for a second, scrubbing at my body as fast as I can.

Opposite me, his palm opens and I sense the pull in the space between us.

The crystalline dust immediately gravitates to him, directed as if by a magnet.

Then it's like a cascade.

I don't second-guess it. As long as the ash is rising from my body, I'll let it go.

As I scratch at my body and face, leaving red welts across my skin, each subsequent crystal rises more easily than the last until they form a stream of glittering ash floating toward the keeper and settling, not only on his palm, but on his arms and chest. Even on his jaw. Covering every visible inch of his pale, gray skin.

Frantically swiping my hand across the remaining ash on my arms, I push the final crystals off me. The moment the last smear leaves me, the heaviness in my heart eases completely.

I exhale a groan of relief.

My legs buckle, but it doesn't seem to make any difference to the way I'm standing, given that there's nothing beneath me.

Finally free of the dust, I turn my mind to Micah and Beatrix.

My goals are simple. Basic impulses geared toward our survival: Remove the dust from them and get the hell out of here.

But first, I turn to the dark magic keeper. "You said we have to give the ash to you. Does it count as 'giving' if I scrape it off their bodies for them?"

Glittering light spills out from behind his crown, as if his eyes suddenly lit up. "You have that power," he says. "You may remove whatever darkness you like from them, and I will accept it as a gift from you, Sophia Dragon."

His use of my name is startling—and also puzzling that he gives me the surname of my species. What's more worrying is the implication that *I* have the power to take this darkness from them where another supernatural might not.

I shake off my uncertainty and my questions. I don't have time to waste. My only goal now is saving my family.

"Allow them to come to me," I snap at the keeper, gesturing at Micah and Beatrix, taking a guess that he can control their movement. "If you want the magic from them, you must bring them to me so I can give it to you."

A cold smile touches his lips before he crooks his finger at them and they both glide toward me.

I reach for Micah first, since he was most badly affected, pushing my hands across his body in large sweeps, starting with his torso. Then I hurry to clean his face, shoulders, arms, neck, and finally his legs.

The last crystals of ash lift off him.

I was hoping he would wake up, but although color returns to his cheeks, his eyes don't open.

I swallow my despair and quickly reach for Beatrix, brushing at the ash on her hands and arms, searching for every patch where it covers her skin. As I scrub at the last crystal, her eyelids flutter and my heart leaps—but it falls again when she, too, remains unconscious.

The final stream of dust floats to the keeper's body, thickening the coating that already lies across his arms and legs until he glistens with power.

"You got what you wanted," I say, struggling to turn toward him. "Now, let us go."

He leans toward me as if he's going to say something more, but then, suddenly, he stiffens and twists to the side.

His shoulders are tense, his lips pressing into a sharp line. "I must go," he says, although his voice is low and soft once more and doesn't betray any sort of worry on his part. "Whether or not you escape this place is up to you. But do not worry. If you die, I will claim your magic, too."

Don't worry?

My eyes widen when the darkness begins to swallow his retreating form. "No. Wait! You have to help us. We don't belong here!"

With a cold smile, he stops and snarls back at me, "I know better than most the strength in a dragon's heart. You, of all dragons, do not need my help."

With that, his body appears to disperse into the darkness, melding with the nothingness around us.

His crown disappears last, light glinting off its metallic surface and sparkling before it, too, is gone.

CHAPTER SEVEN

I never thought I'd wish for the return of such a malevolent being, but I'd give anything for the keeper of dark magic to reappear.

Fear and panic rise within me, a horrible force.

I take another deep breath, but it does nothing to steady me. Probably because it's not real air I'm breathing. Not a real breath I'm taking.

But *I'm* real.

And so are Micah and Beatrix.

The keeper left them floating next to me.

With a grunt of effort, I reach out as far as I can, managing to hook one arm around Micah's waist and my other arm around Beatrix to pull them closer to my sides. Micah's wings ripple in the air and it makes it difficult to hang on to him, but I'm determined not to let go.

Swimming seems impossible, but I haven't tried flying and right now I'm not going to ignore any options. Especially after the dust came off our bodies by scraping it—an action that was impossible in the outside world but worked in this place.

All of the laws of gravity and nature seem different here.

I release my wings with a *thump* that doesn't so much as

make a sound as it vibrates through me. Somehow, the sensation gives me hope.

Beating my wings as hard as I can, I focus on the darkness above us, praying that I'm headed in the right direction.

Please.

I try to push through the nothingness with every muscle in my body, fighting the increasing pull that attempts to drag me right back down, tugging at me and breaking my hope.

Still, I fight to rise, beating my wings savagely, over and over until I'm silently screaming within my mind.

I can't die in this place. Not when I had a glimpse of a future where true happiness is at my fingertips. Not when I fought for my survival for so long.

Not when I survived Tyler and my mother and found peace and hope with Micah.

But the longer I beat my wings and the harder I try to escape this abyss, the more I find myself going nowhere.

A thread of despair cuts across my hope, but I refuse to give in to it.

That's when the keeper's voice echoes back at me. The way he'd told me he knew the strength in a dragon's heart and that I was perfectly capable of escape.

If I imagine for a moment that there is a shred of mercy in him, then perhaps he was trying to give me a message in a dark-as-fuck way.

I can't really rationalize anything right now, since my body is at breaking point and my mind feels like it's tearing apart, but I latch on to the fact that we fell through water to get here.

There's a river up there. If I calm my fears, maybe I'll be able to sense it.

Maybe I can call it to me.

Use it as some sort of conduit to help me move.

It's a last thread of hope that I latch on to before I close my eyes and seek again the feeling that flooded my body in the moments before I kissed Micah. I'd been acutely aware of my new power and had opened my senses to the beauty around me. The touch of his lips, the sheen of sweat across his body, the soft breeze on my skin. All of those had become intense sensations for me.

I seek the same sensations now, expanding my mind and my senses beyond my immediate location.

I gasp when the immense body of water above me is suddenly clear within my mind. It swishes and swills against the otherwise imperceptible boundaries of this place.

When Bella Vorago was my dragon, I could walk in the rain and a pocket of air would form around me, keeping the downfall at bay. When I first met Micah, I attempted to latch on to that rain and throw spears of it at him—only succeeding in soaking him. But now I need that same skill.

I need to call the existing water to me. The whole enormous body of it. If I can somehow make it form a tunnel into this place, then I'll have a path to follow back to the river's surface.

Still beating my wings, but more slowly now to conserve my remaining energy, I focus on the incredible weight of the river far above me and the energy within it, the rush and swirl of it.

Come to me, I whisper in my mind. *Fill the darkness and surround me. Become my tunnel to climb out of this place.*

The water's weight increases in my mind and I sense it responding to my command by pressing down hard on the invisible boundary high above.

I shout within my mind: *Come to me!*

A single drop of liquid lands on my upturned cheek. I can't pinpoint exactly where it fell from, but I'm hoping it means that whatever opening we fell through to enter this place has a weak point.

I can force it to open again.

"Water!" I scream, casting my entire will upward. "Churn and boil! Cut and tear! Come to me! Become my escape!"

A thin stream of water pours down onto my face, rushing down my neck and across my wings, and it's all I need.

Suddenly, my wing beats carry us higher, propelling us upward.

The air changes and then—

Water rushes around us. Real, glorious water that swills and churns. Far above, I can see the surface, but now...

It's as if we're at the bottom of a deep ocean.

I tell myself to keep moving. Beatrix and Micah are still unconscious and the returning danger is that they'll inhale the water and drown before I can make it to the surface.

I can't use my arms to swim, so instead, I beat my wings, telling myself they can be my arms, convincing myself it will work.

I didn't escape oblivion only to fail now. I refuse to believe that there's no happy ending for me or that peace is nothing but an illusion—

Light suddenly slices through the water above me, pure beams as bright as sunlight.

I push toward it, sensing that I need to reach out and take hold of it, but that would mean letting go of Beatrix or Micah and I won't do that.

I will never leave them behind.

Ever.

With an exhalation that tears out of my chest, I give a final beat of my wings and propel myself upward, straining toward the light.

The edge of it brushes across my face, my exhaled breath bubbles through the bright water, and then I'm breaking the surface.

I gasp for air, my wings cutting through the swill.

Above me, an angel coasts the air, his hands outstretched. Pure, white light streams from his palms. It's too bright to see his face, but I recognize his silhouette, his alabaster wings, and the white hair that frames his face.

Isaac.

He's the Sentinel allied with Lana. I don't know how he

found us, but he's flooding the space around me with his soul light. It's like a lifeline back to myself from the darkness that had been cutting into my heart.

In the next moment, I'm aware of a rush of air coming at me from both sides. A storm of movement so sudden that ripples rush across the river's surface.

Two powerful forms dive toward me, their wings tucked to their sides to give them speed, their arms outstretched, their bodies a blur of black and gold.

Callan shoots toward Micah on my right, spreading his wings momentarily to halt above the water's surface. He's dressed in black jeans and a black T-shirt, but his skin shimmers with golden scales where it's visible. He's also wearing bands of dragon's gold around his arms. Threads of silver weave through his golden wings, catching Isaac's soul light and intensifying it.

Callan's chocolate-brown hair is slicked back and his cinnamon-brown eyes are piercing, but I don't miss the tense furrow in his forehead. Or the worried press of his lips as he plucks Micah from the water, heaving him upward in a spray of liquid.

"Hold on, Sophia," Callan calls. "We'll get you out."

"Careful!" I cry to him, recalling Tyler's punch to Micah's chest. "Micah has broken ribs!"

Callan give me a quick nod as he coasts in the air for another moment, and I gasp with relief at the realization that Micah is safe. Then I quickly turn my efforts toward keeping Beatrix's head out of the water.

On my other side, Lana dives toward Beatrix, her hands closing around Beatrix's shoulders before she whisks her up into the air. Lana's long, black hair flies around her face, flicking across her blue eyes.

Her tresses hang loosely down her back and, like Callan, she appears to have dressed in a hurry. Her black clothing blends seamlessly with the dark-as-night scales glistening across her skin and the inky feathers that make up her wings. She's wearing a harness and her golden weapon is visible at her back.

"Take Isaac's hand," Lana calls to me. "He's here to help."

She and Callan rise up into the air on either side of me, sweeping toward the wide, concrete ledge beneath the nearby bridge.

Whatever circumstances led them to find us, I'm so grateful they're here that a deep sob makes me inhale dirty river water. Then I'm coughing and spluttering and even with my apparent power over water, I can't seem to stop myself from becoming a choking, weeping mess.

Isaac's soul light fades. "Sophia! Take my hand!"

Without the bright light in my eyes, I can finally focus on his features. His high cheekbones; stormy, gray eyes; and flawless skin that make him appear ethereal.

His outstretched hand lowers to me, beckoning me to trust him, and I don't hesitate to grasp it, even though only days ago, I would have turned in terror and tried to swim as far and as fast as I could away from this angel.

I retract my wings, reducing the water's resistance as Isaac pulls me upward and into his arms. He carries me with one arm under my knees and the other supporting my back, cradling me against his chest.

This angel was once my enemy, but now I trust him with my life. If I weren't *still* coughing out river water, I'd thank him. While I recover my breath, we descend to the wide ledge in the shadow beneath the bridge.

Isaac places me back on my feet, but my legs wobble and I sink to my knees, my strength finally failing me.

"It's okay," Isaac says. "We've got you."

Opposite us, Lana and Callan are laying Beatrix and Micah down on the hard stone. Beatrix's short hair splays around her as her head turns to the side.

Callan crouches over Micah, whose wings are now tucked to

his sides, carefully checking his chest—probably for the cracked bones I warned about.

Both Micah and Beatrix remain still.

Their eyes are closed, their faces pale and gray.

Isaac's calm expression falters as he takes in Beatrix's still form. The worried tension around his eyes and mouth increases. From the first moment he met Beatrix, they've grated on each other, a friction that seems to fill the space between them even now. Except that this time, I also sense fear on Isaac's part.

Lana has remained between Beatrix and Micah, kneeling behind their heads, facing me. She looks up at me, her face framed in her black hair, and I'm shocked to see tears in her eyes.

"I feel their torment," she says, shuddering and wrapping her arms around herself. "It's pure darkness. I haven't felt anything like it since I threw myself into oblivion to escape the veil."

My eyes widen at her mention of an *oblivion*, which is exactly how I would describe that dark space we plummeted into where the keeper of dark magic appeared.

"You've been there? To the oblivion with the dark keeper?"

She nods. "A long story. It's how I escaped the veil after Atrox and Dominus trapped me."

I need to ask her all about it—I need to tell her everything that happened—but I freeze at the tears trickling down her cheeks.

She never cries. She's tough and hard and fearsome and she never gives up. To see such a raw sadness on her face only triggers my own fear.

"Death," I whisper, as the memory of the ash and the abyss threatens to swallow me. "This darkness is like death."

CHAPTER EIGHT

My heart is hurting in a way it never has before. Micah gave me a moment of happiness and now he lies mere paces away from me, injured and unconscious, and I can't help him. I'm powerless to protect him or rescue his mind from the darkness that must be ensnaring it. Just as, in the past, I was powerless to escape my mother's cruel intentions, or my father's scheming, or my own dragon-less body.

Opposite me, Lana shakes herself before she swipes at her tears.

"Isaac," she calls, "come quickly. They need your soul light. You're their only hope."

Isaac bursts into action, the tension rising off him in palpable waves, his focus on Beatrix more intense with every passing second.

He drops into a kneeling position between Micah and Beatrix, in line with their chests, one hand outstretched on either side of himself. His back is to me while his soul light glows softly up across their faces.

If only his light could calm me, too, because awful thoughts are taking over my mind.

What if Micah never wakes up?

What if Beatrix has sacrificed her life to help me?

All because they cared about me.

Me. The most useless of all dragons. The least worthy to be saved.

I can't stop my tremors as I wrap my arms around my chest. I want to be near Micah, crawl across the stone surface to his side, but I'm too afraid that everything terrible that occurred has happened because of me. Because of Tyler's hatred of me.

My shoes are waterlogged. My clothing is saturated. My dragon's power could probably repel the water from my body, but I can't seem to make any part of me function properly. Not my arms, or my legs, or my power that seems so inadequate right now.

I huddle at the edge of the stone ledge within the shadows, the soft swishing of the river water filling my ears, but my own internal voice is louder.

I rebuke myself for my choices.

When Micah offered me his heart, I should have turned him away. I should have protected him from all the poison that remains in my life.

When Beatrix offered to help me stand, I should have said *no*. I should have told her to fuck off like I would have only weeks ago before we'd built trust and kinship between us.

If I'd kept my walls up, they wouldn't be hurt now.

My teeth start to chatter as my hair drips water onto the stone, each splash magnified in my hearing.

Drip. Drip. *Drip.*

"Stop." Lana's quiet voice breaks through my misery.

She drops to a crouch in front of me and I'm shocked I didn't hear her approach, but then, none of my senses seem to be functioning properly right now.

She reaches out for me, her warm hand closing around my arm. "The path your mind is following is leading you into darkness." Her blue eyes are clear and calm as she continues speaking, compelling me to listen to her. "Whatever you're telling yourself—stop. This guilt doesn't belong on your shoulders."

As an Avenging Angel, Lana can sense guilt in others. I've never really understood how she does it, but she's proven to be acutely aware of what others are feeling—sometimes even emotions they've buried deep and may not be aware of themselves.

She continues. "I don't know what happened, but I know that you didn't do this, Sophia. This isn't your fault."

She carefully draws me into a hug, extending her wings and wrapping them around me like a feathery blanket.

I accept her gesture, shivering against her as I struggle to do what she commands. To let go of my fears and the burden of my culpability.

"The ash kept dragging us down." My voice wavers as I try to pull my thoughts together and fail dismally. "I need to... I have to..."

I jolt at the memory of Tyler's threats and the fact that we're exposed in this location. He asked me where Lana and Callan were. He *wanted* to fight them, but only when I would witness it.

By being here with them, I'm putting them in danger.

"I can't be near any of you," I say, trying to push Lana away from me. "You're in danger because of me!"

Lana holds on tightly, casting an alarmed glance back at Callan, who has remained beside Micah. He responds to her glance by jumping to his feet and hurrying toward us.

"You're going into shock," she says, returning her attention to me while rubbing my back in a calming motion. "We need to take you to safety, where you can get warm and tell us what happened."

"I'm afraid we can't leave yet," Callan says quietly, crouching beside us.

His presence is a source of warmth, the heat of his fire dragon nature radiating out from him, but the tension around his eyes brings all of my worries back to the surface. "Isaac's soul light isn't working."

"What?" Lana's whisper is shocked. "How can that be?"

Callan shakes his head. "We don't know. But there's a more immediate problem. Something's wrong with their breathing. Sophia, is it possible they inhaled water in the river?"

Water!

This new fear is like a shot of adrenaline and I jump up with such force that Lana's wings fly wide and she lets me go.

My mind is rapidly working through the chances of Micah and Beatrix inhaling liquid on our way back to the surface. After we emerged back into the river, we hadn't been under water for long enough to drown, but even a little water sucked into their lungs could slowly kill them.

Rushing toward Micah and Beatrix, I focus on their bodies, trying to ignore the nearby river so I can detect if there's unwanted water within their bodies.

As I get closer, I can hear them both softly wheezing and it scares the fuck out of me.

Isaac quickly repositions himself so that he's kneeling at their heads facing me, giving me the space I need to drop to my knees between them.

Quickly, I place one hand on Micah's diaphragm and my other hand on Beatrix's stomach, both at the base of their lungs.

My senses are going haywire. Despite my efforts, the river dominates my mind, the churning liquid filling my thoughts. So, too, does the dark space that lurks beneath the river's surface.

If I hadn't been so desperate to get to the water in the first place—if I hadn't been numb because of the ash painted across my body—I might have sensed the void we were about to plunge into.

A void that doesn't belong in this world. I know I need answers about that place, but now is not the time to ask for them.

I take a deep breath, calming myself as I drag my focus away from the abyss beneath the waves and to the two dragons who now lie on either side of me. Beatrix, who has become a sister to me, and Micah, who offered me his heart.

The longer I concentrate, the more their bodies appear as streams of energy within my mind—energy carried around their bodies by blood and oxygen. But it's being disrupted by the unwanted droplets of water where air should flow.

My palms tingle as I call gently to the river water in their lungs, coaxing it to give itself over to my power.

Return to the river where you belong, I whisper to it within my mind. *Come out into the night. Leave them and let them live.*

I sense the water respond and a moment later, Micah and Beatrix convulse, one after the other. Their chests heave and hacking coughs leave their lips as they both jolt onto their sides.

Water splashes from their mouths while they stay lying down.

Isaac has quickly leaned away from them, although his soul light remains a gentle glow around his palms.

I want to believe that Micah and Beatrix are okay now, but I keep my hands pressed to their chests as best I can despite their sudden movement. I need to confirm that the water has been completely expelled.

For a second, I sense a heaviness within them both, but I'm certain that the water is gone, and in the next moment, they're opening their eyes.

I sag with utter relief. "Micah?" I lean toward him, reaching for his shoulders, careful to avoid his injured ribs on his left side.

His forehead is creased as he squints up at me. "Sophia?"

A second later, he wobbles into a sitting position, his wings retracting fully as he reaches for me with his right arm. "Are you okay?"

A sob-laugh wrenches out of me. "Am *I* okay?"

I slip my arms around him, curling up against his uninjured side while he adjusts his position, wincing as he moves. His left arm folds protectively against his chest, but his right arm pulls me close.

"I thought I lost you." That's all I can say because my throat is choking up.

He rubs my back, pressing his cheek to my forehead, his voice muffled. "I'm here. I'm not going anywhere."

I can't fight the hot tears running down my cheeks.

I'm vaguely aware of Beatrix sitting up on my other side, of Isaac crouching over her, and of Lana and Callan remaining standing like protectors over all of us.

Beatrix's low whisper cuts through me. "Fuck, I thought my life was over before it even really began."

She tries to stand and promptly sits down again. Her face remains pale as she looks up at Isaac, whose arms hover around her as if he's about to catch her.

A little of her old spark returns as she smiles up at him. "Oh, hello there, *pet*."

Isaac scowls at her and I'm reminded of the moment they first met. Isaac was in chains at the time and Beatrix had looked him up and down before she announced that she didn't take Lana as the type to keep a pet. Isaac stiffened and rebuked Beatrix, making it clear that he'd chosen to wear the chains out of respect for his leader. Not because he was anyone's toy.

His glare now would make even the toughest dragon quail.

It quickly fades when Beatrix sniffles, hurriedly swiping at the tears leaking from her eyes. Her gaze is luminous as she leans in his direction. "I followed your light back to myself."

He gives her a quiet nod, his arms lowering to his sides. "Give yourself time to stand. Your legs will be wobbly."

Her short hair slips to the side as she smiles up at him through her tears.

When Lana crouches beside Beatrix, Isaac stands again.

I can't help but notice how he takes up position at our backs while Callan keeps guard on our other side, both of them keenly alert to our surroundings.

Lana considers us all and doesn't direct her question to any particular one of us. "What happened?"

"*Tyler* happened," Beatrix says, speaking first, her face paling again as she wraps her arms around herself. "His dragon is like nothing I've seen or felt before."

"Tyler." Lana makes a low, growly sound in the back of her throat that reminds me she's half-dragon, even though she has the appearance of an angel.

"Tell me as much as you can, as quickly as possible," she says. "We can't linger here and you all need to get dry and warm, but it's important that we understand what threats await us."

Beatrix looks to me. "Sophia?"

"I was conscious for all of it," I say, and then I proceed to describe Tyler's sudden appearance on the rooftop of Zahra's home and the impossible fight with him.

I explain about the ash and how it clung to us and spread between us. How Gisela and Dane fought him off with Beatrix's and Felix's help. Then about our plan to wash the ash off in the river.

Lana, Callan, and Isaac listen intently, but their brows furrow more intensely, their expressions becoming more worried with every word I say.

By the time I reach the part where we plummeted into the dark space within the river, they're all incredibly tense.

I struggle to describe the oblivion we fell into and to explain my encounter with the keeper of dark magic. The way he claimed the ash and seemed surprised I didn't fight to keep it.

I finish by describing my battle to bring us all back to the surface.

Throughout my story, I speak quickly, but I have to take deep breaths to hold off the cold fear that returns at the raw memories.

Finally, I say, "I saw Isaac's light and I followed it upward."

I finish to silence.

Lana is the first to break it. Despite the deep furrow in her brow and the worry in her eyes, she's no-nonsense and to the point. "We have two goals now: The first is to protect Sophia. The second is to protect the dragon's light. Tyler wants to destroy both."

"The safest place to hide the dragon's light is within the veil, but we can't take it back there," Callan says, turning briefly toward us from his surveillance of our surroundings. "That would only repeat the mistakes of the past. But we also can't place the burden on Zahra to guard it now. Not when she needs to protect Emika against this new threat."

Lana is nodding. "The dragon's light is my responsibility. I can stay with Zahra and guard it."

Callan doesn't appear happy with that suggestion. "Zahra's my sister. Let me do this."

I take glances between them, not liking what I'm hearing. "Neither of you should stay out here," I say. "Tyler wants to provoke you. He *wants* a fight with you. The dragon's light gave him his new power. I don't think it's in his interests to destroy the stone. He may want to possess it, but it isn't his target. *You* are."

Lana gives me a small smile. "As are you," she says to me. "Which is why we're sending you behind the veil."

CHAPTER NINE

A protest rises to my lips.

Logically, I know that disappearing into the veil is my safest option. But I've been forced to give up so much in my life. I've been made to accept too many compromises. Worse, I've been thrown into situations where my wellbeing was damaged by other people's choices.

I can't accept that Tyler will tear me away from the people I love. Not when he spent so many years isolating me from my own clan.

"No," I say. "I won't hide. Tyler can't take my new life away from me. I won't accept that I'm destined to be alone." My voice breaks. "*Abandoned.* I won't let him do that to me, because then he's won."

Lana's lips part with a quickly indrawn breath as she rises, crosses the distance between us, and reaches for me.

"You have no need to fear being cast out," she says, taking my hand as she settles into a kneeling position beside Micah. "You're family to me, Sophia. And I..." She glances at Micah. "*We* will never abandon you. Not the Dread and not the Grudge. You have two clans now who will watch your back and protect you."

Micah's arm tightens around me, but I'm too agitated to look up to see his expression.

"Then why send me away?" I ask.

"This is not about pushing you away," Lana says softly. "And you will absolutely not be alone. It's about giving you the chance to grow stronger."

I swallow hard, fighting the fears of my past. Lana takes a deep breath and continues.

"Before Bella Vorago became your dragon, your presence was like twisted vines in my senses," she says. "There was a web around you from which it seemed you couldn't escape, and the harder you tried, the tighter the web became. But I also sensed a tidal wave."

Her lips rise in a gentle smile. A determined smile that challenges me to believe her. "There's an immense power within you, Sophia. Even now, I sense layers that need to be peeled back to reveal what you truly are. I don't think you've even scratched the surface of what you can do."

She gives my shoulder a gentle squeeze. "You need time to find your power and allow it to flourish. We can give you that time."

My eyes widen at the conviction in her voice. *She* is the strong, powerful one and for her to speak about me as if she believes I'm capable of more makes me feel hope. But also terror at the thought that maybe I can't be what she thinks I can be.

"And then what?" I ask quietly.

"Then you'll be ready for the fight of your life," she says, her jaw tightening. "If Tyler's goal is to make you suffer—to *control* you with suffering—then he'll strike at everything and everyone you love. He'll strike at Micah. He'll strike at Callan and me. And Beatrix and Felix. And most of all, he'll strike at Emika because he witnessed firsthand the lengths to which you'll go to protect her."

Emika is precious. She's the only child born to dragon shifters in the last five years. In one instance, I threw myself in front of her to protect her from Callan's flames—flames he had no control over.

I suffered severe burns since I didn't have dragon wings to protect me at the time. I've recovered from those burns and from the pain, but what's important now is that Tyler saw me do it. He knows that losing Emika would mean losing all of my hope for the future.

It isn't despair that rises within me now. It's anger. "He'd better not touch a fucking hair on that beautiful child's head—"

"And *that* is the rage you need." Lana's blue eyes are suddenly bright. Black scales shimmer across her cheeks. "Hold on to that anger, Sophia. Let it quietly grow while you give yourself the chance to become as strong as you can be. Then *you* will be the one protecting us."

Hot tears brim in my eyes as I try to accept the extent of her conviction. "How can you have this much faith in me?"

One corner of her lips rises. A small smile. "Because you once had faith in me." She leans back a little, finishing firmly. "You deserve the chance to train and grow. The veil will give you that chance."

I press my lips together, thinking through what Lana is proposing to give up for me. "What about you and Callan? You deserve peace, too."

Lana gives a soft sigh. "I'll admit, I was hoping for at least one night without conflict. But this is what I was born for. And I won't be alone in my fight. Callan and I will remain out here to protect the dragon's light and study Tyler's movements. We need to know what he's planning."

She exchanges a quiet glance with Callan and the connection between them is so strong that I feel a little of my peace returning.

"Who will train me?" I ask. "If you need to be here." I glance at Beatrix with a grimace. "Given that others might not be so keen to help."

Beatrix widens her eyes at me. "Damn right. I'm not doing it. We'd end up wanting to kill each other."

I roll my eyes at her. Not so long ago, I had a conversation with Lana about the possibility of Beatrix teaching me self-defense and we both agreed it wouldn't go so well.

Micah has remained quiet throughout the conversation so far, but now he says, "I'll train you."

The bond I formed with him tugs at me instantly. The idea of tumbling with him on a training room floor brings more than a little heat to my cheeks. But I'm even more conscious of his injury.

"You're hurt," I murmur, turning my gaze up to him. "Your ribs are broken."

He looks surprised. "Bruised, not broken."

I blink at him. "But I heard them crack."

He grins. "The sound you heard was Tyler's knuckles breaking, not my ribs. My dragon powers seem to have given me bones like steel. It was the ash that knocked me out, not the punch."

My relief is so intense that I exhale heavily. "Well, that's good news."

"Besides," he says, a soft, slow smile forming on his lips, "exploring things with you sounds like a good idea to me. If you would also like that?"

Things.

Suddenly, I don't think we're talking about combat training. I'm increasingly conscious of the way I'm curled up against him and of all the little droplets of water across his body and mine. "I would very much like."

Beatrix clears her throat loudly and I remember where we are.

Damn, Micah has a way of making me fall into the peace and safety of his presence and forget every other worry in my life.

But, as much as I want to accept his offer, I have to focus on the realities of his position as alpha of his clan. "What about the Grudge? They need their alpha."

He nods. "They do. But Leon is a very capable beta. I know that he and Melisma will ensure my clan remains strong and stable in my absence."

Melisma is Lana's mother. She and Lana were recently united after Melisma spent years in hiding with the Grudge dragons. As for Leon, he is an older dragon, strong but sensible.

"Okay," I say, making a quiet decision. "I'll go to the veil. But only for a week."

Micah looks like he's about to argue and so do Lana and Callan.

I hurry on. "Micah, it's incredibly generous of you to offer to leave your clan for a time, but it can't be indefinite. They've suffered too much already. They need their alpha and I won't be the one who takes you away from them."

His expression softens, and I quickly turn to Lana and Callan. "As for my own needs, I need to know that I'm coming back out. If I'm going to train, then I need a deadline. A goal."

They still look like they're going to argue, but I hold up my hand. "If I need more time, then I promise I'll ask for it, but for now, I need to put a limit on hiding. Otherwise... it feels like I'm running away from the world. I don't want to do that."

Lana's expression also softens. "*Two* weeks," she says to me. "You'll need at least that."

I give her a sly smile. "I don't know. If you recall, I'm a quick learner."

When Lana first started training me, I picked up combat skills quickly—far faster than I think she anticipated. I even managed to knock her flat at one point, although I'm a hundred percent certain that was beginner's luck.

At Lana's firm stare, I capitulate. "Okay, two weeks, but if I'm done earlier, then I'm coming out."

"Agreed," Lana says.

At that, Micah turns to her. "Can you get a message to

Melisma so that my clan knows what's going on? It's important they understand my decision."

"We'll explain everything and warn them about this new danger," Lana says. "They need to know about Tyler."

"Thank you," Micah replies. "Please know that if you need a safe place to keep the dragon's light or if you're worried that Emika may be in danger, my clan can hide you in our stronghold. They're accustomed to staying hidden and our hideout has never been breached. The same offer goes for Gisela, Dane, and Felix."

"I appreciate that, Micah," Lana says. "But we won't take the fight to your clan unless we need to."

Beatrix huffs loudly and narrows her eyes at Micah. "I notice you didn't extend the offer of sanctuary to me."

Micah gives her a brief smile. "I don't need to because you're coming into the veil with us."

She arches her eyebrows at him. "Am I?"

Isaac's shadow falls over her, his features stern. "You are."

CHAPTER TEN

Beatrix turns a hot glare up at the white-haired angel, apparently completely unfazed by his ethereal features, her lips pursed and a scowl on her face.

I expect a strong retort from her—nobody tells Beatrix what to do—and I'm not disappointed.

"Like fuck I am," she snaps. "I'm staying here to fight whatever battles need to be fought while Sophia trains in peace."

Isaac crouches to her again, his big hand reaching slowly and carefully toward her.

She watches him approach, warily eyeing his hand, but she doesn't back away, stubbornly glaring back at him until he slips his palm to her cheek.

Her dark eyes clash with his stormy ones.

He speaks, low and soft. "Tell me you don't feel any remaining darkness in your soul and you can stay here."

Beatrix's lips part as if in surprise, but then she shivers. And rapidly scowls. She lifts her head high, although she doesn't push his hand away.

Before she can speak, Isaac continues. "If you have any doubts, then you need to come with us to the veil, where your heart can heal."

Her jaw tightens, a stubborn response. "I'm fine. I don't need your help."

Isaac's other hand flies out toward her heart, a quick movement that slows at the last moment as he gently presses his palm to her upper chest.

She gasps at the contact, but again, doesn't push him away. "What are you doing?"

His response is vehement as he continues to arrest her gaze. "Do not sacrifice this heart because you believe it's too broken to be worthy of saving."

She inhales a quick breath, her chest rising rapidly. Her eyes suddenly fill with tears. "My heart... I don't..."

She presses her lips together, visibly swallowing as she squeezes her eyes shut. Slowly, she inhales and then exhales, relaxing and swaying into the hand Isaac presses to her chest.

I wait for her response, understanding her inner struggle. She and I never saw eye to eye in the past. In fact, we actively antagonized and hurt each other. But in recent weeks, I've caught glimpses of the inner feelings she kept hidden. The pain she felt at her original clan's betrayals, the loyalty she has for Callan, and the fact that, if it comes to it, she'll fight to the death for everyone here. Including me.

Her voice is small as she says, "I'll come with you, Isaac."

For a moment, they stay like that while she slowly opens her eyes and bites her lip, and he responds by giving her a small nod.

Nobody seems to want to break the moment, but Lana turns to our surroundings, her eyes narrowed. Both she and Callan appear suddenly focused on the same point at a distance along the riverbank.

"We can't stay here any longer," Lana says. "I sense malicious intent coming from that direction. Multiple sources. I can't be sure if it's Scorn dragons because dragon shifters are still undetectable in my senses, but we can't take any chances."

Isaac rises to his feet. "We shouldn't use the main entrance into the veil. There's a second access point this way. It's in an exposed location, which isn't ideal, but we'll be able to see anyone coming after us. It also requires more precision to access it so nobody should be able to follow us in."

Lana exchanges a quick, quiet glance with Callan. "We'll run interference."

"If it's Tyler, don't get any ash on you," I say urgently.

"Don't worry," Lana replies. "Until we know more about his power, our purpose will be to distract and evade. We won't engage him unnecessarily and even if we have to fight, we'll use our weapons so we don't come into physical contact with him."

She reaches back to tap her glaive, which rests in the harness around her chest. It's a polearm made entirely of dragon's gold, shorter than a spear and with a blade on each end. The larger blade is sharp enough to cut a dragon's head from their shoulders while the smaller one is shaped like a dagger.

Beside her, Callan also indicates the bands of gold resting around his arms. He can use them as weapons if needed.

"Okay," I say, breathing more easily.

"I'm determined to find out everything we can about Tyler's new power." Lana gives an uncharacteristic shiver as she scans our surroundings again. "I sense the darkness…"

"Close?" I ask, alarmed in case it means Tyler's closing in on us.

"It's everywhere." Her forehead creases. "And nowhere."

She shakes herself, her focus returning to us. "Callan and I will go hunting now." She pins Micah with her fierce gaze. "Micah, I expect you to train Sophia to the level that she can hunt with me."

If anyone other than Lana can teach me the skills I'll need, it's Micah. The Grudge were long considered the most brutal of all the clans. There was a time when Micah's father, Solomon Grudge, was intent on capturing and killing Lana. I wasn't there the night he trapped her, but those who were told me he very nearly succeeded in ending her.

I'm filled with determination, not fear, as I turn to Micah. "Will you?"

He makes me a vehement promise. "I will."

We hurry after Isaac along the city streets, keeping to the shadows where we can.

Even though we no longer have to fear that dragon shadows will appear and betray our supernatural status, we're bedraggled and wet and it's difficult not to attract attention. I'm not exactly sure of the time, but judging by the height of the moon, it must be a little past midnight. The city is alive with nightlife, humans exiting restaurants and night clubs, and we're soon caught in the stream of pedestrians. Luckily, the more people there are, the less they pay attention to us, since they're busy maneuvering past and around each other.

I envy them and the lives they get to live while I'm headed into hiding.

I can only hope that when I learn to fully control my power, I'll be able to whisk water away from my body, and away from my shivering friends, with a mere thought.

But for now, I feel like a water magnet.

It's as if the effort of pulling the water to me in the oblivion has somehow stuck my power in one gear and I can't switch to any other.

Isaac leads us four blocks away from the river, and by the time he gestures to the block ahead of us, my teeth are chattering again.

Micah pulls me close, rubbing my back, but his clothing is as waterlogged as mine, so there isn't much he can do.

Our destination is a well-kept park, at the center of which is an enormous ornate stone fountain. The base of the circular fountain takes up as much space as a pool would, although the water appears very shallow, while the center of the fountain is built up in levels.

Four forest-green statues in the form of mermaids rest at equidistant points around the center of the fountain. The edges closest to us sport statues of turtles and frogs with water shooting from their mouths.

Isaac heads straight for the nearest turtle statue.

I follow more slowly, warily surveying our surroundings. Humans continue to pass by, but it's the nearby building that worries me the most.

We're uncomfortably close to the Cathedral, which is the angels' stronghold. It was once a place I wouldn't dare venture this close to. Now that we've formed a truce with the angels, I tell myself that I don't need to be as worried as I might once have been. But it's difficult to let go of past fears.

Isaac pauses at the edge of the fountain, keeping his voice low. "It's very difficult to gain access into the veil. The Avenging Angel's realm will open automatically to me because it's part of territory that belongs to me. It will never open to you alone. You must maintain contact with my body as we step through or the veil will reject you."

He quickly removes his boots—a curious action—before he says, "It's best to take off your shoes. Trust me."

He holds out his free hand to Beatrix. She quickly slips off her ballet flats, tucks them beneath one arm, and takes Isaac's outstretched hand without hesitation.

Her gaze clashes with his and she seems to have regained some of her haughty spirit when she throws back her head, side-eyes him, and croons, "Thank you, pe—" Her eyes twinkle at him, as if daring him to be offended before she emphasizes his name. "I mean, *Isaac*."

A smile plays around his mouth, but he doesn't otherwise react.

I already tipped the water out of my sneakers but I tap them on the ground a couple of times for good measure before I tuck them beneath my arm like Beatrix did.

Then I take Isaac's elbow on his other side. "We're not stepping into the fountain, are we?"

I'm not unhappy about removing my shoes since my toes had turned to prunes within them, but I have to wonder if we'll draw attention to ourselves from the humans passing us by.

"Don't worry," Isaac replies. "Humans have been known to dip their feet into this water from time to time. They won't think anything of it. As for when we disappear from sight, the veil protects itself with a pulse of magic that will make anyone nearby forget we were here."

While Isaac speaks, Micah also removes his boots, and when Isaac turns back toward the water, Micah grips Isaac's shoulder so that we're all now maintaining contact with him.

Just as we take a step forward, the back of my neck prickles, and it has nothing to do with the humans.

A sudden chill rushes through me like a palpable force.

I jolt, nearly dropping my shoes, my senses going haywire.

"Death," I whisper as the cold creeps over me.

Isaac swivels and so does Micah, their attention drawn to the same spot I'm now staring at.

At the edge of the park on our left, two figures loom, both dressed in dark clothing, both focused on us.

Their faces aren't covered, and I recognize both of them, even though I don't know their names.

The woman has light-brown skin with dark-brown hair that's braided back and has pink streaks through it. The man has pale skin while his black hair is cut close to his scalp with a pattern shaved into it.

It's the pattern that resembles the symbol of his clan.

I met these two dragons on the same night I first met Gisela.

They're Scorn dragons.

A beat later, they break into a run toward us.

CHAPTER ELEVEN

*I*saac's grip on my hand tightens. "We need to move. Now!"

He steps toward the edge of the fountain. "Once we enter the veil, they won't be able to follow us. But we have to hurry."

Checking that we're all with him, he steps lightly over the short, stone edge and into the shallow water.

His shoulders are tense, and I sense his growing worry. He won't be able to move too quickly or he'll risk breaking the contact with the three of us.

"Stay close to me," he says, his voice urgent. "We need to pass right by this statue at a very particular spot. It isn't far. We'll reach it in time if we stay calm."

The water is so shallow that it barely covers my feet, but it's the least of my concerns right now.

Isaac told us to stay calm, but it's fucking hard when Scorn dragons are breathing down our necks.

Risking a backward glance, I catch sight of our pursuers closing in. They're near enough to us now that I can make out a faint mark across their faces. It looks like a smear of dirt. Some sort of smudge.

The closer they come, the greater the chill that rides my body.

But then I catch sight of the figures racing up behind *them*.

Relief floods me at the sight of Callan and Lana moving swiftly and far more quietly than either of the two Scorn dragons as they close in on our pursuers.

"Nearly there," Isaac says as we approach the nearest turtle statue. "Stay close... Stay with me..."

Water pours from the statue's mouth in a long stream and when I take my next step, the spray catches the surrounding artificial lights and forms brilliant rainbows in the air.

The colors blend and blur, obscuring the buildings in the background and even the Scorn dragons where they skid to a stop, seeming to have become aware of the fact that they've become the hunted.

Then the rainbow widens until it consumes my entire view, blocking out my surroundings entirely.

I blink to clear my eyes and—

I step into pure, white light.

The sudden change in our environment stills my breath.

The space we stepped into feels as vast as the abyss beneath the river, but it's so bright, and the air is so crisp, that we could have stepped into clouds.

There's a pause and then hot air billows around me. The gust is strong enough that it would have knocked me over except it's coming from all directions and basically pinning me upright.

It's deliciously warm, and now I understand why Isaac told us to remove our shoes.

Every drop of water on my body, on my clothing, in my hair, and even between my toes evaporates, leaving me warm and dry.

I can't see a thing beyond the bright, white light, but I'm so much more comfortable now that I'm not drenched and freezing. I don't even care that my hair is sticking out at all angles.

Isaac doesn't move away, remaining like an anchor beside

me. His voice reaches me through the intense, white glow as he seems to speak to all of us. "We've arrived safely. Please don't worry about Callan and Lana. They will take care of the Scorn who were following us."

His voice softens. "It's important that you take your time now to let your eyes adjust. Embrace your surroundings and allow the light to become yours."

His voice calms any lingering anxiety and, after a few long seconds, my vision clears enough to make out his silhouette, then Beatrix's form, and finally Micah's smile.

I step into Micah's open arms, resting my frizzy head to his chest, both of us nearly losing hold of our shoes in the process.

"This is the veil," Micah says, and I'm reminded that he's been here once already.

As my eyes finally adjust to the brightness of the air around me, I make out the shape of what appears to be a sun shining far above us and a hint of wispy clouds. The sky is tinged a crisp blue and the soft breeze carries a hint of summer. The floor is shiny like white marble, but it isn't cold beneath my bare feet. I consider my still-damp sneakers and opt to remain barefoot for now.

"It's beautiful here," I whisper, taking a deep breath of the clean air and inhaling the scent of summer.

Opposite me, Isaac continues to hold Beatrix's hand, and she makes no move to break the contact.

He slowly releases his wings and shakes them out, appearing more comfortable in this form.

"Now that the Avenging Angel has returned to us," he says, "the veil is regaining its original beauty. The sky has started repairing itself and soon, I hope, some of the trees will return to this area. It's difficult to imagine now, but there was once a meadow right here, with grass instead of stone."

"You went a long time without an Avenging Angel, didn't you?" Beatrix asks, gazing up at him.

"Too long." Isaac sighs. "When the dragon's light was stolen, it didn't only impact the dragons. It affected the fabric of our world too. Even the veil's core started to degrade—starting with the prison levels and extending into the space around the core."

"The core?" I ask.

Isaac gestures to the lone structure that rises into the air about thirty paces away.

It's a spiral staircase that seems to hang by itself in the middle of the bright space. Its lower step is positioned on the white marble floor, while the rest of it soars upward for about fifty feet and curves to the right. Each plank is wide and appears deep enough for several people to stand on at the same time.

It doesn't appear to have railings at the sides for safety or, for that matter, any beams supporting it from below. At the top, it simply stops, the uppermost step suspended in nothing and appearing to lead nowhere.

Beatrix cranes her neck to see around it, quietly exclaiming, "How is it staying upright like that?"

"I'll explain everything," Isaac says. "But for now, I'd like to take you all to the infirmary so I can make sure there are no lingering effects of the ash. We can talk on the way. I'm afraid there are some warnings I must give you so that you can proceed safely around the veil."

He grimaces. "As I said, the core started to degrade, so there are a number of dangers you need to be aware of."

He proceeds toward the staircase with Beatrix at his side while Micah and I follow. Still holding my shoes, I reach out for Micah at the same time he reaches for me, our free hands entwining, our arms pressing together and brushing comfortably as we walk.

Isaac continues. "Micah has already experienced this space, but Sophia and Beatrix, you need to know that these steps are currently the only way to move around the veil's core. The bottom step begins your journey. After that, you must take each step to your destination."

"Every step?" Beatrix's dark eyes are narrowed and her forehead creased. "Do you mean we can't skip steps?" At Isaac's nod, she asks, "Why not?"

"I'll show you." Isaac's right wing edges closer to her, as if he's on the verge of wrapping it around her. Possibly to allay her concerns.

"Leave your shoes here and follow me," he says, bending to place his boots neatly beside the bottom step before urging Beatrix to do the same.

Then they ascend the bottom step together.

I'm confused when nothing happens when they step on it, but I'm startled when, the moment Isaac's foot ascends onto the second step, a door appears on both sides of that step.

The bottom of each door sits flush to the surface of the wide, wooden plank but otherwise hangs in space with nothing around it.

I catch Micah's smile, and I pick up my jaw.

Then I focus on Isaac as he explains, "Behind each door is another pocket of the veil. Some are vast and some are small, but you must trigger each door in turn or the doors on the next level won't appear to you."

"So we can't fly up," I surmise.

"Correct." It's Micah who replies. Even though the bright light is exposing the exhaustion in his expression, his smile lights up his eyes. "I had the same question when I first saw this staircase, but I'm told that here, in the veil, the path is as important as the destination."

Isaac inclines his head. "That's right. This staircase leads to wonders as well as to darkness. The prisons are located through the doors on these lower levels and I advise you not to go near them."

"The Roden-Darr are imprisoned here, yes?" Beatrix asks as she takes the next step up, at which two new doors appear. She pauses there for a moment while Isaac joins her.

The Roden-Darr were the rogue Sentinels who rose up against Lana. They were supposed to be her followers—her army—but they betrayed her and followed the fire dragon, Dominus Audax, instead.

"They're behind that door," Isaac says, pointing to his right. "For now, they're suspended in soul light. A kind of hibernation until they can be returned to the heavenly realm for final judgement. While they're in that state, they don't require sustenance and for that reason, they can be left alone."

"What about the other prisoners?" I ask, glancing at the door to the left of the step Isaac and Beatrix paused on.

Isaac is suddenly stiff, his lips pressing together in a grim line. "They're gone."

My eyebrows rise. "Dead?"

"No," he says. "They were freed while Atrox and Dominus controlled the veil. We don't know who did it—if it was the dragon brothers themselves or the angels—but when we came back, we discovered that the prisons were all empty."

Beatrix appears as alarmed as I feel. "Fuck," she whispers. "These prisons are meant to hold the worst of the worst."

"How many escaped?" I ask, dreading the release of hundreds of monsters into the world.

Isaac sighs. "At least in that regard, we are somewhat lucky. There were only three supernaturals—all witches—and four animals still alive. All of the other prisoners had already passed away due to old age. But every escapee is extremely dangerous. Particularly the animals."

I can't stop my shiver this time, imagining the potential bloodshed. "The release of even one would be bad news."

Isaac holds up his hand as if to calm me. "These supernaturals, and especially the animals, are extremely cunning. They won't draw attention to themselves by rampaging through the city killing innocents and leaving a trail of blood by which they could be found. They know they'll be hunted. They will try to disappear."

He flashes me a determined smile. "But Lana already has a sense of where they are. She'll find them."

While also trying to deal with Tyler?

I can't stop my worried thoughts.

All I know for certain right now is that I need to train as hard as I can so I can get out of here and help her. As fast as I can.

CHAPTER TWELVE

Isaac gives a deep exhalation and shakes himself. "For now, let's focus on what we can control: Settling you into your temporary home."

He turns back to the stairway. "The infirmary and living quarters are located near the top of the stairs. But this is where I must warn you: The only way to leave the staircase is to either go through one of these doors or to descend each step back to the bottom. Never step off the stairwell into the air around it, particularly at the top."

He pauses to scan each of us as if he's checking that he has our full attention. "This stairwell is surrounded by a dark space that exists between Earth and the heavenly realm. It's a darkness that grew while we didn't have an Avenging Angel. If you step into that space, you will fall into the oblivion, in which you met the keeper of dark magic."

"This veil is connected to the oblivion within the river?" I ask, recalling that Lana said something similar earlier.

Isaac gives me a solemn nod. "Darkness attracts darkness. Once the dark space around the veil's core grew strong enough, it formed a connection with the dark realm within which the keeper exists."

"Is that how you found us tonight?" I ask.

A new shadow falls over Isaac's expression. "There was a disturbance within the dark space that was so strong, it shook the staircase. We went immediately to investigate."

"A disturbance," I murmur, wondering what, exactly, caused it. Maybe when we were pulled into the oblivion. Maybe when I scrubbed the ash off our bodies and it accumulated on the keeper's skin.

I might never know for sure, but whatever caused it, I'm grateful.

Isaac returns his attention to ascending the stairway, causing new doors to appear as he continues. "It's important to understand that the veil is impenetrable. The barrier between the Avenging Angel's territory and the living world can't be breached. Nothing from the outside world should be able to be felt in here. Even if the dark realms are connected."

My eyes widen. "Then... how could any disturbance out there be felt in here?"

Isaac replies. "Asper believes it has something to do with the damage that was caused when the dragon's light was kept behind the veil. She described to me the place where she found the dragon's light—the power from the light was burning through the veil wall. Literally.

"It's my belief—and hers, too—that the force of its rage has interfered with the balance of light and dark in this world. There may well be other openings between realms that we have yet to discover. Openings through which any number of creatures could appear." He gives himself a shake as we reach the midway point up the stairs. "Please step carefully and all should be well."

As we proceed, Isaac points out the doors leading to a library, training rooms, and a food hall before he finally stops outside a door on the left that's located closer to the top of the staircase.

"This is the infirmary," he says. "It's a healing environment that was denied to Asper when she was first brought here."

He immediately opens the door and ushers us inside.

I expect to find myself in a clinical and sterile environment filled with medical beds and medicinal apparatuses like the bed I rested on when my back was burned the night I was caught in Callan's flames.

I move through a short hallway and then the beauty of the room around me takes my breath away.

The walls are painted a peaceful blue with a swirling, white overlay that's sculpted as if to mimic clouds in the sky.

Beds are positioned at intervals along the far wall, each one covered in layers of plush-looking blankets, the topmost one with a texture like feathers on its surface. Off to the right is a table and chairs, along with a wall of cupboards. To the left are multiple open doors, each appearing to lead to a bathroom.

The air is warm, immediately relaxing my tense muscles, and the soft light glowing around us feels like the sun is setting across the opposite wall, even though there are no windows.

And above us... *Oh.*

The ceiling looks like a canopy of stars.

I exhale all of my anxiety, calmed simply by standing inside this room, and take a deep breath for the first time in... Well... It feels like a lifetime since Tyler broke my peace on the rooftop.

Micah, too, relaxes beside me, the tension finally leaving his shoulders, although he slumps a little now that it seems the fight is going out of him.

"I know you will each want to shower and get some sleep, but first I need you to lie on the healing beds," Isaac says. "They'll tell me the extent of any lingering injuries so I can administer the right medicine if needed."

Without hesitation, I head for the nearest feathery bed, although Micah hangs back a little.

Reaching the side of a bed and reluctantly letting go of Micah's hand, I sink onto the bed's soft surface. It's warm and soothing and the feathers gravitate toward my body, brushing my sides. Slowly, their movement stops and most of them seem to flatten against the bed again except for the ones next to the parts of my body where I came into contact with Tyler: my arms and legs.

Beatrix sinks onto the third bed with a contented sigh. It's difficult to see from where I'm lying, but it looks like the feathers surrounding her also wrap themselves up against the parts of her body where she touched the ash.

Micah perches on the side of the bed next to mine, remaining sitting as he rubs his shoulder.

Isaac seems to assess us quickly, murmuring quietly to himself as he heads to the cupboards at the side of the room, from which he removes a number of vials.

He hands the first one to me. "You're dehydrated. This will help."

He also takes one to Beatrix, who sits up to drink it, before he returns to Micah, where he pauses the longest.

Micah has chosen not to lie down and Isaac eyes him with apparent caution. I'm reminded that the alliance between the two men is new and fragile. Micah is the alpha of a brutal clan and Isaac may be wary of giving him orders—even commands that are intended to be in Micah's best interests.

"I'm fine," Micah says to him, taking the offered vial and quickly swallowing its contents. "But if I lie down, I won't make it back up. I don't want to fall asleep in these clothes."

"I respect your decision." Isaac gives him a brief nod and doesn't push it. "Your dragon bodies may be new to you, but you're best placed to understand your own limitations."

He returns his attention to Beatrix, whose head is tipped back as she stares upward. "That painted ceiling is something else," she whispers.

A smile flickers around Isaac's mouth. "The sky above it is real."

She immediately sits up wide-eyed. "What?"

"There's a transparent barrier with an opening you can pass through if you want to fly," Isaac explains. "It was made that way so you can safely test your wings after an injury. There are buffers all around in case your wings fail."

"I'm definitely going up there." Beatrix gives a soft groan as she tears her eyes away from the sky above us. "But I really need a shower. That river water was disgusting."

Isaac's stormy eyes appear calm for the first time since he pulled us out of the river. "Take your pick of bathrooms. There are plenty of towels and robes. I'll see what clothing I can find that might fit each of you, and I'll have food waiting when you get out."

Beatrix promptly slips off her feathery bed and heads for the bathroom nearest to the back wall.

Isaac checks if we need anything else before he hurries from the room to get the promised clothing and food.

Suddenly, Micah and I are alone.

It's our first private moment since we kissed. After that, we were fighting to stay alive. Even walking up this stairwell felt dangerous.

We haven't had a chance to talk, let alone settle into the bond we formed. My feelings for him, this sense of peace that I have with him, is so new to me that I'm not sure how I'm supposed to behave.

Do I ask for what I want? Or do I wait for *him* to ask?

How do I know if our needs will align?

Hell, I know what a toxic relationship looks like, but I don't know how a healthy one works.

I slip off my bed, taking a step toward him, my lips parting as I prepare to take a leap of faith and ask him if he'll come with me into the shower, but he speaks first.

"I'll take that one," he says, standing and pointing to the middle bathroom.

"Oh." I inhale a quick breath and pivot my thinking. "Okay."

I turn toward the remaining bathroom, my footfalls a little wooden.

I sense him pause behind me, but when I glance back, he's already making his way to the other room.

I tell myself we have time. I've committed to staying here in the veil for two weeks. There's no need to rush into anything.

We aren't in danger now. We're safe. That's what really matters.

But I can't quite quell my insecurities.

Fuck it. I need to say what I'm thinking. Now. Or I'll continue to second-guess myself.

I turn back, firmly pushing my hair out of my eyes, preparing to call out to him.

He's halfway through the doorway to the other bathroom already.

"Micah."

Just as his name leaves my lips, he stumbles, landing heavily against the doorframe. He grabs it, his knuckles turning white and his biceps flexing with the apparent effort of keeping himself upright.

I'm at his side in an instant. "Micah!"

"No," he growls. "I'm okay. Leave me be."

My eyes widen. "But—"

His voice softens, although he doesn't look at me. "You deserve some comfort. A warm shower. Clean clothes. You don't need to worry about me. I'm fine. Really."

He pushes himself off the doorframe as if to prove his point, his back to me and his shoulders hunched.

A wash of unwanted confusion passes through me.

Is he pushing me away?

He promised he wouldn't hurt me and I won't forget the conviction in his entire body when he said it. He spoke with honesty and integrity. Nothing like the guile and subterfuge of Tyler's games—the emotional push and pull that would leave me spiraling and uncertain.

Micah isn't Tyler. If he's telling me to leave him alone, then it can't be because he's trying to confuse me.

I have to believe there's something else going on.

As he takes a heavy step away from me, I concentrate on his body language and not on what he said.

He's moving slowly. His breathing is labored. He's keeping his face away from me because… *Fuck.*

The real reason he didn't want to lie down on the feather beds.

He's hurt and he's trying to hide it.

CHAPTER THIRTEEN

My lips set in a determined line before I say quietly, "If you're hurt, then I'm hurt."

Micah half-turns, but the pain lines around his mouth confirm my suspicions: It's taking more effort than he's willing to admit for him to remain standing.

"What did you say?" he asks softly, his voice strained.

Oh, fuck. How long has he been hiding his pain from me?

I don't understand why he didn't say something to Isaac when the angel offered assistance, but the most important thing is that I help Micah now.

I slip toward his chosen bathroom, squeezing myself between the doorframe and his big body. After I wrap my arm around his waist, I pull his arm around my shoulder, grateful when he doesn't try to stop me.

"If you're in pain, then I'm in pain," I say, meeting his eyes.

He was exposed the longest to the ash. He said that Tyler didn't break his ribs, that they're only bruised, and that may be the truth, but the ash was all over his body for far longer than either Beatrix or I were exposed to it.

We don't know enough about what the dust does, or its possible long-term effects, even now that Micah's rid of it.

"I know you said your ribs are only bruised," I say, "but you were exposed to the ash for far too long. I won't leave you until I know you're okay." I try to smile through my worry. "Even then, I'll only leave if you really want me to. But I won't go just because you feel like you can't ask for help."

He exhales heavily and his body weight increases. "You've been through enough tonight, Sophia. I can handle this."

Despite his assertion, his shoulders slump even further. Then, even though he'd started leaning on me, he gives a grimace and tries to move away.

"I should be looking after *you*," he says, his jaw clenching and a hard edge entering his voice. "I'm supposed to protect *you*. Not the other way around."

My chest hurts as I hold on to him, refusing to let him go.

"Why?" I ask quietly, struggling to keep the frustration from my own voice. "Because you're supposed to be the big, strong man in this relationship?"

His forehead creases, his eyes flashing to mine. Stony, hard, wolf's eyes. "I'm supposed to be strong enough to shield you." He growls. "I should be strong enough to stop any threat that comes your way. If I'm going to be your mate, then it's my duty to look after you. I couldn't do that tonight. I couldn't stop Tyler. I'm not the mate you deserve."

Damn. He thinks he failed me.

Nothing could be further from the truth.

I could remind him how hard he fought to keep me safe. How long he stayed alert despite all the ash that would have been sucking the life out of his heart and soul. How much he gave for me tonight.

But at the heart of what he's saying is a belief on which I don't want our relationship to be based.

"No." I rein in my sadness and my fear that my bond with him could break over this. "That's the sort of bullshit Tyler lives by and I don't want it in my life. There's a fine line between protection and control and it's fucking toxic when those lines are blurred."

My arm tightens around him as I push my other hand against his heart, urging him to stay with me. I need to put into words what I'm feeling and maybe I'll fail dismally to get my meaning across, but I have to try.

"That's not you," I say. "And it's not me. We are not going to be like that. I'm going to help and protect you. You're going to help and protect me. Neither one of us is going to feel lesser or incapable or be made to feel like shit when we fail. Because we will never fail to love each other. And that is far more fucking important than winning a fight."

My voice chokes and my eyes fill with tears.

Damn it, but they're angry tears.

They make his face blur, but I plow on. "So right now, Micah Grudge, I'm going to help you take a shower because I care about you and because you need my help and because it really won't be a hardship."

He has become very still beside me. Very quiet. Even his breathing has evened out.

He reaches up to slowly brush his thumb across my cheek, wobbling a little, but he seems determined to make the connection. "Fuck, Sophia, how do you always give me the clarity to get out of my own way?"

I bite my lip with a shrug, grateful that he seems to have let go of his self-loathing as quickly as he did. "I feel like I can be honest with you."

"That's good," he says. "It's important."

He's quiet again.

Then he says, "My father couldn't protect my mother. He put up these walls and they were like…" He shakes his head. "They were like mirrors that I found myself looking into. I wanted to live up to his expectations, but all I found were reflections of myself. It's hard to shake off the expectation of what I'm supposed to be."

I press my free hand to his chest. "You're already there for me. You've already protected my heart with words and smiles and sometimes even by putting your foot in your mouth. I want someone to stand beside me, not in front of me."

He gives another heavy exhale. "It's going to take me time, Sophia."

"I'll be here for it," I say. "As long as it takes."

The corners of his mouth twitch upward. "So you're going to help me shower, huh?"

I try to blink away my tears, surprised by the heat in his eyes, but also welcoming it.

Dropping a slow kiss against his shoulder, I allow my lips to linger as I put on a voice. "Oh, no, what a shame I have to see you naked and run a cloth all over your body. Woe is me."

A laugh rumbles through his chest, but he winces and presses his hand over mine where I rest my palm on his heart.

"Fuck," he says. "I really do need your help."

"Well, then," I say, clearing my throat and attempting to clear my head of all my heated thoughts. "I'm putting my bossy pants on and you're going to do everything I tell you."

"Yes, mate," he says, an intense heat bursting to life in his eyes that takes my breath away, but the desire in his expression is quickly replaced by a grimace as he takes a step forward. "Can you command the shower to come to us?"

I was so worried about Micah that I only now consider the room around us. Sky-blue tiles cover the walls from floor to ceiling. We're currently standing in a small dressing room with another open door between us and the bathroom itself.

The shower is on the far side of the next room with transparent surrounds that curve around it on either side and leave an opening in the middle. The showerhead appears to be removable, so I'll be able to hold it to wash Micah, and the space within the shower looks more than large enough for both of us.

Multiple small seats, which appear to be made from some sort of smooth resin, are scattered around the bathroom and dressing room, including one within the shower itself, clearly designed to allow someone to sit while showering. There are also handrails at the side of the shower and around the room.

A wall of shelves filled with towels is positioned on the near right of the dressing room while basins are on the left.

"We can make it to the shower," I say. "Just lean on me."

I draw on my new dragon strength as we plod across the space, using my foot to kick the first door closed on the way.

Like in the bedroom outside, the ambience in the bathroom is calming, the air is warm, and the walls remind me of a clear, blue sky.

Finally making it to the shower, I brace to take more of Micah's weight as he settles into the chair.

"Sit there," I order him, causing another upward twitch at the corner of his lips.

"Yes, mate."

Every time he calls me his mate, a tingle of excitement passes through me and I have to fight to stay focused.

But focused, I remain.

Hurrying back to the dressing room, I gather up a mountain of washcloths and larger towels for when I need them. On my way back to Micah, I drag another chair over to the side of the shower and drop the towels onto it before I step back inside.

Turning the water on, I wait for it to heat up and fill the space with calming steam before I turn back to Micah. "Tell me where it hurts."

His smile fades. "I wish I could pinpoint it." His forehead creases as he rubs his chest. "It's a strange coldness. I felt it in my arms and legs when we were walking through the city to the fountain, but I assumed I was simply cold. I thought it would go away. Now, more than anywhere else, it's in my chest."

I want to quell my worry, but I can't. "It's in your heart?"

"I don't know how to describe it," he says, his brow furrowing more deeply. "My heartbeat falters. Like it randomly misses a beat every now and then." He shakes his head with a heavy exhalation. "I'm not making sense."

I kneel in front of the chair and take his hands. "We don't know what Tyler's power can do. But we survived it. We're alive."

As my hands close more tightly around his, I make him a promise. "I intend to keep us that way."

CHAPTER FOURTEEN

I rise again, slipping my shirt up over my head and my jeans down over my hips, leaving me in my lacy bra and underpants. Between the steam and the warmth of the bathroom, any cold that threatened to seep into my bones is gone. And it makes no sense standing in a shower fully clothed.

I reach for Micah. "Now, let me get those clothes off you."

His gaze flows down my figure and he takes a moment before he follows my instructions. Standing, he uses the handrail to balance so I can peel his wet clothes from his body.

I try to remain business-like, but damn, it's not an easy task.

He's sculpted all the way from his broad shoulders to his muscular stomach to his powerful thighs. I make a concerted effort to avoid staring at his pelvis, and when I glance up at his face, his expression indicates that he finds my efforts amusing.

I shake my head at him, bite my lip, and get on with it. Or I try to. Despite my best intentions, I find myself lingering as I direct the shower spray and run the cloth over his body.

What really sobers me is how cold his skin is. The tension in his muscles is worse where his body seems coldest—across his chest near the location of his heart and down his left arm. Even a little up that side of his neck.

Worry overcomes desire, and I focus entirely on making him warm, even increasing the temperature of the spray and making sure the water is on him at all times.

I know I'm succeeding when the tightness in his muscles starts to ease and his breathing evens out. When I run my hand across his chest, finally—*finally*—the cold is starting to fade. The pain lines in his face disappear and the tightness of his jaw relaxes.

The difference in him as he warms up is so distinct that I murmur, "Warmth."

He makes a questioning sound in the back of his throat. "Hmm?"

"It's like light," I say, thinking it through. "It banishes the dark."

I remember the way the ash on Micah's cheeks washed away when my tears dripped onto them: my *hot* tears.

Nothing is certain right now, but I file away the possibility that heat could also fight the numbing emptiness that Tyler's power inflicts.

Heat and water. Either or both.

Micah's voice is husky, the deep baritone bringing me back to the present. "*You* banish the dark."

He's standing on his own now, no longer leaning against the handrail. A very good sign.

Slowly reaching for me, he pulls me closer, taking me with him as he steps back toward the chair. When he lowers himself onto it, it's with slow, deliberate movements, and it's clear he isn't sitting because he needs to. His hands linger on my hips as I remain standing in front of him. His arms are extended, but he doesn't pull me onto the chair with him.

"Would you like to come here?" Despite the tug in his hands, the question in his voice sounds genuine and when he still doesn't draw me onto his lap, I know the decision is entirely mine.

Without hesitation, I slide forward, slipping one leg to either side of his hips. The chair is low enough to the floor that my feet can touch the ground, but only with my toes pointed.

It brings my center to his and now there's nothing more than a scrap of wet material—my underpants—between our two bodies.

I don't try to hide my needy moan.

His hands rise from my hips and his fingers splay across my back.

"This isn't how I pictured our first night together," he says, his gaze on my lips. "You looking after me. Me barely able to remain standing."

I arch my eyebrows at him and give a little shrug. "It's not too different from how I imagined it. Steamy shower, lots of touching—"

I gasp as his lips connect with mine and all of the heat I've been stifling surges to the surface. My thighs clench, my core tightens, and it takes determination not to rock against him.

His lips burn a line from my mouth down the side of my neck, where he makes a husky promise against my skin. "I'm going to ask you what you want, Sophia. A lot. Over and over. I want you to tell me what you do and don't like."

My lips part with an immediate response, but then I stop myself.

What do I want? What do I like?

My only experiences of sex were dictated to me. It was all about *him*, not me.

"I don't know what I like," I say, worrying at my lip before I take a deep breath. "Not yet. But I want to find out."

"We'll find out together," he says with a vulnerable smile. At my surprised look, he shrugs. "I'm still figuring things out, too."

I move to close the gap between us, taking it slowly. My hands press to his chest, soaking up the feel of his skin, warm now. His dragon scales ripple across his torso, following the path of my hand, as if his body is reacting to my touch by revealing his power.

It makes my heart warm—and it also makes me curious.

Carefully, I tug his left hand from my back and bring it forward to my stomach, watching as my own scales appear where he touches me, then fade as his hand moves on.

"Look at that," I whisper. "Is this a mate thing?"

He doesn't answer me right away, his gaze following his hand across my diaphragm, across to my arm where his fingers trail up to my shoulder, leaving a blossoming line of scales rippling in their wake.

Then up the side of my neck, tracing the moisture on my skin.

"It must be," he finally says, his voice husky.

I can't stand the distance between us any longer, leaning forward to taste the droplets of water on his lips and inhale his groan. My center presses up against his hard length and gravity sends spirals of pleasure through my core.

My body has never been ready this quickly before. Never.

Any surprise I feel is overtaken by the need building within me. A spark that I don't want to control or stifle, but I know I can't be selfish in this moment.

"You were hurt," I say. "We should get dry and—"

"Sophia," Micah growls against my mouth, stopping my speech with a kiss. "Your body is telling me you want more."

I don't stifle my sigh of need, running my hands to his stomach and wanting to go lower. "But what I want and what you need right now are different things."

"Your needs *are* my needs," he says, reminding me of my vow to him earlier—that we would protect and care for each other. "Give me permission to use my hands and I will."

"Only your hands?" I ask, preparing to give him permission for so much more, but he gives me a firm nod.

The press of his lips and seriousness in his brown eyes arrests my attention as he says, "We need to take this one step at a time. I want you to trust that I'll always put your needs first."

"But I do trust you."

"I know you do," he says. "But it's easy for someone to make promises. I want you to know that I mean what I say. Always."

I take a moment to marvel at the intense desire in his eyes, the way he isn't hiding it, but more than that—the fact that he isn't acting on it. Tyler would have had me on my back by now.

"You want me," I whisper.

"So much," he says, his hands gliding up to the base of my breasts and stopping there.

I close my eyes as pleasure rides my body at his touch. "But you're waiting."

"I'll wait until the end of time if that's what it takes to prove myself to you, Sophia."

I open my eyes. "You have my permission to use your hands."

He doesn't use them how I thought he would, gliding them around to my back and stroking all the way up to my neck, then back down again, a light, tingling touch that makes my toes curl.

His fingers play across my back while his gaze devours my mouth before he leans in. He stops, his lips close to mine, but he doesn't kiss me. With a glimmer of a smile, he says, "I promised I'd only use my hands right now."

Part of me wants to tell him that kissing is fine with me. After all, we kissed only moments ago. But he said he wanted to prove he'd keep his word, and his hands... well, they're doing amazing things to my body.

When his right hand rises to tangle in my hair, his touch sending delicious shivers down my back, my breath catches and I close my eyes, loving every sensation he's creating within me.

How can a touch that doesn't even come near my core lift me so high?

But that's what he's doing. Lightly stroking my neck, my shoulders, tracing the line of my biceps, then back up to my jawline, the underside of my bottom lip, back across my shoulders and down my spine.

His question is low and soft, whispered against my neck, and it sends a thrill through me.

"Would you enjoy it if I stroke you until you cum?"

Dear saints, yes.

As the steam continues to rise around us, I lean in close to taste the water on his lips. My breathing is slow and deep, but I'm barely in control. "I would, yes."

With one hand splayed across my back, he draws his right hand forward, skimming the base of my left breast before slipping his hand down my stomach to my pelvis. Cerulean-blue scales blossom across my skin as he moves, following the path of his palm to my left hip.

Without taking his eyes off mine, he presses his palm to the side of my hip while his thumb slips beneath my panty line. I gasp as his wet skin descends from the edge of my pelvis to my core. A light press that makes me gasp with pleasure.

I brace against the hand he holds at my back as the instinct to rock against his hard length becomes stronger.

I resist it. For now, I want him to control this.

I want *him* to give me what I need.

He seems to sense it, his thumb moving gently from side to side against me with the perfect pressure. Not too hard. Not too soft.

I moan as the need within me builds. My hands find his chest, molding to his shoulders, sliding to his neck and down to his stomach, my senses expanding to inhale the scent of his body, my fingertips feeling like they're taking in the energy of his scales as they appear at my touch.

When my fingertips brush his lower stomach, he groans and it ignites me. Wanting more, I lean forward and whisper, "I want you to kiss me. On my lips and anywhere else you like."

He responds by capturing my lips, and I love the taste of his skin on mine. I'm conscious of every droplet of water beading on his body.

With his hand beneath the elastic, the side of my underpants presses against the back of my thigh, but I don't care. I rock against his thumb, faster as I abandon what remains of my inhibitions and embrace the heat and pleasure that he's giving me.

I'm forced to break contact with his mouth when my breathing increases. Too fast to draw breath while kissing him.

I catch the heat in his eyes before he lowers his mouth, his tongue flicking over the top of my sodden bra and lower. When he closes over my left nipple, sudden warmth spears through me.

It tips me over into an orgasm that bursts to life and ripples through my entire body, a release so pure that it leaves me gasping and trembling against him.

I'm aware that my scales are rippling across my body, pulsing in time to the waves of the crash, which lasts…

Long seconds.

It feels like a lifetime.

Long enough for my heart to swell and the bond I feel with him to grow.

The intensity fades, but the feeling remains.

I've never felt so calm and safe after any sexual interaction before.

I lift myself a little, giving Micah enough space to slide his hand free. But he doesn't put me away from himself. Both of his arms close around me, drawing me closer. He plants kisses against my cheeks and chin and lips. The same light touch that only makes me want more.

So much more.

My hand has remained, palm flat, against his stomach, and now I ask him, my voice a husky whisper, "May I touch you?"

He draws back a little and the flare of desire in his expression belies his words. "Not tonight. One step at a time. Is that okay with you?"

"Of course it's okay." I take a deep breath, quelling the rising feeling of selfishness that comes with taking and not giving. "It's just that your body is telling me… you need me."

Damn, he's hard beneath me.

"I can take care of me," he murmurs. "But first, let me take care of you."

I'm not sure what else he means to take care of, but he lifts me from the chair and places me firmly on the ground before he reaches for the nearest towel where I left them.

He wraps me up in it before he takes a towel for himself and slings it around his hips. It doesn't really hide anything, but he seems determined to ignore his body for now.

After reaching for another towel, he slowly runs it through my dripping hair before he sets about rubbing me dry. Well, as dry as I can get with my underwear still on.

I step into his arms, reaching up to kiss his lips before I tell him, "I'll give you space." My forehead creases as some of my worry for him returns. "But if you don't feel well, or you need help, promise me you'll call out."

His expression also sobers. "I promise."

"Okay, then." I tug out of his arms but pause at the adjoining door between the bathroom and the dressing room.

With my back to him, I slip out of my underpants and unclasp my bra, pitching both to the side of the dressing room before I throw him a smile over my shoulder.

He meets my gaze with a heated grin.

Then I tug the towel back around myself and close the door.

CHAPTER FIFTEEN

When I finally emerge from the dressing room, wrapped in a warm bathrobe, I find fresh clothing sitting in neat piles on the end of one of the beds.

Plates covered in silver domes rest on the far table and the scent of cooked vegetables drifts over to me, calling to me more strongly than the need for clothing.

I expected to find Beatrix and Isaac waiting, and my cheeks are flushed about what they might have heard through the closed door, but they're nowhere to be seen.

The door to the bathroom Beatrix went into is open and that room is also empty. I take note that *three* covered plates sit on the table, not two, which makes it look like she hasn't eaten yet.

Trusting that she's okay, I head to the food first.

Micah emerges soon after and rifles through the pile of clothing, quickly choosing a shirt and jeans that fit him. Well, mostly. The shirt is a little tight, but he doesn't seem to mind and I certainly don't.

A mouthful of stew hovers at my lips, nearly forgotten as I watch him dress.

The nearest bed suddenly looks very inviting.

"I wonder if this room has a lock," I say.

He turns at my question, his gaze heating me to my core. "I'm not sure I give a fuck if it doesn't."

My cheeks warm and my toes are already curling.

I lower my fork and rise to my feet, but before I can take another step toward him, the far door opens.

Isaac and Beatrix are having an animated discussion, their voices reaching me before they appear at the end of the short hallway. I quickly tug my bathrobe back into place and return to my seat while Micah focuses intently on the pile of clothing.

Beatrix pauses at the end of the hall. If she senses the tension in the air, she doesn't say anything about it. Her hair is windswept, her lips are turned up in a sparkling smile, and her eyes are brighter than I've ever seen them. She's dressed in long, white pants and an ivory tunic, a combination that accentuates her height.

My jaw drops at the lightness in her expression, the complete absence of dark cynicism I'm used to experiencing from her.

"Beatrix?"

She walks ahead of Isaac, who hangs back with a smile on his face.

Beatrix drops into the seat opposite me and declares, "That. Was. Amazing."

"What was?" I ask.

"One of the doors leads to a forest that stretches for miles," she says. "There's a lake in the middle of it that looks like diamonds in the moonlight. There are animals and fish of kinds I've never seen before. And the air—fuck, it's clean. I felt like I could truly breathe for the first time in my life."

"We keep many ancient species safe here in the veil," Isaac explains, leaning up against the wall while Beatrix reaches for her plate. "To ensure they don't become extinct. The Avenging Angel's realm is far more than a prison. It's a safe haven for many creatures. The forest we flew over just now is home to several extinct species. There's even an old cabin there that once belonged to an ancient wolf. We salvaged it before humans could tear it down and transported it here."

Beatrix's eyes narrow. "Well, now I want to see it."

Isaac laughs. "All in good time."

I don't want to break the moment between them, but I'm dying to ask. "You flew across a forest?"

The mere thought of it seems impossible. We've spent our lives hiding. Even for the short time I've had wings, it's been unbearable having to curb my instinct to fly. Zahra's daughter, Emika, has had to wear a clip on her wings her whole life to stop her from revealing them in public.

Beatrix gives a happy sigh. "I flew more freely than I've ever been able to fly. Without fear of being seen. Without having to navigate from rooftop to rooftop or to wait for a stormy night."

"When can we go?" I ask, trying not to sound impatient.

Isaac gives me a smile. "One of the training rooms has a flight area. It isn't as vast as the forest, but it's designed to test your skills. It could be a better option while you're developing your abilities."

"Okay, then, how soon can I start training?" I ask, nearly bouncing on my seat.

Damn, the idea of flying freely makes me feel like a little kid hoping a birthday wish will come true.

Micah approaches from the side, takes a seat, and sits down to his meal.

"As soon as we eat," he says.

"And sleep," Beatrix adds pointedly, covering her mouth as she yawns.

I don't want to wait. I feel like I'm ready to burst out of my skin, but I'm reminded that only an hour ago, Micah was hurt. He seems completely well now, but I shouldn't take any chances with his health.

"First thing in the morning," I say to him. "Beatrix is right. It's been a long day. We need to rest."

Once we finish our meal, I grab some fresh clothing and duck into the bathroom to change.

After that, Isaac shows us to our rooms.

He leads us several steps up from the infirmary. We're nearly at the top now and there's a sense of emptiness in the space above us.

Isaac points to a door painted a soft-green color. "Sophia, you and Micah can stay in this room. Beatrix will stay in that one opposite you." He falters a little. "That is, assuming you and Micah wish to stay in the same room."

There's a question in his voice. Micah shifts his weight beside me, giving me space, but there's no doubt in my mind.

"Yes, thank you, Isaac, we do. I mean… I do." I turn to Micah. "Do you?"

He gives me a grin. "Fuck, yes."

With a brief wave of his hand, Isaac points to the step that will trigger the door for the training room and tells us we're welcome to use it when we're ready. He also points out the door to the forest, as well as the one to the food hall for when we're ready for breakfast.

Finally, he points to the topmost step. "The highest quarters belong to the Avenging Angel. My room is opposite hers on the right. If you need anything, please knock."

After saying good night to Beatrix, I enter our room, not knowing what to expect.

I'm greeted with walls coated in soft-green hues, the texture of them appearing like branches covered in leaves and vines. The short entryway opens into an opulent bedroom, larger than any I've ever slept in with an adjoining lounge area, and a closet the size of the bathroom, which is to say that it's huge.

I pause just beyond the entryway, taking in the room from the gorgeous, wooden furniture to the plush bed and lounge suite, all the way up to the high ceiling, which has the appearance of a canopy of lush branches within a forest.

Micah's arms slip around me from behind. "If I could give you a home like this, I would."

I turn in his arms. I haven't seen the Grudge clan's hideout, but its location has remained secret for so long that it can only be underground somewhere. Far from the sky and fresh air. Far from the comforts I grew up with.

"It isn't the walls that matter," I say, reaching up to clasp his shoulders. "It's the people."

He gives me a nod, but I'm not sure he's convinced as he releases me and prowls around our new room.

Within the closet, we discover more clothing of various sizes. The shirts are bigger and Micah quickly replaces the one he's wearing. I choose a large tank top to sleep in, but I eye the smaller shirts and pants hanging in the closet, hoping some of them will fit me. Clean underwear is a dilemma I'll face soon too.

Micah turns away while I get changed, and then the bed is beckoning.

Slipping under the covers, I reach for the nearest lamp and switch it off.

Micah takes a beat longer to join me, sitting on the edge of the bed with his back to me for a moment, rubbing his left shoulder.

"Are you okay?" I ask, slipping across the large expanse of bed to reach for him.

"Yeah," he says, finally sliding under the blanket and into my arms.

We both end up lying on his pillow, but it's huge enough to accommodate both of our heads. The bed is somehow just the right firmness and I'm immediately warm without being too hot.

"Fuck, this bed is amazing," Micah murmurs, his eyes closing. He tugs me closer, whispering against my lips. "More so because you're in it."

I stroke his jaw before I lean forward to drop a kiss on his lips. Then I carefully reach across him to turn off the lamp on his side of the bed.

The room glows softly for a few seconds, as if moonlight is filtering between the branches overhead, before it settles into a comfortable darkness.

Micah pulls me back against the crook of his shoulder and I settle there, trying to smother the growing need in my core triggered by his nearness. I convince myself I can overcome it with the sensations of warmth in other parts of my body. My cheek where it presses to his chest near his heart. My lower arm cushioned neatly between us. My legs where they fit perfectly against his side.

This bed, this room, it isn't my home, but right now, it feels like we belong here.

In this moment of peace. We belong together.

CHAPTER SIXTEEN

I wake to find the bed beside me empty.

My heart lurches and uncertainty fills me until Micah's shape moves in the early morning light. He's quietly pumping out pushups beside the bed, his body partially hidden from my line of sight because of the bed's height.

Somehow, this room is lit up as if the morning sun is glowing softly around us.

Turning onto my side, I listen to his inhalations and exhalations, noting the evenness of his breathing, before my focus is drawn to the slight sheen of sweat forming across his naked back.

He's only wearing sweatpants—he must have changed when he first got up—and they're slightly too large around his waist. When he finishes his push-ups and rises to his feet, he has to hitch the pants up to keep them from sliding down.

"I don't mind if they slip right off," I say without censoring my speech.

His light-brown hair is tousled and his cedar eyes are bright. "Good morning, Sophia."

His gaze passes across what must be my very messy hair to my tank top, which has slipped to the side and reveals the curve of my breast. Then down to my legs, where the blanket has tangled around me.

I smile back at him. "Morning."

He rubs his left shoulder for a second, and I'm about to ask him if it's still causing discomfort, but before I can speak, he scoops me up into his arms, nuzzling my neck and sending delicious shivers to my core.

"We need to eat," he says. "Then we can start training."

Despite his declaration, he pulls me higher and the temptation to wrap my legs around his waist and never let go is high.

"Fuck, you smell good," he murmurs, grazing his lips across my skin.

Damn. How am I supposed to focus on training now?

I groan against his mouth when he presses his lips to mine. "Micah, I know you want to take it slow, but I want more of you. I want *all* of you."

His arms tighten around me and the hard press of his pelvis against my thigh tells me he isn't immune to my nearness. He lowers me to the edge of the bed, where he kneels between my legs, a tantalizing position.

The bed is low enough that we remain face to face. One of his hands rises to the back of my neck, while he continues to plant kisses across my face. He inhales deeply against my cheek before he pulls back a little to see me.

"I want that too," he says, his gaze steady. "But my wolf's senses are telling me you're fertile now. We don't have any contraception, so your chances of becoming pregnant are high."

My eyes widen. I'm not so much concerned with how he can tell what's going on with my body, but the fact that I could conceive.

None of us dragon shifters have been able to have children in recent years—Emika was the last—and it's a dream I forced myself to forget. The dream of becoming a mother.

"We could have a child?" I can barely breathe, let alone speak. "But that's incredible."

His lips rise into a crooked smile, but it quickly fades. "Right now, though?" he asks. "Is it the right time?"

It's a sobering question. I force myself to swallow some of my joy—but not all of it.

His arms tighten around me and his voice takes on a growl. "We can't stay here forever. We have a battle to fight out there. I'm going to struggle to watch you putting yourself in harm's way as it is. To knowingly bring a child into existence with everything that's ahead of us doesn't feel right."

I chew my lip, fear rising within me, but not of the battle ahead. "Will my body do this again? Will we have another chance?" My anxiety builds. "What if this is a one-time thing?"

His hands glide in soothing strokes down my back as he rears back up. I catch the flash of his brown eyes before he buries his face against my neck again and his teeth graze my skin beneath my ear. It's a weirdly comforting gesture.

"My senses tell me this is just the beginning, Sophia," he rumbles against me. "You don't have to fear losing your ability to have children."

I relax into his touch, allowing every stroke of his palms, every soft brush of his lips, to calm me.

Children. It feels like a wish come true. Of course, I know it won't be easy. Protecting a child and raising a child are challenges beyond anything I've experienced, but I welcome them.

I sigh as he continues to rub my back, drawing me closer to him and once again, I fight the impulse to wrap my legs around him. "How did a wolf survive within you?"

He's quiet for a moment. Doesn't answer me.

"Micah?" I lean back a little, searching his eyes. "If you don't want to talk about it, that's okay."

It can't be an easy topic. Micah has lost both of his parents. His mother died when he was young and his father was recently killed by Sienna Scorn. That was before Lana ended her.

Micah gives a small grimace. "I believe it has something to do with my mother's heritage."

"You mentioned she was a wolf shifter from another city."

He nods. "Dad met her right after he found the *Book of Light Magic*. The book was located in a forest to the west of Portland. She was a member of the Western Lowland pack—one of two rival packs in that city. Dad met her when he was traveling home."

"What do you know about her?" I ask, uncertain if I'm pushing him too far now.

Micah's brow furrows. "Dad wouldn't tell me much. He had so many fucking secrets and my mom was one of them. But I found out that her brother was the alpha of their pack at the time. A very dangerous wolf. Prone to sudden violent outbursts. Like I said, my father wouldn't talk about her, but when I was a teenager, Leon told me that Mom was hiding a dark family secret."

Leon is Micah's beta. I met him for the first time at the battle with the angels. He has a voice like a rusty, old engine and a scent that evokes the dryness of the desert. He has a calm demeanor, but he's as deadly as the other Grudge dragons. Perhaps more so, given that he was also beta to Micah's father.

Micah continues. "When Leon dug deeper, he discovered that there could be old magic in Mom's family. It didn't seem to be a good thing, though, so he stopped asking questions."

I'm startled by this possibility. "Old magic? Creatures of old magic are extinct." I pause. "At least, they're supposed to be."

Micah shrugs. "I wish she were here so I could ask her." His expression becomes even more solemn. "Old magic shouldn't be messed with. Sometimes I wonder about the blood that runs through my veins, but all I know for sure is that some part of a wolf's nature survived within me. I'll never be sure how it happened. Only that I am what I am."

He falls silent and I want to respect that this might be the end of the conversation.

"I understand if you don't want to talk about her any further," I say.

"It's okay." He takes a beat. "I mean, *I'm* okay." His voice hardens. "What happened to her was not fucking okay at all."

"She died giving birth to you, didn't she?" I ask. "Like all non-dragon mothers do."

Callan's mother was human, and she died after he was born. With dragon shifters dying out, some male dragons turned to other species for procreation. They did it knowing full well that the mothers wouldn't survive.

Fucking barbaric.

Even Tyler had a human mistress whom he hoped would fall pregnant when I couldn't give him a child. Not that he ever considered that *he* might be the one unable to have children.

I was grateful when Callan outlawed all relationships between dragon shifters and humans. I didn't want blood on my hands. But... Tyler's mistress drove me to desperation and I'm ashamed of the action I took to try to get rid of her. In the end, Callan bribed her to go away.

She never even knew the danger she was in.

"Lana's mother is the only non-dragon I'm aware of who survived the birth of a dragon child," I say quietly.

Micah gives a small nod, but none of his anger has abated. "Lana's angelic power was stronger than her dragon power, so she was born an angel. That's how her mother survived."

In Micah's case, everything I've heard about his family history indicates that his father was deeply in love with his mother. Taking the risk of getting her pregnant doesn't match with the love I've heard existed between them.

I choose my next words carefully. "Your father must have been devastated when your mom didn't survive."

Again, Micah nods, but he's closed off from me now, his expression far away. "His pain was part of him. But I could never forgive him. He said he loved her, but he knew the risks. He knew her chances of survival were slim to none. I hated him for the choice he made. And then..." Micah swallows. "Then Leon told me what my father wouldn't speak about."

I wait for Micah to continue, not wanting to push him.

"It was Mom's choice. She believed there was a chance of survival and she wanted to take it. She wanted me that badly." He gives a heavy exhale. "Dad never forgave himself for agreeing to it."

"Fuck," I whisper. "Protection versus control."

Micah nods. "He taught me to protect the ones I love, even if it means stopping them from doing things they want to do."

I give Micah a small smile. "No wonder you were so angry that night I was trying to turn myself into bait to draw Tyler out."

My heart hurts to remember it. Callan and Lana had disappeared and I'd thought the Scorn had been responsible. I wanted to get inside the Scorn clan and take them all down. I deliberately put myself in harm's way so that the Scorn would catch me and take me to Tyler. It was my way of getting inside their stronghold.

It was also completely reckless.

But I didn't care about my own safety at that point. My heart was hurting too much.

Now, Micah's rage at my actions makes a whole lot of sense. He got in my way and took the Scorn dragons down. He refused to leave me to face the danger I'd welcomed.

It's also even clearer to me now why he would hide his pain from me and want to be strong for me.

But I need him to know that we can do things differently.

"My father sold me to Tyler," I say, making Micah stiffen beneath me. I hurry on before he can speak. "I mean, of course, that's not how anyone characterized it, but that's basically what happened. I had no dragon power. I was physically weak. Worthless, in my parents' eyes."

I swallow. "My father convinced Tyler that if he married me, he would become the next alpha of the Dread. He gave Tyler everything that should have been mine, including the dragon's gold that belonged to me. Tyler would let me wear the gold to parties or to the Hollow Rose—that's Callan's club—so other dragons saw me wearing it. They'd never suspect I didn't control my own gold. But Tyler took it off me as soon as we got home.

"My mother went along with all of it. She never stepped in. In fact, she told me repeatedly what a shit wife I was. For a long time, I believed her."

Micah's jaw clenches and hard dragon scales ripple across his skin. I might not have the same acute senses that he has, but his anger feels like ripples of heat between us.

"I'm not telling you this to make you angry, or for you to seek revenge on my behalf," I say. "My point is that our parents made their own choices. It's true that we live with the consequences of their decisions, but I'll be damned if I allow their prejudices, their fears, or their actions to destroy *my* future. *Our* future. We can make different choices."

"What are you saying?"

"That we'll wait." I reach for him, holding his gaze with mine. "I want my children to grow up in safety. First, we'll create a safe future for them. Then we can welcome them into our life."

A soft, slow smile forms on Micah's face that lights up his eyes and makes my core heat. He relaxes in front of me, his hands stroking across my back again, slipping neatly beneath my shirt and tracing across my spine. "Okay, then."

Damn it, he's already making it hard for me to keep my word.

CHAPTER SEVENTEEN

When we leave our room in the morning, we find a basket of food on the step outside the door and a note from Beatrix that reads:

Don't expect me to bring you breakfast every day.
B

The basket contains soft-looking bread rolls as well as several pieces of fruit that have the appearance of apples but are the same color as my scales—a bright, cerulean blue.

We take the basket with us to the training room, and I happily gobble down a buttery bread roll along the way.

Neither of us is wearing shoes. We've left them at the bottom of the stairway. But we don't need them. The floor of our room and the planks of wood that make up the stairway are pleasantly warm and comfortable beneath our feet.

We did change into fresh pants and tunics, matching ones. All white today, which makes me feel very angelic.

We'd both raised eyebrows at each other before leaving our

room, but I can't say Micah doesn't look good. The material has enough stretch to allow for easy movement and it clings a little to his biceps and the muscles across his back and chest.

The entrance to the training room has a similar layout to the other rooms—a small hallway that opens out into a much bigger space. In the training room's case, we enter what appears to be an armory while the main exercise room is visible through a wide opening ahead of us.

The weapons in the armory take my breath away, and I nearly choke on the final piece of bread.

I swallow it down as I stare at the left-hand wall.

It's completely taken up with Sentinels' spears, all of them resting behind a transparent panel that has the appearance of glass but shimmers more brightly.

Thank fuck those weapons are secured.

The blade of a Sentinel's spear is deadly to all creatures. Even a scratch can kill. Judging by the number of them all neatly resting on hooks at intervals along the wall, many of these spears would have belonged to the angels who betrayed Lana.

"Isaac insisted that only he should handle those," Micah says, hanging back a little. "The spears apparently only obey the angel they belong to—they're like dragon's gold in that respect—but he has control over all of them in his position as first of the Roden-Darr."

I dare to step toward the wall, fixated on the golden tips. "Could they kill Tyler?"

My question is soft. Hopeful. Spoken on a held breath.

Micah draws level with me, his forehead creased in apparent thought. "There would only be one way to find out. But we'd have to convince Isaac to try. Since we wouldn't be able to use one of these spears ourselves."

"Asking Isaac would be a last resort." I shake my head. "As I understand it, it isn't in his nature to kill."

I force myself to turn away from the wall of spears, eyeing

the alternative weapons on the right-hand wall: daggers, swords, ancient-looking guns, and—

My eyes widen at what sits at the far end.

A set of armor is suspended on the wall. It's made up of golden plates to protect the chest and shoulders, complete with a helmet that has a cross-like opening for the eyes and nose. Two horns extend from the top of the helmet directly backward, each tip appearing extremely sharp.

Beside the armor, resting on a hook on the wall, is a hammer with a shaft that appears to be made of some kind of black bone while the hammer's head is a thick block of gold. Even from this distance, I can make out that there are inscriptions etched into the gold. Some sort of runes, although I don't know how to read them.

The air tingles between me and the armor and my heart misses a beat.

I've had barely any training with dragon's gold, but I know how to sense when the gold is calling to me.

I can't resist the call, hurrying to stand in front of it.

"Is this a suit of dragon's gold?"

Micah is slower to follow me, appearing even warier of the armor and the weapon than he was of the Sentinels' spears.

"Those should be behind glass," he says. "Isaac promised to find a safer place for them."

"Why?" I ask, lifting my hand toward the hammer's handle.

Micah's arm snakes out and he takes hold of my wrist before I can make contact.

"That armor belonged to Atrox Imperator," he says, his voice strained. "The hammer was used by his brother, Dominus Audax. It's a dangerous weapon of light magic."

I inhale a sharp breath. Atrox Imperator was Callan's dragon shadow. Just like Bella Vorago was mine. They'd been reincarnated within us, old souls reborn over and over again because the dragon's light had been hidden from us.

Atrox's power and rage were the reason that Callan couldn't

control his flames for years. The reason he couldn't safely touch another supernatural without his fire being triggered.

It was *Atrox's* flames that burned me the night I protected Emika.

"I should fear this armor," I whisper. "But it feels... lost. Hurt." I turn to Micah. "Dragon's gold isn't meant to be alone."

His expression softens, although he hasn't let go of my wrist. His hold is light and his thumb brushes across my hand, no longer holding me so much as caressing me.

"That's true," he says. "It forms a deep bond with its owner. That's why it can only be controlled by that dragon. But that's all the more reason why we can't use this armor or this weapon."

I tip my head with a growing smile. "Unless you're Lana. Daughter of the Grudge King and Thief of Gold."

Micah grimaces. It was only because Lana had the power to steal the Grudge dragons' gold that she survived Solomon Grudge's bid to end her.

"True," he says. "I'll admit there have been times when I wished that power had been passed to me." He returns his attention to the armor. "Even so, this gold is far too volatile to ever be used again."

"And the hammer?" I ask.

"Dominus used it to give Atrox's soul the power to take control of Callan's body."

I shudder while Micah steps a little closer to the weapon.

"My senses tell me it's made from dragon's gold," he says, his forehead creasing. "But it feels different. As if it's heavy in my mind. Lana described it the same way. She told me she couldn't bend it to her will, despite her abilities."

I nod. "I sense it, too. Perhaps the runes have something to do with that. I'm not sure I've ever seen runes carved into dragon's gold before."

"It's certainly unusual." Micah urges me to step back, inclining his head to the main arena. "Let's get started."

I cast a backward glance at the armor before I enter the training room itself.

The floor has the appearance of wood, but I'm immediately aware of the spongy feel beneath my feet and the bounce in my step. Dropping to a knee, I press the heel of my palm against the surface. "It has a spring in it."

"That's good," Micah says, pressing his palm to the wall beside the opening. "The wall does, too."

I arch an eyebrow. "All the better for avoiding injuries."

As we step farther into the room, the far wall shimmers and becomes transparent, revealing a vast, open space beyond it. "And that would be where we can fly," I say.

"All in good time." Micah plants his bare feet and throws me a challenge. "Show me what you can do."

I take a deep breath before I position myself opposite him.

A buzz of anticipation runs through me.

Any contact with Micah's body is a thrill. Let alone the invitation to put him on his back.

I give him a smile and then I begin.

Three hours later, we're sweaty and hot, and the buzz I welcomed has become a persistent, low ache in my stomach.

Micah hasn't held back, proving to me over and over how many times and how many different ways he can immobilize me. But each time, he also shows me how to free myself. How I can use my smaller body and my lighter weight to slip his hold and strike back. Turn the tables on him and make the best use of his position to inflict damage.

Sometimes, my wings can be used to my advantage. Other times, they're a liability. I'm quickly learning how to recognize which in any given situation.

I run through the last maneuver he taught me, a sneaky

move that puts him on his back and me straddling him, which allows me to land a punch to his face.

Of course, I stop my fist above his cheekbone, since actually connecting with his body with any force would only break my hand. The moment his scales appear across his skin, his body becomes rock-hard.

At the last moment, I flatten my hand, running it down the side of his face. My other hand punches the floor on the other side of his face, taking me low to his body.

My chest is heaving and every droplet of sweat on his body is calling to me.

I pause above him, studying the changing power in his eyes. The slow shifting from teacher to mate. The softening of his lips and the gentling of his hands where they rest against my hips.

"Don't go easy on me, Grudge," I murmur, my lips so close to his that it's becoming unbearable to keep my distance.

I catch his broadening smile before he deftly reverses our position, one hand flying up to cushion my head before I find myself on my back, my legs wrapped around his hips.

He lowers his head slowly to mine, his lips feathering my mouth, the softest touch that sends a shock of sensation right to my core. He deepens the kiss, leaving me gasping when he breaks the contact and trails kisses down my neck.

Finding the upper curve of my breast through my shirt, he asks in a husky rumble, "I'd like to go down on you. Would that be okay?"

Dear saints. Just hearing him ask nearly tips me over the edge.

My core clenches and I bite my lip before I nod. "Uh-huh. Yes."

His head lowers to my stomach, where he plants kisses all along the edge of the elastic band at the top of my white pants, his lips grazing my skin. When he tugs the band lower, his kisses travel to the top of my pelvis and my body responds with a rush of heat.

Damn, I've never wanted to be rid of my clothing this fast.

But he seems content to leave the material right where it is, his thumbs stroking the inside of my thighs outside my pants and his lips brushing over the top of them. His kisses are increasingly insistent across my pelvis and upper thighs, his gaze flashing to mine. It's as if he's waiting for me to take control of what I want.

Without hesitation, I lift my hips off the floor and reach down to push my own clothing off. The elastic waistbands of both the long pants and my underwear only allow me to push them as far as my upper thighs, but he gives a satisfied growl, as if he's pleased that I took control.

My thighs are closer together than I want them to be and it forces my legs flat to the floor, a constraint I want to remove. I'll tear these fucking clothes apart if that's what it takes to give him access to my body.

But Micah doesn't seem at all concerned or deterred.

He's straddling my legs and his position allows him to lower his head to my body. His mouth reaches my pelvis, his tongue swirls between my folds and lightly flicks against my core, and I shiver from the intense pleasure.

Warmth tightens my muscles and cascades through my entire body. My hands find the top of his head and twine in his hair as I wish I could give back what I'm feeling.

I gasp when he responds to my touch by slipping his hands behind my backside and lifting my hips slightly off the floor. It's a gentle arch that tightens my muscles and intensifies the pleasure he's already giving me.

Pure, aching need overwhelms me, and I give in to the sensations washing through me, desperate to rock against him, desperate to feel his tongue against all of me, but I can't find purchase now that he's entirely in control.

And I'm becoming increasingly aware that his touch can only go so far in this position and—*dammit*—it's not enough.

He growls against my core. "Let go, Sophia. Trust me."

The vibration of his voice triggers sensations against my core that are both sharp and soft.

I stop fighting my moan, letting it out, low and needy. I stop trying to control my breathing, accepting how fast it is. And I accept the control he has, trusting him with my body.

I'm breathing heavily, moaning with need as his tongue flicks across me again, but I manage to put words to my feelings. "I trust you."

He responds by lowering my hips to the floor, taking hold of my pants and pulling them all the way off my legs. I gasp with relief when his hands run up the insides of my legs and his mouth follows, finally closing over all of me.

Dear saints, I've never experienced anything like this before. The strokes of his tongue drive every remaining inhibition from my mind. Now that my feet are planted firmly on the floor, I can rock against his mouth and it only seems to please him.

He growls against me, his tongue dragging across my wetness, and it tips me over the edge. My body tenses, my core clenches, and then the release makes me rock wildly against him.

He continues tasting me, drawing out my orgasm in long waves that leave me crying out until I sag to the floor, breathless.

He rears up over me, the desire in his eyes making my stomach tighten all over again.

I reach up to glide my fingertip across his glistening bottom lip. Then I dart upward to kiss him, wrapping my arms around him and drawing him down on top of me, my legs now on either side of his hips.

His kiss is hungry. He's hard between my legs. His body's reaction to me dares me to make a move.

In a swift maneuver—one he taught me this morning—I reverse our positions so that I'm straddling him.

I always thought I'd feel awkward asking for what I want,

but with Micah, it's easy. "I want to taste all of you on my tongue," I say. "May I?"

His lips curve. "Yes."

My heart swells, a thrill rushes through me, and I'm too physically and emotionally fulfilled to be inhibited. I catch the hem of his shirt and push it upward, tracing the hardness of the muscles across his chest and stomach with my fingertips, loving the way his dragon's scales appear at my touch.

When I lower my mouth to his skin, I inhale the heady scent of a wild mountain and the earthy smell of a wolf's fur ruffling in the breeze. Rugged scents that transport me to another place, just like the first moment I met him.

My lips tingle against the stony texture of his skin, my kisses triggering another blush of glistening scales that ripple outward across his chest and then vanish.

Exploring his skin as I go lower, I have no hesitation tugging down his pants, releasing his hard length from the confines of his clothing.

Greedily, my gaze takes in all of him before I lower my head to his hardness and run my tongue along his length, drowning in the taste of a wilderness that no longer feels out of my reach.

He groans my name before his fingers tangle in my hair, but he doesn't try to take control, letting me swirl my tongue across his tip and down the other side. And back again. All while he carefully cups my head and doesn't dictate any of it.

Sinking onto him, I finally take him into my mouth.

I don't have a hope of covering all of him, but I go as far as I can, drawing another groan from him before I rise up again.

As I move, my hands splay on his stomach, sensing the tension in his muscles, the increasing friction. I listen for every catch of his breath, his ragged breathing, every groan that tells me when to ease off or to deepen my touch.

When he comes, it's a heady rush that sends shivers through my own body.

Fuck, he tastes like rain across jagged mountain stones.

I have no trouble swallowing, my own core heating.

Then I glide upward, planting my hands on either side of his head and hovering above him. My hair was tied back, but it's come loose, and now it falls like a curtain to one side of my face, grazing his cheek.

We're both naked from the waist down and our bodies are awfully close together.

How easy it would be to take things further.

My voice catches as I meet his eyes. "There's so much I want to say, but none of it comes close."

Micah rears up beneath me and presses his mouth to mine. I taste myself on his lips and I'm okay with it, especially when he deepens the kiss and it's heavenly, thigh-clenching, sweet, and heady, all at once.

The kiss continues for a long moment until he finally pulls away.

"We should get dressed," he says, his voice husky.

I glance upward. I completely forgot where we are. My cheeks burn when I realize that Beatrix or Isaac could have walked in on us.

Micah pulls my focus back to him, planting kisses on my cheeks and chin before he gives me a heated smile and inclines his head to the far left side of the room. "Want to fly with me?"

Do I ever.

CHAPTER EIGHTEEN

The flight area at the back of the training room is vast and spacious enough that it lends itself perfectly to practicing aerial maneuvers.

I relish the chance to spread my wings and fly without inhibition, and Micah gives me a good few minutes of freedom in the air.

Soon enough, he becomes my teacher again.

By the time our stomachs are growling, I've begun learning how to put my wings to their best use in the air while also using every other part of my body to defend myself.

It's liberating, and I actually enjoy it way more than fighting on the ground. By the time our hunger forces us to take a break, I've learned several maneuvers and I'm feeling far more confident than before.

Finally, we venture out of the training room and up to the food hall, which is more like a large kitchen.

There, we find Beatrix and Isaac cooking lunch at a wide stove. If they notice our arrival, they barely give any indication, seeming engrossed in their tasks and their conversation.

It gives me a chance to look around. I'm surprised at how retro the kitchen appears to be. It's like stepping into a home from the 1960s, complete with a pastel-green fridge in the corner and a pastel yellow kettle sitting on the stove.

A large, rectangular table is positioned in the middle of the room covered in a tablecloth the same color as the fridge while the floor is checkered black and white.

There are windows on the left and right sides of the room, each one framed by short, lace curtains that are clipped back to reveal green fields. A barn is visible in the background through the left-hand window.

I'm startled when I'm sure I hear a cow mooing outside.

"We grow everything ourselves," Isaac is saying to Beatrix. "But unfortunately, without the other Roden-Darr to help, it's going to be difficult tending to the livestock and fields."

Beatrix's hair is windswept again and it makes me think she might have spent the morning flying over the forest—or some other area I don't know about yet.

She cracks an egg into the pan she's heating on the stove. "I can help."

Isaac arches his eyebrows at her before he resumes buttering bread. He doesn't say anything, but it's clear he's doubtful of her offer.

"What?" she asks, glaring at him. "You think I'm too fancy to get my hands dirty?"

He widens his stormy eyes at her, as if to reply with a resounding *yes*.

"Well, I'm not," she says, an obstinate edge in her voice. "And unlike *somebody else*, I don't need to spend my day training."

She gives me a brief glance, confirming she's aware of our arrival, before she returns her attention to Isaac. "If you don't give me a purpose, I'll get bored." She waggles the spatula at him. "And trust me when I tell you, *Isaac*, you don't want me to get bored."

The corners of his lips twitch upward. "Well, I can't have that."

He places two buttered rolls of bread onto plates beside

the stove and continues in the next breath. "After lunch, you can help me gather grains. That should be a good place to start."

I can no longer withstand the mouthwatering scents that are making my stomach growl. Clearing my throat, I opt for a cheery, "Good afternoon, Isaac. What can we do to help?"

"You can sit," Beatrix orders me before Isaac can respond. She points her spatula sharply at the chair nearest to her. "Don't tell me how you like your eggs. You'll get them how I make them."

"As long as they're not burned," I say, drawing a sharp look from her. I give her a sweet smile in return.

Micah pulls up the chair opposite me. He hasn't said a word. Simply leans back with his arms folded across his chest, eyeing Beatrix as she turns back to Isaac and they continue to snipe at each other.

Micah seems increasingly amused by their interactions, but he wipes his expression clean when Beatrix plonks two plates onto the table, each containing bread that smells heavenly fresh and two large eggs sunny side up.

"Don't expect me to cook for you every day," she snaps. "I'm not your maid."

"Thank you, Beatrix. This looks delicious," I respond meekly, drawing a deeper scowl from her.

She suddenly twitches and spins back to Isaac. "I won't have to kill any farm animals, will I?"

He shakes his head, appearing deadly serious. "We don't eat meat. We only take produce from the animals like milk, eggs, and honey. Our bread is made from a special wheat plant that sheds its own, large kernels, but I'll show you how to gather them and grind them into flour."

Beatrix exhales a sigh of relief, but then says, "Honey? As in bees?"

"Don't worry. These creatures are known as 'humblebees.' They're extinct in the outside world. And they don't sting."

"Well, that's probably why they're all dead," Beatrix says wryly. "Survival requires sting."

Again, Isaac arches his eyebrows at her, but it's a gentler expression this time. "Does it?"

Beatrix scowls at him before she continues gruffly. "In my experience."

"Hmm," is all he says.

As they continue their back and forth, I focus on my food.

The size of the eggs makes me wonder if they belong to a bird much larger than a chicken. Either way, they're delicious.

When I've finished eating, Micah inclines his head at the door. I'm surprised to see leftover food on his plate, but that could be because of the cerulean-blue, apple-like fruit he ate on the way up the stairs. Maybe the apples are more filling than they looked.

"C'mon," he murmurs. "Let's get back to training."

I feel bad about leaving all of the farm work to Beatrix and Isaac, and I say so, but Micah gives a shake of his head. "We're here for your training."

We head back to the combat room and spend the rest of the day there. Micah eases up on teaching me combat skills, instead focusing on my understanding of weaponry, including how to care for my weapon. We start with daggers, but Micah tells me I should try out a different type of weapon each day—not for the purpose of mastering it in a single afternoon—but so that I can find my blade of choice.

By the time we return to the kitchen for dinner, I know two things: Daggers are definitely my thing, and I'm exhausted.

Still, I ask Isaac to show me how to use the kitchen appliances, and I insist on cooking the meal, roasting vegetables in the oven and frying enormous mushrooms in butter.

When I serve up the food, Beatrix eyes her plate with skepticism. I guess, just as Isaac never pictured her feeding farm animals, Beatrix never pictured me preparing a proper meal.

She takes the first bite while I hold my breath.

"Well, fuck me," she says before quickly digging into the rest. "Since when can you cook?"

"Since forever." I shrug. "I was expected to spend a lot of time in the kitchen."

Beatrix pauses then gives a soft sigh. "I'm sorry."

Again, I shrug and then begin eating.

"I appreciate this meal, Sophia," Isaac says. "But please don't feel you have to prepare food for us every night. I'm happy to do it."

"I want to," I reply. "It's nice to have a family to cook for."

Opposite me, Micah has also paused, but his expression softens. "Tomorrow, I can help."

Beatrix snorts at him. "A Grudge dragon working over a hot stove?"

Micah arches his eyebrows at her. "There are very few Grudge left. We all know how to prepare food."

She squints at him. "Nope, sorry, I still can't see it."

He laughs. "Tomorrow night, I'll prove it to you."

After we finish eating, I give Beatrix a hug.

I'm tempted to hug Isaac too, but I don't think we're quite there yet.

The next morning, another basket of food is sitting on the step outside our door with a note from Beatrix that reads:

You have to try these.
B.

P.S. I picked the fruit. Isaac did the baking. We've been up since dawn, so you'd better fucking love them.

Inside the basket are multiple large bread rolls with fruit and nuts baked into them. The fruit looks a bit like raspberries and leaves a tang on my tongue.

"I do fucking love them," I mumble around the bread, filling up on the rolls before I begin another round of training.

For the next five days, I work hard at expanding my combat skills, both on the ground and in the air. I increase my speed and agility, along with my ability to defend myself—and to attack an opponent.

I learn very quickly that firearms are not for me and neither are swords or spears. Daggers, on the other hand, continue to suit me just fine, and Micah soon teaches me about all the chinks in a dragon's hide through which to slip a knife.

Each day, I walk past Atrox's armor and fight the urge to step closer to it. Each evening, Micah and I cook dinner, and afterward, I give Beatrix a hug goodnight.

On the fifth night, I hug Isaac too.

But in the bedroom, I fight my body's wants, taking all the pleasure Micah gives me and giving back as much as he's prepared to take, only to find myself wanting more than I can have.

By the sixth day, my speed in combat has increased so much that I force Micah onto the back foot over and over again.

"Good," he says after I put him on his back again.

"But is it good enough?"

His lips press into a grim line. "To fight Tyler?"

I give a short nod.

"That depends on what you're holding back."

He looks me in the eye as if he can see right through me, and I nearly flinch at the challenge in his expression. With a sigh, I slip off him and into a sitting position, pulling my knees to my chest.

"Sophia," he says gently. "Your combat skills have improved to the point where I genuinely think you could challenge Lana to a fight."

I'm both surprised at his assertion and grateful for his encouragement, but I know he isn't telling me this to congratulate me. "But?"

"But your power is still caged."

I quietly consider what has been lurking at the back of my

mind for days now. That I'm no closer to understanding the force within me.

"*My* dragon power is all here," Micah says, pressing his hand to his chest. "I can choose when to reveal my dragon scales and my wings. And my body doesn't break easily. I can pretty much sum up my power in one simple statement: I have physical strength."

He rises to his feet and holds out his hand for me.

Once I'm back on my feet, he continues. "But your power is less tangible. I was hoping that by pushing you to your physical limits, by training you all day, every day, your inner power would reveal itself."

His fingers lace with mine, his thumb stroking my wrist, and I'm distracted by the nearness of his body, the heat that grows within my core so quickly, it's nearly impossible to push away.

His serious expression banishes my heated thoughts. "I should have realized sooner that it would be impossible for you to explore your power while you're confined within four walls. You need a natural environment. Trees. Fresh air."

"Water," I finish for him.

"Exactly." He takes my other hand. "Which is why we should take our training session to the forest."

I'm surprised. "The forest?"

"The only way you'll discover what you're capable of is to be exposed to the elements and find out what you can do."

An involuntary shiver tingles across my skin, triggered by the thought of uncaging what lies within me. "What if... I shouldn't let my power out?"

His forehead creases. "What do you mean?"

I chew my lip for a moment, reflecting on the way I forced the water to come to me in the oblivion, breaking the laws of nature. The way I'm drawn to Atrox's armor—attracted to it while Micah seems repelled by it.

"Not all power is good," I whisper. "Tyler's isn't. And he's clearly embraced it. What if my power causes... damage?"

Micah presses his hand against my heart. "I don't know all the details of Lana's story, but I do know that her power was considered abhorrent to the angels. Her strength was misused against us—and it was also misused against *her*. She would be able to speak to her journey far better than I can, but I know one thing for sure: She took ownership of who she is."

His gaze bores into me. "Your power is in *your* hands."

In my heart, I understand what he's trying to say. How I use my power is more important than what my power is.

But at the back of my mind is a kernel of fear.

Not all power can be controlled. Not all darkness can be repelled. Uncaging the true nature of my power could mean inviting a constant war with myself.

A war I might lose.

CHAPTER NINETEEN

Cold air bursts around my body as I step through the door to the forest and my heart instantly leaps.

The gust of wind is so strong that my hair flies out behind me and my clothing whips tightly against my body. It doesn't let up even after Micah closes the door firmly behind us.

Unsurprisingly, the door leading to the forest is painted a deep, pine green on the stair side, but on this side, it's an unexpectedly bright, crimson red.

We let Isaac know where we were going and sought his permission to come into the forest. He told us to be careful and offered to accompany us since the animals in this place are wild and unused to interaction with angels, let alone dragon shifters.

I carefully considered his offer, but it would defeat the purpose of coming here. I don't plan on taking unnecessary risks, but I can't explore my power without letting go of my boundaries. Or, at least, *trying* to let go.

The breath stops in my chest as I step farther forward onto a jagged, stone surface that extends out into space and ends abruptly only twenty paces ahead of us.

We can only be standing on the top of a sharp cliff.

A mountain range stretches to both sides and far behind us,

while the red door stands benignly upright in the middle of the air, its base barely touching the rocky surface beneath our feet.

It's exactly the environment to which Micah's scent often takes me. The top of a mountain covered in ancient stones where I can picture a wolf prowling between the outcrops, seeking its pack.

The air rushes around me in a tornado, plucking at my body as I spin to Micah. "I thought Beatrix said this was a forest."

My voice is swallowed in the howling wind and when Micah cups his hand around his ear, indicating that he didn't hear me, I repeat myself, this time at a shout. "Where are the trees?"

He points toward the cliff's edge before he moves in that direction, taking each step carefully and pushing against the wind. A few paces from the edge, he cranes his head and peers down. "There!" he shouts. "Below us."

I'm only a step behind him, but I have to stretch forward to see them. Only once my line of sight descends far enough that I can view the horizon do I make out the greenery far below us.

Far, *far* below.

"Fuck," I whisper.

My heart is pumping hard, but a grin is growing on my face. My wariness about coming here is disappearing, and the fear of my power I felt only a short time ago is being pulled away with it.

Fuck, there's something in the air here...

It's instantly intoxicating to my senses.

I've lived my life within four walls and the restrictions of city streets. I've never traveled beyond that concrete and steel world with its carefully trimmed and sculpted parks.

I've never experienced an environment like this before, and Micah was right. The only way I'll discover what I'm capable of is to be exposed to the elements and find out what I can do.

Taking another glance at him, I find a curious light growing in his eyes as he tips his head to the side. I read my name on his lips, even though I can't hear him speak: *Sophia?*

I can't answer him. Not yet.

My blood is pounding, my head is buzzing, and I can practically *feel* the cage around my power straining to break apart.

I'm still fearful of what will happen when it finally opens, but here, in this environment, it feels impossible to continue constraining it.

I take a step toward the cliff's edge, casting my focus inward to the swirling energy within my mind and body, wishing I understood it better.

The white tunic I'm wearing can accommodate my wings, but the instinct to welcome the rush of air across my skin is high. Pulling off the garment, I roll my shoulders and close my eyes as I inhale the scents around me.

The unfamiliar woody perfume of the forest far below, the cold of the air beating across the stony mountain, and then, the earthy scent of wolf and dragon as Micah closes the gap between us.

I open my eyes and now I give him a smile as I allow my dragon nature to surge, my arctic-blue scales blushing across my arms and chest, cooling my cheeks.

Without another moment's hesitation, I burst into a run, sprinting against the wind and toward the cliff's edge.

I launch myself off the rock into the sheer nothingness beyond. I release my wings with a *thump* that vibrates through my body, and for a second, I'm suspended between the opposing forces of air pushing forward, up, and down. I'm cushioned within them so that it feels like I'm resting within the sky.

I'm aware of Micah's presence where he stands on the edge of the mountain, but I don't look back.

In the next heartbeat, gravity takes hold.

I feel it surging through my body, a clutching force that wants to destroy me, but I take control, pushing my hands forward, tucking my wings tightly against my sides and tilting myself downward.

My heart bursts up into my throat as I plunge through space.

Far, far below me are rocky crevices, a stony terrain with a few sparse trees that quickly transforms into the forest. If I don't stop my fall, I'll hit the rocks and break every bone in my body.

If I drift too far forward and don't stop my fall in time, I'll plunge into the trees. At this velocity, I'll be ripped to shreds by the branches. Leaves that may be soft will become like blades.

But if I time my fall perfectly, I can dip into the open area between the cliff and the trees and soar back up in time to avoid hitting either rocks or trees.

Of course, if I were sensible, I could spread my wings right now, slow my fall, and fight the wind to descend to the treetops.

Oh, but this place. It begs me to let go and be wild.

With my wings tucked close to my sides, the speed of my descent increases. The cliff face is a dark gray blur, and now the ground rushes up at me.

At the last minute, I extend my wings, pushing hard against the force of gravity.

With a mighty effort, I sweep my wings backward. A split second later, I throw my arms to the right, forcing my body to twist midair just like I learned in aerial combat training and at the same time, I wrap my wings around myself again.

The result is an upward spiral.

The world spins around me, a dizzying blur of green trees, blue sky, and gray stone as I shoot heavenward.

Finally, my speed slows. I level out, spread my wings, and pump them once. A heartbeat later, I'm gliding across the treetops, close enough to reach down and touch the uppermost leaves.

My heart rate calms, but *damn*, that was reckless.

Also fucking glorious.

I can't stop my satisfied smile as I beat my wings and rise a little higher, giving myself the space to turn onto my back and check the sky for Micah.

He's a distant speck far above me.

Then a plummeting one.

I hold my breath for the seconds it takes him to release his wings—far earlier than I did. His descent pulls to an abrupt halt, his wings billowing a little before he glides down at an angle toward me.

I'm still moving, but he has enough momentum to reach me quickly. Finally positioning himself directly above me, he coasts the air while we face each other.

His wings cast a shadow over me, a sudden darkness, before he shifts position and the sunlight shines through to me once more.

It's not so bright that I can't make out his curious smile.

"How are you doing that?" he asks, his voice raised so I can hear him.

The wind isn't rushing around us here, but even so, our flight snatches the sounds from our lips.

"Doing what?" I call upward.

"Flying on your back. And without crashing."

I consider his question since I simply turned into this position without much thought. Come to think of it, I could be defying the natural laws of aerodynamics right now.

But my senses are so expanded that I'm aware of the treetops close beneath me. The air between the branches and my back feels like a cushion—a buffer. And as for my wings, they're both supporting me and gently swaying at the same time.

I took some swimming lessons when I was younger and right now, it feels a lot like doing backstroke through the water.

It's the only analogy I can think of.

"It's like swimming," I say.

His focus switches to the distance. "Speaking of water."

He lifts upward, giving me space to twist and turn to see the landscape up ahead.

A lake glistens in the distance. It's at least two miles wide and a mile deep, a gleaming, oval shape like a mirror with a rippling surface.

It's the only large body of water I sense, so it must be the one Beatrix mentioned. Anticipation floods me as I wait to see what creatures might be living in it—and within the forest.

Passing across the edge of the trees and the flat expanse of grass, I coast downward and land at the water's edge. There, I stretch out my wings, appreciating the strength and agility I gain from them.

Micah lands behind me, but he hangs back. He's rubbing his shoulder, as if the flight might have strained him, but before I can ask him about it, he says, "I'll check the perimeter. Isaac told us to be cautious and I'd like to be certain we're safe."

"Okay." I venture closer to the water. It shimmers with what appears to be movement right beneath the surface, but I can't make out what might be under there.

Kneeling at the edge, I lean forward, my hands resting on my knees and my wings held aloft. I won't be able to hold them high for long, but like Micah, I don't want to be too trusting of this new environment. I'm ready to fly if I need to.

The water's surface shimmers closer to my location.

I watch the movement, peering hard.

A second later, a swarm of creatures bursts from the water up into the air, filling the space in front of me.

I jolt backward, ready to spread my wings, but the swarm hovers and doesn't make any further sudden moves.

Their wings and bodies are a blue-and-purple blur. Fine droplets of water spray around me like a cool mist as countless little wings beat so fast that they hum like a soft melody.

Taking a deep breath, I look more closely. Each creature is bigger than my hand with a slender body and two gauzy wings on either side.

They're dragonflies.

Hmm... maybe?

My forehead creases as the swarm edges nearer to me and I take a closer look.

They're certainly shaped like dragonflies, but their bodies

are covered in tiny scales and, if I'm not imagining it, I think I can make out gills on their sides between their heads and wings.

In unison, several of them tuck their wings and dive back into the water, swimming just beneath the surface before they pop back up again, spreading their wings and hovering once more.

"Beautiful," I whisper as I dare to lift my hand toward them. It would be unwise to touch them—my body oils could disturb their skin or harm their wings—but the mist they're creating as the water evaporates off them is like diamonds in the air.

I wave my hand through it while another group of dragonflies plunges back into the water and emerges again. They do this in turns and my guess is that they need to stay cool and damp.

"Micah," I call softly. "Come see this."

The forest is quiet behind me. I turn, expecting him to be approaching as silently as I know he can.

I don't see him anywhere.

"Micah?" Quickly, I scan the trees, unease growing in the pit of my stomach.

I listen carefully, wishing I had the ability to hear faraway things like he can.

A moment later, a low, keening cry echoes through the forest.

At the sound, the dragonflies jolt backward, their wings beating faster, the collective hum they're making rising in pitch. A second later, they scatter across the air and plunge back into the water, disappearing beneath the suddenly churning swill.

Whatever that sound was, it startled them.

I jump to my feet, listening and waiting.

The cry echoes again.

I can't tell for sure if it's Micah, but I know pain when I hear it.

CHAPTER TWENTY

I sprint toward the trees, fully retracting my wings to avoid wind resistance.

I fight the regret that's threatening to flood me. Maybe I should have taken Isaac up on his offer to come with us, but I thought I was making the right choice, and it's too late to change it now.

Navigating a path between the low branches and thick bushes, I keep my sense of the lake's location firmly in my mind. If I get lost, I'll be able to make my way back to it.

I want to call out for Micah, but the forest is hushed. It's only now that it's so quiet that I'm fully aware of just how many bird calls filled the air only moments ago.

The cry sounds again, this time louder and sharper.

I'm close enough to identify that it isn't Micah's voice, but it's filled with pain and fear.

A cold shiver passes down my spine. It's the same sensation I felt when Tyler was close by. The same chill that made me shudder when the Scorn dragons were hunting us at the fountain.

Death is near.

I'm not sure how I know that so keenly.

Or why my instincts are telling me that, this time, I should run *toward* the sound and not away from it.

In this place, with my senses so much freer, it's a clear thought. An impulse that I don't question.

I veer toward the location of the cry, identifying small movements up ahead.

Micah's silhouette becomes visible among the foliage. He's crouched beside a tree with a wide trunk and only a little space between him and the thick brush to his left.

He's turned in my direction. But of course, he would have heard me running, possibly as far away as the lake. Maybe even heard me call his name all the way back there.

He holds his finger to his lips.

Relieved to see that he's okay, I follow his lead, remaining silent while I slow down and then creep into the space beside him.

He gives me a brief smile—a reassuring smile, but there's a hint of tension within it—before he points to the clearing ahead.

A creature lies in the thick undergrowth, its legs facing in our direction.

It resembles a horse in size and shape, but its hide is as green as the leaves of the surrounding trees. A perfect camouflage in this forest and, if it weren't lying on darker brown foliage, I might have missed it.

While its body reminds me of a horse—right down to its hooves and tail—its neck and head are that of a stag. Mahogany-colored antlers protrude from either side of its forehead. They're the same color as the deep-red trunks of the trees surrounding us.

The creature's tummy is swollen and it rocks a little back and forth on the ground, groaning into the quiet.

I can't take my eyes off its belly—*her* belly—as I suddenly realize...

"She's trying to give birth," I whisper, my forehead creasing at the way she's breathing heavily, the wideness of her eyes as if she's verging on panic. All could be normal signs of birth, but this chill that remains at the base of my spine is *not* normal. "Something must be wrong."

I'm on my feet in an instant, but Micah's hand closes around my wrist just as quickly.

I meet his alarmed eyes.

"No, Sophia," he says urgently. "We don't know what this creature is or if she'll react badly to your presence. I don't want you to get hurt."

"She isn't dangerous," I say, although I'm speaking out of pure hope, but my next words carry the certainty I feel in my bones. "Both she and her baby will die if we don't help her."

Death remains a cold chill and I sense it within this clearing as surely as I can see the leaves and feel the soft breeze on my now-sweaty skin.

I don't know if I'm making the right choice. I could be about to walk into danger. But my instincts are screaming at me to help this beautiful creature. If I ignore my instincts—if I cage them—then I will have no hope of finding my true power.

Micah's hold tightens. Then loosens. "Remember when I told you I'd have a hard time putting you in harm's way?" He grimaces. "I wasn't lying about that."

I bend to him, turning my hand so that I'm grasping his palm now. "Okay, then, let me promise you what I'll do if I sense any danger: I'll fly away. Simple as that." I incline my head at the deer. "That creature doesn't have wings. It can't follow me into the air. And I promise I won't touch it if I sense that contact with its body will hurt me."

He gives me a crooked smile. "Will you allow me the privilege of watching your back?"

"Not allow," I whisper. "*Request*. Because I *want* you there with me."

I squeeze his hand and now I'm the one letting him go as I rise to my feet again. I take it one step at a time as I move past the thick brush and into the clearing.

"I can hear other creatures. Large ones," Micah murmurs as he follows quietly behind me. "I'll keep watch around the clearing's perimeter."

"Thank you." With a brief nod, I turn my focus completely to the deer.

Her eyes are wide and her nostrils flair as she watches me approach.

It's her fear that could be most dangerous to me.

If she kicks or tries to ram me with her antlers, she could hurt me, and I have no guarantees that my scales will protect me from her.

Between her antlers and her hooves, there isn't really a safe direction to approach her. I could circle around to her back, but then she wouldn't be able to see me and could panic even more.

I veer to the left, crouching low and taking it very slowly, as I approach in the direction of her forelegs—aiming for the spot between her head and chest.

Holding my left hand out as I move, I make shushing noises. "It's okay," I murmur. "I'm not here to hurt you."

She won't be able to understand me—well, I assume she can't—and hell, I could recite times tables and it probably wouldn't make a difference to her, but she seems to respond to the calm tone of my voice.

She watches me with a little less panic.

In the next moment, her body writhes again, and whatever fear she feels for me appears to be overtaken by her distress.

"How can I help you?" Again, I don't expect an answer or for the answer to magically appear to me, but it makes me feel better.

I consider her body from my current distance, but it's impossible to see from the outside what might be wrong. It's not like I trained as a vet or grew up on a ranch to understand how a horse-deer-creature might give birth or what sorts of complications could arise.

Making contact with her body is my first step—and certainly the most dangerous for me.

Reaching forward, I ready myself in case I need to leap back or spread my wings and fly.

Inch by slow inch, my arm extends toward her upper foreleg.

Her hide is softer than I was expecting. It feels like green grass warmed in the sun, and I'm instantly flooded with the scent and feel of summer. Early mornings before it gets too hot and the sunlight is gentle. Glimmers on my cheeks. Earth beneath my feet.

For a long moment, I stay there, my arm extended and my eyelids drooping with the heady sensation of being *alive*.

It's only when the deer moves a little that I realize how close I've leaned in to her body.

It's reckless, but she hasn't attacked me, so I lower myself further, my hand stroking along her side as far as I can reach, my fingertips brushing the edge of her belly.

The movement brings my chest to hers and my head to her neck. I rest there lightly, using my stomach muscles to stop myself from becoming a weight on her neck and side.

It's like resting on a grassy meadow.

I'm aware of the way Micah has frozen nearby, seeming caught between the need to surveil our surroundings and keep watch over me.

I want to reassure him, but I can't break this connection with the deer.

She hasn't fought me or tried to shake me off. She hasn't panicked. The longer I maintain contact with her, the calmer my heart grows.

I can hear her heartbeat, steady and strong, and sense the way her muscles are working hard to deliver her baby into the world…

No, make that *babies*.

There are two of them, surrounded in fluid, but both are

positioned butt-first. I don't know a lot about giving birth, but I know that butt-first is bad news.

I close my eyes and listen to her body, the same way I expanded my senses to dispel the water from Micah's and Beatrix's chests, distinguishing the different liquids within her. Blood, powerful and strong. Fluid, life-giving and now... potentially life-saving.

This water, like the river water, will obey me.

I'm sure of it.

Swirl, I tell it. *Churn gently but firmly. Turn the babies around.*

For a moment, I sense the deep well of power writhing within me, a force so great that I feel like I'm merely skimming the surface.

It scares the fuck out of me and I clamp down on it, focusing only on this one, simple task.

Turn the babies. Gently.

I've barely finished my command when the mother jolts upward.

I leap backward, away from her clambering legs as she shifts up into a kneeling position. Her eyes have flown wide and the concentration on her face is intense.

It happens so fast that I'm not certain I did what I needed to do. My heart is in my throat and it feels like the next seconds extend forever as I wait and hope that I helped her and didn't harm her.

Then, one after the other, two small fawns slip onto the undergrowth. Both head-first. They're partially covered by the birth sac, but their heads are clear. Their eyes are closed and their legs are curled beneath them.

I hurry farther backward, giving the mother space as she immediately turns to them, nudging both of them before she starts licking them all over.

The little ones gravitate toward her, turning their heads and cracking open their eyes. She nuzzles them, making soft, bleating sounds before she rests down on the ground again, continuing to lick their hides.

I'm not sure I've ever seen anything so beautiful.

Also… maybe a little gross…

My nose screws up for a second before I quietly laugh at myself.

More than anything right now, I feel lighter.

The chill in my spine has vanished. Death won't be claiming these creatures today and for that, I'm grateful.

I turn to Micah, but he's facing away from me, his back stiff.

"Sophia!" His call is low but urgent. "There are more of them. Incoming. Fast."

A second later, I hear it, too: The thunder of approaching hooves, many of them, moving through the trees at speed.

Within seconds, the edges of the clearing are filled with green bodies and then we're surrounded.

CHAPTER TWENTY-ONE

*E*very space we could escape through on foot is suddenly occupied with deer, their green hides melding with our surroundings so that it appears as if the forest has suddenly thickened into an impenetrable, chest-height, circular wall.

Micah holds his hand out, a sharp movement, one that tells me not to come closer to him.

A second later, a large stag steps into the clearing right in front of him.

The stag's antlers are long, each tine appearing sharper than the one before, and his hide is sleek, glistening a little more brightly than the other animals'.

Tossing his head and snorting, the stag paws the ground with his front hoof. His focus on Micah is intense, his antlers following a sharp arc in Micah's direction.

"Whoa, okay," I whisper, edging away from the new mother. "That's an unhappy daddy."

The mother's head has risen and she gives a soft bleat. Her babies are snuggled into her side. Instinctively, I know that she won't want us to disturb them. They'll be in the middle of bonding and it will be a critical time for them.

Micah hasn't moved. He calls quietly back to me, "The stag must think we're a threat. We need to move away from the doe and her babies."

"I couldn't agree more," I say.

But as I speak, a row of deer emerges into the clearing in front and behind me, all of them angling toward my location. It isn't a big space and now there's a risk that we'll hit the animals if we release our wings.

"We need to fly," Micah says. "But there isn't space for both of us. Hold your wings tight. I'll come to you and then we can—"

His voice suddenly catches and his right hand wraps around his left shoulder. "Fuck."

"Micah?"

He doesn't immediately respond, but the turn of his head allows me to see that his eyes are watering, liquid trickling down his cheeks as he drops to his knees.

"Micah!"

A gray pallor flows up his neck and down his left arm from beneath his sleeve.

His heart!

My stomach sinks and my own heart thuds in my chest.

No! This can't be happening now.

I need to reach him and get him out of here. Assuming I'm strong enough to lift him into the air. But, dammit, it took both Beatrix and me to carry him when he was unconscious. My power is undefined and so far, there are no indications that it gives me increased physical strength.

My thoughts fly through my head in the space of a heartbeat.

I'm already stepping toward Micah when five smaller deer, most likely females, judging by their smaller sizes, converge around me. Their heads are lowered, their antlers pointed at me.

Their tines appear sharp enough that I'll impale myself if I try to ram my way through them, but there isn't space to spread my wings without hitting them.

Within seconds, they've cut me off from Micah and are pushing me back toward the mother deer.

When I turn, trying to find a gap between them, I discover that all of the deer are positioning themselves the same way, heads down and antlers toward me. All of them converging to form a circular wall around me.

The mother and her babies are now close on my left, and, weirdly, she doesn't seem even remotely alarmed by the events unfolding around her. I'm glad in one sense because I don't want her to suffer any more distress.

The distress right now is all fucking mine.

"Micah!"

He doesn't respond, his shoulders slumping over where he kneels.

The stag hasn't remained idle. Pawing at the undergrowth, it kicks up leaves and debris as it roars at Micah.

Micah's head shoots up and he struggles to rise.

The moment he makes it up onto one knee, it's like a trigger.

The stag charges, its antlers aimed right at Micah's chest like daggers.

A scream leaves my lips, but Micah reacts swiftly. His fist flies upward, his hand wrapping around the longest tine in the blink of an eye.

For a moment, I think he's going to succeed in pushing the beast away, but the second he touches the antler, its color changes from mahogany to icy blue.

The air sizzles and the scent of burning skin is acrid across my tongue.

Micah gives a roar of pain that cuts through my heart.

The stag keeps pushing, its hind legs digging into the earth behind it, and its now-icy tines inching closer to Micah's chest and neck.

Micah strains to keep it at bay, his biceps bulging with

apparent effort. But if the tine he's holding is burning his hand despite his scales, he'll soon lose feeling in that palm. He won't be able to hold off the stag much longer.

I dread what will happen if the stag succeeds in ramming its antlers into his chest. The tines look deadly enough, but their transformation into icy weapons could cause catastrophic damage with a single stab.

My eyes are wide with fear, but I react without hesitation. I leap toward the nearest deer, focusing on its antlers and drawing on the reflexes I've been honing all week.

I prepare for the pain I'm about to feel, the burn that could tear the skin off my palms, and ready myself to push the animal out of my way.

All I want is to create enough space so I can reach Micah and drag him out of here.

Both of my hands close around the deer's antlers.

I'm shocked when the tines warm beneath my touch, remaining mahogany in color.

There's no ice, and I feel no pain. What's more, the deer doesn't react by charging at me. Its eyes widen at the contact and its head lowers even farther, a strangely meek gesture.

I don't have time to wonder why.

Pushing as hard as I can, I command the deer, "Move aside!"

I don't want to hurt it. I stepped into this clearing wanting to save life, not to take it. Of course, I have no idea if it will understand my speech—I highly doubt it will—but my shove should be indication enough of what I want.

The animal complies so fast that I nearly fall on my face with the force of my push. I release its antlers as quickly as I can, allowing it to back away from me while the deer next to it also sidesteps, its head remaining low to the ground. So low that its antlers are scraping the ground.

I stare at both deer in shock, but I can't waste time trying to figure out their behavior.

Five paces away, Micah is straining to keep the stag at bay—and quickly failing.

The air sizzles again as the stag's icy tines reach the Grudge dragon's chest and burn a tear through his shirt.

My heart is in my throat as I launch myself across the clearing. "No!"

The stag's deep-brown eyes widen at my cry, although it's impossible to know if it's because the animal is surprised or confused. Or some other stag emotion I can't possibly understand.

It doesn't back off. If anything, it increases its efforts, ramming its antlers even harder at Micah's chest.

Fuck!

I don't have time to scream, focusing all my energy into my speed as I race across the final distance and throw myself at the stag's neck.

At the same time, I reach out, my hand closing around its sharp tine—the one that's tearing across Micah's chest.

For a split second, I feel the burn.

It's icy. Beyond cold. So freezing that it feels like I've plummeted into the water beneath a frozen lake.

As cold as death and it threatens to consume me.

CHAPTER TWENTY-TWO

The icy power in the stag's antlers collides with the well of power within me and it's like a bullet hitting a target.

Instinctively, my body reacts.

Warmth flows through my palm.

Beneath my touch, the tine transforms back to its mahogany color, the icy-blue vanishing and taking the chill with it.

The beast jolts backward. I release it, but its movement is so fast, and Micah must have been holding on so tightly, that it pulls him with it.

He lands on his hands and knees in the undergrowth.

The beast's eyes are wild as it backs away, but only another step, swishing its antlers from side to side like a warning.

I'm too afraid to stop. For all I know, I've merely startled it and it will resume its attack at any moment. What's more, it's only two paces away from Micah. Not far enough for comfort.

"Keep back!" I cry, holding out my left hand in an attempt to ward off the creature as I drop to Micah's side.

Urgently, I check his chest and hand while trying not to take my eyes off the stag.

Micah has remained partially crouched, one knee to the

ground, the other leg bent awkwardly. A burn mark extends across his chest from his left shoulder to the upper right of his ribcage, where the stag's tine dragged across his skin.

The palm of his left hand is badly charred, the scales burned, and I shudder at the damage.

Wrapping my arm around his waist, desperate to draw him upright, I heave with all my might.

Fuck, he's heavy.

"Micah, you have to help me." My speech is low, hushed, and for a moment, he doesn't respond.

His head is lowered and I'm intensely concerned that he might have passed out in the last few seconds.

I'm relieved when he groans. "That beast really doesn't like me."

The air shifts around me with every sway of the stag's head. It hasn't taken its eyes off Micah and continues to paw the ground.

And yet, when I snarl at it, "Back off!" it jolts and complies. If only for another step.

What the hell is going on with this animal?

Why attack Micah and not me?

Desperately, I seek a way out of this situation. Wrapping my arm around Micah's waist, I ask him, "Can you walk?"

He gives another groan that I take as a *yes*.

"I'm getting you out of here." With my hand still held out toward the stag, I move cautiously backward, supporting Micah as he comes with me.

It's awkward and graceless, but we make it ten paces like that before we near the edge of the clearing.

The stag doesn't stop pawing the undergrowth, continuing to toss his head, snorting sharply as he watches us go.

I take a big risk when I turn away from him to check that our path is clear.

A single deer stands in our way.

Its head is down like the others, its antlers held to the front and low to the ground. It has a dark-green blaze across its forehead, which is different to the other creatures.

It doesn't back off or budge as we approach. But it doesn't attack me, either.

It's standing in the opening to the path I need to take—the nearest gap in the trees that's wide enough to accommodate both Micah and me walking side by side.

Now that Micah's taking some of his own weight, I can reach out toward the deer, even if it's a big risk. I wrap my hand carefully around one of its antlers and give it a gentle push to the side. "Out of the way, please."

The creature steps aside, moving in the direction I push, keeping its head down.

A clear space finally opens up in front of us and I don't take it for granted.

As fast as I can, I plow through the opening and into the forest beyond, taking regular glances backward. I've made it another ten paces before the deer all raise their heads, their antlers held high. The female with the blaze across her forehead moves toward me and tosses her head, but that's all before she calms again.

Then, within seconds, they all step backward. Their bodies camouflage seamlessly into the foliage until I can't make out a single one of them anymore.

They may as well not exist. Not even the new mother, who must have stood up and taken her babies with her.

We don't stop walking. Micah's footsteps are labored, his weight on me heavier and heavier as I trudge back to the lake. Once there, I help Micah to sit down on the grass, praying that it's safer here by the water.

I don't understand what the hell just happened. Possibly one of the strangest experiences of my life.

Micah leans to the side before he lies down in the grass.

"I need to get you back to the infirmary," I say, my mind

working at a million miles an hour as I try to think how I can possibly convey him back on my own.

It's miles to the red door and would take us hours to walk. Even flying would take too long—a longer trip back than the flight here because of the steep incline up the mountain. It would be too draining for Micah in his current state of ill health and the thought of him passing out and falling mid-flight terrifies me.

I briefly consider flying back on my own and getting help, but I quickly dismiss that option. I can't leave Micah unprotected. The deer seem to be gone, but they could reappear just as quickly. Given our experience with them, I'm far warier of our surroundings now.

Micah's breathing is ragged. "It's okay," he says, as if he hears my worried thoughts. "I'll be okay right here."

I'm not so certain. I worry at my lip as I lean over him, carefully lifting and then tearing a little of his ripped shirt to see his wound better. The burn on his chest is a thin welt, not as bad as I feared, although it must sting horribly.

The burn on his hand is more worrying. I carefully bring his arm up to rest it across his stomach.

I can't stop my gasp. "These burns—"

"Will heal," he says, his eyes closed, and his speech stilted. "They hurt like hell, but… I've always healed fast. I don't think that's changed."

I can only pray he's right, although the burns are quickly becoming the least of my worries.

When I pass my hand across his heart, his skin is cold to touch and the gray tinge has worsened, clouding his body all the way down his left arm and up the side of his neck. It's like a dark shadow of the dust he was exposed to.

Just as I move to replace his shirt where it was, he gives a sigh and takes hold of my hand, stopping me.

"The warmth helps my heart," he says.

I glance upward at the bright sky. "Do you mean the sun?"

Now that we've exited the cool forest, late-afternoon sunbeams are shining down around us and the heat is certainly calming to my nerves.

"The warmth, yes," he mumbles.

At his response, I quickly but gently pull the opening of his shirt a little wider to expose more of his skin to the light. I rest my hand beneath it. "There."

He fully relaxes, his eyes closing.

I consider his breathing and it's a little steadier, which gives me the peace of mind I need to let go of some of my anxiety.

Not all of it, though. I need to do more for him, but I'm struck by my inability to help, my reliance on his healing power, and the hope that the sun will warm him enough that the chill will leave his heart.

For a second, I consider if the stag was trying to help him, since its antlers had a burning effect, but I dismiss that possibility too. That burn was icy. As cold as death. Not a warm burn that might have aided him.

No, the stag was trying to kill him.

And yet it didn't try to hurt me.

With a sigh of frustration, I lie down beside Micah, my hand continuing to rest beneath his heart. I'm prepared if I need to jump up quickly, but for now, my body heat can only help him.

Slowly, very slowly, his breathing evens out and when I brush my hand upward, I find his skin warm again.

My relief is so huge that tears burn behind my eyes.

I finally exhale my tension.

Well, some of it.

Not all, because I need to face the anxiety that I've been pushing away.

On our first night in the veil, the aftereffects of the ash seemed temporary. It took effort to help Micah, but the symptoms disappeared. For the last five days, he seemed fine. Until suddenly, just now, he wasn't.

But I have to acknowledge that it wasn't as sudden as it felt. I find myself recalling each time he rubbed his shoulder and every time he pushed food away. And I know it wasn't my cooking because Beatrix and Isaac devoured every bite.

I wanted to believe that Micah was completely healed—that I could focus entirely on training my body and developing my strength—but he isn't.

Lifting myself upward a little to see his face, I find him peacefully asleep. Just now with the forest animals, he accepted my help and didn't push back. He didn't pretend he was okay when he wasn't.

I'm grateful for that.

But it doesn't cancel out the fact that I don't know what's going on with him or really how to help him.

And at the back of my mind is a seed of fear that is threatening to strip away my fragile sense of control. Just as I fear exposing the heart of my power, I also fear losing what I've only just found and can't bear to be without.

Him.

I grit my teeth.

Fuck my fears.

I'm not a powerless dragon shifter anymore.

Micah and I will survive this. Together.

CHAPTER TWENTY-THREE

The sun has set by the time Micah stirs.

I've remained at his side for the last two hours, sometimes standing and stretching my legs, other times sitting beside him while the forest became hushed with the approaching night.

At one point, the dragonflies swarmed over from the lake, circled around Micah, and then dove back into the water.

Since then, they've visited at intervals and right now, several of them are humming around my shoulders. Now that the moon is rising, their wings are even more luminescent, catching the light magic that fills the moonbeams.

At another point—a far more stressful point—the deer with the blaze on her forehead appeared at the edge of the trees. She lifted her head quietly, looking me over with soft, brown eyes while her nostrils flared. Then she turned and vanished and I could breathe again.

After that, there was no sign of any deer at all.

Now, Micah's eyes open slowly.

Then quickly.

He sits up in a rush, his shirt gaping open where it's ripped. "What happened?" He twists to me. "Are you okay?"

"I'm fine." I lean forward to reassure him, gesturing to his chest and hand. "Your wounds healed quickly."

His forehead creases as he looks where I'm pointing. "What wounds?"

I purse my lips at his question. His skin has healed, so it's not like he can see the welt on his chest or the burn on his hand anymore, but it sounds like he doesn't remember being wounded at all. "From the stag."

"The stag…?" He tugs at the torn material, the crease in his forehead deepening. "I remember the doe in the clearing. Then the other horses—uh, deer—surrounding us and then…" He shakes his head. "It's a blank after that."

"Okay," I say, keeping my voice calm as I summarize events. "Let me fill in the gaps. Your heart started to hurt. The stag attacked you. I got you out of there. You've been asleep since."

He rubs his forehead. "Fuck, I don't remember any of that."

I'm not hugely surprised now that I reflect on how dazed he was at the time, but I'm adding this new symptom to the list of things about which future Sophia is going to worry her heart out—and then find answers to.

Now, Micah's focus shifts to the dragonflies, following their quick movements as they dart over to him and back to me.

He sounds wary as he asks, "What are those?"

"Dragonflies. I think." I shrug. "They live in the lake like fish, but they can fly around in the air. It seems like they only need to return to the water when their bodies dry out."

As I speak, the insects do just that, zipping back to the water and diving into it. Within seconds, another group of dragonflies rises and soars across to me. I'm probably imagining it, but it feels like they're taking turns keeping me company.

I take the opportunity before they reach us to lean a little closer to Micah, placing my hand firmly on his thigh—the one farthest from me.

"Be calm," I say, "but you have a friend on your other side."

Micah's focus darts to my hand, then to the grassy patch next to his leg.

A fluffy, little creature about the size of a corgi sits in the grass beside him, its face upturned and its eyes bright. With floppy ears, the cutest button tail, and rich-brown fur furrier than any I've ever seen, it looks like a rabbit. Except that it has a nose like a piglet's.

Micah freezes as the creature snuffles at the air.

Without moving an inch, he whispers, "What. The Fuck. Is that?"

"Rabbit, maybe?" I give an apologetic grimace. "I'm not sure. But it's harmless."

Micah's hands fly into the air when the little creature bounds onto his lap, turns around and around, and then settles down against his stomach, its ears flopping over its face.

I clear my throat. "They're *all* harmless."

"All?"

Two more rabbit creatures venture out from behind my back, eyeing Micah before they snuggle in on either side of me. They each rest a chin on one of my thighs.

"Nope," he says, shaking his head at the creature in his lap. "No making friends with the wildlife."

When he reaches down to pluck it off his lap, he pauses, his fingers barely brushing its body. "Their fur is like silk."

"Could be why they became extinct," I say, suddenly grim.

"Yeah." He sighs and leaves the creature where it is.

He's quiet for a long moment, watching the dragonflies hum around us. Then his jaw clenches, and he exhales heavily. "I need to know what's going on with me."

"Me too." I've had hours to think about it. "Lana and Callan said they'd find out what they could about Tyler's power, but I don't think we can wait for them to bring us answers. Isaac mentioned there's a library here in the veil, and I imagine it has books about all sorts of magic. Tomorrow, I'd like to spend the morning there. We can train in the afternoon. Also…" Now my speech becomes more hesitant. "Isaac may be able to help you. His soul light can banish darkness."

"It can also burn, immobilize, or kill his targets," Micah says pointedly.

I know only too well the danger of a Sentinel's light. When Sentinels attacked little Emika, I was knocked unconscious by their soul light. I woke up to find Lana protecting me from Grudge dragons who had found me unconscious.

One of those Grudge dragons was Micah and, while I would have foregone being knocked out, I wouldn't change any other aspect of my first encounter with him.

"A Sentinel's soul light is a double-edged sword," Micah continues. "It can heal or harm. We're new allies and there's a lot of bad history there. I'm not sure I'm willing to submit to that yet."

I stiffen because Isaac already used his soul light when Micah and Beatrix emerged from the river. He did it at Lana's instruction and I didn't think anything of it except to hope that it would help. I trusted both Isaac and Lana without question. But seeing the intense wariness in Micah's expression now, I'm worried about how he'll feel about what was done.

It does, though, explain why he didn't rest down on the feathery bed in the infirmary. His distrust of angels runs even deeper than mine.

Before I can work out how to tell him what happened on the riverbank, Micah continues. "But you're right. Isaac could help. Even if he doesn't use his soul light, he might have useful knowledge, particularly now that I'm experiencing more identifiable symptoms. I'll speak with him about it. Tomorrow morning. Then I'll come to the library with you."

I let out the breath I was holding. "Okay, then. It's a plan."

A plan woven together with threads of hope and nothing much more, but it helps.

By this point, the moon has risen and the appearance of our

surroundings is changing. Every blade of grass seems to have a bright tip so that we're suddenly sitting in a sea of glowing dots.

"I wish we could stay here, but we need to get back," I say softly.

"Do we?" he asks, his brown eyes suddenly bright in the twilight. "Do we really need to go back?"

Well, clearly, he doesn't remember the stag trying to kill him or he might not be so keen to stay here. All night. In the dark.

"Isaac mentioned a cabin in this forest." Micah glances back toward the mountains. "I think I saw it on the way, halfway between the lake and the door at the top of the mountain. It could be a good stopover point."

I consider Micah carefully. I'd love to believe that his motivations are founded in the chance to be naked in front of a cabin fire, but there's tension in his voice.

Quietly, I ask, "Are you trying to tell me you're not sure if you have the strength to fly all the way back to the door?"

He clears his throat. "I feel fine. Fucking great."

My gaze becomes a stern glare. It's one thing to fly over the forest but an entirely different challenge to ascend at the sharp angle that's required to reach the height of the mountain's peak. It will be arduous, to say the least.

"Okay, I don't feel fine," he says in a rush, his shoulders hunching. "I feel tired."

He shakes his head. "I can't describe it. It's like my body's fighting an internal battle and I have no say in it. No control over it. It's fucking frustrating."

I reach for him, my hand slipping over his heart. "So much more frustrating for an alpha, who is supposed to never tire. Never falter. Always remain in control. But it's just you and me here. There is no weakness. There's only strength."

The anger in his expression fades, his jaw unclenching, his gaze softening. "Your hand is warm."

I meet his eyes with a soft smile. "Will your strength take you as far as the cabin?"

"It will."

"Then that's where we'll stay the night."

Without further fuss, I slip my hand away from Micah and reach down to the rabbit on my right. "Okay, little one, off you go."

I give it a little scratch behind its ear and it leans into me before it hops away. When I nudge the other one in the same direction, it bounds across the grass to join its friend before they both stop and turn expectantly, their ears flopping down beside their faces.

"You too," Micah says, lifting the sleeping rabbit off his lap. It wiggles its nose, blinks its eyes, and then leaps across the grass to join its pack.

Within seconds, their paths along the lake's edge appear as three lines of retreating splashes within the sea of light.

As if on cue, the dragonflies lift away from me and dive back into the water, and then it's just Micah and me again.

We take to the air, our wings beating smoothly as we rise above the trees.

The mountain is a looming presence in the far distance. When I scan the forest off to the left, I make out a brighter patch, where there's a clearing within which is the shape of a cabin.

Keeping Micah within my sights at all times, I veer in that direction. He stays close beside me until we land in front of the cabin's porch and then he takes the lead, scanning the perimeter before heading up the short steps.

I hang back, still studying the forest.

Normally, I would assume that Micah would hear any approaching threats—just as he'd heard the deer before I did. But I can't be sure now if his senses will be operating at full strength.

Closing my eyes and listening carefully, I take in the quiet noises that indicate movement through the undergrowth and within the trees, but it's all quiet rustling, nothing sharp or sudden.

A bird calls softly, then another, and it sounds like some sort of owl—two of them—calling to each other. The hooting fades. I wait another moment for the hush to resume and then I turn away from the forest, as satisfied as I can be that our surroundings are safe for now.

Ahead of me, Micah is pushing open the door. It creaks a little and then catches on its hinges, only opening partway.

He makes an unhappy noise in the back of his throat and when I draw level with him and peer through the narrow opening, I can see why.

There's a skylight in the ceiling and the moonbeams reveal a whole lot of dust and some very old furniture. Two chairs, one broken. A table with cracks in the surface. A tattered rug in front of a blackened fireplace.

It looks like there's some sort of washroom through a door on the left but I don't want to know what could be festering within the cracked, white sink I can see sitting against the far wall.

"Never mind," I whisper cheerfully. "It won't take me long to make it spick and span."

My stomach chooses that moment to growl. Loudly.

Micah gives me a rueful glance. "Maybe we should try flying all the way back after all."

"No." I catch hold of his arm. He can't hide the dark rings beneath his eyes, which contradict the hours he spent sleeping this afternoon. "Let's rest here for a short while at least. Then we can consider flying back. Isaac and Beatrix know where we are—if they're worried, they can come find us—and my hunger can wait. You're my priority. At the very least, if you get some more rest, you'll be stronger for the remainder of the flight."

I reach forward and shove at the edge of the door before angling myself through the gap, trying to ignore the way the dust flies up around me.

Glancing back, I check that Micah's following me.

He steps inside and that's when the light around us changes so suddenly that I swing back to the cabin's interior.

I stop still, barely able to breathe.

The whole place has transformed.

CHAPTER TWENTY-FOUR

The cabin's floor is now made of gleaming wood and the walls are painted navy like the darkest night sky but with golden filigree weaving across them that makes them appear bright.

The fireplace is filled with a warm fire that lights up the iron work around its edges along with the mahogany mantelpiece above it. The table is laden with food and jugs and glittering tableware, all sitting on top of a golden tablecloth. Ornate table legs carved with the shape of vines peek out from beneath the golden overlay.

Every chair around the table has a plush, velvet seat, also golden in color. And the far room—what was a dirty washroom—is now a vast bedroom containing a bed so large, I can only see one side of it.

My voice wobbles. "What kind of sorcery is this?"

Micah takes a quick step into the room, his footfalls quiet on the lush rug that now rests on the floor inside the door. He turns from one side of the room to the other, his head held high and slightly tilted, as if he's listening and inhaling and sensing with every part of his body.

His declaration comes out in a hushed murmur. "This is old magic."

I stare at him. "Are you sure?"

Isaac mentioned that this cabin belonged to an ancient being, but I never imagined it could be a place of old magic.

"I feel it." Micah gives me a smile that lights up his eyes and banishes the shadows that were gathering beneath them. "I feel it in my blood."

He said that his mother may have had old magic running through her veins and now I have no doubt about it. His entire demeanor has instantly changed, as if his body is reacting to something in our environment—or, maybe, our environment is reacting to his presence. Possibly both.

The dark circles under his eyes are gone. So is the hunch that was dragging down his shoulders.

He inhales a deep breath, so deep that his chest expands beyond its already broad width. "I feel stronger here."

Prowling around the room, he brushes his hand across the tops of the chairs, along the mantelpiece, and finally over the windowsill.

A glance through the window tells me that the light from within the cabin isn't spilling through onto the porch.

The back of my neck tingles in response to the energy in the room.

Micah surprises me when he pulls out a chair. "Hungry?"

I eye the food. It looks like roast chicken and vegetables—carrots, potatoes, corn cobs, and peas—all neatly set out in dishes near a gravy boat. It's difficult to withstand the mouth-watering scents rising from it, but I make myself pause.

"Is it safe?" I ask. "What if it's enchanted?"

"That's a fair concern," he replies, his expression sobering a little as he reaches for the nearest bowl containing bright-green peas. He smells it first, then picks one carefully out, dabbing it to his tongue.

I'm on edge until he says, "I don't sense anything magical about it."

"Except for the fact that it appeared when we stepped inside," I say, rounding the table to join him.

The fireplace is now at my back and the warmth is calming, the burning wood making a soft, crackling sound.

I sniff at the carrots before I poke one of them and then dab my finger to my tongue.

Micah waits for my assessment.

"Glazed in butter," I say.

"If you're worried, we can skip the food and get some rest in front of the fireplace."

I notice he doesn't suggest the bedroom and it's probably for the best. That bed looks entirely too accommodating of activities that don't involve sleeping.

My stomach immediately protests at the idea of forgoing food. "Let's eat."

We sit down to the sumptuous meal and, when nothing awful happens after we start eating, I finally relax. The food is delicious and the white wine is sweet. I limit myself to a single glass because I want to stay sharp.

When we step away from the table, I notice once again that, although Micah filled his plate, he didn't eat much of it. Maybe only a few pieces of chicken and some peas.

His lack of appetite brings back my worries.

I take his hand and urge him toward the couch in front of the fireplace, which sits low to the ground. It's covered in thick cushions and is both wide and long enough for me to lie beside Micah.

Once we're settled, he strokes my hair, his eyelids drooping.

"When this is all over, I want to try connecting with my mother's family," he says, suddenly but quietly.

I lift my head to find him relaxed, but in his eyes is a hint of determination.

"I've been thinking about it for years," he says. "I have no real connection with the wolf side of my nature, other than to benefit from its senses. I can't shift into the shape of a wolf. Hell, until the dragon's light was freed, I couldn't control my ability to take on dragon traits. But the wolf is a part of me I can't keep pushing away."

"Reaching out to her family could definitely help with that." I worry at my lip. "But you said her brother—your uncle—was prone to violence. Will he welcome you?"

If wolf shifters are anything like dragon shifters, then rival alphas are rarely welcome.

Micah acknowledges my concern with a nod. "There are no guarantees. I heard that his son is alpha now. But, yes, it's a real possibility that there could be tension. Or that I won't like what I find." He gives me a smile. "But I need to know."

"Okay," I whisper. "When this is over, I'll come with you."

It sounds like a simple thing, but it's far more complicated.

He seems to know it. "I wouldn't expect you to come with me. Not when it could be dangerous."

I peer up at him. "Are you suggesting you'd go on your own?"

"I could."

"Nope." I lower my head to his chest again. Then I second-guess his wishes. "As long as you want me to come with you?"

"I would like that."

We're quiet after that and within minutes, his breathing deepens.

I thought I would drift off too, but I can't sleep.

My mind is churning too much.

After a while, I slip carefully off the couch, stretching out my cramped limbs before I bask in front of the fire.

The crackle and pop of the wood is calming. Until another sound breaks across it.

My ears prick at the soft, crunching noise coming from outside the cabin.

Footfalls?

Suddenly wary, I venture to the window, crouching low in case I'm visible from the outside.

When I poke my head up, all I see is the porch and the quiet forest. As before, the cabin's lights don't spill beyond the glass.

Nothing looks different.

The crunching footfalls sound again. This time, I identify them as coming from the space immediately in front of the cabin steps.

But there's nothing there.

I glance back at Micah. I don't want to wake him just because I *think* I hear something. Especially since it hasn't disturbed him.

Remaining crouched, I venture to the door, turn the handle, and then peer through the gap outside.

Once again, the light doesn't spill, and the forest looks just like it did before.

Fuck, now I feel silly.

What's more, the crunching sound stopped as soon as I opened the door. Instead, the noises of the forest filter through. The swishing of leaves and branches, the rustling of tiny creatures in the far undergrowth. That's what I must have heard. The sound must have been distorted through the cabin's walls and windows.

Still, my training is kicking in. We assessed the perimeter when we flew in, but it can't hurt to double-check it now to make sure we're safe.

I don't want to leave Micah on his own for long, but it will only take me a minute to check our immediate surroundings.

Taking a deep breath, I step outside, close the door behind me, and cross the porch, swiftly descending the steps, intending to head around to my left.

The moment my foot leaves the final step, my stomach lurches, as if I'm falling from a great height.

I land heavily on the ground right in front of me, my knees buckling under the unexpected sensation of plummeting—

despite the porch step remaining right behind me and the distance being mere inches above the ground.

What the fuck?

I look up to discover that, once again, my environment has changed in a heartbeat.

CHAPTER TWENTY-FIVE

A neat garden stretches out in front of me.

It's filled with sculpted flower bushes no higher than my waist, all set out in patterns. Between them is a myriad of smooth, white pathways. Above me, the sky twinkles with a million stars, the light crisper than any I've ever seen.

Only the cabin has remained the same. It's a brightly lit shape behind me—and *now*, its lights are spilling through the windows.

Everything else has changed.

Directly in front of me, a girl with pure, white hair bends to a silver flower growing on a blood-red bush. She's wearing a pearly dress that moves around her as if she's standing in a gentle breeze. Except that I can't feel it. For me, the air is completely still.

Glimmering light twinkles around her silhouette and makes her appear as if she were moving very quickly. Like a hummingbird, whose wings beat so fast, they look as if they're standing still.

I've frozen with surprise, on edge and ready to fight if I have to, but then she speaks.

"You are not dead." Her voice hums like the sound of a fingertip running around the top of a wineglass. "And yet here you are. In my garden."

"What is this place?" I ask. "Who are you?"

She looks up at me. Her eyes are a startling white with only the barest hint of irises. Possibly green, but I can't be sure.

"I thought you might have guessed," she replies, "since you've met one of us before."

Met one of them?

When my forehead creases, she shrugs and turns back to the flower bush, running her hand from one silver rose to the next. "I imagine the encounter with my darker counterpart was very unpleasant and worthy of being forgotten quickly."

Her darker counterpart?

My thoughts click together.

She must be one of the keepers of magic.

"You're the keeper of light magic," I say, taking a guess, my eyes widening at the possibility.

I take another look around. *Did I somehow fall into another oblivion?*

"Oh, no, child, I am not a creature of light magic." Giving a little chuckle, she addresses me as if *I'm* the child, not her. "Although I understand why you might think that to look at me."

White light flickers around her fingertips as she plucks a flower from the bush. Crimson sap drips from the stem as she steps slowly toward me. "No, dearest. I am the keeper of *old* magic."

Right.

I glance back at the cabin, wondering if the old magic within it has somehow created a conduit to this place.

The keeper stops three paces away from me while crimson sap drips from her fingertips. "I think you know why the four keepers of magic exist?"

"To tether the magic that lingers when a supernatural dies," I say, recalling what I gleaned from the keeper of dark magic.

She nods. "All magic must return to its rightful keeper. Otherwise, it will contaminate the earth, and that's when the monsters will rise."

I'm alarmed. "Monsters?"

"Creatures of pure destruction and chaos." Her silhouette glimmers as she darts closer to me and suddenly, she's standing a mere pace away. "But they are not my concern right now." She pauses. "You are here and yet you are not dead. It's perplexing to me how you keep finding the cracks into our realms, Sophia Dragon."

My forehead creases. "I didn't *find* anything. The keeper of dark magic said that the magic I was carrying called out to him."

Just as the magic in this garden must have called me here from the cabin.

Her eyebrows rise. "Yes, that dark ash would have called to him. But I take it you interpreted that to mean *he* brought you into his realm?"

"Well... yes."

She gives a snort. "We do not have power over the living."

I remember the way the keeper of dark magic roared at me to give him the ash, emphasizing repeatedly that he couldn't take it by force while I was alive.

"Otherwise," the old magic keeper continues, her focus shifting to a point past me, "I could simply reach out and call your mate to me. There are strains of old magic in his blood that I would gladly tether."

She gives me a smile that suddenly chills me.

"It's been a long time since that cabin has glowed with magic," she muses. "The angels think they're protecting it, but they're keeping the cabin from the beings to whom it belongs. One of which is your mate."

Scowling at her, I step into her line of sight—turning myself into a visual barrier between her and Micah.

I don't like the way she's talking about him, I distrust her cold smile, and I'm anxious about her assertion that I somehow knowingly *chose* to enter her space. Lana mentioned throwing herself into oblivion to escape the veil, so it must be possible to actively leap into it the same way I plunged into the river.

"Well, then," I say, "I must have *fallen* into this realm, just like my friend fell into the dark magic keeper's realm when she—"

"Oh, no, that was quite different." The keeper shakes her head, her next words proving she knows exactly what I'm talking about. "Asper Ashen-Varr leaped into the dark keeper's realm through an open door that was already well-known to the angels—who, by the way, were complicit in that door's creation and did nothing to stop it from forming."

Her voice becomes a snarl as she speaks of the angels, but her expression becomes more neutral as she continues. "You, on the other hand, have discovered new cracks and slipped through them like an unstoppable ray of light."

The bloody sap from the silver flower's stem continues to drip onto the ground and I'm shaken when I follow its path down to what I thought was grass.

In the moonlight, the earth gleams, but now that I peer closer, I realize I'm standing, not on soil, but on a substance that is white and powdery.

"White ash," the keeper of old magic says. "It's what happens when an environment burns with uncontrolled magic for so long that dark ash turns white." The corners of her mouth tug down. "It begins to resemble powdered bones. It's the consequence of magic that is left unclaimed and untethered. I keep my garden this way to remind me of what will happen if I ever fail in my task." Her voice becomes hard. "We, the keepers, have sacrificed everything to ensure that the ground never turns to white ash again."

"It happened before?" I ask, my eyes wide.

"Many eons ago. In the time when monsters rose from the very soil beneath our feet."

With a sudden movement and an equally abrupt change of subject, she holds out the silver flower to me. "Will you take this?"

It feels like a loaded question and I hesitate, studying her and trying to discern her motives.

Her expression is inscrutable, but her white eyes narrow when I don't move.

She prompts me with, "Consider it a gift."

Warily, I lift my hand, my fingertips brushing the edge of the delicate flower.

As soon as I make contact, heat flares in my palm and a flash of light travels from the tips of my fingers across the petals.

The keeper's eyes brighten and a gasp passes her lips. "Oh! So *that* is how you crept in here."

I stare at her, confused by her declaration.

"What are you saying?" I demand to know.

Frustratingly, she takes a quick step back from me, the flower still clasped between her fingertips, her form flickering and gleaming. "But of course, there can be no death without… *life*."

Her smile fades. "Go now, Sophia Dragon, before I give in to the temptation to claim your magic. Even though I know it would be futile—and the keeper of light magic may rage in her realm—I'm not immune to trying."

I take a hasty step backward. My heel bumps against the cabin's bottom step. The whole time we were talking, I felt like I was much farther inside the garden but I barely moved.

I spin to the steps and the cabin.

A sudden bright gleam of light at the corner of my eye tells me the keeper of old magic didn't keep her distance when I turned my back to her.

Her voice sounds at my ear and sends a shiver down my spine.

"I won't have to wait long for your mate's power," she whispers. "It will be mine very soon."

A shock of anger burns through me.

I twist back to her. "What do you mean, *soon?*"

But my foot has already ascended onto the first step and her garden is gone.

I'm left staring at the quiet forest.

CHAPTER TWENTY-SIX

The keepers can only tether magic from a supernatural who has died. If the keeper of old magic is claiming she'll have Micah's magic soon…

I race up the porch steps as fast as I can.

Now that the keeper's garden is gone, I can no longer see through the cabin's windows. Its exterior looks as old and rundown as it did when Micah and I first arrived.

I can't get inside fast enough, fearful that the interior will have also changed in my absence.

I'm relieved to see that it's just as beautiful as it was before.

Racing across the opulent room and around the lounge, I drop to my knees beside Micah, where he has remained lying on the couch.

My heart is in my throat as I press my hand to his chest.

I need to know that he's breathing. I need to feel the beat of his heart beneath my palm.

His chest rises and falls steadily. His breathing is even but changes at my touch. "Sophia?" His voice is groggy, his eyes cracking open a little. "Is everything okay?"

Damn. I woke him up.

But my relief that he's alive is so intense that I can't bring myself to feel bad about disturbing his rest.

I clamber on top of him, straddling him before I lie down and curl up against his chest, needing to hold on to him as hard as I can.

"Everything's okay," I whisper.

"Hey." His voice is low and soft at my ear as his arms rise around me. "What's wrong?"

"I can't lose you." My throat is constricted. "I *won't* lose you."

I'm trembling and his arms tighten around me, a firm pressure that's anchoring me. He presses a kiss to my forehead, then to my temple, then he reaches my lips and I'm lost to the sensations. Until this man kissed me, I never imagined that there could be so much heat in such a light touch.

"I wish I could promise you that you would never lose me," he says, breaking the contact with my lips to press his cheek to my forehead. "But death is nobody's friend. It claims us all."

One of his hands rises to gently cup the back of my head, the other remaining like a tether across my torso.

"But I can promise you this, Sophia: I will love you for all of my days."

I close my eyes, trying to stem my tears. "I love you, too, Micah."

"Then we'll never be lost," he says.

I raise my head, letting my tears fall. He brushes them gently before kissing the trails they're leaving down my cheeks.

"We'll never be lost," I murmur.

I end up falling asleep beside Micah and when we wake, early morning sunlight pours through the windows.

The table is set with fresh food, but we don't linger. We've been gone from the main staircase for long enough, and Micah's energy has returned. Isaac and Beatrix didn't come looking for us in the night, but I don't want them to start worrying.

The ascent back to the door is challenging, but we approach it at the gentlest angle that we can, alleviating the sharpness of the climb.

Finally, we reach the top of the mountain, both of us sweaty and our chests heaving.

I take a last look at the forest before I proceed to the door.

Micah wanted me to come to this place to connect with my power. I'm not sure if I did that exactly. I don't feel like I have greater control or increased knowledge.

In fact, the opposite could be true. My power has become less quantifiable. I basked in this wilderness, saved a mother and her babies, connected with strange little rabbits and pretty dragonfly fishes, escaped an angry stag, and somehow stumbled into the realm belonging to the keeper of old magic.

If I've gained any knowledge about myself, it's that my power is wilder than I imagined it could be. It feels untamed. Uncontrollable, even.

But I'm no wiser as to its true purpose.

When we push open the red door and step out into the bright stairway, I'm surprised to find Beatrix sitting hunched on a step three rungs up, her head in her hands. Isaac paces along the step above her, his footfalls quiet but agitated.

I'm immediately on the alert—more so when their heads shoot up as soon as we appear.

Beatrix jumps to her feet, eyes bright with tears, her voice harsh. "Where have you been?"

She looks so upset that my imagination goes wild. "What's happened? Is someone hurt?"

"I was worried sick! *That's* what's happened!" Beatrix's brow is deeply furrowed, her glare red-hot. "We looked everywhere for you. We flew over the forest. We even searched the cabin."

Her finger jabs in the direction of the door we came through.

"We thought maybe you'd come out and gone somewhere else. We searched everywhere! Even the prisons. We couldn't find you." Her voice rises with every word until she's shouting. "I thought something terrible had happened."

"But we were right there…" I glance up at Micah.

"The cabin," he murmurs. "The old magic."

Fuck. I should have realized. The light didn't spill out. Nothing was visible from the outside. And only Micah could trigger its true nature. Neither Beatrix nor Isaac would have been able to see inside it.

Concerned only with easing Beatrix's mind, I hurry up the next step toward her, even though her scowl—and apparently her rage—only increases the closer I get to her.

"I'm okay. Really. I was safe." *Mostly.* "Micah was with me. And even if he hadn't been, I can handle myself."

"*Handle* yourself?" she snaps. "Losing track of you was like losing a kitten inside the house and worrying if it got out onto the street."

"I'm not a kitten—"

"But you're as fucking helpless as one!" she snarls.

I pull up sharply as her speech threatens to pierce the armor I've been slowly accumulating around my sense of self-worth.

"Helpless?" I ask, my voice sharpening.

She takes a step down so that now she's standing only one rung up from me and her height means she remains towering over me.

"Why do you think Lana put you in here?" she snaps. "You think it was to train you and build up your strength? Get real, Sophia. She wanted you out of the way so she can get on with the real fight. Out there. Where I should be. Not in here babysitting you."

Micah and Isaac have stayed mostly quiet until this point, but now they both move toward us.

Micah gives a low growl that sounds like a wolf's warning. "Beatrix. That's out of line."

At the same time, Isaac's hand lands on her shoulder. "Don't take your fears out on your friend—"

In the next second, Isaac jolts backward, retracting his hand so suddenly that his wings thump outward. He nearly misses the next step up. He didn't tell us what would happen if we skipped a step, but his face is ashen when he drops to a crouch.

He's nursing his hand against his chest as if touching Beatrix had hurt him.

She whirls from Isaac back to us and I find myself drawn to the color of her neck and her cheek on the left side of her face. Her skin is gray, as though shadows have gathered on that side of her.

Oh... fuck.

Micah's focus on Beatrix appears as equally intense as mine. "Beatrix," he says, "is your heart cold?"

Her lips twist as if she's going to rebuke him, but then her forehead crinkles and she takes a shaky breath. She presses her hand to her chest. "I don't feel well…"

Her knees buckle and she falls forward into my arms.

Micah is suddenly at my back, supporting me so I don't tip down the steps under Beatrix's weight and momentum, but it's Isaac who scoops her out of my arms.

He lifts her close to his chest, where her head rests against his shoulder, and then he rushes up the stairs with her.

With a brief, worried glance at Micah, I follow Isaac to the infirmary, where he lays Beatrix down onto one of the feathery beds.

Both of her cheeks are gray now, and so is the skin down her entire left arm where it's visible around her short sleeve.

"We need to get her warm," I say urgently, tapping into the only solution I know. "Isaac, can you heat these beds somehow?"

"I can do better than that." Isaac hurries to the cupboards at the side of the room. He plants his palm against the front of one of them and waits a few seconds until the door clicks open on its own.

Heat rushes from the cupboard across the air and Isaac turns back a moment later, holding multiple white blankets. The sweat beading on his brow tells me they must be incredibly warm.

Carefully, he lays the first one across Beatrix's unconscious form and then the second blanket on top of that.

Meanwhile, Micah pulls up a chair for me and I slip my forearm under the warm material to hold Beatrix's hand. She's as cold as Micah was when he collapsed yesterday.

"Damn," I whisper. "It's happening to Beatrix too."

Isaac's voice is sharp, his worry palpable as he hurries to cover Beatrix from her neck to her feet. "Micah, how did you know her heart was cold?"

Micah exhales heavily. "Because I've been experiencing the same thing."

Isaac glances at me. "And you, Sophia?"

I shake my head. "My heart is fine."

Isaac finishes positioning the blankets and then he studies the feathers at the edge of the bed for a long moment. "The feathers are telling me…" The furrow in his brow deepens. "But this shouldn't be possible."

"What is it, Isaac?"

He gestures at the way the feathers around Beatrix's head are alternating between pure white—the color they were before he laid Beatrix down—and dark gray.

"White indicates good health," he says, his shoulders stiff. "Gray indicates death."

CHAPTER TWENTY-SEVEN

I can hardly breathe, my voice choking up. "How can Beatrix be near death one moment and completely healthy the next?"

Isaac shakes his head before he runs his hand over his eyes. "I don't know."

Damn. I was hoping Isaac might have answers for us—some knowledge that might help—but it's clear he doesn't.

I consider Beatrix... proud, cunning, quick-witted Beatrix... who now lies helpless beneath heated blankets.

My hand moves from her hand to her chest.

I press my palm over her heart, sensing the flow of blood through her body and the stilted beats of her heart.

The slowing of beats happens in time with the feathers turning gray.

My declaration is quiet, but I feel it in my bones, the same way I can sense the chill of death in the air. "She's walking a path between life and death."

"Then I will keep her on the side of life!" Isaac snaps, a sudden, vehement declaration. "I will not lose her." His soul light begins to glow around his hands. "You said she needed warmth. What else can I do to help her? Tell me what to do next."

The sudden helplessness in his eyes hurts my heart. "Warmth helps, and your soul light might help too, but…"

"But?" Isaac waits for me to continue and I wish I had more to tell him.

"It's a temporary fix," I say. "Not a cure."

His jaw is tight, but the light around his hands glows more brightly. "Then I'll do what I can."

Lowering his hands, one hovering above Beatrix's face and the other above her chest, he takes a deep breath and the light around his palms grows steadily brighter.

"Sophia, you should move back," Micah warns me. "You shouldn't be exposed to soul light when you don't need to be."

I'm not afraid of Isaac's light. Despite my experiences with Sentinels in the past, I trust him. But Micah has a point. I don't know what repeated unnecessary exposure could do.

Just as I slip my palm away from Beatrix's heart, she gasps.

Her deeply indrawn breath is like a scream as she lurches upward, knocking the blankets off her chest and nearly colliding with Isaac's hand.

"*What the fuck?*" Beatrix shouts before she gasps again.

Her hand flies to her chest, her focus moving rapidly from me to Isaac. "What happened to me?"

Isaac drops into a sitting position on the side of the bed before his arms wrap tightly around her. "You're alive. That's what matters."

"I… um…" Her voice is muffled against his chest, but then a sigh sounds and her body visibly relaxes. "Okay, then."

Relief surges through me and I watch them with a growing smile. My happiness is tinged with the knowledge that, as it is for Micah, Beatrix's revival is unlikely to be permanent.

Isaac slowly pulls away from Beatrix but remains at her side as he turns to us. "We need answers. Tell me everything that's happened with Micah."

We describe Micah's blackouts, lightheadedness, and gray pallor. I add the way Beatrix's heart was faltering just now—similar to how Micah had described his symptoms to me. Micah speaks about the feeling of ice in his chest and how he's experienced lost time.

"But you, Sophia, haven't felt any of these symptoms?" Isaac asks me.

"I was affected by the ash when it was on my body," I say. "But not since it was taken away by the keeper of dark magic." I glance up at Micah. "I thought it was only Micah who remained affected. He was exposed to more ash, and for a longer time, than either Beatrix or me. But now it's clear that Beatrix is unwell too, and I'm..."

I've kept it together until this moment, but my voice shakes.

Somehow, I force myself to continue. "I thought everything would be fine after the keeper took the ash from us."

Isaac appears to chew his words. "There seem to be two possibilities here. Either the keeper did something differently when he took the ash from you, Sophia, although I'm not sure why he would."

"Or?" I ask.

"Or your power is somehow protecting you from the long-term effects." Isaac's expression is increasingly stormy. "Did the keeper say anything to you about the nature of the ash?"

My forehead creases as I recall the interaction. "He said that the ash carries destruction and that it was his burden to tether it."

Isaac is nodding. "That matches with my knowledge of the four keepers. They were created in the oldest times, hundreds of years before the era of the Twilight Queen, when magic was causing chaos."

I nod. "But it was strange because he accused me of wanting to keep the ash. He seemed surprised that I would willingly give it to him. In fact, he asked me why I would relinquish it without a fight."

Isaac eyes me warily. So do Beatrix and Micah.

Micah is the first to speak. "That makes it sound as if retaining the ash, keeping it on your body, would be somehow beneficial."

"The kind of power worth fighting over," Beatrix says.

Isaac's eyes have widened a little, his expression unsettled. "For a creature like the keeper of dark magic to speak about the ash in that way, such a benefit could only relate to dark magic."

"It would have to be some evil, fucked-up power," Micah says.

All this talk of dark ash is triggering the memory of my conversation with the keeper of *old* magic. She'd talked of ash and destruction, too. But I'm not sure what the connection might be.

"I agree." I rub my forehead with my free hand as my thoughts become increasingly worried. "What if I did the wrong thing?" I can't bear to look at Beatrix and Micah now. "What if I should have left the ash on you? What if getting rid of it only made things worse?"

"No." Beatrix speaks quietly. "That ash dragged me down into darkness. If you'd left it on me, I'm sure it would have eaten my soul. I'd be dead already."

Micah grips my shoulder, a comforting hold. "You removed it from yourself too, Sophia," he points out. "You aren't sick."

I groan with frustration. "But that only brings us back to the possibility that there's something about my power that's protecting me. In which case, I was never going to be hurt like you were."

Which Tyler could have known.

A shudder stops me from speaking now.

Tyler threatened to hurt everyone I love, one by one, starting with Micah. He told me he would take everyone away from me until I would have to accept that he was the only one who loved me.

Every threat he made implied that he was *choosing* to let me live so I would witness the destruction of my found family and experience heartache because of it.

But now I wonder if, somehow, he knew that his power couldn't kill me. So if he couldn't harm me physically, then he would hurt the people I love instead.

"Could the *Book of Light Magic* give us answers?" I ask Isaac, but the angel shakes his head.

"The book once contained all the secrets of light magic, and it might have had answers for us, but it was wiped clean. The events recorded in it now go back only as far as the evening of the battle at the Cathedral." A shadow falls across Isaac's expression as he speaks. "Also, I fear it isn't the *Book of Light Magic* that would enlighten us in this situation."

"Dark magic," I whisper, fighting the fear that arises within me whenever Micah speaks of uncaging my power. "Where would we find the *Book of Dark Magic*, assuming there is one?"

Again, Isaac shakes his head. "Its location is unknown. Hidden, just like the *Book of Old Magic*. Of the four books, only the *Book of Elemental Magic* is now being kept out in the open, passed between powerful fae. Apparently, they see it as a symbol of prestige to be in possession of the book. Of course, they aren't going to simply leave it lying around, but they make no secret about which family has it."

I dismiss the idea of seeking that book. "Fae magic won't help us here."

Not against the dark power that's draining the life force from the shifters I love.

"Are there any other books in your library that could help?" Micah asks. "We were planning to go there this morning."

Isaac purses his lips. "It's possible. There could be something in the history books, but…"

"But?" I ask.

Isaac sighs. "For many years, I filled my days by enriching my mind with the knowledge in those books. I don't remember seeing anything in them that explains what's happening here."

Frustration threatens to overwhelm me now.

I hoped Isaac might be able to help. I thought I might find answers in his library, or even in the *Book of Light Magic*. And, while I haven't looked in the library myself, and I don't plan on ruling it out, it sounds like there's little hope there.

We're dealing with dark magic and there are only a few sources of truth available to us in that regard.

"Ash, destruction, and death," I say, my declaration falling into sudden silence. "We don't have the answers, but I know where I can find them."

Even if I don't like it. Not one fucking bit.

Micah considers me warily. "Sophia?"

His hand has remained on my shoulder and now I reach up to cover it with my own. "There's one supernatural I can ask," I say. "The keeper of dark magic himself."

Micah immediately shakes his head. "No."

I meet his worried eyes. "I need to return to the oblivion."

I stand at the top of the veil's stairwell, peering down into the chilling space below.

A haze like a thin mist floats in the air between the step I'm standing on and the floor below. It looks like white stone down there, but the mist in the air tells me that when I leap off this step, I won't reach that stone.

I grip a small, purple vial, which is filled with cold water. There's nothing special about the water or the vial, but water was my means of escape last time, so I'm taking some with me.

"You don't have to do this," Beatrix says.

I turn to her. She hovers on the step down, a blanket pulled over her shoulders.

Isaac stands behind her and I'm quite certain he isn't going to let her out of his sight for a while.

Micah is quiet where he remains another step down,

hanging back. He doesn't have to say anything. I know how he feels about me putting myself in danger.

"I don't remember much of what happened before I blacked out," Beatrix says. "But I think I said some pretty shitty stuff to you. If you're doing this because you think you have to prove—"

"I'm not." I want her to know she isn't responsible for my choices, but more than anything, I want both her and Micah to hear me when I say, "I'm doing this because I won't stop fighting for the people I love."

I meet Micah's eyes across the distance between us.

One corner of his mouth hitches up. "Come back safe."

I return his smile, taking in the warmth it gives me. "I'll see you soon."

Then I step off the ledge.

CHAPTER TWENTY-EIGHT

I don't release my wings, allowing myself to drop without resistance.

My bare feet hit the mist first, the bright veil vanishes, and then I'm plummeting through the dark.

I come to an abrupt halt, suspended in what feels like infinite darkness. A vast and immeasurable space filled with spine-chilling energy.

The hairs on the back of my neck stand up, but this time, I'm not in a state of shock or desperately trying to reach my friends. I have the chance to look around—really look around—tilting my head and taking in my environment from different angles.

I'm surprised to discover that there are variations in the darkness. Striations in the air that could mean it's not as flat and endless as it first appeared.

Releasing my wings but keeping them close to my sides, I study the space below me. It looks like it descends forever, but the longer I stare at it, the more I'm aware of disparities in the light at different points.

It's another staircase.

Dark-as-night stairs, but they appear solid and one of the steps is only an inch below my feet.

Pointing my right toe, I brush the solid surface and the contact draws me down onto it.

It's freezing, but I can't regret my bare feet. I need every tactile sense to survive in this place.

Now that I'm standing on solid ground, the gleaming surface reveals itself even further. It's inky dark and reflective, which gives the impression of nothingness, even though it is most definitely *something*.

Carefully, and slowly, I take a step down.

This time, I can move without a fight.

I don't know for sure, but making direct contact with the surface below me seems to have opened up my ability to move around. I resolve not to lift off the ground if I can help it, since it was when I was suspended that I seemed to get stuck midair.

Taking the stairs downward, I arrive in another vast space. I can only see twenty paces around me. Everything beyond that is concealed in gloom.

I stop a few paces from the staircase, not wanting to go too far away from it, and then I raise my voice. "Dark magic keeper!"

The space around me swallows my voice. There are no echoes. Only nothingness.

"Keeper of dark magic!" I call again. "Show yourself."

My cry is met with silence, and it's unsettling when the seconds become longer.

I wait another minute, preparing to call out again, when a figure moves in the gloom opposite me. I anticipate the swish of the keeper's robes, the chill of his presence, the hiss of his wraith-like voice, and the disconcerting way his crown covers his eyes.

Instead, the footfalls coming nearer to me are steady and firm and accompanied by the soft creak of leather and the gentle clang of metal.

I take a quick step back when a female silhouette emerges from the gloom.

A woman with long, dark hair and bright eyes strides toward me. She's wearing golden armor that fits snugly against her curves while a weapon sits across her back, its blades visible over her right shoulder. It's some sort of double-sided axe, a little like Lana's glaive except that the blades of this weapon sit on either side of the top.

In her right hand, she's holding a swath of material, but I can't make out what it is.

"He's gone," she says, coming to a halt five paces away from me.

Gone?

A shiver of fear runs through me. The keeper of old magic accused me of creeping into their realms. Now, I wonder if I somehow damaged the oblivion, or worse—set the keeper of dark magic free. I remember the way the keeper of dark magic had jolted suddenly at the end of our last conversation and told me he had to go.

The stranger drops the material in her hand and I recognize it. It's the dark magic keeper's cloak. As it falls to the floor, it catches the air, billows a little, and then settles onto the ground with a hiss.

The woman holds her head high in the way of a warrior, appearing completely confident as she gives me a sharp appraisal.

"I sense your guilt," she says. "But this was not your doing."

Before I can ask her who she is, or how the hell she can be so certain this wasn't my fault, I sense movement behind me.

I swing as another woman appears within the darkness.

The newcomer is beautiful, her skin flawless. Flowers cascade from a tiara that sits on top of her head all the way down her long, amber hair. She's wearing a flowing dress, and crimson light glimmers around her as she moves.

Quickly stepping to my right, I keep both women within my sight, along with the staircase, since it's my only certain exit.

"Where is the dark one?" the amber-haired newcomer demands to know. "Why is his realm empty?"

Her question appears directed at the warrior woman. Other than giving me a quick glance, she barely acknowledges my presence.

The warrior has stiffened. "What are *you* doing here?"

"The same thing you are," the amber-haired woman snaps. "Trying to find out why dark magic is no longer being tethered."

They begin circling each other like rivals and the closer they draw to each other, the more the magic glimmering around them sparks like electricity. Crimson and gold light clashes in turns.

"He has abandoned his duty," the warrior snarls.

The redhead's mouth twists. "The boundaries between realms are crumbling. Why wouldn't he choose freedom if he had the chance?"

The warrior's eyes shoot wide and her voice carries a deep accusation. "You wish for a return of chaos?"

"Of course not!" the other woman says. "But…" She falters a little, coming to a stop. "Our solitary existence is not to be envied."

The warrior also stops pacing. "That was the sacrifice we made." She gives a long sigh as she returns the redhead's gaze. "It's been a long time since two of us were in the same place." Her voice is croaky, and her forehead puckers a little as she rubs her jaw. "Damn, my voice is rusty."

"Indeed." The woman in the dress nods her head. "But the last time we were *all* together, the laws of nature were broken."

"Not by us," the warrior replies pointedly.

"Oh, but we were younger then." The redhead gives a rueful smile. "Perhaps a little too proud for our own good. We didn't help matters."

"Proud." The warrior nods. "And fearful of failing in our duty."

"We had good reason to be afraid," the redhead says. "But…

if I could go back to that moment with what I now know, I would choose my actions more wisely."

Now that the friction between the two women has come down a few notches, I clear my throat to catch their attention. It's impossible to know what event they're talking about and it sounds like it happened a long time ago, so I file it away and hope it has nothing to do with me.

What matters to me now is the information they can give me about Tyler and his power.

I've already deduced *what* these women are. I just don't know which is which.

"Okay, ladies," I say. "Which one of you is the keeper of light magic and which is the elemental?"

The redhead turns her bright eyes on me. "I am the keeper of elemental magic," she says, smugly tipping up her chin. "I carry the frost and the sunlight, the wind and the rain. I gather up the voices of animals and the bounty of the harvest. I safeguard the magic in the very air you breathe. I am of the fae and the good witches."

"And you?" I ask the other woman.

The warrior quietly scoffs at the elemental keeper. "Sunlight and frost. Ha." She draws her double-bladed axe from its scabbard across her back. "I am of shifters, angels, and, yes, it may surprise you that I'm also of humans. That is, the ones who have a trickle of magic within them. And as for what I carry, I have *this*. The truest weapon of light magic."

Now, the redhead—the keeper of elemental magic—rolls her eyes. "You mean a symbol of it. An *impression* of it. The actual weapon is lost on Earth somewhere."

"Not lost," the warrior snaps. "Carefully hidden. As it should be. Lest it tear civilization apart."

"If you say so," the elemental keeper replies.

As much as the elemental keeper intrigues me, it's the other keeper who interests me the most. One day, when I breathe my last breath, she is the one who will collect my magic.

"So *you're* the light magic keeper," I whisper.

The warrior steps closer, once again appraising me. "And you are the dragon who creeps through the cracks in our realms and brings life into dark spaces."

"I need your help," I say. "I need to know about the dark magic that's being used against my friends."

The keeper of light magic sighs. "Then you need the keeper of dark magic. We can't help you with that."

Fuck.

"Can't you tell me anything?" Frustration billows within me when they respond with silence. "Well, then, how can I find him?"

The light magic keeper's eyes widen. "How can you find a shadow?" she asks. "He is everywhere but nowhere. And I fear, now that he has somehow managed to step beyond the boundaries of his purpose, his form will have been irrevocably changed."

My forehead creases as I eye her warily. "What are you saying?"

"I'm saying that the keeper of dark magic no longer exists."

I'm startled. Suddenly frozen by what this could mean.

The elemental keeper is nodding at her counterpart, her cheeks pale. "If he were still in existence, we—that is, we keepers—would not have been able to enter his realm."

"But if that's the case, what will happen when creatures of dark magic perish?" I remember the warnings the silver-haired keeper of old magic gave me, the way she talked about chaos and said she kept her garden cloaked in white ash as a reminder of her purpose.

The elemental keeper edges closer to me. "I have felt the darkness that is growing in your world," she says. "I sense the ash that fills the air and chills my soul. The dragon who wields this darkness will only grow stronger now that dark magic is no longer being tethered. With every death of a dark magic creature, his power will only increase. After all, darkness attracts darkness."

I try to work through the mire of fear that threatens to bog me down. I came back to oblivion hoping for answers. I didn't expect to find out that the situation is far worse than I thought.

Grasping at any possible solution, I ask, "Can a new keeper of dark magic be created?"

Both women pause for a moment, their heads tilted as if in thought.

"Not in the way we were created," the elemental keeper says. "That magic is the oldest of old, and it no longer exists."

The keeper of light magic is peering at me. "But maybe—"

She stiffens, her eyes shooting wide and a gasp leaving her lips.

I take a step toward her, daring to reach for her. "What's wrong?"

"I can't stay," she cries as the light around her begins to glow brightly. "A powerful supernatural is near death and I must be ready to tether her light magic."

She spins to the elemental keeper. "Sister, we must not falter. The world may fall to darkness, but even in darkness, there is order. If we, the keepers of light and elements, fail in our duty and, saints forbid, the keeper of old magic should fall, then chaos will truly rule us once and for all."

With that, she races away into the darkness. Her footfalls become faint echoes and my remaining hope for answers fades with them.

"Did I cause this?" I whisper to myself, rubbing my eyes. "Did I split this realm apart when I escaped it?"

"The dark keeper's absence is not your doing," the elemental keeper says, edging toward me as she reinforces what the light magic keeper told me.

"How can you be sure?" I ask, my voice bitter.

A cold smile touches her lips. "Because, my dear, your heart is still beating in your chest."

She steps back into the gloom.

"What do you mean?"

She stops, tips her head, and gives a little shrug. "Whoever gave him what he needed to walk the Earth has made a sacrifice with consequences they may not understand."

Hovering at the edge of the gloom, she continues. "Do not stay here for long, Sophia Dragon. This realm was designed with a purpose it can no longer fulfil. Now that its true master is gone, it will become a vacuum from which you may never escape."

She disappears into the darkness, and then I'm alone.

I have no answers now, only greater worries, and her warning spurs me into action.

Quickly, I ascend the dark staircase, although my footsteps become heavier as I go. Only moments ago, I was incredibly pleased to have discovered this way out. Now it's leading me back to a reality I don't want to face.

The keeper of dark magic is gone.

Dark magic will spill into the world and Tyler will grow stronger.

And I still don't know how to heal my family of the magic that has already taken hold of them.

I emerge into the light of the veil without having to use the little vial of water I took as a precaution.

Micah, Beatrix, and Isaac are waiting for me, each of them lurching forward when they see me.

Beatrix was standing right at the edge of the top step and barely waits for me to be fully standing on it before she tackle-hugs me. "You're safe."

Micah is so close behind her on the same step that the three of us take up most of the space and Isaac hovers at the far edge.

Micah hugs me as soon as Beatrix releases me.

"What happened?" he asks.

Before I can answer, the quick thud of boots and frantic beating of wings reaches me.

Beatrix and Micah both spin to the sound, opening up the space between them so I can see another figure racing up the stairs from its bottom rung.

I gasp. "Callan!"

His golden wings are spread as if he's fighting the instinct to fly toward us. His breathing is so harsh, I can hear him from this distance. Sweat drips down his face. His normally calm demeanor has vanished and in its place is... *fear*.

Lana is in his arms, her feathery, black wings tucked around her body. Her eyes are closed and one arm dangles limply outside the cocoon of her wings.

My heart is suddenly pounding in my ears.

The keeper of light magic said...

"A powerful supernatural is near death."

"No," I whisper.

But my voice is drowned in Callan's cry. "Lana's hurt!"

CHAPTER TWENTY-NINE

*I*saac bursts into action, racing down the steps to reach the infirmary door. "This room! Bring her here."

My feet are moving and I'm aware of Beatrix and Micah on either side of me as we hurry down each step as quickly as we can.

I dart through the open door right behind Callan. Micah and Beatrix are close on my heels.

Callan hurries toward the nearest feathery bed and lays Lana down on it, carefully lowering her head and then rapidly straightening her out. He tucks her dark wings on either side of her.

"What happened?" Isaac asks, rushing to Lana's side. "Did Tyler attack her? Has she come into contact with the ash?"

Callan sinks to a kneeling position beside the bed. He's so tall that the bed rests at his waist height. "We were creating a diversion so that Zahra, Emika, and the other Dread dragons could re-locate safely to Grudge territory. We were keeping our distance from the Scorn, leading them away, but we walked into an ambush. Tyler was there."

My hand flies to my mouth. "No…"

"There was no warning," Callan says. "I didn't sense him ahead of us. Neither did Lana. Then he was upon us." Callan rubs his forehead, his expression stricken, his brown eyes filled with rage as he takes Lana's hand. "He went straight for Lana. Cut her face. I used my fire, but she'd already collapsed. I caught her and when I looked up, Tyler and the Scorn were gone."

"Are the others safe?" Isaac asks. "Zahra and Emika?"

Callan nods. "Felix and Melisma went with them. They sent me a message. The diversion worked."

I've plastered myself against the wall inside the door, keeping out of the way. Micah has stopped next to me while Beatrix edges forward. She halts in the middle of the room, her focus on the feathers that are now rippling around Lana's form.

Their soft surfaces stretch toward Lana, their color changing from white to rose pink and then…

Dark gray.

I clap my hand over my mouth to keep from crying out.

This can't be happening.

Around me, everyone has frozen except Callan, but if he hasn't been in this room before, he won't know what the color of the feathers means.

Without another moment's hesitation, I race to the cupboard where the blankets are heated and slap my hand against it. I can't tell if it's working until the door clicks open a moment later. Warmth rushes out as I pull two blankets from the top of the pile.

My hands are shaking, but Micah is beside me and so are Beatrix and Isaac, each of them helping to pull the blankets over Lana's still body.

In the midst of covering her, I lightly press my hand over her heart.

Ice-cold.

So is her left arm between the edge of her sleeve and her golden armband.

I sink into a crouch beside Callan before Micah quietly brings chairs for us both to sit on, and then he just as quietly steps back, taking up position near the cupboards. His presence is calming to me, although his expression is grim.

"Lana's the strongest of us," I say to Callan. "She can beat this."

A hint of amber flames ripples across Callan's skin, making the air shimmer with heat waves.

He reaches for Lana's face, his palm cupping her cheek.

"Wake up, *fire dragon*," he says, his voice becoming more desperate. "Please, Not-Lana. Wake up."

"Put your hand on her heart," I whisper to him. "Your fire is warm and it will help her."

Callan immediately slips his hand beneath the blanket, leaning forward over Lana, his head bowed and eyes closed.

His pain and grief hit me hard. He and Lana already gave everything, risked everything, to be together. Now, Tyler may have taken it all away.

My eyes burn with tears I can't control. I try to stop them, to switch off my overwhelming sadness, but it's impossible.

Despite my declaration that Lana can survive this, the fear inside my own heart is hurting me.

If the ash claims Lana, who is the strongest of us, then what hope do the rest of us have?

A tidal wave of dread is coming for me.

It rises up within my mind, a gigantic swell that rushes toward me, threatening to swallow me and toss me against the rocks. I feel it like a physical pull radiating from Lana's unconscious form, as if the wave is dragging me toward her.

She described me like an ocean of constrained power. She told me to peel back the layers and I've been trying to do that, but now, I feel like I'm right back where I started.

Drowning and constricted.

Around Lana, the feathers ripple once again through hues of white, rose pink, and then gray.

Callan was holding her hand before he moved to her heart and now her fingertips peek from the edge of the blanket.

I reach for her. Close my hand around hers and then—

The tidal wave stops. Everything calms.

In its place is a tingle of gentle energy that I can't quite identify. I've never felt this way on contact with Lana before. Callan is the calm one, the one who always made me feel like everything would be okay.

Lana used to scare the fuck out of me. And yet...

What *is* this?

Testing the sensation, I lift my hand from hers.

The moment I separate from her, fear washes over me again and my hand plummets toward hers once more, an act of pure instinct.

I gasp at the calm that fills me again. A stronger energy now. With it comes the sound of steadily beating wings, the warmth of a fire, and the strength of sunlight. It's an energy I've never felt before.

It's as if it's... *new*.

My eyes flash open.

Oh.

I must have exclaimed aloud because I find myself the center of attention. Callan has lifted his head and Micah suddenly hovers beside me.

They look at me expectantly, but I can barely speak.

I have to be certain.

Slipping my hand and arm under the blanket, I rest my palm on Lana's lower stomach, sensing the ebb and flow of her blood and her own injured energy thrumming through her.

But with it comes another force, separate to her own. New but strong. And incredibly calm. So strong that I can almost feel the beat of young wings and the heat of first flames against my skin.

"Why now?" I whisper, my heart hurting so badly that fresh tears fall down my cheeks.

"What is it, Sophia?" Callan is like stone beside me, an immensely powerful dragon who has even more to lose now.

"It's life," I whisper. "New life."

CHAPTER THIRTY

Callan's gaze flies back to Lana. "A child?"

My throat is so tight that I can barely speak. "Lana's pregnant."

Opposite me, Beatrix and Isaac lower themselves to the floor and so does Micah, stepping back toward the bed so he can kneel on my other side.

A hush falls over us as we huddle around Lana.

"The first dragon to be born since Emika," Beatrix whispers.

The sudden rage in Callan's voice sends shivers down my spine. "If Lana survives the ash."

There's nothing I can say to take away his pain.

He was the first dragon shifter who put his faith in me and believed in me. He spent almost his entire adult life separated from his clan because of his fire. Until a few days ago, we couldn't stand this close to him, let alone hug him. Now, we're huddled around him, yet there's no comfort that we can give.

All we can do is wait for Lana to wake up.

If she wakes up.

I press my cheek to the back of her hand, leaving hot tears on her skin, before I replace the blanket over her.

It's only then that I realize her glaive is nowhere in sight. "Where is her weapon?"

"I dropped everything at the bottom of the stairs," Callan says. "My gold is there too."

"I can bring them to you," I say. "She needs her weapon's strength."

It's an empty promise. I can't touch their gold. I believe that Callan may be able to carry Lana's glaive, but it's likely to chop my hand off of its own accord if I try to pick it up. Callan's gold won't be any more receptive to my touch.

But I can't stay here any longer, watching Lana cycle between life and death.

To lose Lana is to lose a sister.

I need to think. I need to act. I have to get out of this room and decide what I'm going to do, because I won't allow Tyler to take anything more from me than he already has.

Callan gives me a nod. He doesn't say anything about the weapon, even though he will know I can't bring it to him. In fact, everyone in this room will know it. But he rises to his feet, reaches out, and pulls me into a hug.

"I know you love her too," he says.

Fuck. I bite hard on my lip, but it doesn't stop my sobs.

I try to breathe through them. An impossible task. I can't speak, can't push away the pain, can only hug him back.

When he releases me, I swipe at my cheeks and swallow hard. Focusing on the door, I only hope I can make it there before my grief turns to rage.

"Sophia."

My name is whispered and it freezes me to the spot.

It wasn't Callan, or Beatrix, or Micah who spoke it.

I spin to the bed. "Lana?"

Her eyes slowly open, but only a short distance.

Callan immediately leans over her.

Her hand rises toward him, the blanket slipping off. Her

cheeks are pale and her voice is weak. "Callan… I need to speak with Sophia…"

He takes a long moment, pressing his forehead to hers, heat waves radiating between them, before he replies. "Anything you need, I'll do it."

She meets his eyes and the silent communication, the deep bond between them nearly kills me.

Callan rises up again, but he doesn't have to tell the others. They're already moving, Beatrix first with Isaac close behind her, both of them casting relieved looks back at Lana and wiping their cheeks.

Micah stops beside me. "We'll be on the staircase if you need us."

"Thank you."

When the door closes behind him and Callan, Lana holds out her hand to me.

I take it, slipping into the seat Callan was occupying. There's so much I want to say, so much relief I'm feeling at the fact that she's awake, but also too much dread because I don't have a cure for this darkness.

Her blue eyes are only half-open, but her gaze is piercing in its intensity. "You sensed it, didn't you?"

My forehead creases. "Sensed what?" I ask, since there's been a whole lot of fuckery I've sensed lately: death, life, beauty, rage, and dark magic.

"That I'm pregnant."

My eyes widen a little. "You knew?"

She gives me a crooked smile. "Only since last night. My period is like clockwork, one week on and four weeks off. I've been late for two days, but I wanted to be sure before I told Callan."

I want to tell her everything will be okay, but I can't.

She's already continuing. "It's why I convinced Zahra to relocate to Grudge territory. I needed to make sure that Emika and the other Dread dragons were safe so I could come back here to the safety of the veil and figure out what to do."

"You ended up getting hurt."

She sighs. "The irony hasn't escaped me. By trying to seek shelter here, I brought about the harm I was trying to avoid."

Her eyelids droop and she takes deep breaths.

"Why did you want to speak with me?" I ask quietly.

She slowly opens her eyes again. This time, they're full of shadows. "There's a darkness out there and it's growing rapidly."

I nod. The elemental keeper mentioned it too.

"I thought I could handle it," Lana says. "Putting my life on the line has never stopped me. It's in my nature to throw myself into the path of danger." Her gaze suddenly burns into me. "But I can't do that now. I'm vulnerable. And even if I weren't, I have to acknowledge the fact that I'm not the one with the power to fight this darkness."

I ease back from her. "If you mean me—"

"I do."

I'm already shaking my head. "I don't understand my power any more than I did a week ago."

Lana considers me quietly. "Tell me what you *do* know."

Taking a deep breath, I try to steady myself. "I can sense death. I can feel the chill when a person—or an animal—is dying. I can also sense life. New life, that is. I helped a mother deer give birth, and now with you—"

"Back up," she says, her eyes a little brighter. "A mother deer?"

"They live in a forest behind one of the doors." My forehead creases. "I don't actually know what they're called. They look a bit like horses, but they have antlers."

"Mahogany antlers, the same color as the tree trunks," Lana says, as if she knows the animals I'm talking about. "And fur as green as leaves after a fresh rain."

"That's them."

Now her lips press together and she looks a little worried. "I hope you avoided their antlers. They can burn the skin right off your palms. Even through your scales."

I nod but shrug off the danger because it's in the past and the least of my worries. "The stag attacked Micah. He ended up with some burns, but I was able to push the stag away, and Micah healed."

Lana's eyes quickly narrow. "You pushed its body away?"

"No, I held it by the antlers, but really, it was fine. It didn't burn me. I was more confused about why the stag attacked Micah in the first place."

She's staring at me, but with the gentlest smile. "Oh, Sophia, your power is an incredible thing."

I'm even more confused by her reaction than I was about the stag's attack. "I don't understand."

"Nobody touches the antlers of those beasts without burning themselves. Not me. Not even Isaac with all his purity." She squeezes my hand. "As for why it would have attacked Micah, well, I imagine the stag thought Micah was a threat to you."

"Why would it believe that? Micah was just standing there."

Her expression becomes grim, but her piercing blue eyes refuse to release me. "The shadows are growing in Micah, too, aren't they? Just like they're growing in Beatrix. And now in me."

"How did you know about Micah and Beatrix?" I ask, since she only saw them briefly just now and even Isaac hadn't sensed anything was wrong until Beatrix collapsed.

Lana's speech slows, but she seems more careful than tired now. "When they were in this room with me just now, there were moments of nothingness where their presence should have been. Moments when it was as if they weren't here at all."

With every word Lana speaks, my heart is falling. My world is crumbling. And now it's my turn to arrest her gaze and not let her go. "Lana, what is it that you know? What *aren't* you telling me?"

She squeezes her eyes closed. "I've spent every waking moment since we separated tracking and surveilling the Scorn. As you know, I can't sense whether or not someone is a dragon shifter, but I can sense guilt.

"When I interacted with the Scorn on previous occasions, I sensed murder, theft, and violence. But now? The Scorn dragons who are wearing Tyler's mark radiate nothing. They have no guilt. No emotions. It's like observing a stone. They have no *life*."

"Tyler's mark?" I ask.

"A line of ash across their faces." Lana's lips press into a grim line. "I didn't understand it until I felt the ash on my own skin."

She lifts her free hand from beneath the blankets and presses her fingertips to her face. "Right here. The tip of his wing scraped me and that's all it took. Now, I feel my heart slipping away. I feel… a nothingness taking over."

I'm shaking my head. I refuse to believe it, but denial is a cruel emotion.

She continues. Relentlessly. "I sense it in Micah and Beatrix. They're losing themselves. And soon, like me, they will become Tyler's puppets."

CHAPTER THIRTY-ONE

"No." I remove my hand from Lana's. "I won't accept that."

"You must!" she says, shocking me with her sudden ferocity. Gone is my friend and in her place is the angel I once feared. Cold and deadly. "You must face it so you can fight it!"

My teeth are gritted. "Facing it is one thing. But fighting it? I'm not like you or Callan. I've never been a leader. I've never been the dragon anyone turned to—"

She snatches my hand back into hers, a hard grip. "When I brought the dragon's light back into the world, every dragon was given the ability to evolve. I thought that would be a good thing."

"Okay." I give her a cautious nod, uncertain where she's going with this. "We don't have to hide from moonlight anymore. We can shift different parts of our bodies at will. We have dragon souls that are our own—"

"Good things, yes," she says, her voice becoming a snarl. "But what of the dragon who craved power and delighted in cruelty? What sort of evolution would such a dragon experience?"

"You're talking about Tyler," I whisper.

"He has evolved into a source of misery and fear. He has a heart of ash that infects all others so they become like him."

Lana's hard expression falters and now tears form in her eyes. "Now consider: What effect would Tyler's power have on an angel-dragon who was born to be a hunter and a killer? How dangerous could she become if she had no soul and no heart?"

My eyes widen as I realize she's now talking about herself. "You wouldn't hurt us—"

"Wouldn't I?" Her grip on me hasn't eased and now it's painful. "I could kill you right now, Sophia. I don't need a weapon. It's my mind, my heart, and my reason that stops me. It's my love for you that stops me."

Tears burn hot behind my eyes as she continues.

"Soon, I won't be halted by anything. Dark magic delights in death. And I will bring it."

I shudder, but once again, she's relentless.

"As for Micah, raised in the most brutal clan, do you think he would hesitate to break your neck if his mind were gone and Tyler ordered him to do it? Or Beatrix and Felix, who were born into the Scorn clan and taught only violence until the Dread took them in?"

She takes a breath, gasping into the silence. "Or Callan..."

Her voice breaks, but she rallies and continues. "I already faced a future where Callan's power could be used for destruction and it terrified me. But it's nothing compared to a future where we all become soulless weapons."

Lana's fear cuts through my foundations and there's no denying her words now.

I squeeze my eyes closed, praying for courage, before I open them again and ask, "What can I do?"

Her blue eyes sear me like fire and even though she doesn't speak, I feel the power in her contemplation, the silent assessment of my failings and weaknesses. It's as if, with a single look, she can pluck at every thread of guilt in my soul and judge my worth.

She speaks much more quietly than before. "You can heal us, Sophia."

Her words wash over me, her conviction so impossible that I'm sure I can't have heard her right.

I shake my head, my eyes brimming. "I can't heal anything. I'm struggling to heal myself."

And there it is. These wounds in my heart and mind that I've been stitching together for years—imperfect, desperate stitches—have only just begun healing.

I'm still raw and fragile. The past isn't going to magically disappear because I've been offered love and family. Trust takes time. Healing takes time. A lifetime, even. Micah knew it even more acutely than I did. He promised me that he would prove to me how much he loves me every day, even if it takes a lifetime for me to truly believe him.

Lana's hold on my hand finally loosens and her voice softens, but she doesn't let me go. "Sophia, I want to tell you what I felt in the moments before I woke up. And I need you to hear me."

I give her a nod, and she turns her hand over so that it's now resting in mine.

"In the darkness, I was lying on a slab of ice," she says. "My heart was pumping ash through my body instead of blood; I could see the black soot flowing through the veins in my arms. I should have been alarmed, but the ash brought an alluring nothingness. An absence of struggle. There was no longer any need to worry or care. Fuck, it was actually a relief. So much weight lifted off my shoulders.

"Then came a torrent of light. It felt like sunlight was being poured over me and it burned like lava." Her eyes widen as if she's remembering it. "Suddenly, I was screaming to be let up off that slab, to face the struggles again, to feel the fear and pain and loss, to welcome all of it back. Because then I would be alive. Because that is life."

Tears trickle down her cheeks as she continues. "That river of light was *you*, Sophia. Your tears. Your power."

I stare down at our entwined hands. The back of her fingers are smeared where I'd cried. My tears have dried, but her skin glows in subtle streaks where the tears fell.

"I wasn't lying," I whisper, not a denial, but a plea for understanding. "I don't understand my power or how to use it. I don't even know what it is."

She smiles through her tears. "But I think I might," she says. "Because I can see it."

My eyes fly wide.

She gives me a smile that breaks through the tension in her face. "Sophia, you're glowing as brightly as the dragon's light when I first brought it out of the veil."

"I'm what?" I check my arms and hands, but I don't see what she sees.

"When I looked at Micah and Beatrix, I sensed nothing, but when I look at you, I sense everything," she says. "Everything good. Just lying here in your presence, my mind is filled with hope. I have this buzz in my head that tells me not to give up, and a taste in my mouth like I'm chomping down on a bouquet of fucking sunflowers."

Her lips lift into a smile and her eyes are brightening with every passing moment.

"It's joy and bliss and anticipation for a life that could be." Her gaze arrests mine as she continues. "The only explanation I have is that your power is *life*, Sophia."

Her smile grows when I stare at her in disbelief.

"You're the moonlight in the dark. The sunlight in the shadows. The quiet between bursts of thunder. When you finally accept your strength, you will be a force to be reckoned with."

I'm trying to process what she's telling me. I've been afraid of finding out that my power is dark when in fact, it could be the opposite.

She continues. "Your touch must be the reason that Micah

and Beatrix haven't succumbed to the ash yet. Your power must be keeping it at bay."

I remember each time I hugged Beatrix and each time I put my hand on Micah's heart when he was cold. In the forest, I thought it was the warmth of sunlight that helped him, but now I remember the way he'd told me that *I* was warm. When Beatrix lay on this feathery bed, I'd pressed my palm to her heart too. And then I'd cried onto Lana's hand.

For the first time since encountering Tyler on the rooftop, I feel true hope.

"Then... I can fight Tyler," I say. "I can beat him."

I'm still not sure exactly how to use my power, other than simply reaching out my hand, but now that I have more of a sense of *what* my power is, I have hope that I can figure it out.

At the very least, it explains why I wasn't affected by the ash like Micah and Beatrix.

"I believe you can beat him," Lana says, although her smile fades. "But it won't be easy. And the risk to anyone around you is high."

It's a sobering reality. "Because of how easily he can hurt them."

All it took to wound Lana was a scratch across her cheek. Beatrix was hurt by secondhand contact with the dust. And Micah, well, he was exposed to far too much of it, but he's been at my side nearly non-stop ever since.

I square my shoulders. "Will you let me try healing you?"

Not only would I give anything for Lana to be okay, but if I know I can counteract Tyler's power, then I'll be far less worried about taking my family with me into this fight.

Lana relaxes against the feathers. "I'm not about to say *no*."

I exhale slowly since I haven't consciously used my deeper power before. For a long moment, I consider the times when I've felt most in control. Weirdly, it has been when I've embraced risk, letting go of my inhibitions and worries, and I followed my instincts.

Like choosing to dive off a cliff and plummet toward a forest far below. Or to run toward a struggling deer. Or to step into a magical garden controlled by a powerful keeper of magic.

Or... slipping my arm around Micah's waist and finding the courage to tell him that he didn't have to hide his pain from me.

Reaching out, I press my left hand over Lana's heart and, with my right hand, I cup her cheek where her skin is tinged with gray.

At my touch, her black scales blossom across her skin, appearing around my hand on her neck and face, and above the neckline of her shirt.

She stays perfectly still and I close my eyes, seeking the life-giving blood pumping around her body. It's an easy task now and I can immediately identify her heartbeat.

But with a shiver I can't hide, I can now also sense the death in her blood, the lifeless ash she was talking about, and it chills me to my bones.

It's all through her body. Everywhere her heart pumps.

Flecks of death glittering within her.

I grit my teeth and pray that I can feel the happiness Lana described, the bliss that makes her think of sunflowers, because the death that's flowing through her is sucking all of the joy from my own heart.

At the same time, my palms tingle and I sense new warmth pooling in my palms. It's subtle. So mild that I could mistake it for Lana's body heat.

I latch on to it, focusing inward.

I seek the tidal wave within me that could set her free, hoping I have the courage to release it from its cage.

CHAPTER THIRTY-TWO

I inhale. Exhale.

On my next inhale, I feel like I'm pulling at my own heart.

There *is* life within me. So much of it that I feel like I'm going to burst, but there's... something else too.

A trickle of energy that feels darker.

It's the same wild sensation that made me question the nature of my power and its consequences, that made me fear an internal battle within me.

I can't identify it, except that I can now sense it's at the core of my power. Like there's another part of me immersed at the center of that tidal wave and it's that other part of myself that I've been caging all along—

I gasp as Lana's hand wraps around my wrist.

"Sophia!" Her voice is sharp but hoarse. "Stop!"

My eyes fly open to meet hers. Her forehead is beaded with sweat and her scales have come out in full force, the strength in her hand nearly crushing my arm.

I have no doubt that this time, her body is responding defensively to my touch.

As if I'm a threat.

I jolt back from her, needing to break the contact between us, but even though my hands lift off her, her own hand continues to grip my wrist. The force of my backward movement jolts both of our arms and wrenches my shoulder socket. I lurch to a stop halfway out of my chair and leaning over her.

"I'm sorry!" she cries, her eyes piercing mine. "I need you to stop, but I can't let go yet. I'm trying to sense... I can nearly sense..."

"What?" I ask, desperate for her to name this energy that I can't identify but which is thrumming through me like an electrical current.

"I don't have a name for it," she says breathlessly. "But it feels... *beyond.*"

"Beyond what?"

Her forehead is deeply furrowed, the tension around her mouth increasing. "Beyond what should be possible."

I stare at her, my dismay only growing. "What does that mean?"

She opens her fist and releases me and it feels like being dropped into the unknown. I plummet back to my seat.

"I'm sorry, Sophia," she says, worry settling in her eyes. "I can't describe what I sensed. It was overwhelming and wild and full of possibilities, but it was also like being smashed against rocks and broken into pieces."

She stops, and there's silence between us until I say, "I felt it too."

Her black hair spreads around her face. "A little of your power seems to be healing. Too much is—"

"Dangerous," I say bitterly.

Too many fucking sunflowers.

She stares ruefully at my wrist as I rub it. "I'm certain you will come to understand your power and to control it," she says. "You just need more time."

"I don't have time," I snap, and then I try to quell my frustration, try to soften my voice. "*Micah* doesn't have time. Neither does Beatrix. Or you."

Her lips press together and she doesn't utter a denial.

They're all running out of time.

I give a groan of frustration, dropping my head into my hands. "Right now, my power feels like a Band-Aid on a knife wound. And while I'm trying to figure things out, Tyler's out there building an army of fucking soulless Scorn dragons."

I raise my head again. "If my power is dangerous, then I need to use it against Tyler. *That's* when I'll understand it."

I expect her to argue with me, but instead, she says, "I agree."

"You do?"

Once again, her eyes pierce mine. "Your instincts are pure. Trust them."

That's all she says and I consider her carefully. "If I destroy Tyler, will you be cured?"

"His power will no longer exist. He can't turn anyone else's heart to ash."

I narrow my eyes at her, not liking her evasive response. "But will *you* be cured?"

She exhales heavily. "I want to believe that if there's still light in my heart, then the ash will lose its power once its source is destroyed."

My heart is cracking a little at the uncertainty. "But you don't know for certain."

She shakes her head. "I might die with him."

My hands are shaking and all I can do is close them into fists, trying to anchor myself.

Where is this fucking hope when I need it for myself?

Again, I speak carefully. "You're giving me the power to make my own choices, aren't you?"

She inclines her head. "I'm not your alpha. And quite frankly, with the force I sense in you, there isn't an alpha in the world who should rule over you, Sophia. Your choices now must be your own."

Leaning back in my chair and folding my hands in my lap, I consider my options.

None are terribly good.

I could leave the veil and confront Tyler on my own. My family would be safe from the fight—some of them here in the veil, the rest hidden in Grudge territory. But for Micah, Beatrix, and Lana, the longer I'm gone, the colder their hearts will become. A ticking timebomb left behind.

Or I can take them with me, keep them close, and make sure their hearts are safe. But in doing so, I'd be exposing them to the battle ahead. They'd be vulnerable to Tyler's power and he could use them against me.

Even if I destroy Tyler, I might not be able to save my family. Not those who have already been affected by his power.

Fuck it. There is no right answer.

As I contemplate Lana and remember where she came from, I know one thing for certain: I don't want to fight this battle alone.

"I'm taking you with me," I say quietly. "You and Micah and Beatrix. I want you at my side. But Isaac and Callan must either stay here where it's safe or go to Grudge territory to help protect the others. I won't allow anyone else to be exposed to Tyler's hatred."

Lana takes a deep breath. "Help me up?"

I lean forward to wrap my arms around her. It's a difficult mission when her wings are in the way, but I manage to draw her upright. Then I'm hugging her. I press a kiss to her cheek and I can't help but notice the way her natural skin color returns at the contact.

Before I help her to the edge of the bed, I say, "Love you, Lana. You're my sister now, and I'm going to keep you alive."

She tips her chin at me as she slides her feet to the floor, taking a deep breath but remaining upright when I release her. "Love you, too, Sophia."

Not words I ever thought this angel would say to me.

My happiness fades as I contemplate everything I need to tell Micah and Beatrix. Everything about the plan that's slowly coming together in my mind.

Beatrix may well love it.

Micah will hate it.

I have no idea how Isaac will feel about it. But I suspect that Callan will oppose it; only because it involves being separated from his mate.

I exit the infirmary to find my family waiting on the steps outside.

Callan is holding Lana's glaive as well as his own gold. Beatrix and Isaac are huddled together, but Micah is actively pacing. He stops when he sees me.

"Come in," I say. "We need to talk."

Once they're all settled inside the infirmary, I talk them through the knowns and the unknowns of my power. I also tell them all about my encounters with the keepers. Then I finish with the worst: what we know about Tyler's power and my inability to counteract its effects.

I finish to silence and it's as heavy as I expected it to be. I sense rage and grief around me and it's coming from all of them. Except Lana, who gives me a reassuring nod.

Taking a deep breath, I say, "I'm going to fight Tyler, but I can't do it on my own."

Beatrix squares her shoulders and lifts her head high. "As if I'd let you go without me. Besides, one week of gathering wheat while simultaneously fending off unruly thickens is enough for me."

I peer at her. "Um... thickens?"

Beatrix screws up her nose. "They're like chickens but not."

When Isaac presses his lips together, a glimmer of humor on his face, Beatrix rolls her eyes at him.

"They have the nerve to smell like roses while they try to peck out your eyes," she says.

Isaac shifts a little in his chair. "Now, now," he says. "It was trying to nuzzle up to you."

Beatrix twists to him. "Its beak came right at my eye. You'd be terrified too if a big, red bird poked its beak right at your face."

He shrugs. "Good thing I was there to save you, then."

Beatrix clears her throat as she turns back to me. Her cheeks are flushed. "Fucking terrifying."

Observing the connection between Beatrix and Isaac only makes me more reticent about my plan, but I have no choice about what needs to happen.

I turn from Isaac to Callan, addressing them both. "Callan, Isaac, you're not affected by the ash. I need you to go to Grudge territory and keep our families safe."

Callan's expression immediately hardens and so does Isaac's.

"We can help you in the fight against Tyler," Callan says.

I shake my head. "The danger is too great. I won't risk another person I care about being hurt by the ash."

Before Callan can argue further, Lana takes hold of his hand. She doesn't say anything, and her touch seems to convey her wishes to him. The raw grief that washes over Callan's face is nearly too much for me.

I take a deep breath, trying to steady myself as I prepare to let Micah know my plan.

He rises from his seat, quiet but determined, and speaks before I can. "Ask me to fight for you, and I will." He takes my hands and his voice softens. "But if you need to fight this battle by yourself, *for* yourself, then all you have to do is ask and I'll support you in any way you need."

"I need to do this for myself," I say. "But not by myself. I want you beside me, along with Lana and Beatrix. But, Micah..." I hesitate and take a deep breath before I continue. "I need you to go against every instinct in your body."

I meet the increasing wariness in his cedar-brown eyes as I say, "Because I plan to be bait."

CHAPTER THIRTY-THREE

The armory is our last stop before we leave.

Beatrix goes straight for the swords while Micah picks out a combination of blades and firearms.

I choose a single dagger and take a weapon belt from the wall, tying it around my waist. I've chosen to remain in my long, white pants and white tunic. I've become used to the softness of the material and the ease of movement that it allows. Besides, I'll have plenty of access to my own clothes soon enough.

Callan and Lana have chosen to wait outside the armory for us since they already have their weapons, but Isaac heads straight for the wall of Sentinel spears and remains there, staring at it until I step up beside him.

"Isaac? Are you okay?"

"I've never used my weapon to kill," he says. "I have faith in your plan, Sophia, but if it doesn't succeed, I need to consider what I should do. I'm now asking myself if Tyler is an adversary for whom I should compromise my vows."

"Nothing should make you compromise your beliefs."

Despite my assertion, he exhales heavily and continues to glare at the deadly weapons.

I take another moment to think through his dilemma, and

then I ask him a question. "Tell me something… If you use your Sentinel spear to strike a tree, would you kill it?"

"Sadly, yes," he says. "The spear is designed to end life."

"What if you struck a piece of coal? Or a stone?"

He arches an eyebrow and asks me a question in return. "Or ash?"

I nod and give him a moment to ponder his answer.

"No," he finally says. "The ash would not be harmed. For the simple fact that it isn't alive."

"What about your soul light?" I ask quietly. "What impact would it have on ash?"

He gives a slow shake of his head. "Like my weapon, soul light only affects living matter. It can break through darkness, but only in the mind and body of the receiver. It wouldn't reach the heart of a creature made of ash." He exhales a quiet sigh. "Which would be why it has no effect on the ash already hurting those I care about."

His gaze flickers to Beatrix, where she's testing the weight of a sword. The friction that used to exist between them is gone and in its place is a new tension. One I pray they have the chance to explore.

"Then your Sentinel spear is no use against Tyler," I say, "but your soul light is of use to me."

His forehead creases. "But…"

"Your soul light is for the ones I need you to protect," I clarify. "I know it's a lot to ask you to watch Lana walk into this fight without you or Callan at her side. But the Dread dragons and the Grudge, and even Gisela and Dane, will need you. If I don't win this battle, you must do everything you can to protect them."

He gives me a solemn nod. "Then I'll choose a different weapon."

He reaches for a simple-looking wooden rod that rests on hooks to the left of the Sentinel spears.

I leave his side and step toward Beatrix and Micah, who

appear to have finished choosing weapons, but I hesitate.

Lana told me to trust my instincts.

Giving in to my impulses, I gravitate toward Atrox's armor.

The helmet gleams. The plates in the armor are finely crafted but sturdy-looking and interlocked, so they should be able to move without revealing gaps. The entire suit, from the helmet to the chest, shoulder, and thigh plates, is a beautiful piece of artwork, the likes of which I've never seen.

"Sophia?" Micah's voice is quiet, but it also carries tension.

He's concerned about anyone approaching this gold, let alone touching it, but that's because of whom it belonged to.

"This metal isn't evil," I say. "Its purpose is to protect its wearer, whoever that may be."

I dare to brush the chest plate's smooth surface with the tips of my fingers. The lightest touch. All while I prepare to leap backward if the gold reacts badly to my presence.

I'm surprised to find that the metal is warm to the touch, not cold like I expected.

Daring to press my entire palm against its surface, I lean in and speak softly to it. "I don't have any dragon's gold. All I've had has been controlled by others. You would be the first to be truly mine. If you let me, I will give you a home and a purpose."

The gold trembles, shivering at my touch as if it were alive.

It is. A living substance that no longer feels lost in my senses, but there's also a new buzz within my mind. A warning of sorts.

I quickly retract my hand, concerned that I've pushed the gold too far by asking it to become mine. Releasing my wings, I hold my hand out to the others, warning them to keep their distance. "Be prepared to run."

They're on edge, although Micah looks like he's determined to race *toward* me, not *away* from me.

I brace as the gold plates shiver again, this time in a ripple that runs from the top of the armor all the way to the bottom and then, as if it's all part of the same piece, a ripple flows from the bottom of the helmet to the top.

Before my eyes, the entire suit lifts off the wall, and then it begins wrapping and folding itself, compressing inward. The horns on the helmet twist and join across the long sides, then the curved portions that cover the head divide into smaller pieces and begin overlapping each other. The chest, shoulder, and thigh plates do the same, wrapping over each other, making themselves smaller and smaller with every fold.

I consider the suit with wary dismay, worried that I've triggered its destruction.

I didn't mean for that to happen.

"No." My soft cry turns to surprise when the smaller helmet piece adheres to the larger chest piece and then they elongate. The folding movement slows and finally, a single piece floats in the air opposite me, mere inches from my outstretched hand.

It looks like a belt, and the helmet has formed what appears to be a clip at the front of it.

Carefully, I remove the harness I put on earlier, along with the dagger I placed in it.

Closing my hand around the new belt made of dragon's gold, I find it warm and light, as if it's absorbing its own weight.

"Hi there," I whisper to it before I wrap it around my waist.

It sits neatly above my hips, clicking closed easily.

I'm left holding the dagger and uncertain how I'll carry it. For a moment, I consider if I'll need it. Maybe I could leave it behind.

Before I have more time to think about it, the gold at my waist ripples again, becoming fluid for an alarming second before it takes the shape of a new dagger, neatly sheathed and sitting in a comfortable position against my hip.

"Okay, then," I say to the gold, my heart swelling a little.

This gold is mine now.

"Thank you," I whisper to it, pressing my palm to its surface with a silent promise that I will care for it.

I look up to find my family poised on their toes as if they were still prepared to rush toward me.

Now, Micah visibly relaxes and Beatrix shakes out her shoulders.

Isaac doesn't look perplexed at all. "It's good for dragon's gold to have a home," he says. "It isn't meant to be alone."

I replace the ordinary dagger on the wall, and then I carefully consider the hammer that's surrounded by empty space now that the armor is gone. When I bend to the hammer, hovering my hand above its surface, I again sense what Micah and Lana described.

The hammer feels heavy within my senses. Weighed down by its own history.

When I encountered the keeper of light magic, she was carrying a weapon that radiated a nature very similar to this one. She said that the actual weapon was hidden, and for good reasons.

"This hammer must remain alone," I say with certainty. "It should be hidden and never used again."

Isaac gives me a firm nod. "When this is all over, we must find a safe place for it."

We exit the armory to find Lana and Callan waiting.

They're both dressed in white pants and tunics similar to mine. It brings out the darkness of Lana's hair and the brightness of her blue eyes. Callan towers over all of us, both he and Lana radiating an immense power that takes my breath away.

It defies the grief in their expressions.

Lana's cheeks are tear-streaked and Callan's eyes are shadowed, his lips pressed into a hard line.

I'm asking them to separate at a time when they should be together. "I'm sorry," I whisper.

Callan's response is spoken in a deep growl that sends a shiver down my spine. "Fucking kill him, Sophia. If you don't, I will try. Even if it means I die trying."

There's no room for doubt in his words.

Tears are welling in Lana's eyes.

If I can't save her, Callan's rage will be a destructive force to be reckoned with.

Despite all my fears of what the future holds, I tip my head back and meet the deep rage in Callan's eyes. "You were the first to give me a real home and to believe in me," I say to him. "You were there when my dragon first appeared. You held my hand when I was afraid and taught me how to release my wings. You opened the door to my freedom and gave me the chance to step through it. Now, it's my turn to protect you."

I step up to him, tipping my head back, unflinching in the face of the heat waves beating around his form. "Tyler will meet his end at my hand, or I too, will die trying."

Callan gives me a firm nod.

Then I turn to Isaac. "The way out?"

He gestures to the bottom of the staircase. "We'll exit the veil through the most concealed door. We can part ways once we're out there. It's not safe to go back via the fountain. The Scorn have seen us there. They could be lying in wait. We need to go through a door that's rarely ever used." He grimaces. "Only in exceptional circumstances."

"Why is that?" I ask as we follow him down the staircase.

"It lets out into a back alley," he replies. "Humans have constructed buildings around it over time in a way that makes it difficult to access from the other side, but also creates perfect conditions for the veil's magic to conceal it."

At my curious glance, he gives me a mysterious smile. "You'll see."

He descends the final step and then heads to the right. I don't know how he can tell where he's going, since there isn't a discernable path, but he walks ten paces straight ahead, followed by two paces to the left, and then he stops.

A white door appears in front of him, its color so pale that it's difficult to make out against the backdrop of our bright surroundings.

"I'll keep the door open for you," he says. "But remember you won't be able to return to the veil without me."

He takes the handle, but instead of pushing the door outward, or pulling it inward, he slides it to the left.

A misty haze rests over the opening, but beyond it, I can make out faint sunlight. It's midday—a time of day when I might have felt safe.

Traditionally, the Scorn always carried out their kills in dark rooms, shadowed alleys, and grimy basements. Maybe even on rooftops on cloudy nights. Never under bright lights. But the attack on Lana and Callan occurred during the morning hours, proving that the Scorn no longer have any hesitation launching an assault in broad daylight.

The faint sounds of traffic and the hum of city life filter through the haze.

Micah's presence at my back is all the reassurance I need before I step through into the alley beyond.

The moment I leave the veil, a shiver rocks me. The alley is dark, deserted, and narrow, and dirt has gathered around the edges on both sides and formed a layer of sludge beneath our feet.

It's also completely closed off at the other end, which isn't more than ten paces away. It feels like I've stepped into a box. Windowless brick walls rise high up on all four sides. Isaac and the others follow me through, the door closes behind us, and then we're completely boxed in.

"How the fuck did this happen?" Beatrix asks, gazing at the built-in space around us.

Isaac grimaces. "For the most part, entrances to the veil were carefully planned to exist within well-established buildings with a high chance of never being torn down. This spot was a miscalculation. It won't officially exist on any city plan, but the magic in the veil stops it from being blockaded over."

"I see why you don't use it often," I say, picturing myself dropping directly down into this space with enemies on my heels. "The chances of someone catching you or following you into the veil are high."

"That would be true," Isaac says as he steps into the clear space at the other end of the alley. "Except that the veil's magic is able to be amplified within these walls. Sort of like a ball bouncing from one wall to the other in a never-ending loop. It means that this entire space is protected. We won't be exposed until we reach the top."

Well, that's some good news.

There isn't space for all of us to spread our wings at once, so we take off in turns.

Isaac goes first, soaring upward before landing on the edge of the rooftop far above. He takes a moment to check the surroundings up there before he gestures for us to come up.

Micah and I are last. He steps up to me and the darkness in his eyes seems inky in this enclosed space.

I immediately press my palm to his heart, willing the warmth to reach his skin through the soft, white material.

"Whatever you need. Whenever you need it," he says, his voice husky. "Tell me and I'll be there."

"Fight," I whisper, reaching up to press my lips to his, tasting the saltiness of my sudden tears. "Fight against the death that's trying to claim you. Because I need you. I want you. And I want the chance to have a family with you."

He lowers his head, his forehead pressing to mine, and we stay like that for another moment before I force myself to move back so I can release my wings.

Micah is close behind me as we soar upward.

I alight on the edge of the rooftop and quickly scan my surroundings. We're standing at the center of a gently sloping roof, far enough back that there's no chance we could be seen from the streets below.

We're also very high up, which makes it easy to see far across the city. Tucking my wings away, I quickly scan for landmarks I might recognize. I'm relieved to discover that we're close to the center of the city. We're equidistant from Grudge territory and Callan's last home—which is where I plan to go next.

But here, on this rooftop, is where we'll part ways with Callan and Isaac.

Wanting to give Callan and Lana, and Beatrix and Isaac the space they need, I venture carefully toward the roof's edge with Micah at my side.

We take quick peeks down to the street below. It's darker than I was expecting at this time of day and the usual city sounds seem hushed. Above me, clouds cover the sun and the sky is gray. The chill that settled around me when we stepped into the alley is only growing worse.

Everywhere I look, there are shadows where the sunlight should be.

The strong beat of wings draws my attention back to the others. Callan rises into the air, his golden wings shrouded in heat waves, but he stays low to the rooftop.

Lana's focus on her mate prevails until he's a distant figure racing away through the shadows.

Isaac has hung back and now he hurries toward me, arresting my attention with his urgent voice. "It's likely that the *Book of Light Magic* will record your battle," he says quietly. "If Callan sees that Lana's in trouble, I won't be able to stop him."

"I understand," I say, conscious of Lana's gaze on me. She's proven to have hearing nearly as sensitive as Micah's and will be able to hear every word we're saying.

I meet her eyes, even though my answer is for Isaac. "I trust Callan to choose the right path for himself and Lana. Isaac, please focus on keeping everyone in Grudge territory safe."

With a nod to me, Isaac steps back, but he pauses beside Beatrix. He's facing away from me now while Beatrix's face is fully visible to me.

Her whisper is so quiet, she barely makes a sound. "Goodbye, pet."

Isaac's response is soft but determined. "Not goodbye."

At that, he spreads his wings and rises upward, flying low over several rooftops before he also disappears into the shadows.

Now, it's just the four of us. Me and three of the shifters I most care about, each of them fighting the darkness growing within their hearts.

I don't mince words. "We'll go to Callan's home first, but we need to reach it quickly. The Scorn could be anywhere and I doubt they'll hesitate to attack us if they intercept us."

Micah's shoulders are tense, his eyes narrowed at the cityscape around us. "I don't like what I'm sensing out there. It's the middle of the day. The city should be bustling. Noisy. Instead, there's a friction in the air." He inhales deeply. "It smells... *wrong*."

"Death," I say. "It smells like death."

The city might look peaceful from up here, but there's no doubt in my mind that we've entered a war zone.

CHAPTER THIRTY-FOUR

The heavy thump of music masks the pounding of my heart as I weave a path through the throng of humans crowding the dance floor of the Hollow Rose.

I appear to be alone, but Micah, Beatrix, and Lana are right where I need them to be, camouflaged by Beatrix's power and watching over me. Not that I can sense exactly where they are. It turns out that, while I was undertaking combat training, Beatrix found the time to train, too. Now she can use her power not only to conceal herself and others from sight, but from all detection—sound and scent.

I'm proceeding on pure trust that they've remained where they said they'd be.

Around me, the glistening sweat on the human dancers' skin is like diamonds in my vision, every droplet of liquid calling to me.

But I'm not here for them.

I'm here for the dragon shifters milling around on the second-floor loft that overhangs the dance floor.

It's fucking brazen that the Scorn would congregate here.

The Hollow Rose is Callan's club.

But then, Tyler always wanted everything Callan had. He even made a pass at Lana. I'm not sure he cared that I saw him do it.

Of course, it wasn't an easy task to determine that the Scorn were here. Earlier today, after returning to Callan's home and the apartment he gave me, Lana and I set out to scour the city. She can't sense the Scorn themselves, but she was able to single out hot spots of malice and guilt across the city where they might be gathered.

When one of those spots happened to be the Hollow Rose, I made it my first target tonight.

Lana told me to trust my instincts and so far, they're proving to be accurate.

I quickly scan the figures up in the loft, recognizing the two Scorn dragons who followed us to the fountain, along with several others I met on the night Zahra attempted to make an alliance with the Scorn.

But... I don't see Tyler among them.

That's okay. My presence will draw him out soon enough.

As long as I make a show of it.

Holding my head high, I sway deftly through the crowd, choosing a spot right in the middle of the dancers, where I stop and plant my feet.

My right leg is slightly forward, my thigh fully exposed by the high slit in the green, satin dress I chose to wear tonight. It matches the color of my eyes. It's tightly fitted around my torso with spaghetti straps over the shoulders that crisscross down the back to a low waist. A slinky number. The kind that Tyler will like.

I take a moment to center myself before I focus on every droplet of moisture resting on the skin of the humans around me. I'm not totally certain it's going to work—and I have other ideas for drawing attention if it doesn't—but I latch on to the water and mentally request that it move gently outward.

I'm gratified when, at the soft press of my power, the humans gravitate away from me, leaving a gap all around me that will make my presence conspicuous from above.

At the same time, I allow the cerulean-blue shimmer of my dragon scales to gleam across my bare shoulders and up to my cheeks. I have nothing to fear from revealing my scales in this place. The strobe lights make the true nature of my scales visually confusing to any human who might notice them—those who aren't already intoxicated.

My heels tap on the floor as I adjust my balance, ready to move when I need to.

Then I paste a provocative smile onto my lips and tip my head back, allowing my hair to cascade across my right shoulder as I wait for the dragons in the loft to notice me.

It doesn't take them long.

The male Scorn dragon with the patterns shaved across his scalp jabs his finger in my direction. At his gesture, ten Scorn dragons lurch to their feet, including the woman with the light-brown skin and bright-pink streaks in her hair who chased us at the fountain.

She stands and takes a quick step toward the transparent glass that surrounds the loft.

In doing so, she reveals the form of the dragon shifter sitting next to her.

My mother.

I shouldn't be surprised to see her here. She defected to the Scorn when it looked like the Dread would be annihilated. She left me behind when she thought she could save her own skin.

Unlike the Scorn, who are agitated around her, she merely leans back in her chair and peers in my direction as if she couldn't care less.

I tell myself that I didn't come here for her. Not to save her or convince her to come back to the Dread. But—dammit—there are things I need to say to her. Closure I need to reach. I find myself pivoting my plan, plotting out a detour that will take me to her.

Wiping my expression clean, I crook my finger at the Scorn with the pink hair, beckoning to her before I blow her a kiss, Beatrix-style.

A dark scowl settles on the woman's features, and I picture the bullet she'd love to put between my eyes.

She won't, though.

Tyler wants me hurt and groveling at his feet, not dead, so my fear levels are low right now.

It looks like she's shouting orders at the others as she leaves the edge of the loft and hurries toward the elevator at the back. I can't hear what she says—the balcony is soundproof—but I'm sure I'll find out soon. The small, glass foyer will slow her down, but the elevator will soon bring her to the dance floor.

I'm already on the move.

"Out of my way, please," I whisper quietly, pushing at the sweat on the bodies of the humans so they drift aside and open up a clear path directly ahead of me.

I quickly make it to the staff-only corridor, where several of the human staff recognize me.

"Good evening, Ms. Dalton," one of the men says, his greeting forcing me to pause. He's wearing black-rimmed glasses and I recognize him, although I don't remember his name.

"It's nice to see a familiar face," he says, appearing relieved to see me.

The human employees have been taught to respect Tyler, but they aren't stupid. The tension around their mouths and eyes tells me they know something isn't right. Callan is a good employer and always treats humans well. I imagine the Scorn are exactly the opposite, and the staff must be wondering what's going on.

I've already pivoted in my mission, and I tell myself another small diversion won't hurt, so I stop beside the human.

"Thank you…uh…" I scan his name tag. "Mark. It's nice to see you again, too. I'm sure you've gathered that there's been some upheaval, but things should be back to normal very soon."

Thinking fast, I add, "In the meantime, I have Callan's authority to ask you to close early tonight. You'll still be paid for a full night's work, but it might be best to get all of the patrons out of here."

I don't plan on causing problems inside this building, but I can't predict what the Scorn will do, and human collateral is the last thing I want. Now that the opportunity to clear out the club has presented itself, I'm taking it.

Mark looks relieved and so do the other human staff who have gathered behind him. "Thank you, Ms. Dalton," he says. "It's a strange night tonight. We'd like to get home to our families."

It's clear from his words that the humans are feeling the darkness too, although they won't have an explanation for it. I give them a quick nod and that's all I have time for before I need to hurry toward the elevator.

It opens just as I reach it.

The Scorn woman stiffens when she sees me standing right in front of her. Her hand tightens on her gun, which rests at her waist, while she gives me a quick onceover.

It's obvious that I'm unarmed. My slinky dress is so skin-tight that it's impossible for me to hide any weapons under it. I didn't risk wearing my new gold belt because other dragons would sense its nature.

"Sophia Dalton." She curls her lip at me. "If you wanted our attention, you've got it."

"Such an honor to see you again," I say sweetly. "But it wasn't *your* attention I wanted."

I slip into the elevator beside her, making her eyes widen with surprise. I imagine she expected me to either fight her or try to run.

"Going up, yes?" I ask.

She rapidly sidesteps to avoid contact with me, her hand tightening on her weapon.

Before she can speak, I arch my eyebrows at her. "We can fight it out just for the fun of it, but I was sure you were on your way to apprehend me, so I thought I'd save you the trouble."

I jab the button for the balcony floor and the doors close.

"What the fuck are you playing at, Sophia?" she asks me.

"Nothing," I say, looking her firmly in the eyes. "No games. I assume Tyler's looking for me, so I'm giving myself up. All I ask is that you allow me to speak with my mother before Tyler drags me away."

Her forehead puckers in apparent confusion, but her hand eases off her weapon a little. "Why would you surrender?"

I sigh. "Because running is exhausting."

Running from the past. Running from things I can't change. But running toward my future... well... that's fucking liberating.

The crease in her forehead doesn't fade.

I wouldn't trust my answer, either.

Now that she's standing closer to me, I can see the faint smudge of ash across her left cheek. *Tyler's mark.* She's wearing long sleeves to her wrists and a turtleneck, black shirt that reaches all the way up to her chin. If the skin on her left side is gray in tone, then I can't see it.

Her irises are flecked with pink and they're rapidly changing shape, becoming more reptilian with every second it takes the elevator to reach the balcony floor.

For a second, I wonder what kind of dragon she might be with eyes that pretty. A cotton candy dragon, maybe. The kind that leaves you with a nasty stomachache.

"I don't know your name," I say.

"Niah," she snaps. "I'm Gisela's cousin."

"So you're a full-blooded Scorn, then." And could have been

in the line-up of potential alphas before Tyler took control of the clan. "It's surprising to me that you would follow Tyler."

"Opposing him is futile," Niah retorts.

A moment later, the doors open, and I prepare to face a small army of Scorn.

CHAPTER THIRTY-FIVE

I take a step toward the elevator doors, but Niah's hand wraps around my arm, wrenching me to a stop.

"You will submit to restraints," she snarls.

"Of course. Slap them on me." I look at her expectantly. "Unless you don't have any with you right now."

She huffs as she pulls me into the little foyer immediately outside the elevator. It's lined with glass walls, which leaves the room ahead fully visible while also creating a barrier. Callan had it created to provide a protective boundary if his fire was accidentally triggered.

I let Niah push me around, deliberately acting as if I couldn't fend her off if I tried, as she propels me through the foyer and onto the balcony beyond it.

I snatch a moment to study my mother where she sits close to the glass wall on the far side of the loft.

Her tall frame is slouched, her silver-streaked hair spread out in a tangled mess across the back of the chair. She was always well-dressed, but now her silken shirt is creased and there are visible sweat stains around her underarms and neckline. She used to be dripping in gold, but now she isn't wearing any.

She's staring in my direction, but it doesn't feel like she sees me. It's hard to tell for sure in this light, but her emerald-green eyes appear glazed. The glass dangling in her hand across the armrest could be filled with anything.

Anger and pity war inside me.

This is the life she's chosen for herself?

The Scorn dragons around me have all risen from their chairs. Half of them—about nine, at a quick count—are dressed in black up to their necks and have faint smudges on their cheeks. They stand at tables laden with swords, daggers, and guns, along with a variety of drinks.

The other half are also dressed in black, but their faces aren't marked and their forearms are visible. They're the ones who appear tenser, holding their weapons tightly in their hands, an intriguing difference with the marked ones.

"Sit," Niah snaps at me, pushing me into the lounge chair opposite my mother's. She snatches up a chain of dragon's gold from the nearby table, whispers to it, and then she wraps the rope around my wrists.

While she works, she casts an order at the man with the pattern shaved into his scalp. "Gordon, message Tyler that we have Sophia." Then she raises her voice at my mother. "Hey, Martha, I've brought some company for you."

"Huh?" My mother's voice is slurred. She squints up at Niah before her gaze falls to me.

It's like she's seeing me for the first time since I arrived.

"Sophia." Her eyes widen, then her cheeks flush. She sniffs loudly and holds her head higher. "It seems they're bringing me the trash now."

I don't look away. There was a time when her comment would have hurt me. Now it simply washes over me.

Niah laughs and folds her arms across her chest while Gordon finishes up punching a message into his phone.

"Tyler's on his way," he says, pocketing his phone right next to his gun.

I won't have long now before I need to return to my previous plan, so I lean across to my mother. My wrists are now bound, but I reach out for her hand.

"This doesn't have to be your future, Mom," I say quietly.

She snatches her hand away from mine. It's a jerky movement. "What future?" she snarls. "I have no future unless he chooses me."

At her words, a tense silence falls around me. The thump of music continues to vibrate through my feet, although I'm aware of the staff guiding patrons toward the door. They seem to be doing it in small batches, which is clever if they want to avoid attracting attention.

Up here in the loft, the dragons with smudges on their cheeks are smirking, while the ones without marks have stiffened, their features drawn. *Afraid*, even.

"What are you talking about?" I ask, focusing back on my mother.

She points to her pale cheek.

"He didn't choose me," she cries. "He only chooses the strongest ones."

Her lips stretch wide into a grimace—or maybe a snarl, I can't tell which—as she continues. "The rest of us will be left to perish. There's no future in the light."

She isn't making sense and I'm running out of time. I remind myself that taking the time to care about my mother could cost me dearly. Particularly because the chill running down my spine is so much stronger now.

Tyler's coming closer.

"Mom," I say quietly. "I deserved so much better than you allowed me to have."

She scoffs at me. "You always wanted too much. Silly Sophia."

"You deserved so much better, too."

Her eyes widen at me, then fill with tears. She half-lifts out of her chair, a wobbly, uncoordinated movement. Her slap flies toward me, aimed at my face, but my bound hands shoot up, my reflexes firing.

I intercept her, catching hold of her arm and holding her tightly between my hands.

She gasps, flinches, and her lips twist, but she's so unsteady that my hold on her is now keeping her upright.

I'm not sure if she ever loved me. I know she never protected me. I also know that this is the last conversation I ever want to have with her.

I wrap up my memories of her, and I put them away.

"I'm going to forget you now," I say to her, my voice steady and certain. "If I meet you again, you'll be a stranger to me. Not even someone I used to love."

Releasing her arm, I allow her to drop back to the couch. She nearly misses the seat, catching the edge of it before she slides back into it and reaches desperately for her glass.

It's time for me to move.

I remain standing as I turn calmly in Niah's direction. "Thank you for giving me the chance to say goodbye to my mother."

Niah's face screws up in a snarl. "Sit down."

"No." Softly, I clap my hands, an awkward but not impossible movement.

At my gesture, the rope of dragon's gold falls right off me and clatters softly to the ground.

Niah jolts. "How did you—?"

"It wasn't me," I say, but I'm not about to give her any further explanation, certainly not to alert her to the camouflaged dragon shifters currently watching out for me or to tell her that Lana and I made contingency plans if I ended up constrained by dragon's gold. Niah may not even be aware of Lana's ability to control other dragon's gold, and I'm not going to enlighten her.

Especially since Niah and the other Scorn are now drawing their weapons and hurrying toward me.

But I'm ready.

Every droplet of alcohol, every smear of sweat, and every pulse of blood in this balcony is tangible to me.

"*Stop*," I whisper, my command directed to the blood pumping around the Scorn dragons' bodies.

Niah gasps, chokes. She clutches at her heart, her eyes bulging as she drops to her knees.

"You…" She gasps. "What are you doing?"

All around me, the Scorn are falling to their knees, their faces turning pale as I stop the blood from pumping around their bodies, placing enormous strain on their hearts.

Nearer to me, the woman I once called my mother simply stares at her comrades and takes a sip from her glass. I left her blood alone because she's already destroying herself.

Gordon glares up at me, his voice a low rasp. "You can't… kill us…"

I'm a little unsettled by his claim, and even more disconcerted by the darkening hue rippling across his face and hands where his skin is visible.

My intention was to make them all pass out. I haven't quite succeeded and maybe I *can't* kill them this way, but I've done enough to get myself the hell out of here, and that's what matters.

My detour is over.

I slip off my heels, gripping them in my hand as I sprint toward the glass foyer, navigating it as fast as I can before reaching the elevator.

The doors open far too slowly for my liking.

Behind me, the Scorn are starting to move.

I dart into the elevator and turn back to the room. The unmarked Scorn are still down on their knees and several appear unconscious, their bodies crumpled on the floor, but the marked ones are rising to their feet—despite the fact that I'm still holding on to their blood.

The doors finally close and I shut down my power.

I need to conserve my energy for the fight with Tyler.

Exiting the elevator when it reaches the level of the dance floor, I race across the staff-only corridor and through the side door out into the service alley beside the club.

The moonlight is dull, the sky is covered in clouds, and the cobbled alley is dark. It's exactly the kind of night that dragon shifters would have welcomed when they were burdened with dragon shadows.

Releasing my wings, I shoot toward the rooftop, aiming for the eastern side.

I'm only halfway up when the service door below me bursts open and the nine marked Scorn pour into the alley. Niah and Gordon are at the front and they both look up, quickly spotting me.

The sound of beating wings within the alley reaches me just as I land on the rooftop, but it isn't the threat from below that concerns me now.

I hurry to the center of the flat space and take a moment to place my heels onto the ground. As I crouch, I glance at the far corner of the rooftop, where the nearby buildings cast darker shadows.

My armored belt lies there, where I left it earlier. It rests beneath an inconspicuous piece of canvas, which looks like nothing more than rubbish that wafted onto the building.

I sense the gold waiting for me to call it, and it gives me courage. So does the knowledge that I may not be able to see or sense them, but my family will also be making their way outside the building and will be prepared to fight the moment I need them.

As for now, the back of my neck prickles, my chest compresses, and ice trickles down my spine. A freezing wind moans around me, a low, droning sound, as a dark cloud spills across the sky like soot.

Ash floats down in front of me and it's like the sky is already on fire.

"Tyler," I whisper. "Show yourself."

CHAPTER THIRTY-SIX

The cloud of ash in the sky above me obliterates the moon and its light as the ash thickens and takes shape.

Dark wings and clawed hands form, black scales glistening across every inch of Tyler's body while charcoal-colored mist swirls around him.

He lands opposite me with a final sweep of his wings that sends an icy wind across me. We may as well be standing on a frozen lake, not on a rooftop, given the haze of frost rising from the surface beneath my feet.

Tyler folds his wings to his sides, where they drape so heavily that they scrape across the ground as he prowls toward me. His pure-black eyes rake down my form, a slow consideration.

"Sophia," he says, his voice like the whisper of wind through a dark cavern. "You came back to me."

I swallow my retort as the Scorn dragons appear from the alley, landing and folding back their wings. I'm not surprised to see that Niah's wings are a bright, candy pink like the color of her reptilian eyes.

She and the others keep to the edge of the rooftop, fanning

out around Tyler and me. They all take a knee and bow their heads to Tyler, but not so low that I miss the upward curve of their lips. It's as if a slow euphoria is quietly taking over each of them now that he's here.

"We thank you for the gift of your strength, master," Niah says.

Tyler ignores her, his dark eyes twinkling at me as he watches my response to his followers' actions.

I fight my fears as I face him, reminding myself that I'm not his to control anymore. Of course, I could pretend that I still want him. I could disarm him with lies, but the truth is important to me.

"I'm here to stop you," I say. "By whatever means necessary."

He gives a soft laugh, as if he considers me to be foolish. "You can't stop me, Sophia. Nothing can." He gestures at our surroundings. "Darkness is everywhere. *I* am everywhere." His forehead crinkles as he closes the distance between us. "I'm in every dark thought. Every doubt. Every moment of self-loathing. I'm timeless and eternal. There is no stopping me."

He reaches out to run a clawed finger through my hair, drawing the light-brown strands forward. "Life is nothing without death."

His head lowers to mine, his inky gaze falling to my lips as he hovers inches away from me. "You're nothing without me."

I consider his gestures, his words, all intended to make me feel small and insignificant, but I am so much more, and I know it now.

The closer he gets to me, the more in control I feel. At the same time, there's a growing hum within my mind and it feels like the sensation I experienced before I reached for Lana while she was unconscious.

The tidal wave of power is building within me. When I experienced it before, it felt destructive. A current dragging me down to where I'd suffocate, crash against the rocks, and be destroyed.

CLAIM THE LIGHT

This wave I'm experiencing now could very well destroy me too. It's pulling me toward Tyler and I might have thought *he* was making it happen, but the dark core within me is demanding that I make contact—just like I needed to hold Lana's hand when she lay on the feathery bed.

But touching Tyler now is a far more dangerous act. The last time I made contact when he was covered in ash, the dust turned my skin to ice, numbed me, and left me nearly unconscious.

I've taken a long moment to reply and now Tyler's forehead pinches and his head tilts, a slightly puzzled expression. I suppose he thought I'd either respond with anger to his taunts or be hurt by them.

It seems to disconcert him when I remain calm and quiet. Instead of speaking, I lift my hand toward his chest and the location of his heart. He's standing so close to me that I need to angle my arm carefully, my palm slipping between us and hovering an inch from his black-scaled body.

The icy temperature rising from his skin is nothing short of deathly.

I choose my question carefully. "What has this power done to you, Tyler?"

The crease in his forehead deepens and the press of his lips becomes hard. "You think I'm weak."

I smother my sigh. Of all the interpretations he could draw from my question, he leaped to one he would consider the most derogatory.

"Far from it," I say.

As I speak, the warmth of my power grows within my body. A reaction to his continued presence. When I first encountered him in his new form, my power was completely caged. Over the last week, I've opened my heart to it and embraced it, but only to a point, and now…

I need to test its limits. I need to know how far I can go.

A faint glow of energy is building around me, the air

becoming brighter, pushing at the black mist that wafts around him.

Our two powers are very slowly colliding.

I dare to edge forward, the warmth of my body pushing at the coldness of his. "Your dark energy has the capacity to obliterate everything around it," I say. "*Nearly.*"

His eyes narrow sharply. "Nearly?"

Again, he takes my words—a statement of fact this time—as an insult.

"You said it yourself," I continue quietly. "Life is nothing without death. But for death to exist, first there must be life."

I take a quick breath, preparing myself for the huge risk I'm about to take.

Then I step in and close the gap between us.

My palm connects with his chest. I brace for my hand to sink into his shadowy body. I'm prepared for the sharp cut of his ash across my skin and the freezing cold of his power that could pull me down into despair.

But the moment my hand meets his chest, warmth bursts through me.

It's instinctive, and I'm shocked that I don't have to call it.

Heat bursts beneath my palm and shoots out across his form, transforming his ash in an instant.

My fingers now splay against very human-looking skin, which extends for at least three inches in every direction around my hand.

His eyes fly wide, and he gives a roar that sounds like pain.

Leaping back from me, he lands in a cloud of soot several paces away, crouching in swaths of dark mist as he glances at his chest.

I'm a little dismayed to see that it has returned to ash, but I'm certain I can turn him to flesh again.

I can make him vulnerable.

At the edges of the rooftop, the Scorn have lurched forward, some toward me and some toward Tyler.

His hand shoots out and he snarls at them. "Stay back! I'll handle this."

I'm conscious that my family will also be watching—and waiting for my signal to enter the fight.

Not yet.

I made them promise not to join this confrontation unless I was outnumbered. I'm painfully aware of how hard it will be for them to wait. They're all incredibly strong dragons who have never backed away from a battle. I can practically *feel* Micah's rage beating down around me like the shield he wants to be for me.

But I need them to give me space to test my limits, while also providing the assurance that I'm not alone.

I don't waste another second, storming toward Tyler as I give a cry to my dragon's gold within my mind.

Come to me!

The golden belt is a blur at the edge of my vision as it rises up and shoots toward me.

Within a heartbeat, it has wrapped around my waist, the pieces unfolding as I continue to move. Plates of armor rise up across my chest and down my thighs, molding to my shape and cinching my dress close to my skin. The helmet wraps across my cheeks and forehead, along with the back of my head, fitting neatly around me without obscuring my vision.

Then the final piece—the dagger that the gold created for me—flies into my right hand.

I'm gratified by the hint of alarm in Tyler's expression before he covers his reaction. "You think you can fight me, Sophia? You're fooling yourself. I'll crush you like the worthless trash you are."

I don't deign to respond to his taunt. Micah taught me to stay focused, to see my target and all of their vulnerabilities without the emotional crap that comes with who they are.

Tyler is an opponent to me now. Not the man who once controlled where I went, what I wore, and often what I ate.

He is a creature of bones and flesh with wings, a chest, arms, and legs, all of which can be broken. If I force them to become solid, living matter first.

My left hand flies out as I make contact with Tyler's still-outstretched arm. Power bursts through me, his arm becomes solid, and I upset his balance and nick his arm with the blade at the same time.

Blood splatters the rooftop and his eyes widen.

I don't stop.

Flipping the blade so that it points toward my elbow and allows my right fist to connect with his chest as fully as possible, I follow up with a flurry of blows that force his body into flesh and take the brunt of my new strength.

He rallies and fights back, but I evade his hits and my armor protects me from the rare punches that he manages to land. He may have acquired his combat skills in a gym, but he wasn't taught by a Grudge dragon who was forced to survive by his fists.

I beat Tyler around the rooftop, cutting his arms and legs, nearly slashing his wings, until I manage to fully upset his balance and knock him onto his back.

He lands heavily, but I'm in position, straddling him as we fall, one knee bent to take the impact without breaking my own bones.

I've switched the dagger to my right hand and now my left presses to the center of his chest.

Intense warmth pools between us, cutting through the ash covering Tyler's chest and all the way across his shoulders. He is living skin. Muscles. And a heart with beats that thud through my palm.

My dagger is poised above his chest, and even though his hands are wrapped around mine and he grunts with the effort to keep my blade at bay, he doesn't seem to have the strength to stop me.

I'm conscious of the Scorn rushing to their feet again, but their reaction only angers Tyler.

"Stay the fuck back!" he roars at Niah. Then to me, in a snarl, he adds, "Get the fuck on with it, Sophia. Let's see if I still have a heart."

He lets go of the dagger.

I'm startled by his move, but the force I'm exerting on the blade drives it down.

It slices through his skin, right into his heart.

Thump.

He stiffens beneath me. His breathing slows, and the light within his eyes grows darker, like an encroaching night.

My chest is heaving, my muscles are aching, and my hands shake.

I have nothing left to say to him as I wait for his heart to stop beating.

I wait…

And wait…

The tension around his mouth smooths out. The hint of pain in his eyes fades. The dagger rests deep in his chest and his heart has stopped beating, but he continues to breathe, and now his sigh cuts through the growing confusion in my mind.

"I've been trying to tell you, Sophia," he whispers. "You can't kill me."

No. It's impossible.

His heart is real. I used my power to change his form from ash to flesh. The dagger cut right through it.

He should be dead.

A soft chuckles leaves his lips as I stare down at him.

Dread is rising within me, stronger than my fear of my own power, and it's threatening to crush me.

His chuckle becomes a laugh. A cruel, victorious laugh. "Silly Sophia. I tried to warn you. While there is life, there is also death."

He pulls the dagger from my numb fingers, sliding it right out of his chest.

There isn't a drop of blood on it.

I struggle to speak as fear rises up within me. So much fear. "But… how…?"

He drops the dagger to the rooftop with a clatter and I don't yet have the focus of mind to break through my shock and call it back to me.

Tyler wraps his hands around my shoulders and, if it weren't for my armor, his claws would be breaking my skin.

"Let me spell it out for you, sweetheart," he says, his voice becoming hard. "Your power is life. My power is death. While you live, so do I."

CHAPTER THIRTY-SEVEN

Tyler's arms close around me and he lurches upright, lifting me off my feet.

If I weren't in shock, I would have reacted already. *Should* have reacted already because one of his hands closes around my neck, and his other fist collides with my cheekbone.

The force of his punch to my face is so great that the armor caves. The pain is like a burning rod cracking across my cheek and it's only because of the protective layer of gold that my bones don't break.

Of course, he would have been counting on it, since it seems he needs to keep me alive.

The impact of his fist propels me out of his arms and I land heavily on the rooftop.

I have to get up.

Get the fuck up!

But my moment of shock, of collapsing on this rooftop, must have been the final straw for my family.

Multiple shadows drop across the rooftop as Lana, Beatrix, and Micah appear in the air above me. Their wings are a flurry of black, red, and silvery-gray as they storm down toward Tyler.

Micah reaches him first, his fist connecting with Tyler's jaw.

Tyler reacts instantly, disintegrating into a cloud of ash that billows outward, and Micah's attack sails right through the soot.

Micah isn't deterred, rising up again and soaring down for another attack.

Lana and Beatrix have veered to the side, aiming for the Scorn, who are now racing toward the fight.

My family's attack is swift and sure.

I've barely made it back to my feet before Lana drives her glaive through Niah's chest, and Beatrix deftly stabs Gordon through the throat. The Scorn dragons' deaths are so quick and brutal that it takes my breath away.

Both Scorn fall to their knees as Lana and Beatrix turn to the attacking dragons beside them, meting out death to another two shifters within seconds.

Confident that Lana and Beatrix will watch my back, I'm about to turn back to Tyler when my focus is drawn to Niah.

She should have fallen to the ground already, but she hasn't.

There should be blood pouring down her chest, but there isn't.

I take a quick, disbelieving step toward her, but my heart is already sinking.

Ash wafts up from Niah's wound, and from Gordon's throat, and they raise their heads, their eyes completely black for the seconds it takes them to stand up.

They blink, and the darkness is gone, but so are their wounds.

It will only be seconds before Lana and Beatrix realize what's happened, but in those seconds, the awful reality of Tyler's power crashes down on me.

It's suddenly clear to me why the keeper of dark magic was so certain I would want to keep the ash. And now, my mother's earlier cry also makes sense. *"I have no future unless he chooses me. I will be left to perish."*

Tyler's power is invincibility.

He can't be killed and neither can those he marks.

Of course, this may well include Micah, Lana, and Beatrix, but it's not a power they would welcome. Even now, I sense Micah's movements slowing, his hits becoming sluggish, every speck of ash covering his skin destroying his heart and mind.

I sense his life fading. The cold chill of death.

All while I live.

I take a step back, scoop up my golden knife, and press it back into place on the armor. Then I quietly ask the armor to retract because I need to expose as much of my body as I can.

I sense its reluctance. It takes moments to obey me, but I command it more firmly. "Thank you for protecting me, but now I need you to stay with my family."

The gold peels off my body, plate by plate, returning to the shape and size of a belt, which I unclip and place on the ground.

Across the rooftop, Tyler has remained a cloud of dust, his gleeful face appearing and disappearing with every failed attempt on Micah's part to subdue him.

"There's no shame in surrendering, Grudge," Tyler calls to him. "You will only be one of many."

Micah ignores him for a moment, wobbling in the air opposite him, appearing on the cusp of attacking again, but he has paused.

His fists are dripping with ash. His skin is dark gray—not the silvery color of his dragon scales. His shoulders are hunched, and his wings are held low.

I suddenly realize that I spoke aloud when I commanded my gold to stay with my family and, even in the din of battle, Micah would have been able to hear me.

I tip my head back to meet his eyes.

He can't possibly read my thoughts, or know what I'm about to do, but the way he looks at me tells me he senses the finality that's settling within my heart.

His wings are shivering, he's clearly struggling to stay aloft, and his voice is raw. "Whatever you're thinking, don't do it, Sophia. There has to be another way."

There isn't.

I try to smile through the burn of my tears. "I love you, Micah Grudge. I'll miss the life we could have had together, but I'll see it in my dreams."

With that, I charge toward Tyler, my feet flying, my power bursting through every limb in my body.

My breathing is calm, even though my heartbeat is jumping all over the fucking place.

I collide with Tyler's ash, my power forcing him to become solid. I sense his sharply indrawn breath and the way he tries to wrench himself out of my hold, but my arms have clamped around his naked chest.

All I have to do is push him down.

Down through the dark.

The keeper of old magic told me I have a knack of finding cracks into their realms, but this time, I plan on *making* one.

As the force of my shove propels us both a few feet across the rooftop, I throw my right hand forward, reaching into the space between spaces, feeling for the energy I know is there.

My fingertips brush the edge of the vast nothingness that exists within our world, and that's all I need.

Closing my fist, I tear a rip in the wall of the dark keeper's realm and take Tyler with me.

Into oblivion, where I intend to destroy us both.

CHAPTER THIRTY-EIGHT

We fall forward into darkness.

Tyler's body cushions my landing, the air audibly knocked from his lungs as he lands beneath me.

I spring up and away from him, no longer needing to keep his body solid. In fact, his ashen shape belongs in this place.

I release my wings and fly backward, putting a solid five paces between us.

He jumps to his feet with a roar. "Where the fuck are we?"

"Where we belong," I say, swiping at the hot tears on my cheeks and fighting the constriction in my throat. "An oblivion that exists outside the knowledge of most supernaturals. The darkest of spaces, where the bodies of the dead can be picked over and their magic claimed."

Tyler turns left and right, his black wings folded against his sides, while his wild eyes take in our surroundings.

"You can't escape," I say. "Not without my help. And I will never help you."

He rages toward me. "Take me back!"

"No."

His fist lands on my face, rattling my bones and sending me

flying backward. I land on the cold, marble floor, too dazed to get up. Staring at the endless night above me.

The pain doesn't last long. It seems that my body is becoming better and better at healing itself.

Tyler's footfalls are coming closer, but I take a moment to lie still and catch my breath.

Specks of ash waft across my vision and I follow their path to my left.

I'm puzzled when the ash gravitates toward an uneven mound that lies a short distance away from me. A few more flecks of soot join them. They float in the same magnetic fashion that the ash wafted toward the keeper's body when I encountered him. But he isn't here.

I squint at the strange shape the ash has settled onto, trying to make sense of the shadows, before I finally recognize the folds of the keeper's cloak.

The elemental keeper warned me that this place will now become like a vacuum. She told me not to stay long or it could destroy me.

Well, that's what I'm counting on.

Tyler grabs me and hauls me upright, his face ugly in anger, but I knock his hand to the side, landing a quick sequence of blows to his chest that force him to release me.

I'm not in shock anymore and I'm prepared to fight back for as long as I must for the energy in this place to trap us both.

Every time I touch Tyler's body, he becomes solid flesh that can be hurt and bruised and I make the most of the moments I have before he lets me go with yet another howl of pain.

He roars at me. "Take me back!"

I repeat. "No."

With a growl, he spreads his wings and tries to fly upward, but he doesn't make it farther than the height of my shoulders before he seems to hit a barrier. His arms strain, he grunts with effort, and then he drops back to the marble floor.

A flurry of ash wafts away from his body, all of it having lifted off him while he was thrashing.

Each speck glides through the air toward the keeper's cloak.

He doesn't appear to have seen it, and he won't understand what it is. His hand darts out toward his own loose ash, his fist closing around the nearest flecks before he tries to press them back to his chest.

They simply float away from him again.

Interesting.

I catch one of the flecks in my hand, feeling the chill within the substance, cold as a little cube of ice.

My forehead creases when my fingertips suddenly feel wet.

My hand snaps open. The ash is gone.

Instead, bright-blue snowflakes rest in my palm, their delicate shapes melting against the warmth of my skin.

I blink at them in surprise as the water drips through my fingertips, the liquid forming sparkling droplets in the air.

What just happened?

Opposite me, Tyler draws himself upright, his chest heaving, threats spewing from his mouth that might have once scared the shit out of me.

"I'll fucking kill you, Sophia. If you don't do what I want, I'll break every bone in your body until you can do nothing but scream."

I let his threats wash over me, my focus on the droplets of water now dancing in the air. Droplets I created.

"Tell me again about the balance between life and death, light and dark."

My sudden command silences him. A deep scowl forms on his face. "Light and dark must always be in balance," he snaps. "If life exists, so must death. Your life guarantees mine."

"Yes," I murmur. "For death to happen, first there must be life. But what if life isn't what you expect?"

I catch another fleck of ash and close my hand around it,

feeling the sharpness of its edges like rough pebbles. When I open my hand, glittering rocks rest in my palm.

Oh...

The picture of my life is coming together in my mind like a puzzle, all of the important pieces becoming clear.

This power I've been caging...

I close my eyes, remembering when I tried to heal Lana. I felt all of the life in my heart. Too much life and at its core was a wild energy. A power without boundaries that, once released, could cause irrevocable damage.

I remember the flash of fear in Lana's eyes when she asked me to stop, as if I'd somehow struck at her very being, and I recall the way she described what she felt as something *beyond*.

Tyler has risen to his feet, his fists ready at his sides, his black eyes fixated on me, but he doesn't compare to the threat within me.

"You were wrong about me," I say quietly. "Lana was, too. She said my power is life. You thought the same. But that's only partially correct."

He's shaking his head, obstinate in the face of my assertion. "I'm not wrong. I was never wrong about you, Sophia."

I stare at the pebbles in my hand. Objects that came into being with a mere thought on my part because I wanted one thing to become another. I wanted the ash to change.

"The dragon's light is a source of evolution," I say, studying Tyler's swirling form. "Lana asked me what impact it would have on a dragon who craved power and delighted in cruelty."

I shake my head with a quiet, unhappy laugh. "We were so focused on you. But what *I* should have been asking was what might happen to a dragon who was desperate for change."

Tyler is eyeing me warily now. Maybe, in the midst of all his prideful thoughts, his instincts are finally alerting him to the fact that he's in danger.

For the first time in my life, I don't care about his response because whatever he chooses to say or do, it won't change what matters—the choice I now face.

I can unleash the power within me and save myself, or I can continue caging it and die in this place.

"I was afraid of my power," I say. "I didn't embrace it like you embraced yours. I avoided it, despite how deeply I craved it." I take a step toward him, my anger rising, the pain in my heart increasing. "Despite how deeply I *deserved* it."

He inches away from me, all the glittering mist swirling around him making him appear wraith-like as he glides backward.

Dropping the pebbles to the ground with a startling clatter, I spread my wings, testing their strength, only a hint of what they're truly capable of. "Now I understand that, yes, I should be *very* fucking afraid of my power."

I make my choice.

Finally, I decide to shake off the shackles of my old life, the perceptions of strength that plagued me from the day I was born. Finally, I accept that I deserve to be loved and respected and treated with kindness. That I can find happiness in things that don't cost anything. That I can give love and expect my love to be valued and cherished in return.

Right there and then, I strip off my dress and underwear, since I'll need them intact later.

I expect Tyler to comment on the fact that I've removed my clothing, to make some degrading remark, but it seems he's fixated on my claim that my power should be feared.

"Your power is nothing." His lips twist with derision. "Life is weak. It's fragile. I can crush it in a heartbeat. I can crush *you* in a heartbeat."

He blusters when I don't react to his taunts, screaming at me. "You're nothing without me!"

"I'm *everything* without you," I say, and then I set my power free.

CHAPTER THIRTY-NINE

My perspective changes as my body transforms, my line of sight rising higher as the shift consumes me.

Cerulean-blue wings spread at my sides, growing in length and width proportionate to my chest, which expands exponentially. My arms and legs and neck thicken and my tailbone extends, and all of it happens so smoothly that there's no pain.

Only a blissful release as my body takes the shape of the dragon I want to be.

A full dragon shift.

Tyler stumbles backward. "Impossible! No dragon can shift like that anymore."

"I can," I rumble, marveling at the deep growl in my voice as I lower my enormous head and consider his... well... rather puny body.

My claws alone are as large as his forearms and my tail could slap him a mile in any direction.

I consider my scales for a moment. Not quite the color I want...

So I change them, lightening the shade to an icy blue.

At that, freezing air frosts across my back and forms a flurry of snowflakes. They lift around me, sparkling and new, before I warm my breath, breathe out, and turn the snowflakes into rain.

It patters to the marble floor.

Tyler tries once again to rise into the air, frantically beating his wings. Despite his ability to move across the floor, he still can't fly.

"What the fuck *are* you?" he shouts. "How are you doing this?"

"My power isn't life," I say, lowering my head to his again and baring my teeth. "It's evolution."

He's shaking his head, a vigorous denial, but I expected nothing less.

My body shivers as I will myself back to my former humanoid shape, but this time, I give myself cerulean-blue hair and a violet-colored dragonfly tattoo on my left shoulder. Just for the hell of it.

I pull my clothing back on, briefly testing my power on it, and confirming that I have no effect on inanimate objects.

"I cried out for change, so that's what I was given," I say. "I can change any aspect of myself. I can evolve back and forth according to my whim. But the thing is…"

I narrow my eyes at Tyler, who has regained a little of his bravado now that I'm not a towering dragon anymore. "I believe I can force you to change, too."

Heading straight toward him, I stretch out my hand.

He backs away, slowly at first, and then faster as my approach pushes him in an arc around the dark space.

"I could give you the ability to fully shift," I say. "Or the power to breathe fire. Or I could make your heart kind. But I won't do any of those things because you don't deserve them. All you deserve is what you chose for yourself: death."

He digs in his heels, snarling back at me. "You can't kill me. Not while you also live. I proved it."

"True," I say, taking a quick glance at the cloak on the floor, which now rests at my feet. "I can't kill you, but I can give you what you want. All the dark magic you could possibly crave. For eternity."

I crouch and pick up the keeper's black cloak from the ground.

Now *this* is not an inanimate object.

The power in this cloak is ancient, visceral, and filled with pain and sacrifice, the kind of magic that should never be messed with.

"This cloak belonged to a powerful creature of dark magic," I say. "It's my gift to you, Tyler, for helping me see what I am."

His forehead creases and he hesitates, clearly thrown by my offer.

I'm sure he won't remain quiet for long, so I glide up to him quickly, sweetness dripping from my tongue. "A powerful cloak for a powerful dragon."

I press the material to his chest with one hand and, at the same time, brush the fingertips of my free hand across his heart.

It's enough for my will to take effect.

With a single thought, I remove his memories of me and of who he used to be, leaving his mind empty of attachments.

But I refuse to shield him from the pain I'm certain he's about to feel.

Of its own accord, the cloak slips around his neck and shoulders, attaching itself to his body.

His eyes widen and a scream leaves his lips as the material settles over his wings, forcing them inward and compressing them against his sides. Every speck of ash and dust that was covering his body sucks inward, thumping audibly against his chest.

His body seems to implode for a moment and then his figure stabilizes, now tall and thin and hardly there.

His scream fades and, when he falls silent, a band of dark light appears around his eyes. A blindfold that will keep him from seeking a life beyond his new purpose. It isn't a crown as such, but it will hold all of the dark magic it needs to hold, along with every other part of Tyler's body.

"Well, hello there, new keeper of dark magic," I say.

A shudder passes through him, and then he blinks at me, as if he's trying to place me.

His voice echoes, wraith-like and perplexed. "You should not be here, dragon. You are not dead."

"No, I'm not," I whisper, stepping away from him. "I'm very much alive."

With a single thought, I will myself into the shape of a dragonfly, a large, golden one. My dress floats to the floor now that my form is smaller, but I give myself a pair of clawed feet and scoop up the material with them.

Then I dart upward through the darkness to the future that's waiting for me.

~

I shoot upward into a strange calm.

The fight on the rooftop I left behind looks like it must have spilled across multiple roofs in the time that I was gone.

Dark scorch marks sear the surfaces around me, a sign of the savage burn of dragon's flame.

Golden bullets circle the air nearby. In the center of the cage the bullets create, Niah stands with two other Scorn dragons. On the rooftop behind them, the remaining Scorn are gathered in a tight circle, all of them on their knees. Another circle of golden bullets zips around them, clearly forcing them to stay where they are.

Gisela stands beside the first group, her hands outstretched, and I sense the energy streaming between her and the bullets, which are keeping Niah from making a move.

Dane stands near the second group, his hands also outstretched.

I'm not surprised to see the rest of my family dispersed

around the two groups of captives. Lana and Callan stand near Gisela, while Beatrix, Felix, Isaac, and Lana's mother, Melisma, stand with Dane.

Isaac warned me that he wouldn't be able to keep Callan from this fight if Lana's life was in danger.

They're all sweaty and breathing heavily, their shoulders tense and their weapons raised.

But it's Micah who draws my attention.

He paces back and forth along the far edge of the rooftop I'm currently hovering over. His location puts him between the two groups of captives.

A single body lies at his feet.

I recognize Gordon, the Scorn with the patterns shaved across his head, his neck twisted at a bad angle.

His death indicates two things.

The first is that Tyler's power must have been destroyed when I condemned him to the oblivion. The Scorn are no longer invincible. And I can only hope that also means that Micah, Beatrix, and Lana are free from Tyler's power.

The second thing is that Micah may have been responsible for the death that ended the fight. As soon as one of the Scorn died, I suspect the others would have surrendered quickly.

"Who's next?" Micah roars, his voice raw with pain. "Who will fight me?"

My heart cracks.

Callan warned me what would happen if something happened to Lana, but I should have considered what Micah would do if he'd thought he'd lost me.

It looks like he'd be willing to walk through the wall of golden bullets and snatch Niah out of there, just for the chance to fight someone. The bullets streaming around the Scorn suddenly seem more like a protective barrier than a restraint.

Closer to me, Callan exchanges a look with Lana and I read their unspoken messages clearly. They're trying to decide which one of them will tackle Micah—literally.

I begin to call out, but I forgot I was still in dragonfly form. And, even with my silken dress hanging from my little feet, I won't attract attention from my location.

For a heartbeat, I consider the danger I pose to all of them.

If I accidentally use my power, the consequences could be catastrophic. They are all perfect in their imperfections and I would never want to change any of them.

I'm filled with self-doubt as I hover quietly at the edge of the group.

I have a choice to make. One that's tearing my heart apart.

Can I return to my family?

Am I a threat to them now?

My power came into existence when the dragon's light was brought into the world. In the moments that followed, all I wanted was peace, but it was the dragon's light that made this happen.

Suddenly, I realize what I need to do, and I'm determined not to do it alone.

With my heart in my throat, I fly around the back of the group, heading toward Micah, remaining in my dragonfly form so I can reach him without being intercepted.

The moonlight shines down around me, its brightness another sign that Tyler's power is gone.

I land in the space directly in front of Micah, letting go of my dress in the air and dropping my dragonfly body down through it. As I will myself back into my humanoid form, my arms extend through the armholes of my dress and it neatly covers my body once more.

The shift happens seamlessly and in a stream of light.

Micah comes to an abrupt halt as I appear right in front of him. His hair is disheveled, his shirt is torn, and his long pants are badly scuffed. It all reminds me so much of the first time I saw him that I'm transported back to that moment in an instant.

The memory of the rain and his wolfish scent will stay with me forever.

His rage beats across me, and I sense how broken he is. A dragon with cracks in his heart.

Then he focuses on me and the pain in his face eases. "Sophia."

I want to take away his hurt, but I clamp down on my power. Sadness is important. It's meant to be felt. Even if every part of me wants never to feel it again.

He steps toward me and I badly want to hug him, but I hold up my hand, keeping him at bay.

My palm is inches from his chest but I won't make contact until I know I'm not a threat to him.

"Micah," I say. "I need you to trust me."

"I do." His declaration is spoken without hesitation and makes my eyes burn. "Tell me what you need."

"You have to keep your distance from me," I say, my voice wobbling a little. "But only for now. Not forever."

His jaw tenses, but he gives me a firm nod.

Beatrix has edged toward me on my left, while on my right, Lana has also gravitated in my direction.

Lana's blue eyes are wide as her gaze takes me in, and I have no doubt that she can sense the immense energy within me. She gestures to the others to stay back. "Give Sophia space."

I incline my head in a thankful nod.

She returns it with a gentle smile. She, of all dragons, will understand what it's like to struggle with the nature of one's inner self.

I take a moment to sense the location of my armor, safe on the other side of the rooftop but it, too, could be harmed by me, since it's living metal. I send a mental command to it to go to Lana when I leave this place. I trust that she'll keep it safe.

Turning to the others, I raise my voice and speak to all of them. "Tyler's gone. His power is destroyed. He's never coming back. The Scorn clan is now without an alpha."

My focus moves to Gisela.

I'm determined that the peace I craved will be achieved tonight.

Once and for all.

"Gisela Scorn," I say. "Do you claim the right to lead your clan?"

She holds her head high, her blue-black hair shining and her golden bullets glittering in the air. "I do."

My voice becomes hard. "There is a right of challenge. Does any dragon here wish to fight to the death for this right?"

Within the circle of bullets, Niah is the only one who twitches.

Gisela lifts her hand and the bullets return to her side, leaving Niah free to move.

"Cousin?" Gisela asks.

Niah's lips press together, the corners of her mouth turning down. Her chest is rising and falling faster than it should be, her forehead deeply creased. If she weren't a Scorn dragon, I'd believe she was distressed.

"I've woken up from darkness," she says, her voice rising. "My mind was caged within my own body, and I was compelled to act without autonomy. I had no control. In fact, I've never had fucking control. Not once. Now you're asking me to submit to being ruled again." She thumps her chest. "I *cannot*. Not when I finally have the chance to rule myself."

At her declaration, my family tenses, and Gisela's expression is fast becoming resolved to the inevitable battle.

Across the way, Dane is watching Gisela closely—watching her back—but it's Felix who makes a move.

He has always been quiet but scarily so. A dragon of few words and a sharp mind.

His hair hangs loose around his face as he steps around Dane, releases his wine-red wings, and lands in front of Niah.

She tenses but doesn't back away.

"Niah," he says, greeting her quietly. "Do you remember me?"

She considers him warily, her lips tightening briefly before she answers. "Of course I know who you fucking are."

"No," he says gently. "Do you remember when we were little kids?"

Her face falls and her eyes suddenly fill with tears. She looks away, blinking rapidly, but the tears trickle down her cheeks.

I don't know a lot about Felix's history. I know that he and Beatrix were born with strength that rivaled that of the Scorn family, who had ruled over their clan for generations. Beatrix and Felix were a threat to the existing hierarchy, so when they were only seven years old, they were sent on a mission to steal from Callan's father. It was expected that Callan's father would kill them, but he didn't. He gave them a new home instead.

When Felix waits for an answer, Niah tips up her chin, sniffing angrily through her tears. "I remember you didn't come back. I remember you weren't there to protect me. I had to protect myself."

"Not anymore," he says. "You don't have to live like that any longer." He takes a step closer to her. "The boundaries between clans are coming down. There's family waiting for you if you're willing to help pull down the walls."

"I don't..." Her forehead crinkles. "I can't just..."

He holds out his hand to her. "Just one small step. That's all I'm asking."

She stares at his outstretched hand for the longest moment.

"I'm here for you, Niah," he says, so softly I almost miss it.

Her expression crumples for a moment before she rallies and reaches out. She clasps his hand. It's the briefest hold before she withdraws, but it seems to be enough for Felix.

He gives her a silent nod.

Niah's chest rises with a deeply indrawn breath before she turns back to Gisela. "I will not challenge you. I ask only that you let all of us live."

"Granted," Gisela says before she, too, raises her voice. She's barely fourteen, but she commands her clan like a queen. "This is a new day for the Scorn. There will be changes."

She pauses before the smallest smile touches her lips. "Good changes that will only make us stronger." Her eyes meet mine across the distance, then her focus shifts to Lana and Callan. "Never again will we go to war with our own people."

Niah takes a knee and the other Scorn are quick to follow.

Across the way, Dane removes his bullets from around the second group before he exchanges a quick glance with Gisela. He has pledged his life to her and I'm certain that together, they'll face any new challenges that might come their way.

Now, my focus returns to Micah. He hasn't moved from my side but he kept his distance like I asked.

I hate to leave my family without the answers about me and Tyler that I'm sure they're craving, but I know what I need to do next. My speech is quiet. "Micah, can you take me to the dragon's light?"

"It's safe in Grudge territory," he says. "Callan told me where they hid it. I can take you there."

He spreads his wings and lifts into the air.

I rise to meet him, deliberately making my wings a darker color so I won't attract attention in the sky.

His eyes widen a little at the change that flows over my wings, but he doesn't ask questions.

Together, we fly away into the night.

CHAPTER FORTY

*G*rudge territory is hidden well.

I never would have guessed that it's located within a maze of old tunnels hidden beneath a human prison. It also brings home to me the harshness of Micah's upbringing. Not that he didn't have love in his life, but he was surrounded by poverty—and thrived in the face of it.

We meet Micah's beta, Leon, where he's standing guard at the entrance. I keep my distance from the older dragon with the wavy hair, but Micah bear-hugs him.

"Welcome back," Leon says. To me, he gives a respectful nod.

When Micah explains where we're going, Leon waves us through, telling us he'll stay at the entrance in case the others return soon. He'll make sure we continue to have the space we need.

After that, we pass through the main living area, where we find Zahra and Emika asleep in front of the fireplace. Zahra is half-propped up in a chair, as if she was trying to stay awake.

Emika is curled up in her mother's lap. Her sleep appears deep and I sense her peace. Until the dragon's light was restored, old dragon souls were reborn in us, over and over again, and Emika's dragon was one of the oldest souls. A heavy burden to carry.

The stress of the last week would have been intense for both of them, so we tiptoe past and let them sleep.

At the exit to the living area, Micah takes a lamp from the wall and carries it with us, lighting our way through a series of tunnels until we reach a room that feels colder than the others, like it's set deep within the ground.

Micah keeps his distance from me, respecting my wishes, but I sense his growing tension every time he looks at me.

I wish I could say something—*anything*—to dispel his concerns, but it's taking all my concentration to keep my power constrained.

The room we've entered has stone walls carved at regular intervals into rectangles. It takes me a moment to realize that it's a crypt, and that the large, rectangular box in the center of it is a coffin.

Engravings cover both the coffin and the walls. They appear to be the names of dragons, some in writing I recognize and others I can't easily read.

One bears the name of Solomon Grudge, Micah's father.

Micah takes up position against the wall near the door as I make my way toward the round object wrapped in cloth resting on top of the coffin.

Carefully, I unwrap the velvet cover to reveal the diamond within it.

The dragon's light.

It's the size of my fist and it gleams gently in the dark.

Its true origins are a mystery. All we know is that it was created in the time of the Vanem Dragon and the Twilight Queen. It was covered in dragon's gold before it was given to the dragons, so, as far as we can tell, they thought it was made of pure gold and never knew what was really inside it.

Lana expressed a theory that this diamond may have been someone's heart.

I peer at the stone in the hopes that I can understand its secrets simply by being near it.

The diamond merely glints back at me.

"Why?" I whisper, my desperation growing. "Why would you give me this power?"

The light within the stone flickers.

I reach toward it, passing my hand through the rays that are glinting upward.

The moment I connect with them, light bursts around us.

At the side of the room, Micah gives a shout and flings his arm over his eyes.

I leap backward, terrified that I've broken the diamond. Quickly, I adjust the nature of my eyesight so I can see despite the brightness around me.

I gasp.

While Micah continues to shield his eyes, I can now clearly see the silhouette of a man.

He stands directly in front of me, his form transparent enough that the coffin and the stone are visible behind him, but solid enough that I can also make out the details of his face and clothing.

He's as tall as Callan, his broad shoulders held back and his arms corded with muscles. Clad in black pants that cling to powerful thighs, he is bare-chested and wears a pure-white pelt across his shoulders. It's held together by a golden chain at his chest. His hair is walnut brown and his eyes…

I'm startled by their color because I could be looking at Callan's eyes.

My question is a bare whisper as I struggle to breathe through my surprise. "Who are you?"

"My name is Nathaniel," he says. "But what matters more than my identity is the power I gave you."

I wasn't expecting him to get right to the point, but it's a fucking relief.

"I need to know why," I say, lifting my hands as if they were weapons. "If your purpose is to keep dragons in balance with their environment, why would you ever give such a chaotic power to anyone, let alone me?"

The corners of his mouth twitch upward. "Not chaotic in the right hands."

My brow furrows at his response, but he inclines his head in a conciliatory gesture. "You asked an important question and the answer is critical: Because there can no longer be only one dragon's light."

Warily, I study him. "I'm not sure I heard you correctly."

He exhales quietly before he folds his hands in front of himself. "I gave my heart as my last living act before the moment of my death, and I did it for purely selfish reasons."

I'm surprised by his admission and I say so.

Nathaniel gives me a rueful smile. "I was mortal. But the woman I love is eternal. By offering my heart to the dragons, my soul could continue on, and I could be with her for the eternity that she is destined to live."

His jaw clenches, and now I sense a deep rage, the kind that has burned for far too long. "When I was taken from the dragons, I was taken from her, too. Irreparable damage was done. To the dragons, to me, and to her. She lost me and, in the moment before I disappeared behind the veil, I felt her heart break. I needed to get back to her, but I couldn't."

My own heart is in my throat. I wish more than anything that Lana was hearing all of this. She had the chance to only briefly describe to me the fiery hell that the dragon's light was creating within the veil, the pure wrath that was close to burning through the veil's walls.

The man's voice is now a harsh snarl. "Never again will I allow my heart to be withheld from those who need it. That is why I have given you the same power that I control, Sophia Dragon."

I'm sure I'm no longer breathing. I'm certain my heart has stopped.

Somehow, Nathaniel has moved closer to me and now he stands only a step away. "That is why you are also *the dragon's light*."

I drag air into my chest, but he is relentless, although his voice quiets now. "Over time, you will pass your abilities to other dragons, and they will pass their light to other dragons, until the day when the light exists in every dragon's heart."

He steps back. "Then, I can be at peace."

Tears are falling down my cheeks. "I understand."

Even though the enormity of what he's saying is going to take me days, weeks, even months to process.

"How can I make sure I don't hurt anyone?" I ask. "This power is wild and my impulses could lead to destruction."

His expression softens. "It will be hard at first. You will need to seclude yourself completely until you can control your basic impulses. After that, you must follow the path of old magic. It will lead you to those who can help you more fully control and use your power."

I glance at Micah, remembering the way he spoke of his mother's family and how he wanted to connect with them. Now it seems that fate is guiding me in that direction.

Even so, I have doubts. "But what if—"

"The power you control is pure light magic, but it was created in the time of old magic and in accordance with the old laws," Nathaniel says. "You must find other beings of old magic, surround yourself with them, and learn their ways. Your power can't hurt them, and they can teach you how to control it. Then you can return to the dragons you love. Stronger. Calmer. At peace."

My heart swells. I want to believe him.

I want to believe that peace is finally within my reach.

I dare to ask him, "Why do you remind me of Callan Steele?"

He grins at me. "His mother was human, yes?"

I nod.

Nathaniel's chuckle is so contagious that I find myself smiling back at him.

"Well," he says, "my sister had many children, and they had many children, and so on through the ages. All the way to Callan's mother."

He peers at me as if he also wants to ask me something. "You encountered the keepers of magic."

I nod, although it didn't sound like a question.

"The woman I love met them, too." Again, the corners of his mouth twitch upward. "She told them to fuck off. Well, not in so many words, but the intent was the same."

My eyebrows rise, but I suddenly recall the conversation between the keepers of light and elemental magic. They spoke about a time when they'd all been drawn to the same place and a supernatural being had broken the natural order. I can only imagine it was the woman he's speaking of.

His humor fades, his speech becomes cautious, and now he asks the question I sensed he was building up to. "Will you do something for me, Sophia Dragon?"

I reply without hesitation. "Yes."

"Return my heart to the woman I love."

He spoke of this woman as having the power to live an eternal life, which must mean she's still out there. Somewhere.

"But... how will I find her?"

"Your path will take you to her." His eyes twinkle. "For she is also a creature of old magic."

Nathaniel's silhouette begins to fade, but his quiet smile remains burned into my memory. "Claim the light, Sophia Dragon. It will never lead you astray."

Then he's gone and the bright light vanishes.

Micah rises from his crouch, cautiously lifting his arm from his eyes.

Tears are streaming down my cheeks. Tears of hope, but also of responsibility. *Oh, what a thing to cry about.*

"Sophia?"

Nathaniel told me that I can't harm beings of old magic with my power, and old magic runs in Micah's blood. But he also carries light magic, so it might not be enough to protect him.

I edge toward him, feeling more terrified than I've ever felt in my life. I should reach out into the universe right now, tear a little opening into another realm, maybe into the old magic keeper's realm, and take myself away from Micah immediately. Stay away until I can return, in control of myself.

But my legs won't move.

Even though Micah couldn't see Nathaniel, I don't know how much he heard of our conversation, if anything.

Micah's expression smooths out, a look of quiet peace falling over his face as his gaze takes me in, running from my hair to my lips and up to my eyes.

"If you need me to wait for you, then I want you to know, I will wait a lifetime for you, Sophia," he says.

He steps toward me and doesn't stop.

"If you need me to take risks and throw myself into the path of danger, then I'll do that, too."

He's so close to me now, but still, I can't back away.

His arms close around me, arms that are full of acceptance as well as strength. His palm brushes my cheek and I'm holding my breath and shaking because any second now, I worry that I'll change something in him.

His voice lowers. "If you need me to stand at your side and be the person in your life who stays constant and true, I can do that too."

My eyes fill with tears as I trace the shape of his jaw, read the love in his eyes, and sense the power within him. A deep power, an old magic that's like a solid foundation beneath my feet.

Finally, I can exhale.

I press my lips to his, drinking in his kiss and all the heat that comes with it.

When I pull back, nothing has changed.

He's exactly the same. My mate. The dragon who loves me.

"Come with me," I whisper. "But don't tell Isaac I did this."

Micah's forehead crinkles. "Did what?"

I reach into the space beside me, sensing the energy in the air and the conduits between places of magic. I've progressed from stepping into realms by accident to ripping entry into them as acts of desperation, but now I'm beginning to understand what the lines of energy around them feel like. The boundaries between realms.

The dragon's light gave me this power—a power Nathaniel himself would have desperately needed when he was trapped in the veil—but he didn't have the body to carry out his wishes.

Now, the energy is mine.

I sense the boundary around the forest that lies within the prison veil and I slip my hand between the streams of energy surrounding it.

I bite my lip because I think we're about to enter it from quite high up.

"Get ready to spread your wings," I say as I close my arms around Micah and pull him sideways.

A single step takes us through.

"What the…?" His exclamation is snatched away in the wind as we plummet through the blue sky above the emerald-green forest.

His wings thump outward in time with mine.

I'm falling facing upward, but I change the aerodynamics of my wings to accommodate my position, only now recalling the way I've done this before. Although I didn't realize it at the time.

I twist a little to see that below us is the cabin. In the distance is the lake. But farther to the right is a large clearing in the middle of the forest, and I gesture to it. "There."

I turn, adjusting my wings again, and Micah follows me down to the mossy undergrowth.

He's barely folded away his wings before I collide with him, my lips finding his, my hands tugging at his shirt and pants.

I break contact with him, only to ask the question. "Do you want—"

He doesn't let me finish.

"Fuck, yes."

I moan against his lips, needing the connection we've waited for. I don't want to change a single part of myself for this. I am as I was, entirely and completely, with all my vulnerabilities and imperfections. My body just the same as when we stepped out into the moonlight together, and peace was within my grasp.

A peace I can now claim as mine.

Micah's hands tangle in my hair, his mouth burning a trail down my neck and to the tops of my breasts, which are still covered by my dress, although I'm not wearing a bra any longer.

He leans back to pull off his shirt and tug down his pants and underwear, kicking them both to the side.

Fuck, he's beautiful.

I step right back into his arms, needing to explore his chest, his cock, and every other part of him, but he's already pulling me down to the ground so that he's on his back and I'm straddling him.

He pushes my dress up to my hips, his hands stroking my thighs, slowing down a little, letting me take control.

My body was ready from the moment we landed in this clearing and I don't need or want to wait. Without hesitation, I position myself over him and he guides me down onto him.

My body fits around his, my muscles relaxing as he strokes his thumb across my core. Pleasure spirals through me, and I plant my hands on his chest, rise up, and then drive myself down.

I fight not to arch my back at the intensity of the wild need riding me now. Somehow, the more I let go, the more in control I feel, and I don't have a moment of doubt about what I want. Or a moment of fear that I could hurt him or damage the soil beneath us.

The wilder I am, the more my power calms.

The desire in his eyes nearly kills me as he groans. "Fuck, Sophia."

His voice triggers my climax and the release is so complete that I'm trembling and swaying on him while wave after wave of pleasure rocks me, only increasing as he crashes beneath me.

I don't think I could possibly go again, but he begins stroking my hips, nudging my dress up over my breasts, and rearing up beneath me to kiss them.

Heat builds between my legs again, a renewed need that makes me feel heavy and light at the same time.

I can't remove the dress fast enough.

Then we start again, slowly this time, exploring each other's bodies until I can't stand it any longer and take him inside me, draw his hand to my core, and seek all the pleasure he can give me.

He groans my name and I scream his, and then we collapse onto the grass again, our bodies glistening with sweat, our limbs entwined.

I can sense all the life around me and I haven't harmed any of it. Here, in this place, I feel like I fit and I'm determined that I will find that feeling no matter where I go or what challenges I face.

Minutes later, rustling in the forest around the clearing heralds the arrival of the deer. They appear around the edge of the space, their green bodies and mahogany antlers blending with their surroundings, but not so much that I can't see them.

I'm not alarmed.

I sense the peace within them. Particularly in the stag, who steps forward and lowers his antlers in my direction, one front leg extended. The others follow, their antlers nearly touching the ground.

When they lowered their antlers to me the first time I encountered them, I didn't realize what they were doing, but I do now.

Uncaring of my nakedness, I rise to my knees and incline my head, acknowledging the way they're bowing to me.

The stag raises his head, tosses his antlers gently, and then the deer disappear into the trees again. Within seconds, they're gone.

I turn back to Micah, who has remained relaxed beside me. He gives me a crooked smile as if nothing surprises him now.

I know we have a journey ahead of us. First, we will need patience and care as I bring my power under control within the safety of this forest. Then we will be able to leave and seek out his distant family and the beings of old magic hidden in the west.

After that... Well, I have a purpose and Micah has a mission. Both of us need to connect with the past and the future. But no matter what happens, we'll do it together. And always, we will have a family to come back to. Dragons who care about us. Powerful dragons who will guard the future with as much care as we will.

Resting back on the soft grass, I can't resist the impulse to draw patterns on my body, my finger trailing across my skin as I color in the space above my breasts and all the way down to my thighs.

Micah can't seem to take his eyes off me, heat growing in his eyes again.

His voice is a deep growl as he says, "Sophia, you're—"

I rear up and kiss him, needing more, needing an entire future with him, because no matter where I am, if I'm with him...

"I'm home."

EPILOGUE - LANA STEELE

37 WEEKS LATER

I prowl along the dark back street, my black scales rippling across my body and enabling me to blend into the shadows. My footsteps are silent, my breathing is steady, and my wings are tucked into my sides.

My belly, on the other hand, is huge.

It's taken me some time to figure out how to function with my expanding size and the insistent kicking that seems only to increase when danger is nearby. My child behaves as if she—or *he*, we don't know which—wants to join me on the hunt.

A child after my own heart.

My target is fifteen paces ahead of me, a furtive female silhouette darting between buildings, her bony fingers clinging to a small, black pouch. I'm not sure exactly what's in the pouch, but I watched her acquire it from a black-market store that exists within an underground network of supernaturals that I'm slowly tearing apart, piece by piece.

The buildings in this area of the city are decorated with graffiti that itself is peeling as the paint chips off the cracked bricks. Watermarks stain the buildings from top to bottom and piles of trash litter the footpaths.

This area used to be controlled by Scorn dragons. In the

past, I would have been bracing for the possibility of a golden bullet in my back, but now my heartbeat is elevated for different reasons.

The dark witch I'm tracking is the last of the three witches who escaped from the veil prison.

I found the other two more easily since they weren't so cautious about using their powers and left a trail of human bodies in their wake. They were working together, and I imagine they thought their chances of survival would be higher that way. It only made them easier to locate.

But this witch... She's cunning.

She'll know I'm coming for her.

I should turn around and head back the way I came, seek reinforcements, and try to find her again later. This expedition was meant purely for surveillance. In fact, I promised Callan that I was only going out for some air.

But I unexpectedly caught her scent, and I can't let this opportunity pass me by.

I've never been so close to catching her as I am now.

She turns a corner up ahead into another back street, one I'm vaguely familiar with. It's a short street and several of the buildings lining it have been condemned. The streetlights are broken and only one is working at the far end, causing the shadows to thicken around me as I follow her.

Shadows were once my friend, but I shudder at the memory of how dark my world seemed to become when Tyler ruled these streets. That was before Sophia defeated him and banished him to the keeper's realm.

Some of that darkness threatened to continue even after he was overcome. When I returned to the prison veil afterward, I made a disconcerting discovery.

In the level of the prison where I had been kept, next to the cage where the shadow panthers were imprisoned and I fought for my life, I discovered a hole in the wall.

Another cage had been hidden behind that wall.

Someone was being kept there, but I still have no idea who.

Isaac, too, was baffled. And alarmed. He told me he didn't know there was a cage there, let alone another prisoner, and the absence of sour lemon on my tongue confirmed he was telling the truth. Not that Isaac would ever lie to me.

We only have theories about who the prisoner might have been and how their presence was so well concealed. One is that a magical barrier must have been placed across the wall to conceal the extra cage completely. Even from me. Another theory is that the cage was actually a separate pocket of the veil, similar to the one the then-Celestial Ascendant had placed behind my cell, where she put the dragon's light.

Most concerning was what the cage itself told me: a creature of powerful blood had been kept there.

The scraps of discarded clothing on the floor—in fact the very air within the cage—filled my chest and my mind with an overpowering sense of danger. It was a dark creature. Possibly female. Carrying a spark of rage within her that felt as scorching as dragon's flame.

As for the shadow panthers that also escaped, I haven't sensed them within this city. If they're here, they certainly haven't caused any carnage. Unfortunately, Isaac and I can't pinpoint the exact moment when they escaped from the veil. My focus when I first returned to the prison after liberating the dragon's light had been on making sure the Roden-Darr were properly secured. I'd sent Micah back to Sophia that night and then I'd taken the time needed to ensure the Roden-Darr were constrained.

The panthers could have escaped right out from under our noses while we were in the veil and moving between levels. Given the proximity of the shadow panther's cell to the hidden cage behind it, it's possible that the unknown inhabitant of that cage took the panthers with them.

I may never know what really happened.

All I know for certain is that the powerful prisoner, whoever she is, has not remained in my city. I haven't sensed her presence and that's just as well because otherwise, I wouldn't stop until I hunted her down.

Unlike this witch I'm tracking now. This old woman smells like rotten fruit, and I've already connected her scent to multiple human deaths.

Proceeding more carefully along the darker side of the street, I watch the witch flit into a nearby alley. Her movement is so quick that I suspect there's either a hidden entrance to her hideout in that alley, or she knows she's being followed.

I pause at the corner into the passageway, listening intently to the scuffling sounds within it, not far from my position.

My hand lifts to my hair, where my glaive is masquerading as a small, golden pin. I found that as my pregnancy progressed, my back pain increased, and I took to wearing my glaive in my hair, instead of in a harness across my back.

I'm reassured by my weapon's presence, but I now face a difficult decision.

If this is indeed the location of the witch's lair, then I can come back later with reinforcements, because I can be assured she'll turn up here again. But if she's merely passing through, then losing her now could mean months of searching for her again. In the meantime, she's bound to kill again. Dark magic thrives on death. She won't stop.

I quell my inner groan. I don't want fatalities on my hands when I can prevent them.

At the same time, I don't want to endanger my child.

Damn. There was a time when I would throw myself into danger, but that version of myself has given way to my need to protect the child I'm carrying and to honor the love of a dragon whose heart would be torn out if he lost me.

Fighting any witch who controls dark magic is no easy task. They're unpredictable and can never be defeated by brute force alone.

I hate admitting it, but I have to come back with reinforcements.

Just as I make the decision to leave, the choice is taken out of my hands.

A shriek sounds from around the corner and the witch flies at me from the shadows, her cloak billowing around her bony form. The scent of rotten fruit envelops me at the same moment that her left hand reaches for me, clutching at my shoulder. Her other hand is clenched tightly around the shaft of an arrow with an ivory tip, which she aims at my heart.

Her attack isn't the fastest, and I evade it easily, leaping back at the same time as I snatch my glaive from my hair. The weapon takes shape within my hand and I prepare to swing it across her throat and end her.

Dark light blasts from her free hand and hits my weapon arm. My scales thicken across my skin and protect me from her magic, but the impact slows my swing. The witch ducks and sends another blast of magic at me. This time, I deflect it with my glaive, sending the dark energy into the nearby brick wall. It sizzles across the surface, burning like acid, and I'm incredibly grateful for my scales that will protect me if I'm hit.

I'm on the back foot, but I recover my balance, deflecting each of the quick blows she sends in my direction before I push forward again.

I sense her fear as I get closer to her.

Her efforts become more desperate and another explosion of light rockets past me.

I narrowly evade it and prepare to deliver the strike that will kill her, but at that very moment, my womb contracts.

It's a painful tightening more intense than any Braxton Hicks I've experienced before.

Oh... fuck me. Not now!

Without the distraction, I would have easily avoided the would-be dagger she rams at me once more, easily beat my wings and lifted into the air. I'm close enough to have cut her down already. But the sudden pain and the intense tightening makes my torso rigid and freezes me for a split second too long.

She sees her chance, and she takes it.

The arrowhead she's aiming at me lodges in my left shoulder.

For a moment, I'm relieved, since she rammed it into the fleshy part of my torso and missed my heart, but to my shock, a bolt of what feels like electricity passes through me.

My head spins and my legs give out. Unable to control my body, I thump against the dirty, brick wall and slide down into the filth at the side of the building.

Fuck!

The witch leaped back as soon as she stabbed me, but now she ventures forward. Eyeing me warily as she approaches. Her irises are washed out and nearly completely white, her cheeks are gaunt, and her skin is a sickly gray, all a sign of the dark magic that must be eating away at her.

She cackles as she looms over me. "I've stabbed you with an arrowhead fashioned from the tip of a fingerbone of an ancient titan. It was very difficult to come by. Very expensive. I had to make the shaft myself and attach it."

When I can only stare up at her, she comes a step closer.

"A lesser supernatural would have died already," she says. "But you will need an extra push to meet your death."

Pulling a dagger from within her cloak, she waggles it in my face.

"Fancy this," she says with a giggle. "An old crone like me defeating an angel like you."

My vision is blurring, but I'm no longer trying to focus on her. At the corner of my eye, there is a tiny spark of light.

Within my hearing there is the softest hum of gossamer wings.

A golden dragonfly glides effortlessly across the air and hovers above the old lady's head.

Sophia…

I haven't seen her since she traveled west with Micah five months ago.

But where is Micah?

I make out a shadow on the rooftop opposite our position. If it's him, he's camouflaging himself well. There was a time when he would have been the first to put himself between Sophia and danger, but now it seems that he trusts her to ask for help if she needs it.

It takes a strong man to recognize the strength in the woman he loves. Just as Callan has always respected my strength and autonomy, so too has Micah proven that he will support Sophia in all her choices.

The witch seems completely unaware of the threat at her back.

She licks her blade as if it's delicious. "I will slice out your heart, pretty angel, and then I will eat it."

She bends to me, and that's when Sophia makes her move. In the blink of an eye, the fierce dragon transitions herself from the shape of a dragonfly into her human form. Her hair is longer than it was the last time I saw her with even brighter golden highlights, her eyes are crystal clear green, and her golden belt rests around her hips.

"Careful with that blade, old witch," she says as her left arm snakes around the woman from behind. "You might cut your own tongue."

Sophia's right hand holds her golden dagger. Without a second's hesitation, she slices the blade neatly across the witch's throat, driving it deep.

Quickly twisting and pushing the witch to the side, she ensures that none of the blood sprays on me.

I stay where I am in the dirt, catching my breath and trying to adjust both to the fact that Sophia's here and that my baby has chosen this night to enter the world.

Sophia attaches her dagger to her belt before she kneels

beside me, her gaze quickly taking me in, her arm slipping behind me and supporting my shoulders. "Hey, Night Sky."

I give her a wan smile. "Hey."

"I'm going to pull this out now, okay?" Her hand wraps around the arrow, which has remained in my shoulder, and I brace for the pain, grunting when she removes it.

Blood trickles down my chest, but not enough to be concerned about. It seems the witch was only intent on breaking my skin to let the arrow's magic do its work. My healing power kicks in a moment later and my skin knits itself together.

Sophia continues to support me, but her eyes have narrowed at the weapon she's now holding. "This arrowhead is old magic. The oldest of old."

"The witch said it was the bone of a titan." I grimace. "I didn't believe her."

Micah lands behind Sophia, folding away his silvery-gray wings before he reaches for the arrow.

When she passes it to him, he examines it quietly. "It is what she claimed," he says, his brow furrowing. "This bone is extremely dangerous. We need to put it where nobody can use it again."

"It's a good thing we have just the place," Sophia responds.

I imagine they're thinking of the old cabin in the veil. Before they left to travel west, Sophia and Micah took Dominus's hammer into the forest in the veil, and Micah hid it within the cabin there. Anyone who wants to steal it will not only have to get past the veil's defenses but will also need to be a rare creature of old magic to access the cabin's interior. It's a double layer of security that will prevent the hammer from being misused again. It will be the perfect place to hide this arrow, too.

I let out another groan when a contraction tightens my belly, trying to breathe through it and vocalize the pain.

Sophia's concerned eyes meet mine. "I won't let your baby be born here," she says. "Do you trust me?"

I have no idea what she's proposing, but I speak with all the honesty in my heart. "With my life." My next breath ends in a moan as another contraction squeezes my stomach. "Oh, fuck…"

Sophia's hand presses to my stomach and she closes her eyes. Warmth spreads through me and it eases my muscles.

"Not yet, little one," she murmurs, leaning toward me. "Your mama needs to get home first."

As the warmth from her hands increases, the contraction eases and I exhale with relief.

"I've only bought you a few minutes before the contractions will start again," she says. "This child is ready to be out in the world."

I grip her arm as she helps me stand while Micah keeps watch over us.

"Get Lana home," he says to Sophia. "I'll take care of the witch and meet you there."

She gives him a brief nod and the trust between them is as strong as it was before they left. Stronger, even.

Sophia urges me toward the end of the street. "Our car is this way."

"Car?"

She gives me a smile. "Micah may have come into some money."

I blink at her, and she elaborates. "His mother was from a wealthy family. It turns out she set up a trust fund for him before he was born."

I'm surprised. "Solomon never told him?"

Sophia doesn't hide her grimace quickly enough. "I think Solomon was concerned that the money would come with strings attached."

"Does it?"

She's quiet and I'm not sure how to interpret her silence. I decide not to push it.

"What about the dragon's light?" I ask, changing the subject.

Sophia took the dragon's light with her when she left, and it was hard for me to let it go. There was a time when I believed that guarding the light was my responsibility and I still feel that way a little. A few months ago, I decided to remove the golden lotus from my armor—the place where the dragon's light had rested. The lotus now sits on a table in the living room of my home with Callan. It's a reminder of how hard we fought for peace.

"The dragon's light is safe," Sophia says. "It can never be taken away from dragons again."

I want to ask her more. I need to know where it is and how she's so certain it's safe. It took a lot of faith for me to let her depart with it. But I trust her. She wouldn't keep information from me unless it was for a good reason.

I also trust the immense power she controls. Particularly because I might need it again soon.

When we reach the car and I slide onto the leather seat, I exhale a groan when the contractions return. Giving Sophia a hopeful look while I try to blink away the sweat in my eyes, I ask, "Any chance you can do that thing again?"

She shakes her head as she slips behind the wheel.

"It wouldn't be good for baby," she says, appearing completely calm and confident in her next assessment. "But don't worry. She's still two hours away. I'll get you home in plenty of time."

I'm not sure if I should be relieved or alarmed. *Two more hours of this?*

Also... "*She?*"

Sophia presses her lips together. "Oops."

A moment later, she puts her foot down on the accelerator, and then I'm on my way home.

∼

My daughter's quiet breathing is the sweetest sound I've ever heard.

Scarlett sleeps in my arms, her tiny face peaceful and her perfect, little fingers curled around the edge of her swaddling cloth.

She smells like the purest spring and her scent chases away every thought of darkness.

Callan's calm presence falls over me, drawing my focus upward. He gazes down at his three-day-old daughter with an adoring smile.

"It's time," he says.

"Just one more minute." I stubbornly refuse to break this perfect moment. Even if it's the same response I gave him five minutes ago. "Everyone can wait for us."

The smile plays around his mouth and brightens his eyes. "They can, but the moonlight won't."

I exhale a sigh, accepting my inability to control nature.

Tonight, we take Scarlett into the moonlight for the first time.

That's when we'll discover if she's a dragon or an angel.

If I were a full dragon, there would be no doubt, but when dragons are born to non-dragon mothers, it's not until they're exposed to moonlight that their dragon nature is revealed.

Or not.

Our daughter was born without wings, feathered or otherwise, and with no other signs to indicate her species.

Sophia is sure she'll be a dragon, and I don't doubt Sophia's instincts, so I really shouldn't deprive my daughter of her power for a moment longer.

Well, maybe just another small moment, as I indulge in snuggling her to my chest.

Tonight is a full moon and, judging by the growing insistence in Callan's stance, the cloud cover is finally clearing.

I remind myself I don't want to miss the light.

Slipping out of the rocking chair, I keep Scarlett close. No need to wake her. The trip to the rooftop garden will only take a few minutes.

We chose to stay in Callan's home that has the flowers in the walls—the home where Sophia's dragon was revealed. The level below this one has remained Sophia's, but other than that, we've made a lot of changes. Turning one of the bedrooms into a nursery was the first.

There have been many changes among the dragon clans too. Our alliance with the Scorn and Grudge has only grown stronger, to the point where there is finally trust between dragons. If any dragon needs help, it's given, no matter what clan they're from.

Gisela and Dane have thrived leading the Scorn. To that end, Felix and Niah have been instrumental in maintaining the peace and helping to ease the Scorn's transition away from their more nefarious occupations. There's a connection between them that I hope will continue to grow.

As for the angels, our truce has held. The then-Serene Commander, who became the Celestial Ascendant, has seen the benefits of dragons who are willing to keep other supernaturals in line. Her angels can get on with their intended purpose—bringing peace and hope to others.

Now that the last of the witches has been dealt with, the city feels calmer, at least for supernaturals. Not unbreakably so—it will continue to take work—but for the first time in my life, I feel like I can step out into the night and breathe easily.

Now, Callan opens each of the doors for me on the way to reach the elevator, which we ride to the top level. On the way up, he reaches across to check the golden pin that rests in my hair. I would have checked it myself, but my hands are currently full.

The rooftop garden was another change we made. I finally met Delaney, the witch who helps Callan with structural changes to his homes, and she seemed to enjoy the challenge of making plants grow here.

I'm looking forward to catching up with Sophia more thoroughly over the coming days. Despite promising myself I would find out everything that's happened in her life since she left, she and I have only managed to snatch a few conversations between me feeding Scarlett, changing diapers, trying to get some sleep, and maybe taking a shower…

I pause on the cusp of exiting the elevator.

Wait, have *I showered?*

I can't quite recall…

Too late now.

We step into the atrium immediately outside the elevator. It has a solid ceiling and is lit with soft, artificial lights, but its walls are made of glass. We pause there for a moment.

Outside, in the garden, our closest family is waiting, all of them appearing to be chatting amongst each other.

Callan gave his human bodyguards the night off. The trust between them is strong, but it's best they aren't present for this event.

Beatrix and Isaac are snuggled together on the outdoor couch in the corner of the garden. Isaac's white wings are extended, one curled around Beatrix's side. It took Isaac and Beatrix months to act on what everyone else could clearly see, but the trust between them warms my heart. Now that the veil is healing, and the entrance to the oblivion has closed, Beatrix spends much of her time there.

My mother is sitting on the nearby lounge, talking with Zahra. Mom is in her customary white T-shirt and jeans, always casually dressed despite her warrior nature, while Zahra is gorgeous in a skirt and blouse in a soft amber color that makes her cinnamon-brown eyes pop with color.

Emika kneels on the patch of lawn in front of them, sitting with Sophia, who is running her fingertips through the grass and changing the color of her fingernails as she does so.

It looks like Emika's laughing, which makes me smile, but the tension in Micah's posture is a worry to me.

He's the only one standing, watching over Sophia and Emika, and it's as if he's on guard, his focus rising to the space around them and even to the sky above. He's a formidable presence and I'm intrigued to see the edge of a tattoo peeking from the neckline of his shirt. I didn't notice it on the night he and Sophia returned, but in my defense, I was a little distracted at the time.

"What's going on with Micah?" I quietly ask Callan.

The atrium is soundproof, so I'm not concerned that Micah can overhear us—not even with his incredibly sharp hearing. We may have made this building more like a home, but we've also increased the securities. The glass around us is not only fire-rated and soundproof, but is also bulletproof.

"I'm not sure," Callan says, studying Micah. "Sophia seems relaxed enough, but Micah's been on edge since they arrived. From what he's said, I gather he met his extended family and they're more powerful than he was anticipating."

Oh. Hmm. Sophia said something about strings, but I don't see Micah being easily intimidated, and it doesn't explain his tension now.

I have a sudden thought. "Is Sophia pregnant?"

Callan gives a laugh that rumbles through his chest. "How would I know?"

"Well, he's standing over her like he thinks hounds of hell are coming after her, and he'll tear them to shreds before they get within a mile of her." I stare at Callan meaningfully. "Just like you did with me."

"I didn't do that. It was totally different." He clears his throat. "It wasn't hellhounds I was worried about. And, as it turns out, I was right to be worried."

I reach up to press a kiss to his chin—the closest I can reach while holding Scarlett. He bends and closes the gap, capturing my lips and kissing me with such heat that it makes me wish we could slip back downstairs and use the time that Scarlett is asleep for other purposes.

I groan against his lips, my focus returning to the garden. "We need to go out there."

"Do we, though?" he asks, his attention remaining on me.

I pull back a little, biting my lip at the desire in his eyes.

Even though peace has finally come to dragons, darkness persists, and it reminds me that these moments with Callan are to be cherished.

"We do," I say, firmly repeating what he told me. "The moonlight won't wait."

It will only take a few more steps and Scarlett will feel the moonlight on her face for the first time.

I gaze down at her sleeping form while Callan proceeds ahead of us, holding open the atrium door for me.

His appearance at the door causes our family to become quiet, their expectant faces turned to us. Emika jumps to her feet and runs to Callan's side, reaching up to hold his hand.

"Is she a dragon?" Emika asks, her voice hushed, her brown eyes turned up to Callan.

"We'll know soon," he says with a smile.

I take a deep breath, cross the distance, and step into the moonlight, allowing it to shine across my daughter.

Scarlett's little forehead creases and her lips purse.

I hold my breath and then—

Delicate, golden scales form across her face and the back of her hand where it peeks from the fold of her swaddling cloth.

I hold on tightly as her eyes slowly open, her irises becoming pure gold as she looks up at me.

"She's a dragon," I whisper.

"A dragon!" Callan says, his voice quiet but loud enough for everyone to hear.

Our family breaks into happy murmurs as I step farther into the garden with Callan and Emika close behind me.

Everyone is smiling and I sense their need to come closer,

but there's one more change that may—or may not—happen tonight.

Kneeling on the patch of grass opposite Sophia, I quickly remove Scarlett's swaddling cloth so that her back isn't constricted, supporting her head and holding her upright against my chest. She's wearing a loose singlet and her golden scales are clearly visible across her shoulders and arms.

There's a part of me that hopes her wings don't appear tonight. Especially since her scales are evidence enough that she's a dragon. It's true that the earlier the wings appear, the more powerful the dragon, but they're also a burden.

Emika's wings developed before she was five and she had to wear a clip on them so she didn't accidentally betray her supernatural status to humans—or to other supernaturals.

I don't want that for my daughter.

Around us, my family gathers. Callan brings Emika to my side. Sophia is now directly opposite me and I don't miss the joy in her eyes—violet eyes tonight to match her currently-violet fingernails. And Mom, Beatrix, and Isaac all slip off their chairs to join us on the lawn, forming a semi-circle as we wait.

Micah, on the other hand, remains standing and I wish I knew the reason for his tension.

Scarlett's back is fully exposed to the moonlight and I count the heartbeats as I wait. If it's going to happen, then it should happen soon.

Theoretically.

The seconds stretch out.

Then she burps. It's the cutest sound and it makes Emika giggle.

I'm about to shrug and lay Scarlett back down because I guess that's it, when a shiver passes through her.

Scorching heat suddenly burns across my shoulder, flames bursting into life at the edge of my vision. My own scales shimmer across my skin, protecting me from the heat while my family leaps backward.

My eyes fly wide. "Dragon's fire!"

I have no idea how to feel about the fact that my daughter can already breathe fire and my thoughts rage thick and fast.

Fuck, how will she control it?

Oh, thank the saints we didn't remove the fireproofing from inside the house.

But while the others are jumping away from me, Callan is launching himself toward me, his arms outstretched, and the look on his face freezes me.

In the heat of my daughter's fire, my senses failed to pick up the other sounds behind me.

I spin in the direction of Callan's focus, and now my reflexes are working at full speed.

As quickly as I can, I pass Scarlett off to Callan. He cradles her safely against his chest and his wings shoot out, creating a wide shield that protects my entire family from the threat that has appeared behind me. Not that my family won't be ready and able to fight if they need to.

I pluck the golden pin from my hair.

Glaive!

The pin resumes its natural shape in my hand, the blades on my golden spear becoming deadly sharp.

The plume of my daughter's flame swirls in the space I'm now facing and it's growing before my eyes, rapidly becoming a whirlwind several paces wide that spirals upward. The growing flames create a force so strong that it knocks me back a step.

I dig in my heels as two figures—a woman and a man—appear in the middle of the firestorm, seemingly protected from the flames by a cocoon of light that emits from the man's palms.

Instantly, I sense that it's the man who took control of the flames and increased them.

He rises upward, rolls his shoulders, and closes his fists.

My eyes widen when he appears to suck the flames into his body, absorbing them completely until there's nothing more than a faint glow in the air. He's as tall as Callan, his shoulders as broad, and he glows like a cooling ember.

The woman has silver-streaked hair and her eyes gleam like metal. She's dressed in entirely black clothing, along with knee-high black boots.

She pulls up sharply at the sight of my weapon but greets me as if she knows exactly who I am. "Asper Ashen-Varr, it's an honor to meet you."

I'm not so sure I feel the same about them. The man reeks of murder—although it's faint, as if those acts were committed in the past—and the woman, well, she's hardly innocent of death.

Before I can reply, Micah appears in the air above Callan, his wings beating briefly before he drops into the space beside me.

His voice is tense. "Ana," he says, greeting the woman first and then the man. "Aiden."

I glance at Micah, but I don't lower my weapon. "Friends of yours?"

His lips press together into a hard line. "They're allies from Portland. Powerful ones. They fight darkness, but they never bring good news."

"Easy, Micah," Aiden says, his hands raised. His palms are still glowing with the flames he absorbed. It makes me wonder how he'd cope against Callan's fire. Or mine, for that matter. "We're not here to cause trouble. Ana needs to speak with the Avenging Angel. That's all."

Micah shakes his head at Aiden before he gestures to my family. "These supernaturals are my family," he says. "This is a time of celebration. They don't need to be part of your war."

"No, but they have a right to know what's coming," Ana says, her silver eyes glinting. "All I ask is the chance to be heard."

I don't detect a hint of a lie. She believes what she's saying and her intentions aren't malicious.

Behind me, Callan has retracted his wings, revealing the rest of my family, all poised for a fight. All, that is, except for Sophia, who has moved to the edge of the group. There's a hint of resignation in her expression.

Her response both worries and reassures me. If these people were a threat to me, I have no doubt she would have leaped to my side already, prepared to deal with them.

Assuming she can.

I'm fully aware that her power doesn't affect beings of old magic, and that thought gives me pause.

I consider the newcomers with even greater caution.

"It's okay, Micah," I finally say. "I'll speak with this woman."

Ana visibly relaxes, but Micah doesn't. He steps back toward Sophia, guarding her once more.

"Is there somewhere private we can go?" Ana asks.

"Just in here." I gesture to the atrium, but I pause to meet Callan's eyes, silent communication passing rapidly between us.

He will watch over me and protect our daughter with his life.

I don't miss the way that Ana also sends a silent message to Aiden. There's a bond between them that feels as strong as the bond between Callan and me.

It helps me relax a little, but not much.

I lower my glaive and lead Ana to the atrium, waiting for her to enter before I firmly close the door.

She keeps her distance from me, watching me carefully. "The first Avenging Angel to be born in hundreds of years," she says. "The weight on your shoulders must be colossal."

"Not when I have family to share it with," I say. A truth I learned along the way.

She inclines her head. "Family you want to protect."

I narrow my eyes at her. "If you've come here to threaten me—"

"Warn," she says, her hands flying up. "I'm here to warn you."

Her shoulders slump a little and she gives a heavy exhale. "I think you must already sense that it won't be *our* choices that determine our children's future."

My forehead creases when her focus shifts to a point past me. I follow her line of sight into the garden, past Micah, to Callan, who holds Scarlett close.

Ana steps nearer to me, but her focus remains in Callan's direction. "Which side will she choose?"

I swing back to Ana, my response vehement. "If you mean to imply that my daughter will turn to darkness, she will not."

Ana's eyes widen. "Oh, I'm sure she won't. Your daughter will follow her heart, just as her mother has done. But I'm not speaking of your daughter."

I stare at Ana with wary confusion.

She purses her lips. "I'm speaking of the old soul." She peers at me, as if she believes I should know exactly what she's talking about.

And I do.

Fuck it, but I do.

I turn back to the garden and my line of sight falls lower than Callan, to the little girl clinging to his hand.

"Emika," I whisper.

I saw her in the *Book of Light Magic*. It was before the pages were erased and the book reset itself. I was confused at the time because it seemed like I was looking into the future at something that had not yet come to pass.

In the images, Emika was at least twenty years old, her straight, black hair much longer and billowing around her face in a wind I couldn't feel. Golden armor rested across her chest, just like Atrox's but with different runes carved into it. The ruby-red wings of a dragon had risen up behind her, a larger-than-life silhouette, its scales glimmering in the light of a fire that seemed to consume her.

She looked right at me, as if she were gazing through time, and she greeted me in the same way that she would acknowledge an opponent. *"Hello, angel,"* she said.

I constrain the shiver threatening to reveal my quiet dread.

"She carries a heavy burden," Ana says, her voice hushed.

"The weight of her choices could shift the balance between light and dark."

I spin to Ana, my vow determined. "Then I'll make sure the burden never breaks her."

Ana returns my vehement glare for a long moment. "That's all I can ask of you." She steps back from me, as if, having delivered her message, she has nothing more to say.

But she pauses at the door, adding, "There's a war on the horizon, Asper Ashen-Varr. A war between old and new gods. I pray Emika never joins it." She takes a deep breath. "With you in her life, I have hope that she never will."

With that, she pulls open the door and hurries to Aiden's side. She gives him a single nod. He pulls a box of matches from his pocket, lights one, and drops it to the lawn.

He takes her hand and to my astonishment, the flames burst upward, their bodies disappear into them, and then the fire immediately extinguishes.

I'm left staring at a swirl of smoke.

I have so many questions about who Ana and Aiden are, what their purpose is, and how the fuck Aiden can manipulate fire like that, but they're gone and right now, my only concern is my family.

I transform my glaive back to the shape of a pin, slipping it back into my hair as my feet carry me swiftly outside the atrium. I race into Callan's arms, where I rest my head next to my sweet child's.

"Lana?" he asks, but I can't speak yet, can only hold on to him.

Across the way, I meet Sophia's eyes.

Her expression strikes me hard now. She fought for peace, but she knows it won't last forever.

Well, fuck that.

Because I will fight to keep it. *We* will fight to keep it.

I watch the determination build in her eyes. The pure fucking willpower that tells me she will defy any threat that comes our way. I recognize the fight growing in Micah's stance as he continues to guard over all of us. The resolve in the faces of Beatrix and Isaac, the way they look at each other with a promise to love and protect, no matter what.

I see the courage in Zahra and in my mother and recognize their strength as warriors.

And in Callan, I find my calm. The kind of calm that gives me resolve, perspective, and reminds me that his fire, his heart, and his strength are precious gifts that I will never take for granted.

Above all, we have love, and we will fight any battles we have to fight to protect each other.

Now and always.

To find out who escaped from the veil prison *and* what happened to the original keeper of dark magic, don't miss **Dark Magic Shifters: Book One**.

If you're curious about Ana and Aiden, check out the complete **Soul Bitten Shifter** series.

And for everything you could want to know about Nathaniel, read the **Bright Wicked** series, a complete fantasy romance.

Turn the page for the first chapter of Dark Magic Shifters: Book One!

WOLF OF ASHES - CHAPTER ONE
(DARK MAGIC SHIFTERS #1)

Dark Magic Shifters: Book One

His dark crown will be mine.

My mother was imprisoned for a crime she didn't commit. She was locked away in darkness, never to see light again.

I was born into that darkness, that perpetual night. I learned to survive without sunlight and to thrive on the scraps that were thrown to me.

All because someone didn't want me to claim my birthright.

Now I'm free. And I'm coming for what's mine.

I'll go deep into the nightmares of an empire built on blood and bones to find the wolf whose name my mother couldn't utter.

A beast who stole my place among shifters.

I'll do whatever it takes to slice his empire apart, piece by little piece.

Even if it means making a deal with a man whose thirst for vengeance exceeds my own. A broken king. The darkest of them all.

In return for his power, he wants more from me than I can give.

He wants my heart.

Content information: Dark Magic Shifters: Book One is a dark paranormal romance, the first in the Dark Magic Shifters series. Recommended reading age is 17+ for sex scenes, mature themes, violence, and language. Ends on a cliffhanger.

Keep reading for the first chapter!

Dark Magic Shifters
Copyright © 2023 by Everly Frost
All rights reserved.

Author's Note

This is the story of how the original keeper of dark magic went missing.

This is also a story of revenge, lust, greed, death, and the power in a heart.

Chapter 1

"*You were loved.*"

That's what my mother whispered to me when I was a little girl shivering in her lap because I was afraid of the scraping sounds that would echo through the damp stone wall beside our cage.

"*You were loved.*"

She'd remind me over and over like a ward against the perpetual night that surrounded us. While she shared her food with me, stretching out the scraps our jailer fed us. While she wrapped her arms around me to keep me warm from the freezing cold in winter.

Even when she struggled to breathe at the end.

"*You were loved.*"

I soon came to understand that she chose her message carefully.

What mattered was not that there was love in my life before I'd been born, but that it was in the past.

I was loved.

She was loved.

Until we weren't.

Now I crouch in the center of my cell, my threadbare, black dress barely covering my backside, listening to the unusual sounds through the solid, stone wall to my right.

I'm accustomed to hearing soft snarls from animals I can't identify, along with the occasional low moan—of pain, not pleasure.

But these are two voices I've never heard before.

Neither of them belongs to my jailer. He calls himself Zadkiel. He's an angel with the blackest hair, the whitest wings, and a smile that makes my stomach turn.

The higher pitch of one voice tells me it's female. The other is male. Both are muffled through the thick, stone walls that make up my cage.

Four stone walls. Impenetrable ones.

There are small air vents in the ceiling, each located near a corner. I have an old mattress on a wooden frame for a bed, a wooden bucket in the corner for a toilet, and a single, wooden chair, which I rarely sit on. Because, well, that would be civilized. Or so my mother told me every time she rested on it, her head held higher, as if it made her feel like her old self.

I am not civilized.

The cage is magically sealed so that the walls defy any sort of deep scraping or attempted burrowing.

Not that I haven't tried.

Like the animal that I am, I have broken my claws on those stones over and over, looking for any weak patch. After my mother died, I turned my quest into a game, managing to scratch out tiny squares as I tested every inch of stone for a weakness.

The scratches remained on the surface, but my claws sunk no deeper.

Zadkiel found it humorous. So humorous that he would slap me once for each square I made since his last visit. The slap itself didn't hurt so much as the light that filled his palm.

His light magic. The power he uses to keep me under control that blazes from his hands whenever he wishes.

A purity of magic that's a contradiction to his rancid soul.

Painful to my dark heart.

He taught me that if I try to escape, he will flood the air with light. Once, I made it three steps past him toward the door he'd left inches open to taunt me. His light burned my back so badly that I couldn't sleep for days.

Screaming never did any good, either. As Zadkiel likes to remind me, sound only passes one way through the wall—inward—and he's the only one who knows I'm here.

But now...

Something's happening beyond my cage.

Something new.

I close my eyes and focus on the sounds, trying to hear what the woman is saying. Hers is the first female voice I've heard since my mother died. The man's voice is raised and threatening.

But still, their speech is inaudible. Rising to my feet and hurrying to the wall, I press my ear up against the cold surface, desperate to make out what they're saying through the magic coating the stone.

Searing heat suddenly burns across the side of my face.

I jump away from the wall with a cry, staring in shock at the way the rock has turned crimson red, as if it's being heated from the other side.

My eyes widen at the power it would take to reach through stone this thick.

The blaze stops then starts again, much lower to the floor. I jump farther backward as it bursts across the stone in a wavy line for several feet, leaving the smooth rocks glowing.

My ears suddenly *pop*.

It's painful and sharp, as if the pressure within my cage changed. My mother once described being carried into the air and the way the weight changed within her ears. I wonder if this is the same kind of thing.

Crouching low, I dare to hold my hand, palm up, toward the glowing stones, but I'm wise enough not to make contact. Not yet, anyway.

Searing heat radiates out from the stone, scorching my palm even at a distance, but it's not so much the temperature that intrigues me now.

It's the way the air around my hand shimmers with energy.

Slowly extending the claw on my right forefinger, I press it against the rock.

To my shock, my claw sinks into the stone.

All the way through until my finger is burning from the contact.

The magical seal is gone!

I wrench backward so fast that I land on my backside. I don't know exactly how it happened. Possibly because of the source of heat on the other side. Or maybe some other magic is at play.

But the seal is gone.

My heart is in my throat, my thoughts churning at the possibility that escape is finally within my reach.

But how to make it happen?

The stone is hot and soft, like heated metal that will soon form a hard surface once more. I know this because my mother taught me all about the properties of metal. All about a lot of things.

She taught me everything she knew. Every miniscule piece of information, no matter how trivial it seemed, in case it would one day help me.

She taught me basic physics, chemistry, and biology. She taught me math and how to read. She convinced Zadkiel to bring us books, although he seemed only to agree because he could subvert her intentions, never bringing what she asked for: like a children's picture book when she asked for a book on natural sciences.

Sometimes he would bring books in other languages that she couldn't read. But she was never deterred. She would use whatever he brought her, even if only for the illustrations, and would simply change my lesson.

She educated me about humans and supernaturals and all the different kinds of magic.

I learned about lust, greed, sex, envy, politics, basic medicine, technology, and food—and *damn*, I want to try cupcakes one day. The pink, frosted ones with sugar decorations on top.

I learned that the sky is blue, not gray like my cage's ceiling, and that there's such a thing as 'fresh' air.

It was also clear that, for my mother, who had lived under a blue sky and breathed fresh air, being kept in this cage was a misery her body couldn't sustain.

For her final lesson, she taught me about death.

But I found out all by myself the meaning of loneliness.

Now, I carefully consider the glowing stone along with the intense growls on the other side of the wall. I make out the sharp clanging of metal—possibly chains, judging by the way the sounds seem to slither and rattle. Then voices again—both the man's and the woman's—followed finally by retreating footfalls, heavy ones.

Silence.

I'm not sure if they've both gone, but if I don't try to escape now, I may never get another chance.

Racing to the lone chair, I pick it up, throw my arm across my eyes to protect them from flying debris, and then I bash the chair against the wall where it's cold and hard.

The chair's legs snap off. One of them shatters. And now they're perfect for digging through hot stone without burning my fingers. Assuming the wood doesn't catch fire, but I'll deal with that if it happens.

Crouching low to the heated portion of wall, I begin gouging the surface as fast as I can, dragging the jagged wood through it. Splinters immediately catch in my palms and I pause to retrieve my mother's old shirt, wrapping the tattered material around my hands and using my teeth to tie it before I resume my task.

The wood isn't as sharp as my claws and it's slower to cut through, snapping off at intervals and frustrating my progress.

I persist until the moment a chunk on the other side falls away.

The opening is only as big as my hand, not nearly large enough for me to slide through, but certainly big enough to allow sounds and smells to rush in.

My moment of elation is destroyed by the savage growls and strong scents of dark beasts.

A mouth full of teeth gnashes at the opening on the other side, silvery teeth gleaming at me in the darkness. A silvery eye flashes across the opening as the creature takes a quick look at me before resuming its gnashing.

Fuck!

I scuttle back from the opening.

The overlapping snarling sounds coming from the other side tell me there's more than one of those beasts, whatever the fuck they are. But the scents are all theirs. Whoever the woman and man were, they're gone.

I sift through my mother's descriptions of dark creatures and land on a few options for what the snarling creatures could be, but I would need to see more of their bodies to be sure.

Like that's going to happen in any safe fashion.

My hopes are now in turmoil.

If I make the opening big enough that I can escape through it, the creatures will also be able to get through to my side.

If I somehow manage to keep the opening small enough only for my body—which is not guaranteed if the beasts are slimmer than me—I'd have to shimmy through headfirst or feetfirst and either way, they'd rip me apart before I made it more than a few inches.

I switch my focus to the door, tentatively pressing on it. It's also made of stone and sits seamlessly in the wall, but it has remained locked. Even if it weren't, I can't be sure I won't step right into the path of the beasts outside.

For all I know, Zadkiel may have placed those creatures there as a second line of defense if I were ever to get out.

Fuck, fuck, fuck!

What's worse, now that I've made a hole in the wall, he will see it. He'll know the magic was somehow broken and he'll punish me for it *and* I'm sure he'll find a way to fix it.

He could come along at any moment now.

I crouch low to the ground as a sense of finality settles over me.

I'm certain I'll die in a fight with him. Of all the things my mother taught me, it's that Zadkiel isn't an ordinary angel. Unlike many other supernaturals, he has the strength to kill me.

But a chance like this hasn't presented itself for twenty-three years. It may not happen again.

If I don't try now...

I retrieve my mother's old skirt. I was saving it for when my black dress got too ragged, but it's time to take chances. Ripping the skirt into smaller pieces, I wrap one of them around my other palm to protect my skin.

I choose the two sharpest planks of wood from the remains of the broken chair.

Now that I'm armed with more than my claws, I wait, preparing myself for when I hear Zadkiel's approaching footfalls.

Long moments pass.

The snarls on the other side of the wall die down a little. Then start up again. The beasts seem to be prowling back and forth. Waiting, like I am.

Time stretches. The long minutes become long hours.

At one point, I nod off, only to wake with a start, but nothing has changed.

The hours become a day and by then, my hands are going numb. I'm forced to put down my weapons, but I'm prepared to pick them up at a moment's notice.

One day becomes two, and now I'm hungry.

I have one chunk of bread left and half a flagon of water.

The beasts continue to move back and forth in front of the opening I made, but the pitch of their snarls has changed. Every now and then, they make a plaintive moaning sound.

Are they hungry too?

Zadkiel has never been absent for longer than two days. When the second day stretches into a third, I begin to consider that he might never return. He hasn't brought me food or fresh water, and I haven't heard him come to feed the beasts, either.

Finally, the snarls outside my cage stop and, when I dare to peer through the little opening, I make out the faint silhouette of a paw and a leg resting on the ground. One of the creatures must be lying close by.

It gives a soft whine, but that's all.

By the fourth day, I have no water left and my choices have run out.

If I'm going to die anyway, better to do it while I'm still strong enough to put up a fight against the creatures outside my cell.

Assuming I can even break the wall open now.

Cautiously, I use the blunt end of one of my makeshift weapons to tap the wall. The stone is so brittle that it cracks off at the lightest touch.

I test it on a higher spot and with slightly more force, expecting the wall to remain solid.

Crack!

The sharp sound is followed by a cascade of cracks and then, to my shock, the fissures extend in all directions, a vibration ripples through the wall, and the surface fractures across several feet.

Chunks fall in both directions—toward me and outward.

I leap back just in time to avoid being hit in the head as a portion of the wall above me also collapses.

I left one of my makeshift weapons on the bed, but I don't dare take my eyes off the beasts now directly in front of me, gripping my remaining plank of wood in my left hand.

On the other side of the wall, multiple yelps sounded as the stone clattered down, and dust fills the air.

As it clears, I find myself facing another cage, but this one has bars and a fully visible door with a latch that looks like it could be broken but has remained in place.

Four shapes move in the darkness. I make out sleek, black bodies, silver eyes that disappear when they blink, and silver claws that extend and retract as they prowl toward me.

They look like panthers and my memory stirs.

But no… They can't be…

Not the shadow panthers my mother told me about. One female and three male. She was convinced these beasts had hidden themselves from the world in a mountain somewhere.

Yet here they are. All four of them. Each with unnaturally silver claws and eyes that betray their species.

Three of them hold back, making it clear that the one in front is their leader. Her slightly smaller bone structure tells me she's the female of the pack.

She's the one whose instincts I have to trigger.

Any other beast could have been a problem for me, but these creatures are the stuff of nightmares and whispers.

Just like I am.

I was born to tame beasts like this, gather them to my side, and give them a purpose.

The female will obey me if she recognizes the nature of my power.

I allow my claws to descend and my teeth to sharpen. If I have to shift fully, then I will, but I'd rather conserve my energy.

Lowering my head without taking my eyes off her, I draw back my lips and utter a fierce growl, pulling the sound from deep in my chest. It's the snarl my mother taught me that signals to another dark creature that they should leave me the fuck alone or face the consequences.

"Back off," I snarl as my growl fades. "That's all I ask of you."

The female panther's head snaps up, her ears pricked and alert. She gives a soft grunt, blinking at me in the dark, her silvery eyes appearing and disappearing as her eyelids close and open.

I growl again, more softly this time. "I want my freedom and I'd rather not kill you."

She sniffs the air, her nostrils flaring, and now a curious light enters her eyes. She takes a small step in my direction, her paw landing on a piece of rocky debris that lies between us, but she doesn't come any closer and her claws retract.

I'm sure it's the only sign of subservience I'll receive from this proud creature.

I take a chance to glance at the cage door. It's so close and the latch is twisted and broken. It will take multiple twists, but I hope I'll be able to lift it—unlike these beasts, whose claws could never achieve the fiddly task.

Carefully, I step up onto the debris, choosing my footing so I don't slip or get stuck. The rocks shift beneath my feet and the panthers twitch, but they don't come after me.

Faster now, I sidestep to the door, keeping the beasts within my sights.

My hand lands on the latch and, after twisting it back and forth and then over its damaged catch, I'm slipping outside the cage and into the corridor beyond it.

With a firm push, I close the door behind me.

Just like that, there are no longer any bars or walls around me.

I'm struck with a sense of space and it's suddenly fucking terrifying.

Rows of cages stretch out into the distance, maybe as many as fifteen on each side of the wide corridor. The absence of sound tells me that, other than the panthers and me, there's no other living creature here.

Directly to left is the solid, stone wall that formed one of the sides of my cell, but facing it from this direction, I would never be able to tell that there's a space behind it. The door's outline isn't visible and all that sits on the wall is a misshapen lever that has the appearance of melted iron.

I turn back to the far end of the corridor. I've never had the chance to look so far into the distance and my vision blurs as I try to scan along the cages to the door that must be located at the end.

I tell myself the impediment to my vision will pass.

I was born an apex predator with the sharpest senses. My

ability to see long distances may have been stunted by my surroundings, but I promise myself I'll overcome it.

Stepping away from the cage, I'm preparing to race down the corridor and claim my freedom when I pause.

Inside the cage, the panthers have prowled forward, their bright eyes trained on me.

The female makes a soft, mewling sound, her head held low, but not in an aggressive way.

"You want your freedom, too." I sigh, hoping I'm not taking a terrible chance when I open the cage door and back away quickly, increasing my speed when the panthers don't immediately leap out after me.

My matted hair slaps my back in heavy thumps as I run.

Behind me, the panthers move quietly, but they pull to a quick stop each time I turn to glare at them.

Finally, I reach the door to my freedom. It doesn't have a handle. It looks like I only have to push it. I'm still gripping one of my wooden stakes and both of my palms are wrapped in the scraps of my mother's clothing.

If only she were with me right now.

My eyes burn with tears I won't shed. Grief is not for me, but rage is and I plan on using its heat to avenge her.

"This is for you, Mom," I whisper, planting my free hand on the door and pushing it open.

I expected to exit the prison into darkness.

Instead, the brightest light streams across me, drawing a scream of pain to my lips. Dropping to my knees, I fling my arm over my eyes, desperately trying to see my surroundings.

All I can make out is an expanse of wood immediately in front of me.

As quickly as I can, I untie my mother's skirt material from around my palm and wrap it around my eyes, trying to dull the brightness.

It helps, but it's not a complete fix.

The brush of fur against my lower back and thighs makes me freeze, but then one of the panthers gives a soft grunt. I recognize the female's voice. The side of her face bumps my knee—at least, I think it's the side of her face. Then her head presses up beneath my right palm—the hand from which I took Mom's skirt.

The other three panthers move around me and I'm completely at their mercy as one of them presses against my back, an insistent movement.

I rise up a little and the female rises with me, her head remaining under my hand.

She gives another soft grunt and then moves forward.

I stay where I am, but she comes back to my hand.

"Do you want me to follow you?" I ask, even though I know she can't answer in my language.

She gives another soft grunt.

I have no other choice.

Around me, the air is so bright that even with the blindfold on, I have to keep my eyes closed. But my ears can hear just fine, and my sense of smell is also helpful to me.

So far, we're alone in our immediate surroundings, but I sense the presence of other beings somewhere beyond us. The faster I can get out of here, the better.

The panther leads me to the right and then her head pushes upward. I don't know what she's trying to tell me until my foot hits a surface in front of me and I find myself sliding my foot upward to figure out what it is.

It takes me a beat to realize… it's stairs.

Stepping upward, I shuffle forward, keeping my hand on the panther's head while the other panthers mill around me, their bodies brushing my legs, urging me onward.

I lose count of the steps as we proceed higher and higher, but along the way, I also realize that the air I'm breathing is pure.

Fresh.

It's filling my lungs for the first time and I fight the dizziness that comes with it, as if this good thing could be bad for me, even though I want more of it.

Finally, I shuffle forward and there is no ledge. I stop abruptly because my toes dip and it feels like I'm standing at the edge of something. I try to open my eyes to see what it could be, but just at that moment, there's a sound behind me.

An opening door.

A voice. The same female voice I heard through the walls of my cage.

The panthers give urgent snarls.

All of them ram into my back and then—

Fuck!

I'm falling through air that feels icy and weirdly welcoming at the same time and then darkness engulfs me once again.

Fucking beautiful darkness.

I rip off the covering over my eyes but keep hold of it because there's no way I'm letting go of a piece of my mother.

My fall slows and I land gently on a gleaming, marble floor.

The inky-black surface extends far into the distance in every direction—left, right, and up, into a nothingness that is so vast, I can't quantify it.

I'm not sure where the staircase disappeared to because it didn't feel like I traveled that far, but here I am, surrounded by night.

Is this the world?

I quickly dismiss that possibility. There is no blue sky, no grass, no buildings.

Oh, and there are also no walls.

In the next moment, the panthers land behind me, but all I care about right now is the endless space in front of me.

"This is freedom," I whisper, stepping across the marble floor, which cools the bare soles of my feet, a soothing sensation.

My walk becomes a run and then I'm racing as fast as I can

across the darkness, taking deep breaths, inhaling the glimmering energy in the air.

An energy that reeks of dark magic.

My magic.

The essence of my heart.

The rapid beat of paws tells me the panthers are close behind, but it's when their footfalls are joined by another sound that I slow and stop, crouching to the floor and listening intently.

In the distance is a swishing noise and it's coming closer.

Rising to my feet, I peer into the darkness, finally making out the shape of a tall figure moving toward me. The newcomer appears to be male, judging by the width of his shoulders and the narrowness of his hips and waist, although his entire frame is thin. A long, black robe rests around his shoulders and it must be the source of the swishing sound because it's dragging across the marble floor.

He seems to bring the darkness with him and a thrill passes down my spine.

Then I make out the shape of the black crown resting around his eyes, obscuring the upper half of his face, its spokes rising up over his forehead and past the top of his head.

My heart leaps at the sight of it.

The immense power in the crown calls to me like food to my starving stomach.

The angry press of the man's lips does nothing to dissuade me from my need to connect with that crown.

Without thinking, I lift my hand, the one gripping the loose material of my mom's skirt, and I reach toward him.

He draws to a rapid stop at my gesture.

If only I could see his eyes; I'm sure he'd be eyeing me cautiously now.

"Keeper of dark magic," I say, greeting him. "I never dreamed I'd meet you."

His lips part, as if I've surprised him. His voice is like a wraith's, a shocked whisper. "You know what I am?"

"Of course," I say. "My mother told me all about you. Everything that *her* mother told her. All the knowledge passed down through the generations from mother to child. All the way from the time of the Vandawolf."

The keeper takes a step back from me, but his shoulders are suddenly hunched. "*Vandawolf*. That's a name I haven't heard for thousands of years." He seems to rally quickly. "If you know what I am, then you know you shouldn't be here."

"Shouldn't I?" I ask, finding my lips curving upward. "Isn't this exactly where I should be? In a place of dark magic?"

He glides forward until we're only a few paces apart and now it feels as if he can see me through the metal covering his eyes. "Not until you die."

"Yes, that's right," I murmur. "It's your burden to collect the magic from dark creatures when they perish. So that their untethered magic doesn't roam free and cause chaos. Technically, I shouldn't be able to step foot here until I die, at which time you will strip the magic from my bones."

He gives me a nod, his lips drawing back from his teeth. "Technically."

"Well, then, I must be here for a reason." I lift my hand toward his face again, my tone becoming a challenge. "Perhaps I'm here to claim your crown."

Now, he jolts backward.

I take a step forward, not letting him widen the gap between us.

That crown.

My mother told me all about it. It contains all of the dark magic the keeper has collected over thousands of years, a power like nothing else. Of course, he can't use it himself. His only purpose is to collect the magic. The rules of his creation stop him from wielding the magic he tethers.

But if I had that crown, I could destroy my enemies. I could cut out their hearts and make them bleed. Death would be a mercy for them.

Growls are leaving my lips and behind me, the panthers are fanning out, as if they're also preparing to attack.

"I forgive you for assuming I would fear you," I say to the keeper. "But I got here somehow, and I'm not leaving without that crown."

His answer is a snarl, but his voice sounds different now. Deeper, more guttural. "Why do you wish to take it?"

"I would use it to destroy my enemies and claim what's mine." My voice is vehement. "I will do anything to make them feel the pain they've caused me."

He stops moving, his robe wafting around his black-clad legs. "Anything?"

"I will cut to the bone if I have to." My lips draw back as I allow my claws to descend. "To get what is *owed* to me."

My threatening stance seems to suddenly please him.

The corners of his lips rise. "Would you cut as deep as your own bones?"

I don't hesitate. "If it means I would see my enemies suffer before I die—*yes*."

"Oh, I'm not talking about death," he says. "I'm talking about the power in your heart."

Now I'm wary. "My heart?"

He suddenly closes the gap between us. I brace for attack and the panthers snarl a warning at him, and he stops inches away from me.

The power radiating from him is intoxicating and my head spins to be this close to him.

His voice lowers, a soft suggestion. "I propose we make a deal, you and I."

"What deal?" I ask, my gaze rising from his lips to the crown, but my focus is not the metal right now.

I want to see his eyes.

His response is a whisper that sends a shiver through me.

"Give me the power within your heart," he says. "By so doing, you will give me life. With life, I will be able to claim the power in my crown. In return for this, I will give you the vengeance you seek. Whatever you need me to do so you can achieve your revenge, I will do it."

My eyes widen at his proposal.

If I give him the ability to use his power, he's offering to use it for *me*. I was determined to seek vengeance on my own, but it was going to be an uphill battle. Particularly because I don't have any means to make it happen. I don't even have a shred of untorn material to my name.

Now, all the power I could possibly want is within my reach.

I reach up, suddenly needing to make contact with his body. My fingertips hover the barest distance from his jaw before I dare to breach the gap.

His skin is cool to touch. Ethereal. Otherworldly. And not quite here. As if his form is paper thin.

I know what he is. I know about the power in his crown. But I don't know who he was all those thousands of years ago before he became the keeper of dark magic. I don't know if his heart was always dark or even what kind of supernatural he was.

But... can I give away my heart in exchange for his power?

"You're asking for the power in my heart," I say, my eyes narrowed, since I need the organ beating in my chest to stay alive. "What exactly do you mean?"

"I'm talking about the greatest power of a heart," he says, as if I should already know. "The power to love."

Of course.

But the decision is easy. All it takes is for my mother's long-ago words to echo back to me.

"You were loved."

Quietly, I say, "What use is my heart if there's nobody left to love me?"

His lips soften. I feel his focus like a burn as his hand rises to my chest, his palm pressing over the location of my heart, his fingertips brushing against the bare skin that's reachable through the rips in my dress. A trickle of pleasure travels through my breast and down to my stomach. It's so unexpected that I fight not to gasp.

"If you want my heart…" I whisper, my voice turning into a snarl as I fight the unusual sensation across my skin, *"Take it."*

His other arm scoops around me, pulling me close. I sense the thinness of his form and I marvel at the way his wraith-like body can carry the weight of so much power. "I cannot take most dark magic from the living, but I *can* take the power of a heart since it only exists during life."

I find myself standing eye level with his chin, my gaze lifting to the crown and, up this close, to the shadows behind the metal.

My lips part with surprise when I catch a glimpse of the empty expanse behind his crown, a cavern of pain and despair.

Agony strikes through my chest so suddenly and sharply that I jolt, but his other arm tightens across my back, forcing me to stay where I am. My focus flies down to my chest, where his fingers are clawed and blood is soaking my dress.

A second later, the pain ends as quickly as it began, and his palm flattens against my skin, the final droplets of blood trickling across the back of his hand.

Black blood. The evidence of my heritage.

He lowers his head to mine and whispers against my lips. "I'm sorry if that hurt, but I promise it will be worth it."

That's it?

My forehead creases. "It's done?"

His lips are so close to mine that when I sway forward as I speak, my mouth brushes his. Tingling sensations flow all the way from my lips to my core, making me blink with surprise.

"It's done," he says, the movement of his lips against mine sending another stream of pleasant sensations through my body.

He breaks the contact, leaving me perplexed as he steps back and reaches up to his crown, his hands closing around it as if he's going to take it off.

I lean forward in anticipation, but a second later, he crouches to the floor and his head bows, and I can no longer see his face.

He slips the crown upward. The moment it leaves his head, black hair appears, falling across his face.

Remaining crouched, he rolls his shoulders. His cloak parts at the front, revealing his chest, but clings to the tops of his shoulders as if it's attached to his body.

His frame is thin and transparent.

But then he rises slowly back to his feet.

Now, the cloak floats to the floor and settles on the smooth surface with a soft hiss.

My breath catches when his body transforms rapidly as he moves.

His chest fills out, gaining breadth, and his shoulders broaden. His neck thickens, his biceps grow, and his thighs and calves fill out with muscles.

My eyes widen even further when his transformation doesn't stop there.

Flames suddenly flicker around his chin and chest, fire streaming from his mouth as he exhales.

In the next moment, the fire stops and his fingers extend into black claws that appear deadly sharp and then just as quickly retract.

Next, scales shimmer across his skin, first black in color, then ivory white, then just as quickly, they morph into a dusting of fur that covers his arms and legs before it, too, disappears.

Deep-amethyst wings burst across his back, feathers so long, they drape to the ground before they fully retract. The wings haven't even fully disappeared before electricity crackles between his fingers on both hands, charging the air around us so that it feels like a lightning strike is seconds away.

I can only stare as his form shifts through the characteristics of countless supernaturals from dragons to wolves, bears, harpies, warlocks, and finally…

His skin smooths out to take on a human appearance, settling into a pale-brown color. His tall, muscular form remains sculpted, every perfect muscle gleaming in the dark.

He's completely naked and it's impossible to miss the size of the length between his legs. That is, before energy crackles around his fingertips and clothing appears. Black pants and a gray T-shirt cover his nakedness and cling to his muscles.

He holds his crown in his left hand, but with another crackle of energy, its shape changes, shrinking until it's the size of a ring, which he slips onto the forefinger of his left hand.

Then his head rises, revealing a sharp jaw, high cheekbones, and lips shaped like a god's. He considers me with eyes that flicker through forest green, fiery amber, and finally settle on the darkest brown.

My heart is pounding in my chest, confirming that the organ is healthy and functioning as it should be, but *damn*, it was disconcerting watching this man shift his form through so many different shapes.

He gestures to the cloak, which remains abandoned on the ground, as if it's evidence of his next words.

"Our deal is done," he says, his voice a deep rumble, the wraith-like hiss completely gone. "I am free of my former limitations. Tell me what vengeance you seek and I will make it so."

My lips part. I'm ready to speak, but I pause.

Deals are tricky. The keeper of dark magic has taken the power in my heart and now I need to assert my claim in return.

Despite all the lessons my mother taught me, the only information she refused to give me was the identity of the man responsible for her imprisonment when she was six months pregnant.

Oh, she talked about the supernaturals in her life, but she never told me which man betrayed her. Which man so coveted the chance to rule the most powerful empire of dark creatures that they would condemn her to die in a cage.

I think she must have known that, if I ever escaped, I would seek revenge against that man.

But her final words will never leave me.

"We may be creatures of dark magic, but we were loved."

Now, I allow my hatred to rise as I voice my answer carefully. "You will help me kill the man who murdered my father, imprisoned my mother, and stole the empire that should have been mine."

The dark magic keeper smiles. "Then let the age of dark magic begin."

To find out what happens next, don't miss Dark Magic Shifters: Book One.

THIS DARK WOLF (SOUL BITTEN SHIFTER #1)

A complete series!

I am a wolf shifter born with a human soul.

Packless. Mateless. Unable to bond.

Cast out of my pack, I live in a supernatural safe house filled with broken women. Other women come and go, but I remain.

I'm waiting.

For him.

Tristan Masters—the ruthless alpha of the most vicious pack in the city.

He fought for my life when my pack wanted to kill me. He saved me. I should be able to trust him.

But I know better.

Tristan Masters wants my wolf; my killer soul. When he's ready, he will use me to destroy his enemies.

Tristan thinks he owns me. He thinks there are no consequences because I can't bond to him.

He's going to discover that I am nobody's to command.

This dark wolf will bite back.

Content information: This Dark Wolf is dark urban fantasy romance, the first in the Soul Bitten Shifter series. Recommended reading age is 17+ for sex scenes, mature themes, violence, and language.

BRIGHT WICKED

A complete series!

One forbidden touch.

I am the Bright Queen's Champion. The only fae to control the power of starlight, I am sworn to protect my people from the dark Fell who live in the wilderness beyond our border.

But when a Fell more powerful than any other challenges me, I'm not prepared for his fierce strength and skill.

Or the dangerous desire in his eyes when he looks at me.

Two champions bound to destroy each other.

One misstep is all it takes for me to invoke an ancient law that binds my fate to his. Suddenly, my life is no longer my own.

I am tied to him in a promise of pain and destruction.

Three days to live.

Now, I have only three days before I must fight him in a battle to the death that will determine the future of our two lands.

Every heartbeat counts.

But how can I kill the only man who sees me for who I truly am?

Content information: Bright Wicked is a fantasy romance, the first in the Bright Wicked series, a trilogy told over three consecutive days. Recommended reading age is 16+ for heat level.

STORM PRINCESS SAGA : THE COMPLETE COLLECTION

The complete Storm Princess Saga.

I am no ordinary princess. My crown is lightning, my tears are rain. I am robed in thunder and my voice is the howling wind.

Despite the power raging around me, the greatest storm is the one inside my heart.

Taken from her family to be the chosen Storm Princess, Marbella Mercy spends her days subduing the storm that was sent to destroy her people. But the storm is growing stronger and soon it will be beyond her control.

Each House sends their strongest champion to battle to the death for the right to stand by her side. Some fight for power, others seek glory.

Only one fights for Marbella's heart.

Baelen Rath is the last warrior from the feared House of Rath.

Determined to protect Marbella from the darkness creeping across their land, he will risk everything to reclaim her heart.

But when forces turn against them and powerful enemies are revealed, Baelen and Marbella will face dangerous betrayal to break open the secrets that keep Marbella bound.

This complete series is over 330,000 words and contains:
The Princess Must Die
The Princess Must Strike
The Princess Must Reign
Plus exclusive bonus scenes and a life after story.

ALSO BY EVERLY FROST

KINGDOM OF BETRAYAL
(Fantasy Romance)
1. A Sky Like Blood
2. A Sin Like Fire
3. A Soul Like Glass

DARK MAGIC SHIFTERS
(Dark Urban Fantasy Romance)
1. Wolf of Ashes
2. Book Two
3. Book Three

BRIGHT WICKED - COMPLETE
(Epic Fantasy Romance)
1. Bright Wicked
2. Radiant Fierce
3. Infernal Dark

SOUL BITTEN SHIFTER - COMPLETE
(Dark Urban Fantasy Romance)
1. This Dark Wolf
2. This Broken Wolf
3. This Caged Wolf
4. This Cruel Blood

DEMON PACK - COMPLETE
(Dark Paranormal Romance)

1. Demon Pack
2. Demon Pack: Elimination
3. Demon Pack: Eternal

SUPERNATURAL LEGACY - COMPLETE
(Angels and Dragon Shifters)

1. Hunt the Night
2. Chase the Shadows
3. Slay the Dawn
4. Claim the Light

ASSASSIN'S MAGIC - COMPLETE
(Urban Fantasy Romance)

1. Assassin's Magic
2. Assassin's Mask
3. Assassin's Menace
4. Assassin's Maze
5. Assassin's Match

ASSASSIN'S ACADEMY - COMPLETE
(Dark Academy Romance)

1. Rebels
2. Revenge

STORM PRINCESS - COMPLETE
(Fantasy Romance)

Complete Set: Books 1 to 3 (with bonus scenes and a life after story)

1. The Princess Must Die
2. The Princess Must Strike
3. The Princess Must Reign

MORTALITY - COMPLETE
(Science-Fantasy Romance)

Mortality Complete Set: Books 1 to 4

1. Beyond the Ever Reach
2. Beneath the Guarding Stars
3. By the Icy Wild
4. Before the Raging Lion

Stand-alone fiction - dark romance

Corrupt Me: Immortal Vices and Virtues

ABOUT THE AUTHOR

Everly Frost is the USA Today Bestselling author of fantasy romance, urban fantasy romance, and paranormal romance novels. She spent her childhood dreaming of other worlds and scribbling stories on the leftover blank pages at the back of school notebooks. She lives in Brisbane, Australia with her husband and two children.

amazon.com/author/everlyfrost
facebook.com/everlyfrost
instagram.com/everlyfrost
bookbub.com/authors/everly-frost
goodreads.com/everlyfrost

Printed in Poland
by Amazon Fulfillment
Poland Sp. z o.o., Wrocław